LIFE IN MY FATHER'S SHADOW

A Colombian Revolutionary's Daughter

Rocío Velásquez Dresser

*'La vida no es la que uno vivió, sino la que uno recuerda
y cómo la recuerda para contarla.'*

or

'Life is not what one lived, but what one remembers
and how one remembers it in order to recount it.'

Gabriel García Márquez

Acknowledgments

I will forever be indebted to my colleagues and friends, Dr. Elba Maldonado-Colón and Dr. Jennifer Madigan, for their advice and support. I am grateful to my dear friends Linda Ricchio, Vicki Dronet Alba, Steve McCoy-Thompson, my sister Liliana Rice, and my brother Jaime Dresser for their feedback and for believing in me. Thanks to my beautiful children, Alexandra and Michael, for making my life worth living and for your suggestions, encouragement, and trust. Thanks to the guidance of novelist Tammy Greenwood and the comments of my group at the San Diego Writers, Ink in San Diego, I was able to complete the manuscript. When I felt overwhelmed and thought I could not go on, they reassured me that my story was worth telling, thus giving me the confidence I needed to continue.

To my mother, Cecilia Dresser, who has been a light in my life, I owe my accomplishments. Her eagerness, determination, and selfless love for her children taught me the meaning of perseverance. I am very appreciative of my brothers, Orlando Dresser and Kenneth E. Dresser, because they were always my biggest fans.

I would like to thank my dear uncle Jorge Edwardo Villalba, who is no longer with us, for believing in me and for his insightful feedback. Thanks go out to my dear friends Dr. Miguel Ángel Beltrán Villegas and Manuel Rojas Rubio who guided me along the way. To my dear friend Michele Bass, I owe the French revisions. Thank you for your innovative ideas.

I would like to thank my agent and coach Ken Scott, whose expertise as a respected author, his creativity coupled with his interest in this project helped me transform the manuscript to its current form. Also, thanks to my editor, Joan Elliott, for her observations and keen eye for detail. Additionally, I extend my appreciation to two highly creative individuals, Dan Taylor, and my son-in-law Brian Batugo, for their outstanding work in designing a cover that captures the essence of the story. To my niece, Dr. Janna B. Ropohl Osorio, my sincere gratitude for her insights in refining the cover.

Last, my special thanks to my dear husband Salvatore J. Pettinato, who walked this path with me. He read the manuscript so many times that I am sure he memorized it. His passion for this piece made his feedback invaluable. I love you and appreciate all your support and patience.

This book is dedicated to my family and the children of Colombia.

Preface

1974

On a cold evening, high in the Andean city of Quito, I was reading in the living room when a loud knock at the door startled me. I waited for a moment for our housekeeper, Elisa, but when she didn't come, I went into the hallway, hoping one of my parents would come downstairs. No one did. All I could see upstairs was a faint light. The knocking suddenly became erratic, so I moved forward and opened the heavy oak door. An older woman was standing under the porch light. Her flattened hair wrapped around her head like a scarf while droplets of rain rolled down her cheeks. She stared at me with sunken brown eyes.

'I need to speak to Dr. Jaime Velásquez's children. I have a package for them,' she said. 'His friend Colonel Moncayo told me they live here.'

'I don't know them,' I lied. 'My father is upstairs, and my last name is Dresser. But please, come in, Ma'am. Let me bring you a towel.'

The woman entered the foyer and stood beneath the chandelier. I went to the linen closet; took the largest towel I could find and handed it to the stranger. She draped it around her shivering shoulders. The deep crease in her brow relaxed as she examined my face.

'Are you sure you aren't Rocío Velásquez? You look so much like him.' She pulled a picture out of her wet purse, but I looked away.

'I need to speak with one of his children. It's urgent. He left explicit instructions,' she repeated, tracing my entire body with her round eyes. 'You don't know Dr. Velásquez?' she insisted with an uneasy smile.

My heart was racing, and I mumbled, 'No, I don't. My father's name is Kenneth. But please tell me what is in the package?'

'I can only give this package to one of his children.' The woman shook her head. 'Then I have nothing else to do here.'

She spun around on her heel, and before I could ask her name, she disappeared into the blackness of the night.

At that moment, I thought about the day Papá walked in after what was supposed to be a peaceful protest, his face ashen and his bloodstained shirt untucked. I had tried for decades to shut out what had happened and, for a long time, believed I'd succeeded. But that night, the stranger in the rain had pushed the door to my childhood open. These memories hadn't disappeared, they were engraved in my mind and there was nothing I could do to shake them off.

I didn't want anything from him, the man I had once called Papá, the one who left, who broke my mother's heart and put our lives in danger. He had chosen his political cause instead of his family. Yet I still missed him so much.

I was twenty-four years old and hadn't heard from him in years.

I should've accepted the package. What was in it? What if there was a letter apologizing, explaining why he left, or telling us how much he missed us? My thoughts continued.

I wanted to know, but I only wanted to erase the past. I ran into the street, calling after her.

'Yes. I am Rocío Velásquez! I am her!'

My screams faded away, drowned by the downpour. In desperation, I rubbed the rain and the tears from my eyes as I looked in all directions. The rain was falling in torrents, and it was difficult to see. In the gutters, streams washed away leaves, mud, and trash coming down from the hill. The streetlights flickered. I jumped over puddles while avoiding cars and crossed the street. But she was gone.

Out of breath and trembling I walked back home. I closed the door, leaving the wet towel the woman had used curled on the floor. Then I covered myself with a blanket and collapsed in the reading chair.

How many times have I denied knowing him? Why can't I just continue to pretend he never existed?

Outside, the storm intensified, lightning illuminated the dark sky, and the roof sang as the wind whistled.

A Father's Dilemma

1954

Thinking back, we all saw slivers of Papá's secretive life early on. We lived in a two-bedroomed apartment adjacent to my grandparents' house in Bogotá, when my parents brought home my baby sister, Liliana. I was thrilled. She, on the other hand, didn't seem so happy. Liliana's prolonged sobbing and fussiness kept us awake. Many mornings, I woke up elated to have someone to play with, but when I heard her piercing cry, I pulled the covers up to my ears and went back to sleep.

This went on for a long time until one day I propped myself up in my bed, grinding my teeth, waiting for Liliana to squeal. When she didn't, I went to my parents' bedroom to check on her. The door was open. On Mamá's side of the bed was Liliana's crib. The sour smell of curdled baby milk made me take a step back. I was about to leave when my sister let out a series of coos, then smiled at me, revealing her toothless gums. She began kicking so fast that she rolled over. Our parents walked into the room at that moment.

Mamá asked Papá, 'When did you get home from school last night? I didn't even hear you come in.'

'We stayed late at school,' he said as he paced. 'I am sorry I wasn't here for dinner... we had a problem.' Papá stopped pacing and looked at me. 'Good morning, my girl.' He kissed me. 'Please go to your room.' I was about to complain when he pointed to the door and said, 'Now.'

On my way out, I glanced at my sister, who was frowning.

'But I was going to play with Liliana.'

'Go on.' Mamá patted me on the back.

When Papá cleared his throat, I made a hasty retreat to my bedroom and sat on the floor where I could see my parents' bed. There was something about my father that made me uneasy, something I'd never seen before. He was frustrated, a feeling that would follow him for years.

'We were in the middle of the yearly commemoration of Gonzalo Bravo Pérez's death when we were blocked by a line of soldiers!' He slammed his fist against the wall.

'Jaime, the girls,' Mamá snapped.

I'd never seen him lose his temper before and so I buried my head in a pillow. When I heard his firm steps approaching, I stretched my neck as far back as it would go to see all six-foot-four of him standing by me. He was holding my sister.

'Sorry. I was upset,' he said. 'How about if you watch Liliana while I speak with Mamá?'

I nodded. Papá bent down, arranged some cushions, and sat my sister next to me. He spun around and went back to his room, closing the door behind him. I listened as he told Mamá the story I have heard more times than I care to remember.

Hundreds of young people, including my father, who was a medical student, had marched to the central cemetery to pay their respects to Gonzalo Bravo Pérez, known as the Fallen Student. The police had killed the law student in 1929 during a demonstration. Gonzalo and his fellow marchers were demanding justice and reparations for damages to peasants and other workers, and in particular those killed and maimed in what was known as the Banana Massacre.

By the end of the 19th century, the banana business was huge and competition fierce. The biggest players in the world had formed the all-powerful United Fruit Company. They had purchased vast swathes of farming land and there were few regulations as they cut costs and took control of the supply chain, leaving many of the former employees without work or, if employed, barely surviving on starvation wages while the shareholders and investors grew rich. The workers had no choice but to go on strike to force the company's hand for better working conditions. They held out valiantly for a month, until, on November 12, 1928, the United Fruit Company, pressured by foreign investors who wanted to protect their assets, convinced the Colombian government to send in troops to break the strike. After many weeks of tension, the army opened fire with live rounds on the striking demonstrators in the small-town square of Ciénaga on December 6.

That day was a bloodbath, with nearly 50 striking workers killed and 2,000 murdered in the aftermath, as government troops cracked down on anyone who sympathized or supported the strikers.

At the end of the march to commemorate the fallen, my father and other students had returned to the university to socialize. Midafternoon, a group of policemen entered the university and ordered everyone to leave the campus. The students resisted complaining that they were there to enjoy the carnival events. The police responded by firing into the crowd, killing one of my father's classmates, Uriel Gutiérrez.

I heard my father say, 'I can't look the other way while Rojas Pinilla and his puppets destroy our country and kill our students. We must do something. Can't you see, Cecilia?'

'Why you? Why can't someone else do it? What about *your* family?' Mamá said.

The argument continued for some time. I buried my head under the pillow until I heard the front door slam and at last there was nothing but the deafening sound of silence.

That evening, I heard the voice of a man blaring through a loudspeaker. He was demanding Pinilla's resignation. I went out of the kitchen to see what was happening, but Mamá's arms swept me to her.

'No. We can't be part of that. This is not good.'

She closed the heavy curtains and prayed quietly.

I heard other protesters chanting and shouting, the clanging of what appeared to be cymbals. The sound grew louder as they approached. It was almost as if they were standing in front of our porch. Minutes later, we heard police sirens followed by a stampede of frantic protesters, this time the police bellowing out their instructions through a different loudspeaker, threatening arrest and prosecution.

Eventually, the sirens and the voices faded. Mamá turned the light off and peeked through the curtains but closed them immediately.

'No one should see us.'

At that moment, the front door flew open and Papá walked into the apartment. His expression pained. He stared at Mamá for a moment, walked to the dining room, and dropped his books on the table. He lowered his gaze and sniffled.

3

Mamá hurried to embrace the shattered man who had previously turned heads when he entered a room.

When I saw the bloodstains on his shirt, I covered my mouth with my hands. His voice sounded like gravel as he spoke to Mamá. She turned, pointed to my room. Instead, I walked into my parents' room, where Liliana slept. I pulled myself into my sister's crib and held her. We fell asleep wrapped in the same blanket.

That night, my little sister and I had our first eye to eye contact and even though she couldn't talk, we understood each other.

I learned later that, earlier, thousands of students, including my father, had marched the city streets peacefully while singing the national anthem, protesting the murder of Uriel Gutiérrez. People along the way opened their windows cheering and waving white handkerchiefs. A few blocks into the demonstration, a battalion of troops ambushed the group and began shooting. The students fled, but the soldiers chased after them.

Carlos Arango, one of my father's classmates, and my father took cover in a nearby building to hide. Gabriel Sanchez was there hiding behind a tree and Papá tried to warn him that a soldier was coming. When Gabriel finally saw the soldier, he ran in the opposite direction, but the soldier lifted his rifle, took aim, and fired. Gabriel fell face down onto the ground, blood oozing from a wound in his back. Despite the shooting, the shouting, and the screaming, Papá and Carlos ran to his aid. They took the injured man to the office of a nearby dentist. He asked no questions and showed them to an empty room. While my father frantically tried to save his friend, Gabriel coughed blood. The dentist joined in attempting to remove the bullet, but it was too late. Gabriel took his last breath and passed away on the operating table. By the end of the day, another eleven medical students had lost their lives, scores more were badly injured.

Gabriel had been a regular at our house. He showed up carrying his acoustic guitar, or Luisa, as he called it. He'd sit down and pretend to play it upside down. When I shook my head and called him silly, he'd turn it around and begin playing. A cascade of ink-black bangs fell on his glasses. His rolled-up sleeves freed his arms and unerring fingers so that he could pluck Luisa's strings. He'd play a flamenco piece, his fingers moving so fast it looked like they were running away from his hands. After we cheered, he'd slow down

4

and play Cielito Lindo, also known as Lovely Sweet One. Papá would then join in singing, and the two men serenaded Mamá, Liliana, and me.

Gabriel's last breath sealed Papá's allegiance to the revolution. That day, he swore to fight government corruption and oppression. His friends tried to dissuade him from his relentless activism, warning that it was too dangerous to confront the authorities. He ignored their pleas and assured them nothing was going to deter him from his promise to his dead friend.

Puerto López

Long after Gabriel Sanchez's horrific murder, Papá still talked about it. The regime tightened its grip and outlawed festivals, sports, and other types of youth-led activities, accusing the organizers of being communist sympathizers. The production and distribution of propaganda were forbidden and those who broke the law were condemned to five years in prison. Tensions between activists and the dictatorial government exploded after a retired army colonel exposed what the government was doing in the concentration camps where they held the so-called rebels. There, they were exposed to brutal treatment, regularly tortured, subjected to electric shock treatment, and executed. Protestors were taken to camps and never seen again.

For most people, life went on as usual. But not for us. Every time Papá raised his voice at the radio or Mamá out of exasperation, my sister and I shut the bedroom door. We jumped on my bed to look out the window, which faced our grandparents' backyard, hoping to see our grandmother tending to her plants. If she wasn't around, we played games until it all calmed down.

If Grandma Emilia was in the garden, we'd bang on the window to get her attention. A few minutes later the doorbell would ring and Lola, my grandparents' live-in-maid, would walk us to our grandparents' home, to the sanctuary of some peace and quiet. Lola, the round lady with protruding cheekbones had become an orphan at thirteen, the same year she came to work for my family. One day when I asked her why she had stayed, she smiled, showing her gold-plated tooth. 'Gratitude. Gratitude, my girl.'

Caught in the middle of the war between the rebels and the government, women and children from her reservation had tried to find refuge in different cities. Many of the men joined the rebels. La India, as some people called her, lived in the streets until a social worker took her to an orphanage where Grandma sent her donations. 'The rest is history,' Lola said.

Once inside our grandparents' house, we let go of her plump hands and sprinted to the garden to find Grandma. My sister and I would fall into her open arms and embrace her petite body. The sweet scent of jasmine and spices stayed on our clothes long after our visits. We filled two small water cans with water and proceeded to drown the potted plants while Grandma watered and pruned her golden yellow trumpets and rose bushes. 'Sing to the plants and they'll be happier,' she told us. We did.

When we finished, we went to the dining room, where we found two cups of hot chocolate and a cup of tea for Grandma. Liliana stared at the small basket with warm rolls as we passed it around. 'Only one. We don't want to spoil your dinner,' Grandma said.

She showed me pictures and filled me with endless stories about her childhood growing up as General Francisco Villa de Alba's beloved daughter. He called her Negrita because of her golden-honey complexion.

I learned that my father wasn't the first one in our family to fling himself into politics. In my grandparents' entrance hung my great-grandfather's picture next to his brother's, Captain Jorge Villa de Alba. The brothers had fought in the Thousand Days' Civil War, incredibly, on opposite sides. The general was a leader in the liberal party, while his brother joined the conservative party. After the victory of the conservative party, the general lost his job as mayor and was forced to take a lower-paid post until there was a party change in the government. After the war, the general and the captain never spoke to each other again. It was a sad story.

Next to the captain was the portrait of the brothers' mother. She was a light-skinned, almond-eyed, young Spaniard who was as playful as my grandma and an avid equestrian. However, one day the young woman was riding when her horse was spooked by a snake and threw her to the ground. She died soon after the fall. Two large paintings hung on the opposite side of the hallway, the general's wife, and her sister. The two Jewish sisters had converted to Catholicism in the 1930s.

The family were more than aware of a madman in Germany called Adolf Hitler who was soon to become Chancellor of Germany. Hitler capitalized on the economic woes and popular discontent of the time, and his virulent anti-Semitism and obsessive pursuit of Aryan supremacy was quickly gathering pace. The sister's parents had already read about political prisoners, communists, Roma Gypsies, Jehovah's Witnesses and homosexuals imprisoned in concentration camps in places like Dachau. They sensed it was only a matter of time before Hitler came for the Jews. The family ended their

Sephardic traditions, but secretly practiced Judaism at home with their parents. They went to church only when someone died, for a wedding or christening.

I wondered if my parents' pictures or even mine would one day be added to these walls. I would be a fifth-generation Villa de Alba.

Liliana was still a toddler when my brother Jaime was born, surprising us all. Although premature, he grew fast. One quiet afternoon, Mamá, Liliana and I were in my parents' room watching baby Jaime trying to roll over. He grunted while he swung his arms around and kicked. Papá came into the room singing a ballad, but stopped when he saw Jaime's sweaty, red face. 'You can do it. You are strong,' Papá cheered him on.

Jaime grabbed one of his own feet and chuckled. We laughed when he swung his lower body to one side, rolling over. Once facedown, he growled again.

'Good job, that's my boy,' Papá said, lifting Jaime into the air.

'You're home early. What's going on?' Mamá kissed Papá.

He held Jaime on one side and wrapped his other arm around her and said, 'I was just informed that I will be completing my social service program in Puerto López. It was my first choice.'

Mamá moved away from him.

'I've done everything for you and this family… even staying up late at night typing your school notes so that you can sell them to other students, but this is too much. I've heard things about that town I don't like,' she said. 'They say rebels have taken over the place and besides, I don't want to move. At least not now. I'd prefer to live near my parents, at least until the kids are a little older.'

'Please, Cecilia, there is nothing wrong with that town. You know that the social program is obligatory, and if we don't go to Puerto López, we would have to go to another place, perhaps one even farther away. This is the best option. Once I'm done, we will come back to the city. It would be good for the children to learn more about life in the countryside, don't you think?' He grinned, handing my brother, who was yawning, to Mamá. 'Rocío, are you all right?' Papá approached me.

I blinked fast, trying to hide how uncomfortable I felt. 'Are you mad at Mamá?'

'No. We are just having a discussion.'

'But she was mad.'

'Maybe. But we will work it out.'

'But I don't want to leave Grandpa and Grandma.' I rubbed my eyes, hoping to contain the tears.

'We don't always have what we want. Be strong, my girl,' Papá said as he walked away.

One morning, we were packing Papá's station wagon when I dropped what I was holding.

'Why do we have to move?'

'I told you; I have to complete my social service program.' He stuffed a suitcase deep into the trunk of the car.

I didn't know what the service program was about, but thoughts of going to some strange place, away from my grandparents, the only refuge my sister's and I had, was eating me inside.

'I want to stay here,' I mumbled.

Papá placed a box on the floor and cast his eyes on mine, making me shiver. 'There are things you have to do in life that you might not like, but you do them anyway.'

I pouted.

'That's enough.' Papá tilted his head. 'I know your grandparents are important to you, but this move will be good for our family. Besides, I'll have more time at home.'

Before long, a truck with our other belongings was on its way to our new home and we continued packing the car in silence until there were no more bags.

'We need to go now before it gets late,' he said as he closed the trunk. 'I'll be back.'

I ran up the eighteen steps to our apartment, the steps on which Grandma taught me to count. Our now barren apartment felt raw, so I turned around and went to join the rest of my family outside. Mamá picked Jaime up from the stroller;

Papá held Liliana's and my hands, then we went to say goodbye to Grandpa Miguel and Grandma Emilia.

Lola opened the cathedral-like front door, drying her hands on her white apron and said, 'Come in, please, don Miguel and doña Emilia are finishing their lunch.'

The aroma of fresh-baked bread filled the air.

My family made their way inside, but I stayed behind, wandering the hallway for a while and saying goodbye to my ancestors. There were no pictures of Grandpa's family. His father had died young, leaving his mother with eight children and a small tailoring shop. The older brothers teased Grandpa because, as a child, he was mute. To hide from them after school, he roamed the streets with boys from the other side of the avenue. When he came home late at night, his mother was waiting for him with a belt, and he always missed dinner.

The story goes that one afternoon, Grandpa changed his plan. He decided he would eat before the family did. This way, he could stay out late and not have to go to bed hungry. He went into the kitchen and poured himself some soup. When he turned around, he came face-to-face with his mother. Terrified, he dropped the bowl, which shattered against the tiled floor.

He spoke. 'I'll go to my room.'

Overjoyed to hear her son's voice for the first time, she threw her arms around him and showered him with kisses. Still, years after her passing, Grandpa didn't speak of her or his family.

When I went into the dining room, Grandpa was speaking with Papá.

'You must know that I'm not very happy you are taking my daughter and my grandchildren away. If there is an emergency, it would take hours for us to get to your place. Are you absolutely sure you have to do this?'

'Yes, we do,' Papá said, 'but it will be only for a year. Cecilia and the kids will visit you whenever possible. Puerto López is less than five hours away by car. Don't worry, we will be fine.'

Grandpa Miguel signaled to Papá with his head to join him on one side of the room. The two men whispered for a few minutes. Grandpa's back was toward us. His hands waving in the air. Papá stopped talking after a while and stared into the distance. It looked like he had turned into stone. Grandma tried to distract us with her farewell gifts, but I couldn't take my eyes off the men.

'We look forward to your visits, then.' Grandpa walked toward us and embraced me tight against his chest.

As an amateur comedian, Grandpa used to make fun of everything and everyone. My sister and I would laugh until our stomachs hurt. Sometimes we put curlers on his thinning hair while he was watching TV. He'd pretend not to notice until we were finished. He then would stand up and walk like a woman. 'Those hideous apparatuses.' He'd take the curlers off and throw them at us.

When he fell asleep in his reading chair, I'd take a feather from one of Grandma's decorations and put it up his nose. He'd wake up sneezing and then chase after us.

Grandpa was not smiling that morning. He let go of me and hugged the rest of my family. He shook my father's hand.

'Remember, family comes first,' he said.

My grandparents walked us to the front door and blew kisses as we drove away.

The drive to our new home didn't feel long. Perhaps it was because, at almost six years old, I was distracted. Puff-like clouds sat on the peaks of the Andean mountains. The winding road was terrifying. At one point, I looked out the window and noticed our car was close to the edge of a cliff that looked bottomless.

If our car rolls down there, it will be swallowed whole. I couldn't escape my thoughts.

After we drove for a couple of hours, the mountains disappeared, and vast grasslands extended as far as the eye could see.

We stopped to watch six horsemen herding hundreds of cattle across a river. The men whistled at the cows as their horses circled around the large animals. Three dogs ran around barking. When the first two horses approached the shallow part of the river, they trotted into the clear waters, splashing one another. The herd followed. The dogs and the other horsemen stayed behind until all the cows were in the water; then they crossed.

'I didn't know that cows liked water,' I said.

'Yes, they actually know how to swim.' Papá extended his left arm outside the window. 'This is just one thing you cannot see in the city.'

A little later, the clouds turned gray, and it drizzled. Like a colorful kite, a flock of reddish-orange birds flew over us.

'See that flock of birds? They look like egrets, but they are actually scarlet ibis,' Papá told us, pointing at the sky. 'This is why this area is so beautiful.'

Mamá rested her head on his shoulder. 'It is pretty... so different from other places we have visited.'

'See, I told you,' he replied.

And they kissed. Liliana and I giggled. The weather changed and howling wind and rain accompanied us the rest of the way.

'Look. We're almost home.' Papá pointed to a house in the distance.

It was like a lighthouse on an island. Our new house stood alone in the middle of a sea of tropical grassland. Even squinting, I couldn't see any other buildings. Empty fields were our new neighbors. 'Where are the other houses?' Papá looked at me in the rearview mirror. 'The closest town is Puerto López, which is about twenty minutes away by car. But do not worry, we will have plenty of visitors.'

No one said anything. For the first time, we were going to be by ourselves, no people, city lights, or traffic noise. What would that be like? I began breathing fast at the thought. So different from our life in Bogotá.

When we finally arrived, the rain had ceased. Papá helped Mamá out of the car, and then he took Jaime into his arms. Liliana and I jumped out and ran behind our parents as they made their way to the small brick building.

When Papá opened the front door of the house, I grabbed my sister's hand and ran inside. Mamá told us the movers had already assembled the beds. Our old couch was against the front window. Across from it, there was a matching chair, and in the middle of the room, there was a round oak table. We went to the left of the living room, where we found the kitchen. There was a door next to the refrigerator. Liliana opened it and stepped out onto a short path that connected our house with a separate structure. I tried to stop her, but she ran towards it. When Liliana heard our father's voice, she spun around and came back into the kitchen. She then stared at him with troubled eyes.

'I am not upset, Liliana. That is the infirmary, the place where I will be taking care of patients.'

My sister smirked, relieved she wasn't in trouble.

Papá opened the metal door to the one-roomed structure to reveal a large room with a creaking wooden floor. There were two beds, two chairs, a sink, a fan, a lamp on a stand, and a large metal medicine cabinet. Everything in the room was white, including my father's coat, which hung on a coat stand. Papá showed us some of the equipment, but told us never to touch it. 'You need to stay out of this room, girls.'

My sister and I nodded.

'Only Dr. Hugo Gutiérrez, the dentist; Lorena Pérez, the nurse; and I, aside from the patients, of course, will be allowed in the infirmary.'

Before we left the city, I'd heard Mamá tell Grandma that Lorena became a nurse after her older brother had been killed. The young man disappeared after joining the leftist local group. A few months later, his body was returned to the family. The authorities claimed he had been found face down in a ditch; he'd been sprayed with bullets. No one claimed responsibility for his death.

Haunted by her brother's horrific passing, Lorena left her small town and went to Bogotá, where she became a nurse. The dentist, whom Papá called Rich Boy, had attended the best schools in the city. But just like my father, he too had to complete his social service.

Mamá came in.

'Large room,' she said, dusting the cabinet with her fingers. 'How about if we check out the rest of the house?'

Papá closed the door of the infirmary behind us. In line, we went back through the kitchen and into the hallway. Liliana and I inspected every room in the house. In the first room, Jaime was sleeping in his crib near my parents' bed. A small, tiled bathroom was next to my parents' room. I held my sister's hand and walked on to where we found Mamá's sewing machine, ironing board, and two hampers packed with clothes. On one side of the room, there were boxes stacked up, almost to the ceiling.

In the last room, we found our twin beds, which were parallel to the window. 'I'll take this one.' I sat on the one next to the window.

Liliana climbed onto the other bed. I stood on mine and looked out the window. I could only see grassland. My heart felt heavy for my grandparents. They seemed so far away.

The first few days in our new house were busy. Mamá and I organized the closets while Liliana played with Jaime. Soon, Papá's patients began coming to the infirmary. One day, shortly after midday, Papá came home for lunch to escape the windless, fierce summer heat. I jumped out of my seat with delight when he came in. Now that he was working next door, I didn't have to stay up late to be with him. He was home for most meals.

We had just begun eating when we heard a woman squealing for a doctor. We rushed outside, where we found a woman collapsed on the steps of the infirmary. She had the largest stomach I had ever seen. She was bigger than Mamá when she was pregnant with Jaime. Lorena came out of the infirmary and tried to pick her up, but the woman seemed lifeless. Lifting her up with his arms, Papá carried the woman inside. Lorena joined them, closing the door behind her.

'Everyone inside,' ordered my mother, nuzzling Liliana and me back into the house.

But when she was bathing Jaime, I left. I had to see what was wrong with the new patient. I had never heard howling like that before. She sounded like a wounded animal.

On tiptoes, I snuck out the back door and went around to the infirmary, where there was an open window. I dragged a stool over and stood on it. But before I could see anything, I stumbled and fell onto a knitting needle. Now I was the one screaming. I screamed even louder when I noticed that the needle, like a skewer, was sticking out of my right foot. Mamá immediately appeared and held my bloody and throbbing foot with a cloth. 'Didn't I tell you to stay in the house?' she snarled.

I became even more distraught when I heard Papá's unmistakable footsteps approaching. When he saw my bare, bloody foot, he threw his arms up in exasperation. 'I told you to wear shoes.'

He lifted me up, carried me into the infirmary, and laid me on the empty bed next to the young woman. Mamá stood by the door. I was in pain, but happy to have my father's attention.

'What were you doing out there? Didn't your mamá tell you to go inside with her?'

'Yes, Papá. I'm sorry.' Tears burst out of my eyes. 'I just wanted to see what was wrong with the lady.'

Mamá walked in and kissed me on the cheek. 'Don't be upset. You know your papá only wants to keep you safe. Rest now. I must feed the others, but I'll see you later.'

She left the infirmary, closing the door behind her. Lorena was standing near the sink, cleaning a baby.

I had some understanding of where babies came from because my father explained it to me before Jaime was born. He used every opportunity he could to teach. Whether we were interested in the subject, or whether we understood the sometimes-complex concepts, didn't matter to him. It was as though we were running out of time and had to learn it all at once.

Papá went to the medicine cabinet and brought alcohol, cotton, and two syringes.

'The alcohol is going to sting, but I want you to be brave,' he warned.

'I will.'

'Good. The first shot will prevent an infection. The second one will help you sleep so that I can remove the needle and suture you up,' he explained, as he patted me on the shoulder.

I wanted him to forgive me and to be proud of me, so I didn't react when I felt a prick in my arm. My foot was throbbing, but I didn't say anything about that either. Then I felt the second prick. I fell asleep moments later.

When I woke up, the needle was gone, and my right foot was bandaged. Papá was speaking to the young mother.

'Miss Ortiz, you need to go back to your parents' home now,' he told her.

'They didn't want me to work, so I left. And now, with a baby, they will never let me back in the house.' She exhaled and looked away. 'Thank you for your help doctor, but I need to leave as soon as my boyfriend gets here.'

'That is not a good idea. I recommend you stay tonight; it could be dangerous for you and the baby.'

'My boyfriend doesn't want me to. Our neighbor will take care of me.'

'All right, but if you have excessive bleeding or develop a fever, you need to go immediately to the hospital in town. Here is your medication.' Papá handed her a small paper bag.

From my bed, I looked out the open door and saw the nurse carrying a bundle. Papá helped the lady into a waiting car. Then Lorena gave her the baby, closed the door, and the car sped down our dusty driveway.

Late that night, a loud hoot awakened me. I sat up in bed and opened the curtains. I saw the silhouette of an owl perched on a branch of a tree. My parents were sitting out on the porch. They stayed quiet for some time, maybe waiting to hear the owl again, but I think it was scared, because it didn't hoot anymore.

Mamá kissed Papá and walked away from him. I lay back on my bed and kept my eyes closed until I heard Papá breathing evenly. When I opened my eyes again, I scouted my room and found him on a mattress by my bed. I smiled. Under the glow of a full moon from an open window, a sudden breeze caressed my face. The owl must have felt the same gust of wind, because it let out a loud hoot.

An Unwelcome Intruder

It seemed that everyone who came to our door was running away from something or someone, and Papá was there to help them. He treated everyone as if they were his most important patient. No exceptions. But one sweltering afternoon when the wind had died down, Mamá, my siblings, and I were left alone to fend for ourselves. Papá, Lorena, and Hugo had gone to the hospital in town to treat patients in critical condition.

With little to do inside the house, I went out to the porch and saw a large hawk hovering over the endless savannah. The bird suddenly swooped with great speed, straight down with claws out, snatched what looked like a mouse, and flew away. The initial admiration I felt for the wide-winged bird faded when I thought about that small mouse. Unsettled, I called out. Mamá and Liliana joined me immediately and I pointed to the sky, but the bird had flown away.

We stayed together until minutes later when we saw a car on the road, approaching fast. Under a cloud of dust, a beat-up pickup sped into our driveway. A heavyset man wearing leather boots and a dirty, untucked shirt stepped out. 'I need a doctor, now!' he demanded.

Pressing a bloody rag against his face with one hand, he held a gun in the other. He looked at our house first, then at the other building with his attention on the sign: *Infirmary*. Then he kicked the door open so hard that it came off its hinges. Mamá turned around with her eyes locked on mine.

'Rocío, you take care of your siblings and *do not* come out of this house. You understand?'

Liliana and I rushed to our parents' bedroom where we found Jaime. I planned to obey, but the thought of the man hurting Mamá made me sick.

Should I go find help? Where can I go? Our closest neighbor is outside of town. My thoughts were muddled.

Jaime cried out.

'Bottle.' Liliana ordered.

I ran to the kitchen on the opposite side of the house.

That was when I heard the man screaming at Mamá, 'You fix me, lady, or I will kill you!'

I stopped. I took out a knife from a drawer and was about to go out to the infirmary when I heard Mamá pleading, 'But I'm not a doctor. You need my husband to help.'

'I don't care, just do it,' the man bellowed.

I thought about the hawk and his prey, then shivered. Jaime's whimpering became louder. My mouth was suddenly dry, and I shook, dropping the knife on the floor. Grabbing the bottle from the refrigerator, I hurried back to the bedroom.

I plugged the rubber nipple of the bottle into his small mouth. He cried once more and then sucked. A moment later, he started fussing again. I went back to the kitchen and put a tablespoon of sugar into the bottle, shook it, and darted back to the room. I inserted the nipple back into my brother's mouth. He twitched a little, but his breathing became more rhythmic. He sucked the milk with such force that it looked like he was afraid someone would take the bottle away. When he finished, he turned over and fell asleep. Now I had become the one drenched in sweat. Liliana had also fallen asleep on our parents' bed.

I went out to the porch and, with my heart racing, I peeked inside the infirmary. The broken door rested against the doorframe. Mamá was pleading, 'Please allow me then to give you some anesthesia before I suture you.'

'No injections. I want to stay awake.'

'But the cut on your cheek is so deep, I can see your molars. I'm telling you; it's going to hurt a lot. I'll sew you up, but understand that I have never done this before. My husband should be back soon. Why not wait until he arrives?'

'Just do it, lady.'

I went back into the house and peered through every window, trying to figure out what to do. I grew angry with my father.

Why isn't he here? This man could kill the whole family.

Sometime later, I noticed, far in the distance, another car approaching.

I sprinted towards the oncoming car. It was Hugo, the dentist.

'Help! He's going to kill my Mamá.'

Hugo stopped the car and got out. His expression tensed.

'Who? What are you talking about?'

'There's a man… a man in the infirmary, and he… he's going to hurt Mamá,' I stuttered.

We dashed through the house to the path. Hugo lifted the unhinged infirmary door and opened it all the way. Inside, Mamá, wearing a bloodstained medical gown and rubber gloves, stood next to the man. Pasty-skinned, he was getting up from the chair. Hugo stepped back when he saw the gun.

'Rocío, go in the house!' Mamá screamed.

I stood frozen to the spot.

The man lunged at Mamá, pulling her towards him. She gasped as he pointed the gun at her. 'You two, move away and don't try any tricks or she dies.'

Hugo pushed me behind him. I grabbed onto his slacks and noticed he was trembling. My heart pounded hard inside my chest and I let out a scream.

'Shut up girl, or I'll kill you too.'

I buried my face in Hugo's leg, trying to be quiet, but a sob escaped me.

'Stay there,' the man ordered.

'Please, let me go… I have children,' Mamá pleaded.

I glanced around Hugo's legs. The man pushed my mother away from him so hard that she fell onto her back. He ran past us and out of the infirmary, staggering. Once in his truck, he raced out of our driveway. The dentist and I turned to help Mamá.

Who is Fidel Castro?

The next evening, when the darkness had engulfed the vast plains, I woke to the sound of the chirping crickets. I stood on my bed and looked out of my window to see, under the porch light, Papá welcoming a stocky man in an army uniform, Colonel Moncayo. He had brought two others. He removed his hat and shook Papá's hand. 'Dr Velázquez, meet el camarada, Manuel Marulanda.'

Marulanda was dressed like other peasants in the region, with light cotton pants and a wrinkled shirt. From his left shoulder hung a discolored poncho. A pencil-thin mustache outlined his narrow upper lip. The man took off his straw hat and shook Papá's hand vigorously. 'It is a real pleasure to meet you, Doctor. You are the talk of the town. Apparently, you are helping lots of people.'

'Please, call me Jaime.'

'And this is Leonel González; you probably remember him. You saved his hand,' said the man.

He gestured to the second man who had two German Shepherd dogs on a leash. The bearded, husky man extended his right hand, then flipped it to show both sides.

'It was a nasty cut, but now, it's like new thanks to you.'

'I am glad to hear that… and the dogs?' Papá asked.

'I brought these dogs from my farm because I already have too many. They're great guardians, so I thought of your family. It is the least I can do to repay you. I'm sorry your wife had an incident with that man.'

I felt an uncontrollable desire to run out and hug my new pets. However, I knew Papá wouldn't approve, so I stayed in my room thinking about what to name them and how to teach them to do tricks.

Perhaps they'd like to walk with me.

I felt butterflies in my stomach just thinking about the adventures we would have. Papá thanked the colonel, who cleared his throat. 'As we discussed, I've also made arrangements for a soldier to guard your house when you're at the hospital.'

'Thank you, Colonel. That will give us all peace of mind.' Papá motioned to four wooden chairs on the porch. 'It is cool here. We will not wake up my wife and children.'

I sat on my bed, and moved away from the window that faced the porch, so that the men wouldn't see me. The colonel was everything my father wasn't, loud and awkward. His gaze wandered when people spoke to him. Papá was gentle and attentive.

'How are things in town?' Papá asked.

'Nothing has changed. The time has come to fight back. The same injustices keep happening. Our people disappear all the time.'

The word *camarada* spun in my head. There was something about these men that made me uneasy. They were not ill, nor did they look like Hugo Sanchez or the other friends Papá had in the city.

Outside, I heard one of them say, 'I know you're not a drinker, Jaime, but today I hope you'll make an exception. We brought guarapo.'

The four men talked for what seemed like hours. I lay on my bed, listening in the darkness. When my body relaxed and I began to twitch with sleep, I forced myself to stay awake and looked out the window again. Papá was still sitting down. But his face was tight now, and he was bouncing his right leg up and down. He did that when he was mad.

He took a drink and said, 'Fidel Castro sent a plea for combatants. The word is that the attack on Fulgencio Batista's army is imminent. We need to move fast. This is our opportunity to support the revolution.'

He raised his glass. The colonel followed.

'We're ready.'

What on earth are they talking about? I thought to myself.

I listened as the men drove away, then climbed from my bed to sneak a look. The dogs were tied to the railing.

Papá then looked towards my window; it was almost as if he knew I'd been watching and eavesdropping. I quickly dived under my covers. He paced up and down for a couple of minutes. When I heard him move a chair, I peeked again. He had unleashed the dogs that were now drinking water from two metal bowls.

Under the faint light, with his long fingers, my father packed a leafy paste inside a wooden carved pipe. He lit the paste with a match. I'd never seen him smoke before. Puzzled, I thought about the conversation I'd just heard and now the image of Papá smoking. My thoughts were somehow disturbing to me. The one thing that kept me joyful was the thought of our new dogs. I was wrestling with my feelings when the sweet smell coming from Papá's pipe crept into my room. Soon, small, ashen-like clouds of smoke rose, dissipating into the night air.

The following day, my growling stomach woke me up. I sat on the porch stairs in my pajamas. The two dogs soon appeared, sniffing at me and wagging their tails. I showered affection on them and soon they curled up next to me, one on each side. Their chocolate coats felt like satin on my hands. While watching the sunrise cast orange and yellow strokes across the light blue sky. I heard heavy footsteps approaching,

'What are you doing up so early?' Papá yawned and sat next to me. 'I see you have already met your new pets.'

The two dogs jumped up and wagged their tails, sniffing Papá's pajama pants. 'I did. Thank you, I love them.' I leaned on Papá's arm. 'I even have names for them, Catia and Nala.'

'Where did you get those names?'

'I don't know, they just look like Catia and Nala.' I giggled.

'They are lucky to be females, because those names would not work for male dogs,' he said, embracing me.

'I'm hungry.'

'Well, I don't have an early appointment, so we can all make breakfast together.' He kissed my head.

'Really? We'll cook *together*?' A wave of fresh air filled my lungs. My father was making breakfast with me.

'It will be fun,' he nodded. 'I would also like to teach you about healthy eating habits.'

'Can we have scrambled eggs?' I asked, playing with a strand of hair.

'Yes, we can make eggs.'

At that, Mamá came out of the house.

'What are you doing up this early?' She rubbed her eyes, then sat next to Papá and kissed him on the lips. 'First, tell me about your friends. Who are the two men who came with Colonel Moncayo?'

'Just acquaintances. They brought us these guard dogs.'

'Who was the man with the poncho? He doesn't look like someone I'd imagine being friends with the colonel.'

'Well, appearances are often deceiving,' he replied. 'Rocío and I will make breakfast today; scrambled eggs are on the menu.'

They glanced at one another with tender eyes; then we went to the kitchen. I whisked several eggs while Papá cut the onion, garlic, tomato, and scallions. When the oil in the frying pan was hot, he added the ingredients together with salt and cumin. The smell of the *sofrito* soon filled the kitchen. I licked my lips just thinking about breakfast. We ate fresh rolls with the eggs. I had my usual glass of milk, and my parents drank hot coffee. There was no discussion about healthy eating, and I was glad and delighted my siblings were still sleeping because I had my parents all to myself.

Just like Leonel had promised, at night Catia and Nala barked and chased anything or anyone they didn't know away from our house. When patients came, my father tied the dogs up by the laundry room, behind the house. Once the patients settled in the infirmary, I let the dogs loose so they could play with me. A few weeks after the dogs arrived, Papá sat next to me on the porch stairs and said, 'I want you to know that today I will be operating on Nala.'

She must've heard her name because she came and lay by my side.

My heart began pounding loud. 'What's wrong with Nala?'

'Nothing, she is fine. I will just be removing one of her teeth.'

'What's wrong with her tooth?' I asked, placing my hands on my cheeks as if he were talking about removing *my* tooth.

'There is nothing wrong. I simply want to experiment with an implant.' Papá cleared his throat.

'Why Nala?'

'Well, people and animals have problems with their teeth, and sometimes they lose them. But we need our teeth for nourishment, and animals also need them for survival. If this experiment works, many people will be able to replace their decayed teeth with new ones. We cannot just think about ourselves. Sometimes we need to make sacrifices to help as many people as possible, regardless of the cost.'

I patted Nala's head. 'What's an implant?'

'It is a metal post that has an artificial tooth attached to it.'

'Is it going to hurt her?' I asked, my heart aching for my new dog.

He rubbed Nala's belly. 'No. She will be just fine.'

I had forgotten about his plans for Nala's surgery until after lunch, when I heard my father calling her. I sprinted and found them behind the house in the laundry room. Nala was standing on a short-legged table. Papá was hunched over her. With one hand, he was holding a syringe; with the other, he was touching Nala's head.

'What are you doing?' I asked, tears forming in my eyes.

'Rocío, go with your Mamá,' he said. 'I told you; I am extracting a tooth. She will not feel anything. Remember when you stepped on that knitting needle? Did it hurt when I took it out?'

'No.'

Papá arched one eyebrow.

'All right, then please let me work and go help your Máma.'

I crossed my arms over my chest and walked away. I found Mamá spoon-feeding mashed papaya to Jaime and Liliana in the bathtub. My brother and sister were splashing in the water, playing with small floating toys.

Restless, I asked, 'Mamá, do you need help?'

'Not right now. You can play with your sister after she's done with her bath,' she said, without turning back to look at me.

I left and hovered near the laundry room until Papá came out, drying his hands with a towel. He did not see me because he went directly into the infirmary and closed the door.

I didn't approach him either. Instead, I released Catia, who was tied up, and then together we made our way over to see Nala.

Her limp body was extended across the table, her chest moving up and down with each breath. I sat on the floor while Catia licked Nala. We stayed in the laundry room for some time and, when Nala finally woke up, she tried to stagger off the table, but I stopped her. She looked at me with infirm eyes, then touched me with her cold nose. Catia wagged her tail, circling Nala.

'You should stay in bed, at least for a while, Nala,' I whispered, and stroked her.

Nala walked away almost as if she were lost. I helped her off the table and dragged her bed near me. Gently, I pulled her over.

'Here, here sit.' Nala hobbled towards me, then lay down.

When the rains flooded the rivers, Colonel Moncayo came to see Papá again. I opened the door and asked him to come in. The colonel's hat was dripping water all over his jacket. From inside the colonel's muddy military jeep, another man looked my way.

'Rocío, is your Mamá here?' His nostrils flared as he waited for my response. I was about to respond when Mamá came out of her room. 'Colonel, come in. What brings you here?'

The colonel saluted Mamá, tapping one side of his hat with his fingers. 'Thank you, Ma'am, may I speak with the doctor?'

'He's finishing his work. You can find him in the infirmary.'

The colonel bowed and walked away. Mamá and I stood by the door as the colonel knocked on the door of the infirmary. Papá opened the door and greeted him. I wished I could've heard what he was telling my father, but the roar of thunder and the torrential rain was deafening, drowning their voices.

The next morning, Papá announced at the dining table that we were moving back to our apartment in Bogotá. I raised my arms in joy.

Mamá asked, 'What about your public service? We've been in this town for almost a year. What do you have left, less than two months?'

'I am almost done. Colonel Moncayo will drive you all back to the city. One of his assistants will drive the truck with our belongings.'

My mother's eyes narrowed. 'What about you?'

'I have to stay a little longer, but I will follow you soon.'

I felt a rush of panic just thinking about not having my father around. The fact that the colonel was accompanying us also worried me.

'How soon, Papá?'

'A few weeks, that's all.'

'What if we get sick? Who'll take care of us?'

'You will be fine.'

Jaime began to howl. Mamá pushed her chair away from the table and tilted her head to one side as she said, 'I don't understand why we can't stay here until you finish.'

He said he was going to work night shifts and it wasn't safe for us to be alone at night. He went on for some time. Incredulous, we listened.

'We can discuss this later. I need to feed the baby.' Mamá left the room and Papá stood up.

'Of course.' It was always the same. We did as he said.

The day Colonel Moncayo came to pick us up, I sat on the porch stairs, feeling uneasy. His helpers loaded the truck while Papá and Mamá packed the jeep.

When the house and the infirmary were clean, Papá kneeled and gave me a bear hug.

'Who will the dogs ride with?' I asked.

'Nala and Catia are staying here,' he said.

'Why? They should come with us. They're my dogs.' I moved away from my father.

'The apartment is too small. They cannot come until we find a bigger house. They would not be happy in a small place.'

'But I don't want to leave my dogs.'

Papá held my hand. 'Rocío, your mamá and I have decided that it would be best if the dogs stay with Colonel Moncayo, at least for now. He will take care of them. I will be staying at the medical housing in town. But I will be around to watch them whenever possible.'

'What about you?' I dove into his arms, sobbing.

'Rocío, I need you to be strong. I will come home when I am done here. Please promise me you will help your mamá.'

I didn't want to be away from my father. I didn't want to leave my dogs. But when I looked around, I noticed they were all watching me. Mamá was holding the baby, with Liliana by her side. The colonel and his helpers had finished packing and were standing next to the truck. All eyes were on me, awaiting my response. Gazing into Papá's eyes, I said, 'All right, but promise me you'll come home soon and try very hard to bring my dogs.'

'I promise.'

He got up and walked me to the car. Nala and Catia joined us, their ears relaxed. I let go of my father's hand and hugged both dogs. Papá kissed us all and helped us into the car. I tried to call the dogs, but I was choking with my tears as we drove away. I couldn't help but look out of the back window. Papá looked so alone.

'He will join us soon.' Mamá touched my face.

I had never been apart from my father. I thought of the many colorful birds I'd watched fly in unison, creating patterns across the sky. Like my father, I had become fond of these small creatures, and I would miss this place.

Catia and Nala ran after us for some time, though after a few minutes, they couldn't keep up. They then turned around and ran back to Papá. The more we drove, the smaller they became until they were gone, swallowed by the grassy Eastern Plains.

My Grandparents in Bogotá

Soon after we left the plains, the jeep began to ascend a curvy road. When the temperature dropped, Mamá handed Liliana and me our coats.

'Let's all cover up,' she said as she wrestled with Jaime.

A blanket of heavy, damp fog followed us all the way up the Andes, the jeep leading the way, and behind us, the truck tagging along.

The sun was setting when we finally arrived in Bogotá. A slanted reddish sunbeam was visible on the horizon. A chilly wind was blowing, and dry leaves twisted in the air like colorful pinwheels. I rubbed my hands in joy as we approached my grandparents' home. We hadn't visited them since we left nearly a year ago.

When we parked, I jumped out of the car.

'We're here,' I announced, as I ran up the eighteen steps to my grandparents' place. Lola opened the door before I rang the doorbell. She embraced me.

'So nice to see you, niña Rocío. We were expecting you.'

Grandma Emilia joined us at the door. 'My sweet Rocío, how are you?'

'Happy to see you, Grandma.' I embraced her small waist.

'You are so tall.' She inspected me with her curious, dark eyes. 'Where are your parents?'

'Mamá is down by the car, and Papá—' I swallowed hard, 'had to stay for work.'

'I'm sure he will be here soon,' she said. 'Now let's go help your mamá.'

She held my hand, and we walked down the stairs to the street where we found Mamá carrying Jaime. Liliana stood by her side. Colonel Moncayo and his two skinny, well-mannered helpers were unloading the truck.

'I'm so glad to have you all back,' Grandma said, kissing Mamá and my siblings.

But we weren't all back. Papá was still gone, and so were my dogs. Anxiety filled my chest as I thought of Catia and Nala. The two-bedroom apartment, which was adjacent to my grandparents' home, was indeed too small for them. I remembered the many times I watched them play and chase after one another until Nala, the older of the two, would flop onto the ground in a full doggy snit. Other days, they had roamed around, chasing birds away and looking for hidden treasure. I knew it was impossible for them to live in our little apartment. I bit my lip so I wouldn't cry.

Colonel Moncayo and his helpers didn't leave our place until they assembled the furniture. Mamá walked the colonel to the door.

'Ma'am, do you need anything else?' he asked.

'No, thanks for all your hard work.'

When the colonel was walking down the stairs, Mamá called, 'Mmm… excuse me, Colonel, I've been curious; how exactly did you meet my husband?'

The colonel stopped and slowly turned around. He pulled out his keychain and nervously began to play with the keys.

'In town. You know, ma'am… it's so small that you pretty much know everyone.'

'Aha, well send him my love.'

Impatient, she tapped her foot until the truck and the jeep turned the corner.

That evening, we were pleasantly surprised. Lola had made her Muisca specialty and my favorite, *ajiaco*. The hearty soup had chicken, corn, different types of potatoes, and *guascas*, a herb that tasted like mild oregano. She served a side dish of avocado and rice, which I later transferred into my soup bowl. Papá would have been irritated at the sight. Mixing food all on one plate was something he considered rude.

But it didn't matter to me anymore. I had been unhappy at first, but now I was angry with him. Mamá didn't notice what I had done, because she was busy telling my grandparents all about our ten-month adventure. I ate the mushy soup, smiling inside.

When I was about to finish, Lola appeared, carrying a tray with glasses of juice.

'*Curuba* juice. I love it. Yum,' I said as I slid my tongue across my lips. *Curuba*, also known as banana passion fruit, is originally from Grandma's region. I recalled the first day I saw Lola make the juice. I had been standing in the kitchen watching how she cut the yellow shells in half, scooped the orangey pulp into the blender and then added water. At low speed, the seeds separated from the pulp, and then Lola emptied the mix into a strainer before pouring the juice back into the clean blender and adding milk and sugar. The creamy juice Lola brought to the table that day was just like I had remembered it, sweet and slightly tart. Delicious.

A heaving sound coming from the bathroom woke me up the following morning. The door was partially open. When I looked inside, my mother was kneeling at the toilet, vomiting. With her right arm, she was clinging to the toilet, and with her other arm, she was pinning her long, auburn hair up, away from her face.

'What's the matter, Mamá?' I shouted. She let go of the toilet and without turning around to look at me, waved her hand, shooing me away. A deep sense of disappointment flashed across me. Even if we called Papá, it would take him a long time to arrive. I stood frozen in distress, a stream of questions and what ifs were rumbling around my mind when suddenly, my stomach tightened, and I too began heaving.

Mamá turned around and looked at me with glassy eyes. Her stained nightgown was draped around her body. She wiped her mouth with a towel and moaned, 'Rocío, go take care of your siblings. Go, now, please.'

I covered my mouth with my hand and went to the kitchen. I wanted to go back and help my mother, but couldn't. Watching her like that had left me light-headed and sweating.

Liliana walked in, scratching her head. 'Where is Mamá?'

'She's in the bathroom.'

'I want breakfast.' She looked around the kitchen as if searching for food.

'She's busy. Leave her alone,' I growled.

'I'm *hungry*,' she said, moping.

The unsettled feeling welling inside me didn't allow me to think clearly. All I knew was that there was something really wrong with my mother. But all I could do for now was follow her instructions. I pulled myself together and served Liliana a glass of milk with a biscuit. I took Jaime's bottle, which had been left on the kitchen counter, and brought it to him. He was still in his crib in my parents' room. When I went back to the kitchen, Mamá was standing near the stove, drinking a glass of water. Her ghostly skin now had a light, rosy tint. The wet collar of her oversized shirt, left by her wet hair, drooped to one side.

'I fed the kids, Mamá. Are you all right?'

'I'm fine now. Something I ate didn't agree with me.'

'Do you want me to call Grandma?'

'No. I'll be fine. There's no need to call anyone.'

'I think Papá should know that you're sick.'

'No, that's not a good idea. He's busy.'

'Mamá is sick?' Liliana stopped eating.

Our mother embraced Liliana then me and assured us there wasn't anything wrong. The last time she had been sick like this was before Jaime was born. My chest got tight every time I relived the bathroom scene. It didn't make sense. Somehow, it was the same feeling I had about Colonel Moncayo.

Is Mamá in danger? Is Papá in trouble? I should've told him I don't like the colonel.

Why did I feel so unsettled?

Torn between fear and loyalty to my mother, I told no one about her condition, which quickly became chronic. Every morning, she would lock herself in the bathroom. Then the horrible heaving sounds began, followed by the sound of puke. My heart aching, I thought that my mother could die.

I fed my brother and sister every morning. When Mamá's time in the bathroom increased, I read to them after breakfast. Most of my books were committed to memory and if I didn't know words, I made them up. I pretended to read Mamá's *Reader's Digest* magazines. I enjoyed creating a make-believe world where the heroes were Nala and Catia, in Puerto López, stories just for the three of us. There was also a small part of me that liked to see my siblings' faces look at me with admiration. When I giggled, they giggled back. When I frowned, they frowned. If I clapped, they did too. My brother and sister never found out that all the stories I read to them from magazines were creations of my imagination.

Sometimes if my brother and sister became restless, I'd have them recite snippets of *El niño y la Mariposa*, *The Boy and the Butterfly*, by Rafael Pombo repeatedly. In this poem, a rich boy asks the butterfly for her wings. But the butterfly refuses. She explains to him why they are essential to her life while they would do him no good. She also asks him why he'd want her pretty wings if he was already wealthy. The boy reconsiders and gives her a drop of honey as a symbol of appreciation and friendship. At the end, the butterfly lands on his hand where she dies. I told my brother and sister an alternative ending.

Like Mamá, butterflies are too pretty to die. She'll be fine. She'll be fine, I kept repeating to myself so I wouldn't weep.

My mother's daily bathroom ritual lasted for what seemed weeks until one chilly morning in early in 1956. I was tending to my siblings when I heard a knock. Liliana and Jaime ran to the front door. 'Don't open the door!' I screamed at my siblings and sprinted after them. Each time someone was at the door, I thought of the cowboy who had pointed a gun at our mother and asked her to fix his face. My siblings stopped and looked at me with frightened eyes. The knock persisted.

'It's me. It's Grandma. Open the door.'

Grandma had always made me feel safe. Her voice was as soothing as cool water on a hot summer day. We let her in. She bent over and hugged each one of us. 'So nice to see my little darlings. Where is Mamá?' she asked as she walked into the living room. A mild jasmine scent came in with her.

'Mamá is in the bathroom. She's taking a shower… I think.'

I felt like an accomplice. I bit my lip, thinking about Papá. Liars infuriated him. But was I really lying? I didn't know. Nervously, I began playing with my hands.

Grandma walked towards the bathroom as she said, 'Rocío, you go play with your brother and sister in your room while I speak with your mamá.'

The sharp clacking sound of Grandma's heels traveled across the hardwood floor. I did as I was told and didn't come out until I saw Mamá and Grandma talking and walking into the living room.

The following day, Grandma walked my brother, sister, and me next door to her house. The sound of the cowbell on the side door greeted us.

'I have a surprise for you.' Our grandmother grinned.

At this, Liliana, Jaime, and I darted into the large and well-manicured garden. On one side, near the fig tree, was a wooden playhouse the gardener had built for us. Inside was a kid's table with four matching chairs. Lola came out of the main house carrying a tray with chopped fruit, cheese, rolls, boiled eggs, and three small glasses of *curuba* juice. 'Good afternoon, niños.' A cheerful toddler, her son, walked by her side.

'What's his name?' I held his small hand inside mine.

'Rodrigo,' Lola said, while she set the table.

I felt sorry for the boy. I'd heard that his father was a drunk and Lola wanted nothing to do with him. 'Can he stay with us?' I asked.

Grandma glanced at Lola. 'For a little while, if it is all right with Lola.'

'Yes, for a little while.'

For some odd reason, Lola seemed uncomfortable with the idea of leaving her son with us. 'Just a few minutes,' she said, as she walked back to the kitchen.

'Why can't he play with us?' I asked my grandmother.

'Remember what I told you before? We all need to keep our place and his is in the kitchen with his mamá.'

I stared at her, not knowing what to say. I thought of the days when I had helped her pack large bags of clothing and bags with food and other donations she later sent to orphanages and shelters.

And now she wants to keep Lola and her son in the kitchen. That doesn't make sense. Is my own grandmother one of those rich people Papá despises? I shook my head, trying to get rid of the conflicted feelings tearing me apart.

'Rocío, are you listening to me?' Grandma snapped her fingers.

'I'm sorry. What did you say?'

'I am taking your Mamá to the doctor today. Please watch your brother and sister. Lola will also be around.' She waved and left.

We spent the day playing store. The figs became the currency, and I was the store manager. I sold my siblings dishes, rocks, leaves, and treasures I found in the yard. Hours later, Mamá and Grandma came into the yard looking for us. They had good news; we were going to have another brother or sister.

I didn't remember Liliana's birth, perhaps because I was too young. But this felt different from when Jaime was born. I was nervous.

'Is it a boy or a girl?' Liliana giggled.

'We won't know until the baby is born. You haven't said anything Rocío, are you all right?' Mamá asked.

'Sorry, Mamá, I'm happy. I was just thinking... what about you? Are you going to get cured?'

'Pregnancy is not an illness,' Grandma hurried to explain.

'We need to tell Papá. He has to know,' I said.

'I already called him, and he knows we are expecting another child. And don't worry, morning sickness is normal.'

Late one evening, I heard a key clicking inside the lock of the front door, followed by a squeaking noise. The sound of heavy footsteps made me jump off my bed. I looked around the room. Liliana was on her side, breathing steady. When I heard Papá's voice. I darted out of the bedroom and saw him bent over my mother in her bed, giving her a kiss.

'It is so great to be home,' he whispered.

Mamá lifted her head off the bed, and bending her elbows, propped herself up. Papá held her hand and helped her sit, then he sat next to her.

'Papá, Papá,' I said, embracing him.

The tears I had been holding back trickled from my eyes. He held me against his powerful chest.

'Why did it take you so long to come home? Is your work done? Are you staying with us now? Where are Nala and Catia?'

'Rocío, you have too many questions. It has been less than two months. That's not very long when you are working. And yes, I am home for good. I have successfully completed my service. That means that your Papá is officially a doctor.'

'Congratulations.' Mamá kissed him.

Our father's face lit up as he told us all about completing his degree, and the plans he had to find work in the city. He also mentioned that the summer in Puerto López had been especially dry, and Colonel Moncayo had taken Catia and Nala to his farm near the Orinoco River, one of the largest rivers in the Eastern Plains. When my eyes felt heavy, I pretended to be asleep. Just as I hoped, Papá carried me to my bed. At least for that evening, I didn't worry. All I had to do was be me.

A New Arrival

I became aware of Mamá's every move, the way she navigated the stairs, her shallow breaths when doing simple things, the naps she took after breakfast and lunch. All I heard my father talk about was the baby and our living arrangements. It seemed, however, that I was the only one unsettled by her condition.

Will it be a boy or a girl? Where will he or she sleep? What about the name? What about hiring a maid?

But when Papá wasn't around, Mamá took more naps and moved slower.

On a day when large raindrops drummed on the roof, I found Mamá lying on the couch. Her maternity skirt and blouse fell loosely on her body. Worried that she might be cold, I brought a throw, and when I was going to cover her legs, I noticed her ankles were swollen.

'It's normal. I'm just retaining water.' She covered her legs with the shawl and put a wet towel over her forehead. 'Liliana and Jaime are taking a nap, so please be quiet. Let them sleep so I can rest.'

I went to my bedroom. And looked out the window. The rain had stopped. The water trapped on leaves sparkled like tiny crystals. A hummingbird went on with its day, feeding from flower to flower, then flying away. I envied the peacefulness of the garden.

My father is a doctor. He'll know if there is something wrong with Mamá. My thoughts were meant to calm my restlessness.

A few hours later, Papá came home singing. Mamá and I were folding clean clothes in her bedroom.

'Why are you so happy?' Mamá asked.

He bent over to kiss me, then kissed Mamá.

'How about if you and I go to the movies?'

'What about the kids?'

Papá took the shirt she had in her hand and placed it on the bed. He then held her hands in his.

'It is all arranged. Lola will stay here with them until we come home. Her sister will stay at your parents' house with little Rodrigo.'

Mamá smiled. 'We haven't been to the movies in a long time. As a matter of fact, I don't remember the last time we were out together.'

'Tell me how you are feeling,' Papá put his head to one side and looked at Mamá.

'She's not good,' I said.

He leaned over. 'What do you mean? She is not well?'

'She—' I was going to tell him about her headaches when Mamá interrupted us.

'Don't be silly, Rocío. Such a worrier,' she scolded. 'I feel fine. Perhaps I had a little indigestion.'

'What did you eat for lunch?'

'Lentils, rice, chicken, and salad. Nothing new.'

'That should not upset your stomach. You should see the gynecologist right away.'

'I will call him tomorrow. Today I want to go out.'

'Are you sure?'

'Yes.' Mamá smiled.

'All right, but I will call Dr. Galindo to schedule an appointment.'

I looked at my parents, back and forth. It was as if they didn't see me.

How could Mamá tell him she was fine? Why wouldn't she mention the headaches or her swollen legs?

Raising my voice, I said, 'But Papá, her legs are swollen.'

Papá lifted her skirt enough to see her knees. Mamá tried to brush his hand away, but he insisted. 'Yes, they are. But she had some swelling with other pregnancies as well. Dr. Galindo knows what he is doing, so do not worry.'

I felt relief pouring from me, so I embraced Papá. He hugged me back.

When Lola arrived, she went straight into the kitchen where I heard Mamá giving her instructions. Then my parents kissed my siblings and me goodbye. When they closed the front door, my brother and sister went to play. I sat on the couch and wrapped my arms around where Mamá's favorite throw pillow had left a lavender scent behind.

After dinner, Liliana and I were playing with Jaime in the living room when we heard someone trying to unlock the front door. The person fumbled with the key several times, then stopped.

'Lola, Lola, someone is trying to open the door!'

Thinking that it was too early for my parents to be back, I picked Jaime up and pulled Liliana away from the door. Lola came out of the kitchen, drying her hands on her apron.

'Who is it?' she shouted, looking at us.

'Lola! Open the door quickly,' Papá's deep voice surprised me.

When Lola opened the door, we let out a yell. Papá had Mamá in his arms. She looked like a rag doll, unconscious, head tilted back and arms dangling.

'What happened?' Lola yelled.

Liliana and I rushed to our mother's side.

'She fainted. Luckily, I was able to hold her, or she would have fallen down the stairs.' Papá held her right wrist, then looked at his watch. 'Lola, put the kids to bed, please.'

'But I don't—' I wanted to say that I needed to stay with my mother.

With his brows furled together in a scowl, he said, 'Now!'

Mamá cleared her throat as her eyes fluttered open. 'What happened?'

'Don't move, *muñeca*, everything will be all right.'

The last time I'd heard Papá call my mother *doll* was after the incident with the cowboy, which made me realize she was in real danger.

'You fainted. Let me see what is going on. I will get some samples and take them directly to the hospital.'

'We should wait until tomorrow. It's late now.' Mamá tried to sit down.

'No. The hospital is not far. I know people at the lab who can expedite the process. I want the test results as soon as possible.'

Lola took Jaime from my arms and tilted her head towards our room.

'Come on, niña Rocío and niña Liliana.'

I stomped away.

Why hadn't Mamá told Papá how ill she was?

In bed, I closed my eyes. I feared for Mamá. I feared for the baby. But wasn't it my father's job to take care of them? She was probably just tired, and that's why she fainted. After thinking about many scenarios, I dozed off.

The next morning, I bounced out of bed like a spring, hoping to hear one of my parents in the kitchen. I put my ear against my bedroom door. Silence. Goosebumps peppered my skin. Then a chill that crept up my spine made me shiver. I ran back to bed and pulled the blankets over my head. Papá startled me when he opened the door.

'Rocío, are you awake?'

'Yes, Papá. How's Mamá?' I pulled the blankets off my head and sat up.

Father's hair was wet, and he had shaved. It was the first time I'd seen him wearing his light-green scrubs at home. He sat on the edge of my bed.

'She has a condition called preeclampsia. It is a pregnancy complication. She needs to start treatment immediately so she can feel better. And it will all go away once the baby is born.'

'What treatment?'

'Well, she is going to have to rest a little more, take medication, and eliminate salt from her diet.'

I wanted to ask him more questions, but he kissed me on my head and walked out of the room.

From then on, Papá cooked when he could, always leaving one portion aside for Mamá. She made faces when she ate, complaining that without salt, nothing tasted the same. When he was unavailable to cook, Grandma had us over for dinner. Lola had a list of all my mother's dietary restrictions.

Every week, Papá and I went to the market and brought back bags filled with vegetables, fruits, and other groceries. I'd make sure he bought a lot of mangos; the ones that turned peachy yellow when they ripened were the juiciest. At home, I waited until he was gone. Then I washed the soft mango and ate it without peeling it, creamy juice rolling down between my fingers.

I'd suck on the pit until there was no more pulp left, then licked my fingers. At the end, annoying yellow strings hung between my teeth. But I didn't mind.

The day Mamá finally went to the hospital to have the baby, Grandma walked Liliana, Jaime and me to her home. 'Pretty soon, we'll find out if you have a brother or a sister.'

Skipping and swinging her arms, two-year-old Liliana sang, '... a girl... a girl.'

It didn't matter to me whether it was a boy or a girl. All I wanted was for my mother and the baby to be healthy.

'Let's go to the backyard first. I have another surprise for you,' Grandma said, smiling.

The three of us darted outside, Grandma behind us.

'But wait, close your eyes.'

We didn't stop. From the oak tree, which was across from our playhouse, hung a swing. With my help Jaime swung first, then Liliana. When it was my turn, I went as high as I could. Going up, I tilted my head and body back, and my legs forward. On the way down, I pushed my head forward and my legs back. The chilly breeze was soothing to my worrisome heart. I thought of Mamá. It seemed she had been getting a little better. Her skin tone changed from pasty white back to caramel. The morning sickness had gone away, but her legs still looked heavy. I was relieved the baby would be born soon. A call from Grandma brought me back from my thoughts. 'Rocío, I'm taking your brother and sister into the house so that they can have an afternoon snack. Don't stay out too long and be careful.'

'I'll come inside soon,' I said, swinging even higher.

In some mysterious way, I felt I had wings. Below me, bees were buzzing among Grandma's alfalfa plants. The fresh smell of the eucalyptus tree sweetened the air.

When I went into the house, I found Grandma staring at the TV screen in the living room. Lola was by the kitchen door with her hands covering her mouth. A newscaster with thick-framed glasses read from a paper he held in his hand. 'We just received this report. There has been a massacre in Bogotá.'

Grandpa Miguel and Papá came in at that moment. At the word *massacre,* they stopped talking and sat on the sofa next to Grandma. Lola hurried into the kitchen. The newscaster continued reading.

'It is with great sadness that we report the killing of thirty people who were attending the bullfight at the Plaza Santa María.'

'We need to get rid of this tyrant.' Papá clenched his fist.

'Papá.' I walked over and hugged him. He hugged me back. I extended one hand and touched Grandpa on the shoulder.

Papá stood up. Taking my hand, he walked me out to the hallway.

'Rocío, go see what your siblings are doing.'

'But what about Mamá and the baby?'

'They are fine. It is going to take some time before the baby comes home. I came back for a few minutes because I wanted to check on you, but I need to go to the hospital soon.'

He gave me a bear hug, the type that made me feel everything would work out. Liliana and Jaime were in Grandpa's office, sitting on the rug. Liliana had a book upside down and was pretending to read a story.

I stuck my head out into the hallway and heard Papá's voice. Through the open living room door, I could see him pacing. 'That assassin... the word on the street is that in January, the dictator's daughter went to a bullfight at the Plaza Santa María. The spectators responded with boos and catcalls. Today the same thing happened during the bullfight, but this time Rojas Pinilla's assassins were prepared.' Papá's voice cracked. 'They killed those who were hissing at the dictator's daughter.'

I knew how much Papá disliked the man called Pinilla, but I couldn't understand why he acted like it was his responsibility to make things better.

The phone rang across the house like a high-pitched alarm. No one spoke as Papá picked up the receiver. Then I heard him say, 'I will.'

Click.

'How is my daughter?' Grandma looked at Papá.

'That call wasn't from Cecilia's doctor. They need physicians to treat those wounded at the Plaza Santa María. I can probably—' Papá scratched his head.

'You aren't thinking about going, are you?' Grandma frowned.

'Well, someone has to help.'

Grandpa confronted my father.

'Cecilia needs you. Your wife and children need you.'

Papá sighed. 'I will ask some of my colleagues to see who is available.'

The phone rang again, startling all of us. I felt a rush of panic.

'Mamá?' I asked as I walked into the room.

At the second ring, Papá lifted the receiver. 'I am on my way.'

'What's happening?' I stood by his side.

'The baby is coming earlier than we thought, so I have to go now.'

I embraced one of Papá's legs.

He kissed me on the cheek and then shook Grandma's hand. 'I will take care of her.'

History Lessons

After Mamá came home with baby Orlando, her legs went back to normal, and the headaches stopped. She beamed with joy when Papá sang songs in the shower, singing along with him as she folded laundry or changed Orlando's diapers. Papá enjoyed grocery shopping, but when he was busy at work, Lola ran his errands so that Mamá could take care of the baby. Liliana and I joined Grandma every afternoon for hot chocolate, cheese, and rolls. Sometimes she read children's books to us. On other days, she surprised us and taught us songs and popular dances.

Los Gitanos was a Spanish Gypsy song we loved. We tapped as our skirt ruffles flooded the air and we sang along to a vinyl record Grandma kept in the record player. Life was back to normal.

Early one morning in 1957, I went into the kitchen where I found my parents eating breakfast. The radio was on. 'The people of Colombia have spoken. This regime has come to an end!' shouted the announcer.

'That's a blessing.' Mamá smiled.

'Hmm, religion again?' Papá rolled his eyes.

'Well, I believe in God.'

'I am just happy to know that justice has been served.'

When my parents saw me, Mamá turned off the radio.

'What's happening?' I yawned.

'First, you kiss us good morning, then you can ask questions,' Mamá said.

'Good morning.' I hugged them both. 'Why was that man yelling?'

Papá crumpled his napkin in his hands. 'A group of generals have replaced a lunatic and a murderer.'

My mother pressed her lips together and crossed her arms.

'Cecilia, it is important that she learn.' My father stood and picked up his doctor's case, then kissed us both. 'We will continue this conversation another day.'

He closed the front door behind him.

Mamá scowled. 'Your papá means well. He just gets too involved, and that worries me. He has ideas about how the government should take care of its people. It bothers him to see people suffering from hunger and a lack of other necessities.' Her expression softened.

'So, why are you upset with him?'

'I'm not. But you are young and right now all you should worry about is school and being a good girl. I don't want you concerned about politics. The time will come for that.'

She walked to her room. I followed her.

We found Orlando awake and playing with the small clown doll Grandma had bought for him the day he was born. Liliana and I had named the clown Pepe. His red nose sat in the middle of his round face. Soft, colorful hair made of yarn framed his oversized head. What I loved the most about Pepe, though, was his big, bright smile.

'Come on, you need to take a bath.' Mamá lifted Orlando, my now one-year-old brother, into her arms. Jaime had been a small baby when he was born; Orlando, on the other hand, had broad shoulders and big dimples.

Liliana and Jaime stayed behind, but my stomach felt empty, so I went straight to the kitchen, poured a glass of milk and picked up a fresh roll from a platter. I was enjoying the sweet taste of the guava-filled pastry when I saw the radio. I listened to the bathwater running, confirming my mother was still busy with Orlando, and then turned the radio on.

'This dictator has arrested his political opponents, assassinated and gassed protesters,' said the commentator.

The clicking of high heels startled me, so I quickly turned the radio off.

'I want breakfast.' Liliana came into the room, dragging Pepe.

'Why are you wearing Mamá's shoes?' My heart was still beating fast.

'Because I want to.'

Suddenly, the sound of hundreds of people singing the national anthem outside our home startled Liliana and me. We hurried through to the living room where we found our mother with our two brothers peering outside. Some people were waving large Colombian flags. Others waved handkerchiefs.

'What is happening? Why are all of those people singing?' I asked.

'They're happy Rojas Pinilla is no longer the ruler of this country,' my mother explained.

When she opened the front door, we followed her out. Lola and my grandparents came out of their house, singing. Grandpa gestured for us to join them on the stairs, then said something about Rojas Pinilla being a Nazi because he had visited Germany in 1936 as a military attaché.

One by one, people from the surrounding houses opened their windows or doors. We all sang as if we were one large choir, standing proud, muscles tight, chins lifted. That day I understood the meaning of victory, of freedom.

At the end of the singing, my grandfather rubbed his rounded belly.

'We finally did it. This is the end of the dictatorship. We'll have *tamales* for lunch today.'

Later that afternoon, we were in the backyard playing when I heard next door's dog bark. My chest hurt. There was an ache that came every time I thought of Catia and Nala.

Will I ever see them again?

'Lunch is served,' Lola called, standing by the back door.

Liliana and Jaime dashed inside. I didn't. Instead, I wandered around the yard. The flowers were blooming, and the air was fresh.

Grandma and Grandpa might allow Catia and Nala to live in their home. That way, I could see them every day.

I imagined them sniffing every corner of the yard. I was bursting with excitement when I went into the dining room. Everyone else was sitting. I joined them.

'You're late, Rocío.'

'Sorry, Mamá.'

'Today is a happy day, so no long faces. Only smiles allowed,' Grandpa cheered.

Lola walked in with a large platter of tamales, a dish that was reserved for major holidays and celebrations. The tamales came wrapped in plantain leaves. When I unfolded mine, the steam, smelling of cumin and garlic, made my mouth water. The masa was filled with chicken, peas, potatoes, and carrots.

Most of the conversation that day was about who was going to be the next president. The country was united; everyone wanted free elections. But I had no genuine interest in politics. I stopped listening and began rehearsing in my head what I was going to ask my grandparents to do for me.

'Rocío, how're you doing?' Grandma took a sip of water, keeping her gaze on me.

'Can I bring Nala and Catia?' I blurted out.

All eyes turned to me.

'The dogs?' Grandma asked.

'Can they live in your house so I can play with them?' I pleaded, looking back and forth between my grandparents.

'Rocío, we already discussed—' Mamá started.

'Two dogs would be too much. Perhaps one?' interjected Grandma Emilia.

Only one dog? How can I ever choose?

My grandfather cleared his throat.

'Cecilia, what do you think? It's not a problem for us to bring one dog.'

'Wait a minute,' Mamá said. 'We need to ask Jaime when he comes home tonight. We can't decide this now. If he agrees, that would be fine with me. But let's not make any decisions now. Is that understood, young lady?'

Silence filled the room. I looked at Grandma through a glazy layer of tears. She winked at me. 'Perhaps I can speak with my son-in-law?'

'I think it's best for Rocío to speak with her papá,' said Mamá, shaking her head.

Papá came home late almost every night after our dinner at my grandparents' house. It wasn't until the following Saturday that we could spend time with him. He had packed a small picnic basket with fruit, water, milk and *arepas* the tiny corn pancakes with melted cheese. He threw in a blanket, while our mother dressed Jaime and Orlando.

'Girls, get ready. We are going to the park,' Papá yelled from the kitchen.

'Yay!' Liliana and I giggled, jumping up and down with excitement.

The cloudless sky, bright with sunshine, welcomed us. Mamá pushed Orlando's stroller and Liliana and I walked, one on each side of her. Papá held Jaime's hand and carried the basket of food in his other hand. We walked a few blocks until we arrived at Nogal Park. Under a tree, our parents laid out the blanket and placed the basket on top.

'Can we go play?' Jaime fiddled with his sweater.

Liliana and I knew better, and so we waited to be dismissed. Our father asked us to sit, then told us all about walnut trees, which apparently had grown in this region for hundreds of years. They had named the park after the trees.

'Can we go now?' Jaime begged.

'All right, go. But stay nearby where I can see you.'

Liliana and I grabbed Jaime's hands and sprinted to the seesaw. When the sun was in the middle of the sky, Mamá called, 'Rocío, Liliana and Jaime, come and eat.'

We ran back to our parents, thirsty and hungry. No one complained as Jaime threw himself onto the blanket and Liliana glided on top of him. I pretended to fall over them.

Trapped under his two sisters, Jaime moaned, 'Help me, Papá!'

Papá tickled Liliana and me until we let go of our brother.

'Okay,' Mamá said. 'Enough, all of you. We need to eat before it begins to rain.'

Holding Orlando with one arm, she began taking food out of the basket.

'But I don't see clouds,' I said.

Papá studied the sky too.

'Oh, they will come, trust me. You know how it is here. One minute can be sunny and a few moments later, you are caught in a downpour.'

We were enjoying our food when Mamá laid Orlando on the blanket and, raising her arms, said, 'Children, we have some good news. We are moving to a bigger house.'

A bigger house? Now I wouldn't have to choose between my two dogs. Surely, there would be room for both of them. I was so excited I almost choked on a piece of arepa I had in my mouth.

I tried to speak, but Liliana beat me to it. 'What about our toys?'

'Can I bring my dogs?' I begged.

My parents turned around and looked at one another.

Papá pressed his lips together. 'Well, the house will not be here in Bogotá. We are moving to Chicago. They have admitted me to the Department of Surgery at the University of Chicago.'

'Where is *Chicago*?' I blinked back my tears.

Papá lifted my chin with his index finger.

'Chicago is in the United States, a country in North America. You will like it. I will go before you to make sure the house is ready when you arrive.'

That day, I didn't confront Papá about not traveling with us. Instead, I tried to convince my parents, with no success, to allow my dogs to come with us. They refused. They agreed it would be too costly. When I challenged their decision to move away from my grandparents, Mamá looked away and informed us Grandpa and Grandma agreed with the move.

My bottom lip quivered. I was flabbergasted.

Why is she so cheerful about moving again? Why isn't she upset? Moving to Puerto López hadn't been easy. What about our grandparents? I thought nothing made sense.

Papá explained, 'Rocío, we are moving because this is what is best for the family. The University of Chicago offered me a surgical scholarship, and I accepted. Right now, all I need is your help. Remember, I told you that sometimes we need to do things we don't like in order to support those we love? Well, this is one of those times.'

I collapsed in my mother's arms and sobbed. No one said anything for a while until a roar of thunder filled the void… just like my parents had warned. We rushed to pick everything up, but the angry rain began splattering us.

Even though my heart throbbed with sadness, that night I chose my family. Moving to Chicago was important to my parents, so when the frosty moon shone behind the trees, I said goodbye to Nala and Catia. That's what Papá meant when he said that we had to make sacrifices. I had to leave my dogs behind. I closed my eyes and imagined them leaping over the tall plains grass while their fur blew in the wind.

Chicago

Our new home was part of a housing development in a neighborhood near the hospital, only available to junior doctors and their families. I was disappointed because I'd envisioned a large house with many rooms and a lush backyard, like my grandparents' home, where we could play hide-and-seek or spend time in a playhouse. Instead, our house had one story and our backyard was small, framed only by broadleaf shrubs. Two apple trees stood in the middle of the lawn. I was pleased to see a swing hanging from a tree, a wooden seat suspended by thick rope. It wasn't very comfortable, but it went as high as the one in Bogotá.

The house had four bedrooms and two bathrooms. I still had to share a room with my sister. Liliana woke me up often, trembling with fear. According to her, monsters came out at night from under her bed, from inside the closet and through the windows and doors. She wouldn't let me sleep until I lay in bed with her. Liliana and I had twin beds, a wooden night table, and a small desk with a matching chair. My brothers' bedroom was identical to ours. Both rooms faced the backyard. The master bedroom and Papá's office faced the street.

When Mamá first walked into the kitchen, she tapped the tile counter. 'This is a spacious kitchen compared to the one we had in Bogotá.' She grinned when she opened the refrigerator. 'The fridge is like my parents' one. It's so big, we can keep gallons of milk in it.'

I didn't share my mother's excitement. I missed my grandparents and even our small apartment. At night, I tried to see my dogs in my mind, but my memories of them had begun to fade away. Once, in a dream, I found myself standing over a frozen lake. Under the ice, Nala and Catia gasped for air and tried to swim out of the icy water. I dropped to my knees, weeping and punching the ice with my fists as hard as I could. I woke up breathless and with ice-cold arms. My parents had forgotten to turn on the furnace.

When the leaves on the trees turned golden, Mamá came into the living room where the four of us were watching cartoons.

'Rocío, I'm going to take a shower. Don't open the door to anyone, and watch your siblings, please.'

'Yes, Mamá,' I said, keeping my eyes fixed on the TV screen.

We were laughing at mischievous Daffy Duck when I looked around the room and noticed that Jaime was gone.

'Jaime, where are you?' I called out. 'Mamá told us to stay together.'

I waited for his response but when he didn't answer, I went looking for him. I found him in the laundry room. He was standing on a stool and had turned on the electric clothes wringer. His face tense with anticipation.

'Stop!' I shouted, as he inserted a shirt and then his right hand between the rollers.

When the rollers caught his fingers, he tried to pull them away as he howled. Blood splattered the shirt and the washing machine.

'Mamá,' I screamed, searching frantically for the release lever.

Seized by panic, however, I couldn't remember where the lever was. Jaime's four fingers went through the rollers, leaving his thumb dangling outside. When he saw his dislocated thumb, he slammed his eyes shut and screamed again. Drops of sweat mixed with tears rolled down his splotchy face.

'Mamá. Mamá,' I hollered again, this time with increasing panic in my voice. She heard our shouts and ran into the room in her bathrobe, her hair in a towel and yelled, 'Oh, my God!'

She immediately pressed the emergency release. The rollers stopped moving, followed by a sharp click, freeing my brother's hand. His bloody thumb, which hung limp to one side, looked like a chewed-up piece of meat. Mamá swathed his hand with the towel that had been on her hair. Jaime moaned, glancing at his hand.

'Didn't I tell you to watch your siblings?' Mamá barked at me.

'Yes, Mamá,' I said, holding my tears back. 'And you; don't move,' Mamá growled at Jaime, who was blinking fast. 'Stay here until I come back.' Her bathrobe hung loose over her small body, tiny shampoo bubbles still swinging from her knotted bangs. 'I'm going to put something on and take Jaime to the hospital. Please watch Orlando and Liliana.' She stared at me. 'Do not take your eyes off them this time.'

Jaime was sniffling and pressing the bloodied towel against his hand. The bright blotches on his face faded away, leaving only his ghostly-looking skin. When Mamá scurried back into the laundry room, she was dressed. Her unruly red hair left a wet spot on the back of her cotton dress. Curling her arm under my brother's right arm, Mamá walked Jaime out. I stood still in the hallway. Mamá stopped by the door and looked at me.

'I'll talk to you later, young lady.' She slammed the door behind her.

Visions of Jaime without one hand spun in my head.

It's all my fault. I should've been watching him. Why didn't I see him leave the room? What was he thinking? Suddenly, I became light-headed and began shaking with a mix of fear and anger. *He didn't obey, and now I'm the one in trouble. Not fair.*

I shook my head, and that's when I saw the neatly folded notepaper on the floor of my parents' bathroom. After picking it up, I walked back to the living room where I found Orlando and Liliana consumed by the TV show. I unfolded the notepaper and noticed it was written in Mamá's delicate handwriting:

March 4, 1958

Dear Mamá and Papá,

I am sorry to have caused you so much pain. I know how much you love your grandchildren and me. I also know you will miss us. But all I need now is your support. We love you and will miss you too. But as I told you before, I did not want to stay in Colombia. I had become afraid of Jaime's socialist inclinations. As you know, our country is not ready, and probably never will be ready, for that type of change. My husband means well but he is an idealist, and people who take that path, even with the best of intentions, are often in danger. I hope that spending a few years out of the country will help him understand that a revolution is not the answer to our problems. Plus, this move is a great opportunity for him to advance his career.

I know that, early on, you did not like Jaime, perhaps because he was from the coast or because he was not rich? Your dream was that I married a wealthy Bogotano. But I fell in love with Jaime. He is not wealthy, but comes from an educated family, just like ours. I never told you this, but it really hurt me when no one in my family attended our wedding. Only two of Jaime's friends were there. I promised myself I would never say anything to you, but with the distance, I have changed my mind. I understand that Grandpa had just passed, but I am your daughter, and all I wanted was for my parents to be there.

Now Jaime must complete his studies, this is important to him and good for our family. When he is done, we will move back to Colombia, and hopefully one day you will be as proud of him as I am.

I dropped the letter to the floor. I couldn't believe what I had just read.

My grandparents disliked Papá!

I wanted to scream. I didn't want to choose between them and my father. I felt the urge to question my mother about my grandparents' feelings towards him and about how he could be in danger. But I couldn't. She would be furious if she knew I'd read her letter.

First my brother's hand and now this. My hands shook as I picked up the letter and then tried, unsuccessfully, to refold the paper to its original state. I did the best I could and threw it back where I found it.

I joined my siblings. For the first time, I understood why Mamá had been willing to move so far away.

We had been running away. I almost said the words out loud.

I knew nothing about communism. What did that mean? All I could think of was it had something to do with Colonel Moncayo and his friend Marulanda or perhaps with the massacre at the bullfight. Whatever it was, it frightened me.

When Mamá returned, she scooped up the letter from the floor and put it in her pocket. I worried she would reprimand me, but she was no longer upset. 'I left Jaime with your papá. Sorry I got angry at you, Chio. You are just a child, and I shouldn't expect you to be responsible for your siblings. I love you. I was just worried about Jaime.'

She kissed my cheek. I didn't say anything. For an instant, I forgot all that had happened. My mother had called me *Chio*, just like Grandma did. A warm wave filled my unsettled heart.

Later that afternoon Papá returned, carrying Jaime in his arms. My brother's hand was in a sling. Mamá kissed my brother. Papá's shoulders sagged. The procedure, which took over five hours, had gone well. However, there was an issue with his thumb. 'For now, we have to wait and see,' he said before taking my brother to his room.

Mamá took a deep breath, pulled out a loaf of bread, and placed two slices in the toaster. 'You should eat something, honey.'

Papá nodded.

The crisp scent of toasted bread was all that was left behind after everyone had gone to their rooms and Papá back to work. I stayed behind by the bay window, watching how the autumn crept over our backyard, as if our old life was slowly peeling away. Everything in this new city was different. We didn't eat fresh rolls anymore, and the food was not like Lola's. The geese migrated to warmer places. Flat land covered with leafless trees had replaced the dramatic lush Andean mountains where I first saw a condor glide high in the sky. I couldn't run to Grandma and tell her about Jaime's hand or ask her why she didn't approve of Papá. And all for what? Somehow, I knew Mamá was wrong. Papá would never give up so easily. I'd never heard my father's voice as determined as that night when the colonel and his men came to see him.

'This is our chance to support the revolution,' he had shouted, the sound of clinking glasses echoed in the night.

The Redheaded Girl

One day, Liliana and I attempted to sell homemade apple juice, what we thought was an exotic drink, only to find that no one was interested. Apples were a rare fruit in Colombia, but not so much up north. We also made our first rag dolls out of material remnants our mother gave us. Those dolls never left the house. Jaime said they'd scare other kids away. Orlando spent hours in the dirt making roads for his toy truck. Jaime climbed the trees, hoping to see what was going on in our neighbors' houses. Snippets of Mamá tending to us and Papá coming home from the hospital carrying goodies, like yogurt, flicker in my mind.

My face burned with anticipation each time I saw the mail truck coming up the street. Weeks earlier, I'd sent a letter to Grandma asking her if she had any news about my dogs. I also told her all about this strange country where kids chewed gum and baseball players spat during games. I had memorized the postman's routine. Every afternoon, he parked the truck, pulled his heavy bag out and then walked the nearby streets, inserting envelopes into each of the mailboxes. I waited until he drove away, then sprinted out of the house with the excitement of a treasure hunter ready to unlock a chest found in a sunken ship. But each day, I opened our small metal box and slumped back in disappointment when I realized that none of the letters were for me. One day,

I returned home holding the only letter in the box, which was addressed to Papá. 'What's wrong, Rocío?' Mamá must have noticed my discontent.

'I wrote Grandma a letter a long time ago, remember? I was hoping this was from her.'

'You'll get one soon. But the mail coming from Colombia is slow,' she reminded me, then read part of the return address aloud. 'Evangelical Hospital of Chicago, the hospital where your father works.'

I followed her to the backyard, where we found Papá playing soccer with my brothers. Jaime was trying hard to get the ball away from Papá's large and agile feet. Orlando's rounded cheeks shook as his little body chased after them. 'Honey, this letter is for you. It seems important. It is from the Evangelical Hospital.' Mamá handed him the letter.

Papá glanced at the return address and then ripped the envelope open. He squinted, trying to read the letter under the bright sunlight. 'It's from the medical director. He's observed me operate on several occasions and he's sent his congratulations on my work so far.'

'Let me see,' Mamá said, extending her hand.

Papá pointed to the middle of the page as he handed the letter to her.

She smiled as she read aloud, ''A highly skilled surgeon.'' Then she read the rest of the letter in silence. When she finished, she embraced Papá and kissed him. 'You're a genius. That's why I married you.'

I hugged both of my parents. In some odd way, being proud of my father made me feel bigger.

The air was cool and brisk, but we ate lunch outside to celebrate the good news. Mamá brought a tray with turkey sandwiches, milk, and slices of melon. Even though Orlando was the youngest, he ate just as much as my other siblings, and I did. 'He's going to be as tall as you,' said Mamá, looking at Papá.

For the first time, I realized Orlando looked just like my father, only in miniature. They both had broad shoulders, curly hair, and long legs. Jaime fiddled in his chair and teased Orlando. When Orlando pouted, Papá intervened. 'Jaime, remember your table manners, hands on the table, elbows down; we do not play or move around. Respectable people behave everywhere they go, especially at their own dinner table.'

The four of us stared at Papá. It was as if his grave voice filtered right through us, leaving us all breathless. When Papá was upset, I felt uneasy, so I snapped at Jaime. 'Yes, Jaime, remember what happens when you don't obey?'

Jaime protested.

'That's enough,' Mamá said. 'We're celebrating the fact that your papá is doing a great job at the hospital.'

'That's correct; we should have a good time. However, I expect you all, from now on, to remember your table manners.'

When our father noticed that my siblings and I had stopped eating, he tried to cheer us up. 'How about if we tell you how your mamá and I met?'

We'd heard this story before, but we acted as if it were new to us. Perhaps we did it to spend more time together or to watch our parents buzz with joy. Whatever the reason was, our parents had our attention.

Papá had been twenty years old when one day Gabriel Sanchez and Carlos Arango, his friends from college, changed their usual bike route to the library. They took a shortcut through a single-family home neighborhood. Suddenly, they saw a young woman crossing the street, her long, red hair waving in the breeze. She and my father locked eyes.

'She had the prettiest and smallest turned-up nose I had ever seen,' Papá reminisced.

When Gabriel Sanchez noticed my father was staring at the girl, he had yelled, 'Hey, man, close your mouth.'

Then the three friends laughed and rode away. Mamá was curious, so she stayed by the porch of her house and watched them until they turned the corner. After that day, he always took the same shortcut, hoping to see the redheaded girl again. Sometimes he walked the busy streets, surveying the crowds, looking for her. Other times, he rode his bicycle, pretending to look for an address.

One day, when the holiday lights glittered around the city, he finally saw her again. This time, she was wearing a blue-and-white school uniform. She had graduated from Santa Teresa, a Catholic boarding school located fifty miles away from the city, and was coming back home. She and Grandpa Miguel were carrying luggage out of a station wagon and into the house when Papá approached them and offered to help. Grandpa, who was a stout ex-army captain, snapped, scaring Papá. But my father calmly introduced himself. He told Grandpa he was a medical student and meant no harm. All he wanted to do was to be of help. Skeptically, Grandpa accepted Papá's offer.

When they finished, Papá shook Grandpa's hand and asked permission to visit Mamá. Grandpa looked at my father from head to toe, then glanced at my mother. She was grinning. Grandpa became pensive for a few seconds, twisting his mouth to one side and then agreed.

For several months, Mamá's grandmother, abuelita Emira, sat on a rocking chair, nestled by a window in the parlor and knitted while the young couple visited. My mother's grandparents lived in the apartment adjacent to the main house. Four months into the courtship, Mamá's grandmother caught pneumonia, and the visits were suspended.

Abuelita Emira's health continued to decline. One chilly afternoon, she asked her nurse to bring Mamá to her room and then to leave them alone. Abuelita Emira gazed at her granddaughter, signaling her to sit by her side. Mamá said she would never forget the sweet scent of a bouquet of violets that stood on the nightstand. Mamá's grandmother explained she had had a dream Mamá was going to marry my father and that her first child was going to be a girl named Rocío. She also pulled a letter from under her pillow and gave it to my mother. It was from Papá. The letter was a formal marriage proposal.

Mamá embraced her fragile grandmother. That evening, abuelita Emira passed. Everyone in the family mourned her. That is, except for her husband, General Villa de Alba, it was too much to bear. A month later, he was found dead, sitting on a chair, wearing his uniform.

Soon after the general's passing, Mamá's father, Grandpa Miguel, bought a large home in the northern part of the city. Without notice, early one morning, two trucks arrived to move Mamá's family to their new home. Mamá confronted Grandpa, but he refused to let her inform Papá of their move. Grandpa had found Papá's marriage proposal letter and decided to keep the couple apart, arguing they were too young to marry.

The family moved to the two-story Victorian house at the center of El Nogal, a suburban neighborhood in the city of Bogotá. Just like their previous home, the new house had an adjacent apartment, the one we lived in before moving to the United States. Mamá's siblings and parents were thrilled with the new house. But for my mother, it was a prison.

Meanwhile, Papá tried desperately to find my mother. He spoke with friends and neighbors, but her family had left no trace of their whereabouts. He kept investigating until the gardener, who had worked for the general, gave him the name of the moving company after Papá promised not to reveal his source.

Papá found the new house and surveyed it for days, until one day, he saw Mamá standing by the window. He waved an envelope until she saw him. She raced downstairs, but when she got to the tree he had been leaning against, there was no one there. On the grass sat a small stone with a white envelope underneath. Mamá hid the envelope in her pocket and rushed back to the house. The letter contained wedding plans.

One Sunday morning, before sunrise, my mother knocked on my grandparents' bedroom door. Without waiting for a response, she went in. She kneeled next to Grandpa and told him she was marrying my father. Grandpa dismissed her and told her to go back to bed. Mamá insisted and told him they would get married that day at 9:00 am at the Porciúncula, a nearby church.

No one in the family attended the wedding. There were two witnesses, Gabriel Sanchez and Carlos Arango. When my grandparents found out that she had gone through with the marriage to Papá without their blessing, they were appalled. To them, it was a disgrace. Bogotanos considered Costeños (or coastal-born people) loud and lazy, although my father was neither. My paternal grandparents were unaware of my father's relationship with my mother. They wouldn't have approved of a Bogotana as their daughter-in-law either. The division between the coastal regions and the capital had existed for a long time. Wealthier Colombians used to live in Bogotá. Some people referred to them as snobs, even though my mother wasn't. What Papá didn't realize then was that, ultimately, these differences were going to separate the two families forever. Papá stood up and finished the story.

'From the beginning, we knew we wanted to be together, and we persisted until we married. One day you, too, will know that you need to do something or be with someone. And I hope that, when that day comes, you have the grit to endure the challenges that come your way. Do not stop. Remember that only people who have a firmness of purpose can achieve their goals. Most of all, we should never make assumptions about people based on where they were born or how they look.'

Like my grandmother, Papá was a storyteller and a teacher. In each story, there was always a hidden meaning. Even though I enjoyed both of their tales that day, I wished I could have understood everything he had said. Because somehow, I felt he was letting us into the deepest corners of his heart.

Outside, the yellowish-brown, feathery leaves flirted with the wind as they swung back and forth before touching the ground. The smell of rain made me think of Grandma and her issues with Papá. My eyes burned. I wanted to tell her that my Papá was a great man, a good husband, and a wonderful father.

Lost for Words

Early one morning, when the birds were already chirping, and the air was still cold, Liliana and I walked two blocks from home to our new school, Hinsdale Elementary. We carried our small, metal lunch boxes, and on our backs hung identical backpacks filled with pencils and notebooks. At the entrance of the enormous building, Liliana gazed at me with dark, fearful eyes. Her bottom lip quivered. I, too, felt the tears dancing in my eyes. So, I held her hand until we arrived at her preschool classroom. Once at the door, she walked in without saying goodbye. The loud bell brought a mob of children into the hallways. I hurried to the other side of the building where I found a sign on a door that read: *Ms. Bell 4th Grade.*

Boys and girls were laughing and chattering inside as they placed their belongings in their desks. When I entered, the room went quiet, and all eyes followed me. I thought of Papá who had shown us around our school the previous day.

'Your English is limited, I believe, and it is going to be awhile before you become proficient, but determination is key to success,' he assured us.

I walked in a straight line without looking at my classmates.

Determination, determination, I kept repeating in my head.

Finally, I reached a tall, blond woman. She looked at me, smiled and said something I didn't understand. I stood next to her, wondering how to respond. After a few seconds, which felt like forever, I mumbled, 'Rocío Velásquez.'

'Ms. Bell.'

The teacher asked me what seemed a series of questions. I stood still, paralyzed by embarrassment.

'No.' The word finally jumped out of my mouth.

I wanted to tell her I didn't understand anything she had just said, because I didn't speak English. The teacher moved her head as if she were confused. She took a step closer to me, shook my hand then indicated that I should follow her. I felt my classmates' curious stares. Once we were at the back of the class, Ms. Bell assembled an easel and pointed to a small table with watercolors, brushes, and a cup of water. She handed me an apron, said something else I didn't understand, and went back to the front of the classroom.

After the other students sat down, she began teaching the class. A sinking feeling swept over me when I realized I didn't have a desk. Ms. Bell's gaze roamed around the classroom as she interacted with the rest of the students. I tried to make eye contact with her, but she looked right through me. Humiliated, I began to sniffle. I wanted to make my parents proud, but how could I do that if I didn't even understand what the teacher was saying and how could I work without a table and chair? Wiping my tears off with the apron, I decided to paint. I assumed that's what Ms. Bell had wanted me to do. *Determination*, I kept thinking.

I picked up the metal watercolor box to open it, but it slipped, clattering to the floor. The other students turned around and laughed as I clumsily tried to pick up the metal container. A moon-faced boy with freckles on his nose, sitting in the last row, hurried to help me. But as soon as he stood up, Ms. Bell said something to him and pointed to his desk. The boy looked at me, shrugged, and sat back down.

It seemed I had two choices: run out of the school and go home, or stay and try to do what I had, apparently, been told to do. I knew that the first choice would get me in trouble with my parents, so I made the best of what I had. I was going to paint the garden that was outside a nearby window. Once I began applying the colors onto the large sheet of paper, the voices in the room faded away until I couldn't hear anyone. Minutes or hours had passed when a light touch on my shoulder startled me. I turned around. The freckle-faced boy pointed at my lunch box, then at the open door. All the students had gone, and Ms. Bell was sitting at her desk, reading papers. I followed the boy to the playground and, as soon as we stepped outside, I felt the freezing wind carve into my bones. 'I'm Sam,' he said, pointing to himself.

Through chattering teeth, I responded, 'Rocío.'

We sat on the sunny side of a bench and ate our snacks, but said nothing. The winter sun seemed to offer no heat. Sam could tell I was cold because he moved closer to me. I grinned.

When the bell rang, I followed him back to the classroom. He went to his desk, and I retreated to my painting. That day I discovered that, as with literature, I could also escape into the make-believe world of art. At home, we were reading *Le Petit Prince* in French. Our father stopped at every page to teach us words and to translate the text into Spanish.

'The more languages you know, the more successful you will be,' he insisted. I felt like the prince, uncertain, lonely, and lost, but now I had my own rose - painting.

After recess, I looked at the large paper and smiled when I noticed everything I'd painted had been a product of my imagination. Instead of the school garden, I had painted a mountain in the background. In front of it, there was a tiny house with small human figures standing next to it. On the other side were two dogs, and the garden had one red rose. The sun was shining behind scarce clouds.

At midday, I went outside and ate a piece of my sandwich. Later, I went to one of the monkey bars in the playground. From above, I looked at the groups of children. Most kids were white like Sam, and the girls had their hair pulled back in ponytails or pigtails. Liliana and I seemed to be the only ones with short, wavy hair.

After lunch, I was delighted to find four fraction problems on the blackboard. I bounced to the back, took out my notebook and added the fractions. Once I finished, I looked around the classroom. The other children were still working on the problems. I stared at Ms. Bell, hoping she would ask me to solve the problems on the board, but her gaze passed by me repeatedly. I sat on the floor and quietly sobbed. Sam glanced back at me, too afraid to leave his desk.

When the last bell of the day rang, I went to Liliana's classroom to find her. She was on a bench with her lunch box opened, the sandwich and banana intact. I helped her close it. When she stood up, she glanced at me with bloodshot and puffy eyes. We held hands and walked home in silence.

My siblings and I were helping set the table for dinner when Papá came home. He put his medical bag down in the hallway and held out his arms. The four of us ran to embrace him.
'Girls, tell me all about your first day at school.'
He looked at my sister, then at me. Neither of us spoke. I couldn't disappoint him, although neither could I lie. I felt the blood rushing to my face.
'Dinner is served.' Mamá came into the hallway.
She kissed Papá and sent us to the dining room.
'Wash your hands first, then we can have dinner and talk about school.'
My brothers, sister and I crammed into one bathroom, trying to share the sink. I stayed behind and lathered my hands with soap until I had no trace of paint. When we approached the table, we stood in line as Papá checked our hands and nails. When he was satisfied, he said, 'Hands are like the door of a house. You can tell by the door who lives inside.'
'What do you mean?' I asked.
Suddenly, everyone was staring at me. Biting my lower lip, I looked around the table, apologetic. No one would dare start eating until Papá responded.
'It is a metaphor which means you can tell who is a tidy person by his or her appearance. Now your hands are clean. Let's eat.'
A sense of relief filled the room.
Our brothers and parents were enjoying Mamá's interpretation of Lola's old recipe, pasta with chicken and peas, while Liliana and I, on the other hand, twirled the pasta around our plates, still distraught about our troubles at school.

We had not touched our food when Papá licked his lips, then blew a kiss to Mamá.

'Great dish. Thank you, honey. Now girls, tell me about your day.'

'It was fine,' was all I could manage.

'Did you like the school?'

'It was different.'

I remembered my father reminiscing one day about how difficult it had been to move from his neighborhood school to a private school.

'What was your school in Barranquilla like?'

Papá chewed the food in his mouth slowly before responding.

'That was a good but challenging experience.'

'What was good about it, and why didn't you like it?' I asked, hoping he would not continue asking about my day.

Papá's eyes narrowed. He put his knife and fork on the plate. He wiped his mouth with a napkin, blinked several times, then spoke.

'I learned a lot at Coastal Academy. When I graduated, I was well prepared for college, but some students were cruel. They mocked me when they found out I was attending on a scholarship. Children should all have the same schooling opportunities. Wealth should not determine your success in life. Many of my friends also applied, expecting to receive grants but were rejected. I felt sorry for them because they were also intelligent, but I feel that those difficulties made me stronger.'

He pushed his plate away.

Mamá moved in her chair, then asked, 'Anything new at the hospital?'

'Yes, as a matter of fact, there is going to be a family day in a few months. All relatives are invited for lunch.'

He pulled the plate back to him and continued eating.

'Can I go?' asked Jaime.

'Yes, everyone is invited.'

Papá didn't ask any more questions about our school, and I was glad. However, I wanted to know more about how he had adjusted to his school and if those children ever stopped being cruel. Mamá filled the silence by telling us all about the new fabric she had bought and how she was planning to use it to make us new clothes. When we were dismissed from the table, Liliana gazed at me. I smiled back. My sister and I had our first secret.

That night, Liliana and I told one another about our first day of school. Apparently, her experience had been just like mine.

'Girls. No more chatting.' Mamá opened the bedroom door. Liliana and I turned away from her and pretended to be asleep. Soon after, I heard Liliana's rhythmic breathing. I, on the other hand, tossed and turned. Papá's comment about problems making you strong made me unsettled. I didn't want to be strong if that meant being ignored by the teacher and mocked by my peers. But I did have a friend. At the thought of Sam, a warm wave filled my chest. Restless, I sat up on my bed and moved the curtain to one side. In awe, I watched for the first time small, cotton-like snowflakes shower the streetlight, making it twinkle like a faraway star.

Some snowfalls later, I went to the back of the classroom and found out that my easel and paints were gone. By then, I had painted many landscapes with dogs, grandparents, rivers, and mountains. I'd also sketched the faces of some of my neighborhood friends. The only thing that made me forget how invisible I felt in the classroom was spending time with them after school. I played hide-and-seek and ball tag. The winner of the hula-hoop challenge got to decide which activity or game we would do or play next. We rode bikes, and I practiced my English, which was by then at an acceptable level. I could at least understand most of what my teacher was saying.

The figures in my artwork were usually distorted and primitive due to my limited art training, but I had become fond of my paintings. They were like a diary in watercolor. I had kept them at school so my parents wouldn't ask me why I had so many of them. All I had taken home was my notebook with math problems and a list of isolated words I'd copied from the board.

So, the day I came into the classroom and didn't see my artwork on the little table, my heart ached. I still didn't speak enough English to ask Ms. Bell where they were. I looked around the room and saw Sam showing me the empty desk that was next to him. Confused as to what to do, I sat down on the floor like I had done when I was tired of painting. Suddenly, I heard heels approaching. I looked up, and Ms. Bell was staring down at me. I stood up. She motioned for me to follow her. I did. She tapped the empty desk next to Sam. Inside, I was glowing as I smiled and sat down.

Mamá overslept one day because she was coming down with a cold. When Papá arrived from an all-nighter at the hospital, he woke us all up. Liliana and I ate our breakfast and raced to school so that we wouldn't be late. The first bell rang as soon as we entered the building. The few students left in the hallways were scrambling to get to their classes.

'Go to your room. Quick!' I gave my sister a light push.

'No. You take me.'

'Then I'll be late.'

Liliana dropped her lunch box and poked out her bottom lip. 'I don't want to.'

I looked around at the empty corridors.

'All right,' I growled.

I grabbed Liliana's lunch box and, without waiting for her, I ran to her classroom. Behind me, I could hear my sister's shoes clicking against the linoleum floor. Her teacher was standing by the door. Liliana looked at me as if I had to save her from one of her imaginary monsters. I was about to tell her she was safe when the teacher approached Liliana and placed her arm over my sister's shoulders. Before they left, Liliana turned around and smiled at me.

The sound of the second bell reminded me I was now very late, so I sprinted through the school until I saw the open door to my classroom. I walked in, out of breath. Suddenly, everyone turned toward me. I felt my face burn as if I had eaten one of Lola's spicy peppers. 'I'm sorry.'

Ms. Bell was sitting at her desk.

'We were waiting for you.'

All the students, including Sam, were smirking and wouldn't take their eyes off me. I checked my skirt, blouse, and my black strap shoes, thinking that something was stained with milk, but my clothes were clean. I felt my body go rigid.

Ms. Bell got up and walked toward the blackboard.

'Have a seat, Rocío.'

I strode to the back of the room, wishing I could become invisible, and sat at my desk. The teacher waited until I had put my belongings away.

'This week's most original work is Rocío's,' she announced.

Ms. Bell had taped two of my favorite pieces, which depicted Colombian landscapes, onto the front classroom wall. I leaned forward and buried my face in my hands, trying to hide my burning cheeks.

'No need to be shy. You did a good job,' Ms. Bell said.

I glanced at Sam, who was pointing towards the blackboard.

'Look up.' He smiled.

I did.

Students whispered.

'Quiet.' Ms. Bell crossed her arms until she noticed everyone was paying attention. 'Let's give Rocío a hand for her creative work.'

Everyone clapped. I giggled, overflowing with happiness.

At recess, Sam and I went to the playground and jumped on the swings. We held hands, laughing, trying to go as high as we could.

On our way home, Liliana said, 'I'm going to tell Papá you were holding hands with that boy. I saw you.'

'What's wrong with that?'

'He's your boyfriend.'

'No, he is not.'

'Yes, he is,' she repeated all the way home.

'Papá, Papá,' Liliana called the moment he walked into the house that evening. 'Rocío has a boyfriend at school.'

Papá squinted, then turned to me.

'Is that true?'

'No, Papá. He's just my friend,' I blurted out.

'You are too young, and I forbid you from having boyfriends. I just finished a long day. I need to take a shower and then I will talk to you, young lady.' Papá stormed out of the room.

I glared at my sister with such anger that she darted to the kitchen, where Mamá was washing the dinner dishes. In my bedroom I lay on my bed, baffled.

I didn't think of Sam as my boyfriend. He was my only friend, but I couldn't tell Papá that because he would ask more questions about what had been going on in my classroom.

I stayed in my room until Liliana came to bed, and when she entered the room, I dashed out. There was no way I could have slept if my father was still mad at me, so I went looking for him. I was surprised to find him sitting next to Mamá in the living room, absorbed by a TV program.

The American news commentator announced, 'We must know that we are not alone in our resistance to the communist threat of domination. That resistance must be a cable of steel that unifies the entire free world.'

'Ha.' Papá chuckled. 'All they are trying to do is to convince people that communism is a threat to them, but the truth is that the greedy American businesses are the real threat. They want control over everything so that they can become even wealthier.'

The commentator continued, 'We provided military assistance to Thailand, Vietnam, Laos, Cambodia, the Philippines and Taiwan.'

Papá stood up and turned the volume on the TV down. 'This government knows they will never win the Vietnam War. Yet they are trying to convince everyone that they will. It is all about their interests.'

'Stop it, Jaime. Just stop it. We came here to have a better life, not to criticize this country or to try to fix anything.' Mamá held her head in her hands.

My father raised his voice and said something I'd heard him say before. 'Not doing anything is just as bad as being part of the problem.' In that instant, he turned around and saw me. I must have had a perplexed look, because he gasped. 'Rocío, were you waiting for me?'

'Yes, Papá. You said you wanted to talk to me,' I whispered, frightened by his outburst of anger.

'I am sorry. I became distracted. Kiss your mamá good night, and I will accompany you to your room.'

I kissed her and walked away. Papá followed me. I got into bed, and after tucking me in, he pulled a chair next to my bed.

'Rocío, you will not be allowed to have a boyfriend until you become a mature woman. Do you understand?'

'Yes, Papá, but he's only my friend.'

'I forbid you from holding hands with him or any other boy. He is your classmate and nothing else.'

'I understand,' I said, but I didn't. Sadness filled my heart. 'If you hate the Americans, why are we in this country?'

'North Americans,' he corrected me.

I bit my lip.

'I mean North Americans.'

Does he also hate Sam, the only one who understands how difficult school is for me?

Papá hunched over and, with his chin resting on his hand, sighed. 'This country offers work and schooling opportunities for its people. And, no, I do not hate

North Americans. Actually, they are good people. They just have a corrupt government.'

'I don't understand.'

'One day, my girl, you will.'

'Are you upset at Mamá?' I choked out.

'No. We were just discussing an issue. But it is getting late now, and we all need to sleep.' He kissed my forehead and left the room.

Like a kaleidoscope, images of my new school, Sam, my paintings, and my parents, swirled in my head, making it impossible for me to fall asleep.

Liliana's coughing reminded me I wasn't alone.

'I know you're awake,' I said. 'But I'm not sleeping in your bed with you ever again, even if you are attacked by all the monsters in the world.'

'I'm sorry.'

'I'll let the monsters eat you.'

'Please,' she whimpered.

'Go to sleep.'

I heard Liliana grumbling herself into slumber.

Dr. Torres

The following spring, as Papá had promised, the board of directors at the hospital hosted a family day, which included children's activities and a luncheon. That day, we wore new outfits our mother had made for the occasion. Liliana and I jumped up and down with anticipation when we put on our pink cotton dresses with white bib-front collars. Orlando complained that the collar of his shirt scratched his neck and that his pants were too short. It surprised me to see how much my brother, who was almost four years old, had grown. Mamá arranged his collar and assured my brother that his pants were perfect. She then winked at me.

I bit my lip so I wouldn't smile, then said, 'They should be fine; they cover your ankles.'

Orlando relaxed and allowed her to help him button his trousers.

Mamá pulled Jaime away from his stick horse. He ran around the house, pretending to be Little Joe from *Bonanza.* Mamá's long hair hung on one side of her face as she helped Jaime dress.

'We need to hurry, or we'll be late. We don't want to disappoint your papá.'

When we were finally ready, she made us twirl around. Liliana and I spun so fast that our skirts puffed up, making us laugh. Orlando twisted his mouth to one side.

'Do I have to?' he asked reluctantly, then turned around once.

Jaime was back on his horse.

Pulling the reins with his left hand, he said, 'Come on, Cochise, we gotta go.'

Then, clucking at his wooden horse, he trotted around us.

'Ayayay.' Mamá stood up and placed her hands on her waist. 'I wish your papá was here to help.' She held my brother's hand. 'Jaime, stop playing. I'm going to get ready. Don't get dirty, you understand?' she warned, squinting, and pointing a finger at us.

The staff had decorated the hospital corridors with children's paintings. When I saw them, I thought about my paintings at school, the ones my parents knew nothing about.

'You look so pretty, Rocío.' Papá's perky voice pulled me back from my memories. He lifted me into the air and kissed me on the cheek. Like a gliding kite, he slowly put me down, leaving a faint, spicy scent around me. He turned around and embraced Mamá, kissing her lips. 'You are the most beautiful woman here.'

She indeed looked pretty. Her auburn hair fell on her shoulders, held back only by a white headband peppered with tiny pearls. Her turquoise dress with white lace trim and belt enhanced her already slender figure.

'Thank you.' She beamed with delight and squeezed Papá's hand. 'You look handsome yourself.'

'Oh, really?' With his nose in the air, he swelled his chest and adjusted his uniform. We all chuckled.

'Let's goooo. I want to play.' Jaime pulled Papá's sleeve. Mamá rolled her eyes, grinning at my restless brother.

Papá grabbed my brothers' hands. 'Yes. Let's start with the games.'

The long hallway with its shiny floor was now crowded with small children and parents, all dressed in their best clothes. Papá stopped when we came face-to-face with one of his colleagues.

'Dr. Torres, these are my children and my wife.' Papá smiled as he introduced us one by one to his friend. 'Dr. Rosanía Torres is also Colombian. He joined us a month ago.'

Dr. Torres and my father looked somewhat alike. They both had long legs and short, dark hair outlining their broad foreheads. The one difference between the two of them was that Papá had an unmistakable sparkle in his eyes, whereas Dr. Torres had an icy gaze.

'Very nice to meet you, Rocío,' the doctor said, extending his hand towards me.

Suddenly, a chill went up my spine. I looked at Papá with pleading eyes.

'Rocío?' Papá tensed his jaw and scolded, 'Say hello.'

'Hello,' I said, shaking Dr. Torres's dry and cracked hand, which reminded me of the farmers in Puerto López.

'It's a pleasure to meet—'

'Let's go!' Jaime interrupted.

Papá excused us, and together we continued walking the long corridors until we arrived at a large room filled with tables. There was a nurse or a parent at each table, moderating board games, finger painting, arts and crafts, and marble games. My siblings and I ran to different tables.

While I was making a picture frame, Mamá fluttered around the tables with the elegance of the blue butterflies I had seen in Colombia. Papá, on the other hand, had concentrated all his attention on speaking to Dr. Torres. The two retreated to a small sitting area located on one side of the games room, away from everyone.

When I was finished making a picture frame, I went to find Papá. He was talking to his friend. I came from behind, so neither one of them noticed I was there. When I approached, I overheard Dr. Torres say something about going to Havana, telling my father about a man called Castro who needed help.

Papá replied, 'I know that there is a lot to do, but it is impossible for me to leave now. I have work to do here. My family…' Papá stroked his head with his hand like he did when he was watching the news or reading the newspaper. Astounded, I took a step back.

Will he leave again, just like when he left us in Colombia, to come to Chicago? We didn't see him for months.

The two men sat in silence for a while.

'But if we don't support him now, the Yankees will overthrow him,' Dr. Torres insisted.

Papá's face tensed. 'Excuse me, if you recall, you have this fellowship because of me. And I am also coordinating the Canadian front.'

I knew Mamá would be very unhappy if she knew Papá was still involved in politics. Wasn't that one of the reasons we left Colombia? I thought about the letter she wrote to Grandma telling her that being away would keep him from pursuing his political interests.

Unnoticed, I went back to the craft table and sat down. At first, I couldn't figure out why the well-mannered, pale, slender Dr. Torres reminded me of the husky, wheat-skinned colonel. But then I figured it out. They were both secretive. It was as though they stood in the shadows.

Mamá made me flinch when she touched my shoulder. 'Lunchtime.'

Papá joined us.

'So, what did you make?' he asked.

'I can't tell you; it is a secret.' I wasn't sure if I wanted to give him the picture frame as a present anymore.

'All right, then let's go to the cafeteria with everyone else.' Papá scoured the crowded room, looking for my siblings. 'I do not see them.'

'You told me they would be safe.' Mamá pressed her lips in anger.

He began walking.

'They are safe, relax. They are here. We just have to find them.'

Mamá and I followed him across the busy room. We found Orlando and Jaime playing marbles on the floor. Liliana was dressing a doll on the other side of the room. Once we had gathered everyone, I was happy to see my parents relax again.

We found the noisy dining area with lingering smells of spiced BBQ hamburgers and chicken, baked pies, and bread. Adults and children held trays carrying food and drinks. When it was our turn, Papá placed the food on our plates, grilled chicken, peas, and mashed potatoes.

When Orlando asked for dessert, Papá leaned forward. 'What you eat is who you are. Too much sugar will give you diabetes.'

'But—' I was going to tell Papá that a little wasn't so bad, but he interrupted.

'There is no but. You need to trust that your mamá and I know what is best for you. You may have a choice of fruit.'

Orlando tightened his lips while blinking fast.

'No need to get upset,' Mamá said. 'Your papá is right. Let me get you a nice orange or apple. You should all be happy that we get to spend time with your papá.'

I was. When I was around him, I felt important and protected. I was Dr. Velásquez's daughter. But today was different. The thought of him leaving us again left me with no desire to eat. So, I stared at my food for a while.

When Mamá returned, we were almost finished with our lunches. She placed the tray of fruit on the table and sat next to my father.

She asked, 'What were you talking about with Dr. Torres? You looked pretty serious.'

He looked away and replied, 'International issues, that is all.'

'What about *international issues*?'

'The world is changing rapidly, and for the better. Batista has left Cuba, and Doctor Martin Luther King Junior. gave an eloquent speech on the integration of schools.'

Papá stretched his legs while Mamá's posture suddenly became rigid.

'Who is Batista?' I asked.

Mamá explained, 'The ex-president of Cuba. Let's change the subject. The kids don't need to know any more than that.'

'It is fine if they ask questions. They should be critical thinkers.'

My father rested his chin on his hand.

Still shaken by the conversation I had overheard earlier and unsure of how to ease the tension between my parents, I babbled, 'When I was in Ms. Bell's class, she posted two of my paintings on the front wall.'

The words spilled out of my mouth, almost as if someone else were speaking for me. I covered my mouth with one hand, but it was too late. They were all staring at me.

'Congratulations!' Papá proclaimed.

'What did you paint?' Mamá asked, tilting her head to one side.

'Just rivers and mountains.'

'Great, I would love to see them if you still have them. I am proud of you.' Papá smiled.

'Yes, me too,' Mamá said.

Relief washed over me when my parents turned to my sister and brothers, who had finished eating and were ready to leave the table. They didn't ask me why I had painted them. They probably assumed it had been part of a classroom activity, and I was not about to tell them otherwise. I didn't want my parents to know that I wasn't given a desk or included in class activities during my first weeks at my new school.

After lunch, my mother went back to the games room with my brothers and sister. I asked my father to take me on a tour of the hospital. Walking proudly behind him, we first entered some type of meeting place with an enormous oval table in the middle. Papá poured half a cup of coffee into a mug. 'Would you like something to drink?'

'No thanks, Papá.'

'All right, then. This is the conference room.'

Large black-and-white photographs of the hospital's original buildings covered the walls. Circling around the table, we stopped in front of each picture as he recounted the history of the hospital.

When we were finished, I whispered, 'Can I see your office?'

'Yes, of course.'

He led me to a small room on the other side of the hallway.

In the middle of his office was a desk, a chair, and a small wastebasket. Papá walked straight to his desk and began separating a stack of files into two piles. 'Aside from seeing patients, I also need to do the paperwork. See, these are the files that are ready to go.' He straightened the files in the small pile. 'And these others,' he said, moving on to straighten the files of the largest pile, 'are the ones I have to complete later today.'

Papá's office had an empty feeling about it. At first, I couldn't tell what it was, but then it became clear to me. The walls were bare. Other doctors displayed pictures of their families. My father had none. When my frame from the craft table dried, I knew could place a picture of our family in it and give him a present. That way, he'd have something to hang on the wall and think of us.

Perhaps I could also give him one of my paintings. I smiled just thinking about his face when he opened his gifts.

'What is so funny?' he asked.

'Nothing.' I held my smile back.

'Are you ready to go?'

'Yes.'

'I am going to show you something you will enjoy. Follow me, young lady.'

He showed me out. We walked onto the second-story outdoor terrace. There, we found a nurse who was giving away balloons to the children.

'Can I have one?'

'*May* I have one?' Papá corrected.

'May I? Please?'

'Yes, you may.'

We waited in line for some time until it was my turn.

'May I have a red balloon, please?' I asked the woman.

'I wish all the kids were as polite as you are.' The lady winked at me. 'One red balloon coming up.' Two large hairpins, deep into her bushy hair, kept her small, white, wing-like hat from flying away. 'Here it is.' She handed me the balloon. My heart leaped with joy, so I embraced my father.

'Thanks,' I said.

He hugged me back and turned away to greet some of his colleagues who had just arrived. In the meantime, I tried over and over to tie the balloon's silky ribbon onto my left wrist.

After a few failed attempts, I finally asked, 'Papá, can you help me?'

At that instant, a sudden gust of wind came and blew the balloon away. I struggled to catch the twirling ribbon with my clumsy hands, but it eluded me. I watched it float into the light blue sky.

'My balloon!' I moaned.

Papá looked up, then at me.

'What happened?'

Without taking my eyes away from my balloon, I explained what had happened.

'I want another one,' I pleaded.

'But look, now there is a long line of kids waiting to get one. I am sorry you cannot have another one. Yours is gone.'

Young children chirped with happiness while waiting in line for their turn. Perhaps others wondered why an older girl would want a small, rubber, inflatable bag. But toys at our house had always been scarce. Our father limited them to one or two per year, for birthdays, holidays, or on a special occasion as a prize. So this balloon was special.

I cried and argued, 'But I was careful.'

'I love you, but all children should have the same opportunities. And if you get another balloon, there might not be enough for the other children.'

Papá hunched over and embraced me, but I didn't hug him back. I was so upset with him that, clenching my jaw and whipping my eyes with my sleeve, I turned away from him.

'I am sorry but—' another of his acquaintances interrupted him, so he patted me on the back and then turned around to speak with the older man.

All I could think of was how much I wished I could have wings to fly after my balloon and bring it back. Boys and girls giggled as they strutted before me with their balloons. I covered my face to stop myself from bursting into tears again. I was angry at Papá and hated to see the other children showing off, so I moved to one corner and stared at my balloon until it eventually vanished from sight.

We left Papá at the hospital and on our way home, Mamá handed me a paper bag.

'I picked up your frame and put it away so Papá wouldn't see it. He's going to love it.'

I took the paper bag and crinkled it inside my fist. It was difficult for me to think about giving my father a gift when I was still so upset with him for his plans with Dr. Torres and for my balloon. Mamá was busy entertaining my brothers, so she neither asked questions nor continued speaking to me about the frame.

That evening, I went to my room, lay on my bed, and reread Grandma Emilia's letter, which I had received days earlier.

April 15, 1959

Dear Rocío
The days seem longer since you all left. I often look out to the yard as if somehow, I will see you with your brothers and sister playing there. But I am not sad anymore, because I received your letter. I am sorry to hear that the change has been difficult for you, but it will get better with time. You are a

strong girl, and I am confident that you will be able to overcome the challenges life will bring you. You have been blessed with a loving family; always remember this.

With regard to your questions about your papá, yes, I like him. At first, we were concerned because they were too young when they met. But your papá has proven to be a responsible and intelligent man.

On another subject, Colonel Moncayo called and said that Nala broke a paw playing in the river, but she is being treated, and we hope she will get better soon.

Papá walked into my room with a glass of milk.

'Rocío, your mamá told me you did not eat much at dinner, so I brought you some milk.'

I quickly folded the letter and put it under my pillow.

'A letter from Grandma,' I explained.

I didn't want my father to know I was inquiring about him.

'Is everything all right?'

'Yes, only Nala broke a paw playing in the river.'

'I am sure she will be fine. She is strong. Are you still upset about your balloon?'

'Uh-huh.'

I was reminded of the importance of charity. He had bought one bike for the four of us. He gave the money for a second bike to children in need.

'It is not all about us. Other people have needs too. There are times when you have to choose others over yourself. For example, Doctor King; I mentioned him at lunchtime. Do you know who he is?'

'No.'

'He is fighting against discrimination and oppression here in the United States, often putting his own life at risk.'

Papá shook his head. I had no idea what all of that had to do with my balloon, but I listened anyway. He spent some time telling me all about the civil rights movement,

'So, are you going to leave?' I interrupted him.

'I am going to bed pretty soon.' Papá twitched.

'No, are you going to leave us? I heard you talking with Doctor Torres.'

Papá rubbed his chin and said, 'No, of course not. I love you all very much.'

For the first time, I felt he was being untruthful. There was conflict and uncertainty in his voice. I decided not to ask any more questions because I wanted to be alone. The weight of anger, mixed with the respect I felt for his desire to help others, left me breathless.

'I better get Liliana. She needs to stop watching TV and come to bed too. Good night, my girl.'

Papá stood up, kissed me, and left the room, then came right back.

'No... I am not going anywhere. I am not.'

I closed my eyes. Why was it that, for my father, everything was somehow a world problem? Things that were important to me, like the balloon or my dogs, didn't matter to him. I thought of the day Nala had her tooth removed so he could experiment with implants. Groggy, she had lain on her bed for hours. I fed her small amounts of food and water so she wouldn't get nauseous. And now I wasn't there to make her feel better. I jumped out of bed and went to my desk. I pulled out a used box of colored pencils my mother had bought for me at a street sale and drew for a while.

The early sunrays woke me the next morning. I lifted my head, trying to stretch my neck when I realized that I was on my bed with my dress still on. Next to me was a wrinkled sheet of paper filled with multicolor strokes, all going in different directions. A faded-red balloon seemed to be flying away from the page. There were no figures, no mountains. Silence echoed in my ears at the thought of Papá leaving us.

My Best Friend by my Bedside

1960

The new year received us with illnesses and unrest. First Orlando and then the rest of us came down with chicken pox. The same itchy blisters spread as far as our mouths and noses. Our parents transformed the living room into one large hospital bedroom where my brothers, sister, and I spent our days and nights. Mamá did the day treatments, and Papá did the night ones. At the end of each day, Mamá was tired and often fell asleep on the couch while waiting for our father to arrive home from work.

Papá made the rounds at night, going from bed to bed, checking our temperatures, applying lotion, or giving us medication. One evening, I felt unusually hot and sweaty, so I threw the sheets and blankets to one side of the bed. But as soon as I uncovered myself, I shivered. So, I pulled the sheets back up, covering my aching body. I wanted to call my parents, but closed my feverish eyes instead. In a dream, I tumbled down a pitch-black, tight hole and tried to hold on to the slippery walls with no success. The touch of Papá's hand on my face woke me up from the nightmare.

'Rocío, you were screaming.' He checked my temperature, then urged, 'You need to take a cool bath so that we can lower your temperature.'

'But I'll be cold,' I complained.

Papá took my sheets off, and bending over me, examined my neck. His pajamas sagged a little. They were getting too big for him.

'Let me listen to your lungs.' He pulled me up with both arms. Once I was sitting, he placed the stethoscope on my back and listened for a while. 'Your lungs are fine.'

'But my head hurts,' I moaned.

'That is a symptom of this virus.'

At first, the lukewarm water made me shiver uncontrollably, but when my body cooled down, the trembling ceased. Mamá later helped me dress and walked me back to my bed. I fell asleep soon after I took the medication. When the early morning pale rays crept into my room, I heard Papá's soft breathing.

He had slept in a sleeping bag next to my bed, just like he had done years earlier after removing the knitting needle from my foot. Because my fever persisted, along with my nightmares, Papá slept by my side for several nights, and knowing that he was close to me made me feel better.

Neither of my parents fell ill with chicken pox. Mamá was immune and Papá had already had it at an early age. My siblings and I were sick for weeks. Mumps followed the chicken pox. Later came the common cold. Our parents continued their home remedies and, in the end, my parents looked like they had just arrived from a desolated, far away, wild land. Their faces had turned pallid, and their eyes deep-set. It wasn't until the flowers bloomed and the weather warmed up that we were healthy again.

To celebrate, one Sunday morning, we packed Papá's station wagon with our one and only bike and a basket with food, then went to Lake Shore Park. We had been there once before, but I had forgotten how much I liked it.

I couldn't take my eyes off the clear, silver-blue waters of Lake Michigan. The soothing, rhythmic waves crashing against the shore sounded like a lullaby. In contrast, the city seemed rigid, filled with skyscrapers that left the smaller buildings standing in their shadows. Distant sounds of whistling trains, pounding construction equipment, and passing cars traveled in the wind. On the beach, the children played with kites and sand tools.

I took my shoes off and ambled towards the shore while the others ate their lunch. Coarse sand tickled my feet. The water was chilly at first, but eventually I became accustomed to the temperature and so I stayed, mesmerized, watching wave after wave crashing against the sandy beach. Sometime later, Mamá's distant voice reminded me I wasn't alone.

'Rocío, come and eat lunch.'

It was then I realized I was wet up to my waist, so I pretended not to hear. I feared getting into trouble. So, Papá came to see me. When he noticed I was soaking, he burst out laughing.

'Ayayay! Mamá is not going to be happy.'

I mumbled, 'I didn't mean to.'

He looked at me, then towards Mamá, back and forth several times.

Then, with a smile on his face, he said, 'What the heck?!'

He took his shoes off and joined me in the water. I laughed so loud that soon my siblings and Mamá were by the shore looking at us as though we were wild animals. In the end, everyone got wet and when we drove home, we tried to keep warm by snuggling close to one another and singing songs.

Two weeks after our outing, when the birds were chirping outside, I went looking for Papá. I wanted to ask him why the frame I'd made him for Father's Day was still in his office at home. Now, it had a family picture and was sitting on a bookcase next to other pictures. I picked up the handmade frame, but quickly placed it back down when I remembered Papá's conversation with Dr. Torres. I didn't want to entertain the thought that Papá would leave us. So, I decided I'd find Liliana and invite her to swing with me. As I was walking out of Papá's office, I saw, jammed between two books, a folded newspaper *The New York Times*. I checked to make sure no one was coming, then unfolded it. The date was May 6, 1960 and the headline read: **Soviets Down American Aircraft; U.S. Claims It Was a Weather Plane.**

Mamá walked in. 'Rocío, what are you doing?'

'Nothing. I was looking for Papá.'

'He went to work early this morning. What are you doing with the newspaper?'

'Reading.'

I handed her the paper, expecting to be scolded. Mamá didn't. Instead, she leaned the broom against the wall, took the newspaper and began reading aloud. Papá startled us both when he walked in.

'I see that you two have found my newspaper.'

My mother folded the paper like a mischievous child.

He smirked. 'I am only here to collect a file that I forgot. Keep reading that article; it is pretty interesting. Rocío is old enough to learn that it is all a farce... a lie.'

'Jaime, please... she is only ten years old. She'll have her whole life to be an adult and to worry about those things.'

'She cannot grow up with blinders. But that has to be another conversation, because I have to go back to work. I will see you both later.'

He kissed my mother and caressed my face before rushing out of the house.

That evening, while my brothers and sister went to play in the garden, I stayed in my room, trying out the watercolors Papá had bought for us when we were sick. When I went to get water to paint with, I overheard Mamá asking him, 'What do you know about the plane that was shot down?'

'Eisenhower is claiming that it was a weather plane. But I think Khrushchev is correct. It was probably a spy plane.'

'Hm. What are the Americans looking for?' Mamá asked.

'North Americans,' Papá corrected.

'Whatever.' Annoyed, Mamá closed her eyes and shook her head.

'Probably to check the Soviets' military capability.'

'Are they really that afraid of the Soviets?'

'Perhaps. What I *do* know is that a communist revolution in Latin America is one of the Yankees' major fears. They already lost Cuba, so they will do anything to stop the Soviets from supporting revolutionary groups in our countries.' Papá nostrils flared.

I tiptoed back to my room. Peering through the open door, I watched my mother stand up.

'Jeez,' she said. 'I thought we were just talking about an airplane. Why do you care about Cuba and what the Americans do?'

He stopped and shook his head in disbelief. 'We should *all* care.'

'Why? We can't do anything about it,' Mamá pleaded.

'Well, if we all thought like that, nothing would get done. 'The imperialists keep people poor, hungry, and sick, while they become wealthier.'

'Socialism is not the answer to our problems, and don't forget that because of the *Americans*, we have a home, schools for our children and you have a career.'

'It has worked for Israel. Think of the kibbutzim.'

I wanted to scream, *Stop.* But my voice wouldn't come out. Time slowed, suspense enveloped us all, and then finally Papá embraced my mother.

'I am sorry, honey. Please understand how difficult it is for me to look the other way when I know that millions of poor children die every day due to the lack of proper nutrition, proper sanitation… illnesses that could be cured if only our countries provided adequate services for them. What would you do if they were your children? Remember how sick they were not too long ago?' He sat down on the sofa. 'Am I supposed to look the other way?'

'Yes, you are, because your responsibility is here with us.'

'I know that. You and our children are my life, and I would do anything to make this a better world for you all.'

My siblings ran into the living room, bringing my parents' quarrel to an end.

I wished I could somehow fix our parents' problems, but I didn't know how. The anguish left me out of breath. When I opened the window, a light spring breeze came in, replacing the stale air in my bedroom. After inhaling several times, I looked up at the sky. Coral and orange brushstrokes left by the setting sun were fading away into the twilight.

Montréal

Inside our house, the table was set. The scent of baked bread and meatloaf wafted throughout the house. An arctic-like snowstorm was threatening the city when Papá opened the front door. Liliana and I ran to embrace him.

'So much excitement, I feel so welcomed,' he joked, hugging us.

He hung his coat and hat on the wooden rack, left his boots by the entrance, and went to his room.

We were sitting at the dining room table when Papá finally joined us. He had taken a shower and was dressed in casual clothes. He kissed us all, then he sat and ate. That day he didn't inquire about our day. He chewed and swallowed before telling us he was now officially a surgeon. 'I can operate without having someone looking over my shoulder.'

'I'm proud of you.' Mamá smiled.

'Thank you. Apparently, the word is out that I have done a good job here because I just received a job offer from a hospital in Montréal.'

I saw the surprise in Mamá's eyes as she spoke to him.

'Are you going to accept it?'

'Yes, I have to. My contract here will end soon.'

'I thought we were going back to Colombia.'

'We will, but not yet. This is a great opportunity to advance my career.'

'And what about us?'

'The children and you will learn French, which will be advantageous for all of you in the future.'

'When are we leaving?' Mamá asked.

'Well, I will have to go first, get settled and then send for you.'

Mamá pushed her plate away, stood up, and walked out of the dining room.

'Rocío, make sure your brothers and sister finish their dinners, then go to your rooms to read.'

He jumped up from his chair and went after Mamá.

I held my breath for a moment, trying to understand why we couldn't have a normal life. My friends had lived in the same city and sometimes even in the

91

same house all their lives. They had friends who they had known for years. Most of them had attended the same school. Not us.

My siblings and I ate in silence for some time. Suddenly, Liliana followed by Orlando, and then Jaime asked me all sorts of questions. Where would we live? Where is Montréal? Why can't Papá say no?

'I don't know… I don't know… I don't know.'

I was angry at my father for moving us around like we were nomads. Also, I was upset with my mother for not forcing him to stay in one place. When I looked around, my siblings were staring at me in disbelief and had stopped eating. I apologized. It was obvious that we were all in distress. Orlando and Jaime refused to go back to their room. They followed Liliana and me, then climbed onto my bed and got under the covers. Liliana lay on her bed. I sat on the chair that Papá had sat on so many nights while reading to us. I told them a story I made up, about a tree that had lost all his friends in a fire. He was sad for a while, but then befriended a snowman left behind by a group of children. I continued. As spring oozed into the forest, the snowman melted away. The tree noticed that a shoot had appeared where his friend had melted down.

I turned around to ask Jaime and Orlando what they thought about my story, but they had fallen asleep.

Liliana looked at me with heavy eyelids and said, 'I don't want to move.'

That night, my brothers slept in my bed. Liliana was happy to share hers with me because she claimed the monsters were back. My body felt limp. It seemed like everyone in my family expected me to be strong, but inside I was lost and alone, just like the tree.

The first postcard we received from Papá showed the Saint-Luc hospital with a tiny window marked in blue to indicate his office window. Sporadically, we received letters detailing events of his work, but there was no mention of us joining him. Mamá often fell asleep on the couch as if she were waiting for him to call or to come home. But he did neither. One day, impatiently, I confronted my mother.

'When are we going to Montréal so that we can be with Papá?'

'Soon. I hope. Actually, I was thinking about working so that we don't have to wait until your Papá sends us money.'

'Who will take care of us?'

'Ms. Madison.'

Ms. Madison was our next-door neighbor.

'Would that be okay with Papá?'

'I don't care what he thinks.' She could tell her response astounded me because she quickly embraced me. 'I'm sorry. I'm not upset with you. It's frustrating not knowing when we'll see your papá again.'

'Where will you work?'

'There is a clothing shop a few blocks from here; they need a seamstress.'

'Do you know how to make clothes?'

'Well, I'm not an expert, but I make all our clothes.'

'I will help Ms. Madison,' I said, feeling conflicted inside. I wanted to be supportive of my mother, but felt unsettled about my father's reaction to her plan.

For the next few months, Ms. Madison came to our house early in the morning and didn't leave until Mamá arrived home from work. I spent many hours in Papá's office drawing or reading. Somehow, being there made me feel closer to him. I often wondered why he had left behind our family pictures. The thought that he didn't miss us was too hard to bear, so I convinced myself that he had additional pictures displayed in his new office.

I didn't tell Mamá that my brothers fought or that Liliana ate little. Nor did I tell her that Ms. Chatty, as I called Ms. Madison behind her back, was on the phone all the time speaking with friends and family instead of watching us. Other days, she experimented with hair colors. One midmorning, she came out of the bathroom wearing heavy makeup and brushing her bright burgundy hair. Liliana and I looked at one another and burst out laughing. Ms. Madison stopped and fixed a piercing gaze on us.

'What is so funny?'

'Nothing.'

That was the first day in a long time I had seen my sister happy. From then on, Jaime and Orlando mocked Ms. Chatty. We were always thinking of ways to make fun of our babysitter. Pretending to be her, my brothers spoke in high-pitched voices, teasing one another. Liliana and I wore Mamá's spiky high heels and pretended to speak on the phone like her too. I knew our parents wouldn't have liked what we were doing, but we did it anyway. Ms. Madison neither noticed what we were doing, nor did she seem to mind. She was pleased to see we kept ourselves busy.

Late one afternoon, when Mamá came home from work, I overheard Ms. Madison asking my mother why she didn't want Papá to know that we were traveling to Montréal. My mother took a deep breath and told her he had been evasive every time she asked him to send us the airline tickets. He also made all sorts of excuses, including complications with our visas, housing availability, work responsibilities, and so on.

When Ms. Madison commented that those were all valid reasons for postponing a trip, Mamá stood up and said, 'It's just a hunch. Thank you so much for everything.' She shook the lady's hand.

Once Ms. Madison left, Mamá asked us all to gather at the dining table. She opened a large envelope, pulled out some documents, and placed them on the table. 'I know how difficult it has been for you not having your papá around. But I have good news. We are moving to Canada in a few days. Here are the passports and our train tickets.' No one responded. 'We'll see your papá soon. Aren't you happy? Don't you think we need to be together?' Orlando played with his hands. 'Jaime, what do you think?'

Jaime fiddled with the button on his shirt. 'Do we have to learn French?'

'Yes, but they say that the more languages you speak, the easier it gets to learn a new one.'

I should have been happy at the prospect of seeing my father, but I wasn't. I feared his reaction when we showed up unannounced and without his approval. But I said nothing. It was clear I wouldn't be able to deter her from traveling to Montréal. To make matters worse, I dreaded the idea of us leaving our friends behind and everything we had. Again.

A week later, a taxi dropped us off at the Chicago Union Station. Only four bags accompanied us. We had left everything else we owned behind. Mamá sold whatever she could and, what she couldn't sell, she gave away to friends and neighbors. She had bought us new jackets and shoes, but she was wearing her old coat and a beige pillbox hat and matching gloves her coworkers had made for her.

The Great Hall at the station was buzzing with people rushing to buy tickets. We already had ours, so we went straight to the wooden benches where we waited for our train to arrive. The enormous columns and high ceilings were like those I had once seen on the cover of an art magazine. They were massive, and the room was so large, our voices made an unusual echo.

We waited for some time until we heard a man on the loudspeaker announcing the train to Montréal. Filled with excitement, we dragged our bags to the nearest platform and jumped onto the waiting train. Some passengers went to the sleeping car, but we didn't. We sat in our seats and took the small pillows and blankets they gave us, trying to rest as best we could while sitting.

The next morning, they detained the train at the immigration checkpoint. Two Canadian officers walked into the car and began asking for documents. When the shorter officer checked our passports, he snarled at the taller officer.

'One Colombian woman and four children are trying to enter the country without visas.'

When the taller, broad-shouldered officer heard this, he walked back to where we were.

'Ma'am, please step out of the train. We need to ask you some questions.'

Mamá opened her eyes wide and, staring at my siblings and me, said in Spanish, 'Don't go anywhere until I come back, and if someone tries to pull you out of the train, scream as loud as you can.'

We grabbed onto one another in fear as we watched the two officers escort Mamá out and onto the platform. The taller officer interrogated our mother, while the shorter one took notes. When they finished, the shorter one left. A few minutes later, he came back. The taller officer shook his head while Mamá appeared to plead with him. Scared, I cracked the window open to hear what they were saying.

'You don't understand, Ma'am. You cannot enter the country without a visa and to make matters worse, you don't have a return ticket.'

'But my husband is a doctor, and he has a work permit. Please let me call the hospital so that you know I am telling the truth.'

'I cannot do that.'

'I have four children. What do you want me to do?' Mamá screamed, then covered her face with her hands.

'Have her children come with us. We will all go to the immigration office,' the taller officer ordered.

'Don't you dare touch my children!'

When we heard this, Orlando sniffled. Liliana and Jaime moved closer to me. I embraced my siblings, pretending to be calm.

A woman approached us and, smiling reassuringly, said, 'Don't worry. You are with us. I have some homemade cookies. Would you like some?'

Orlando and Jaime nodded.

The woman pulled a paper bag out of her purse and gave each one of us a sugar cookie.

We were enjoying our treat when the shorter officer jumped into the car trying to pull us off the train, but he found a human wall around us. The other passengers quickly stood up and, locking arms with one another, they made a circle around my siblings and me.

'Move out of the way. I need to take the children with me,' ordered the flustered officer.

'Then you have to take all of us with you,' said a middle-aged woman.

The officer surveyed the car with angry eyes and then stormed out. He whispered something to the other officer. Puzzled, the two men stared at one another.

'Ma'am… but even if I allowed you to call, which phone would you use?' asked the taller officer in a calm voice.

'I can use the one in your office,' she said, wiping the tears from her eyes.

'I might get in trouble for doing this, but I'll do it. Let's go.'

'What about the children? We can't leave them on the train,' the shorter one said.

Again, Mamá warned the men, 'Don't you dare touch them.'

Jaime and Liliana sat in silence, looking out the window. Tears rolled down Orlando's cheeks when he saw the two officers drive away with our mother, so I pulled him next to me. Little by little, different passengers in our car approached us and gave us food and drinks. Others patted Orlando on the back.

Suddenly, the train conductor came to collect our tickets.

'Where are your parents?' the man asked me.

My voice quivered when I said, 'Mamá went with the immigration officers, but she'll be back soon.'

'We leave in five minutes, so she better be here by then.'

Now all my siblings were weeping. This time, I didn't embrace them. I gulped down my breaths, trying very hard not to weep. I didn't want to scare my brothers and sister even more.

The other passengers booed the man.

'You can't leave without their mother,' a bearded man shouted.

The angry conductor got off the car and went to talk to the policemen. After almost an hour, which seemed like weeks, our mother arrived in the police car. Cheers and claps broke out inside the train when we saw her waving our passports in the air. Like a heroine, she triumphantly hopped into our train car. We hugged her.

'Rocío, we are going to Montréal.' She embraced us all. 'They called Papá's hospital, and he got us through.'

We were so excited and relieved, but a dark feeling had once more risen in me.

The Greatest Secrets are Hidden Well

I held my breath when I heard the announcement over the loudspeaker.

'Montréal Central Station is our final stop. We will be disembarking onto platform four.'

Soon after, the hissing and screeching of the brakes replaced the steady chugging sound of the train. A loud whistle made me grin with excitement just thinking that we would soon be with Papá.

I felt Mamá's touch as she gathered our belongings.

'C'mon, let's get ready. We'll arrive soon.'

We had been traveling for almost two days. Mamá pulled a lipstick out of her purse and colored her lips strawberry red. She combed her matted hair and perched her hat on her head. She then slipped on her gloves. We all leaped out of our seats, eager to dash off the train. But our mother held us back.

'Wait until most of the people have disembarked. This way, we don't hold anyone back.' We were about to protest when she said, 'I don't want to hear any *but*s.'

Restless, we waited until Mamá finally stood up and asked us to follow her. Liliana, Mamá, and I dragged the bags out of the car. Orlando and Jaime carried their toys.

The platform was overflowing with people, most of whom seemed to be in a hurry. Outside, the steam coming out of the trains blended with the already hazy, cool air, making it difficult to see. I walked on my tiptoes, craning my neck, trying to find Papá in a sea of dark coats and hats. Then, suddenly, from out of the mist, he appeared.

'Papá!'

I let go of my bags and ran to greet him. My siblings trailed along, leaving our mother behind with our luggage. When Papá saw us, he sped up his pace. We raced as fast as we could to him, all of us embracing him at once. He chuckled when he felt my brothers clinging to his legs, and Liliana's and my arms curled around his waist.

'Oh. My ducklings. I missed you so much,' he said in a tender voice.

'Hi, Papá! How are you?' I asked.

'I am fine,' he said. 'It is so great to see you all.'

We tried to talk to him all at once until he interrupted us. 'Wait, we need to go and help your mamá first.'

Holding hands, we ran back to help her.

Papá embraced her. She let go of the suitcases, closed her eyes, then hugged him back.

'I am glad you are all here, even though I am not completely ready for you,' he apologized.

'We are together, and that's all that matters. We'll make do with what you have at home.' Mamá pressed her lips together.

'Nice hat!' said Papá, touching the top of Mamá's hat.

'Nice coat!' she replied. The high-collar, dark blue pea coat and his prominent chin made him look important.

Papá showed us the way out of the station. He carried the two heaviest bags while Mamá, Liliana, and I dragged the other two. We crossed a parking lot filled with cars; many of the newer cars had enormous fender fins, giving the appearance of wings. Papá's car wasn't as shiny and the front and back were rounded. Only three suitcases fit in the small trunk. Once we were sitting inside, Papá placed the last suitcase on the back footwell under my siblings' feet. I sat next to my mother in the front seat.

Even though the streets had leftover dirty snow and Montréal seemed older than Chicago, there was something *distinguished* about the Canadian city proudly displaying ornate buildings with oversized doors.

City Hall took my breath away; it was so beautiful. It looked like a fairy-tale castle with towers, balconies and a sloped roof.

The farther we drove, the smaller the buildings became. Spider web-like power lines hovered over them. A few miles away from the commercial sector, we drove into what was now our new neighborhood.

'This is it!' Papá exclaimed.

Freezing raindrops spattered against the car as we turned into a parking lot. The street was quiet except for the sound of the rain and an empty garbage can rolling on its side, pushed by the wind. The cloudy sky made me shiver.

'I was lucky that a friend subleased this place to me, because there was nothing else I could get in one day,' Papá said, as he parked. 'I have been renting a one-bedroom apartment, which is too small for all of us. Fortunately, the landlord allowed me to get out of the lease. This place is comfortable inside.'

Our apartment was on the first floor. Just as we had in our previous homes, my siblings and I went from bedroom to bedroom, trying to decide which one was ours. There were no beds, only mattresses on the floor. I was disappointed but said nothing to my parents. The family room was empty, and the dining room had a wooden table with six chairs. A small stack of plates, a few glasses, and a box with silverware and some pans were sitting on top of the kitchen counter. Both bathrooms had soap, shampoo, and clean white towels.

'I am sorry, but I did not have time to buy furniture. All the things here have been donated by coworkers,' he said. 'But soon we will have our place nice and furnished, like we did in Chicago.'

Perhaps it was because I was tired, or perhaps it was something about this new place that scared me, but I couldn't be as joyful as Papá was. The apartment felt damp and cool.

'Don't worry, honey. This is fine for now.' Mamá peeled her gloves off and smiled. Then she turned around and told us, 'Go take a shower so you will be ready for dinner.'

'Can we play outside?' Jaime begged.

'I do not think that is a good idea,' Papá responded. 'This rain freezes solid, covering the streets with a layer of ice, which can be dangerous.'

Mamá gave my brother a light push on the back.

'Go clean up.'

Liliana and I chose the bedroom next to our parents' room because it faced the street. We wanted to see who our neighbors were, both of us hoping to make friends. After a warm shower, I got dressed. Later, I took my bag into the room and began placing my clothes in the closet. Through the window, I could see my parents standing by the iron railing next to the outdoor staircase that went to the second floor. The front door was ajar, so I heard Papá say, 'You should have told me that you were coming.'

'Well, you left over four months ago and there was no plan to get us here.'

'I was trying to settle down at work. Perhaps you do not understand how demanding my work is. I hardly have any time to eat or sleep, let alone furnish a house.' Papá's face was tense. 'You took an enormous risk crossing the border without a visa. What if they had deported you all back to Colombia?'

Mamá's head drooped. 'You put the kids and yourself at risk by forcing your way into this country. I had begun the legal process, but it all takes time. And by the way, how did you get the extra money for the travel expenses?'

'I worked.'

Papá threw his arms into the air.

'And who took care of the children?'

'Ms. Madison, the neighbor.'

'You left them with that lunatic?' he asked. Mamá was about to respond, but before she said anything, he spun around and headed back inside. 'I am going to get us some food. Let's talk after the kids go to bed.'

Why wasn't Papá proud of my mother? He didn't even seem that happy we were there. He was right; it had been risky to leave the U.S. and force our way into Canada. But I couldn't understand why he hadn't kept Mamá informed about what he was doing to reunite the family. I was struggling to understand what might *really* be going on. My frustration grew when I thought that there was something neither one of them was telling. I was eleven years old and would have understood almost everything. Didn't they realize that even if they tried keeping us out of their problems, we often heard them arguing? The only thing I knew was that they were drifting apart. My heart was pounding when I heard my siblings come out of the shower. I inhaled deeply. Water always made me feel better, so when Liliana left the bathroom, I took a long, steamy, hot bath.

Once dressed, I went to work on my brother's closet, as my mother had requested. I thought that if she were happy, she wouldn't argue with Papá. When I went to the boys' room, Jaime and Orlando were stuffing their shirts and pants in the drawers without folding them, but I wasn't about to scold them. I simply pretended not to notice. Instead, I filled two drawers with their underwear and socks, hung their coats, then left their room. I went looking for my coloring books, but when I couldn't find them, I searched the new garage. There were mostly empty boxes except for two, which had my father's name written on them. Curious, I opened the one on top and found that it had some books. Under that box was a larger one. So, I pushed the box with books to one side and lifted one flap of the bottom box. There, I found a military uniform. Under it was a pair of muddy boots. There were also maps, a phone book, flyers and newspaper articles. I picked up one article that read: **Cuba**

Seizes Billions of U.S. Oil Assets. The U.S. Sets off Restrictions in Retaliation.

What is Papá doing with these newspapers? I know Cuba is another country, so why is he interested in it and who is Fidel Castro? Is he the leader?

I dropped the paper back into the box as if it had burned my hands. I hurried to close the flap, then dashed into the apartment and closed the door behind me, coming face-to-face with Papá.

He cleared his throat. 'Rocío, what were you doing?' He fixed his eyes on mine.

'I was looking for my coloring books, but they weren't there.' I rubbed my sweaty hands.

'Did you open the large box with my things?'

'Yes, Papá. I didn't mean to,' I said, ashamed.

I didn't want him to think I was snooping around.

'Please stay away from those boxes.'

'Yes, Papá.' My voice quivered.

'Dinner is served!' Mamá called.

'Let's go.' He patted me on the back.

I was relieved that he didn't continue questioning me. However, for the rest of the evening, fear clutched at my heart. What was he doing with that uniform? My mind was spinning with questions when Papá passed me a plate with *viande fumée,* smoked meat.

'This is one of the iconic foods from Montréal,' he said. 'Try it. I think you will like it.'

I had lost my appetite, but to avoid being questioned by my parents, I took a piece of the corned beef-like meat and a slice of bread and placed them on my plate. Papá's watchful eyes followed my every move. He waited until he saw me take the first bite in my mouth, then looked away. It was as though he wanted to make sure I was fine about what I had seen.

What he didn't know was how uncomfortable I felt, suspecting that he was hiding something from Mamá. If I said nothing, I would be disloyal to my mother. But if I revealed his secret, I would be disloyal to him. He would also probably leave because he wouldn't have anything to hide. Puzzled and confused, I ate slowly and mostly listened to everyone talk.

That evening, Papá came to our room. Liliana had turned to one side of her mattress and was breathing steadily.

'Papá, why are you upset with Mamá?' I said, twisting a corner of my pillowcase with my fingers.

'I am not upset. I was worried that something would happen to you.'

'Did you miss us?'

'Yes, of course. Sometimes I sat on a bench by a lake just watching kids and wishing you were here with me. I even saw a duck that made me think of Jaime.'

'Jaime looks like a duck?'

'Well, not really. You know how he is always grinning?'

'Yes. He smiles like one.'

'Is that why you call us my ducklings?'

'That's right, because I love you.'

'What about Mamá? Do you love her too?'

'I do. And she is the best mother in the world. Don't you ever forget that.' He kissed my head.

I tried to appear cheerful, but Papá's secret things scared me.

'Papá.'

'Yes?'

'Why do you have that uniform?'

'I am doing some training.'

'For what?'

'I don't want to discuss it right now. It's getting late. Go to sleep, Chio.'

I felt as though I was peering into a scary pit that was filled with mysterious water, one I could almost smell and touch. But just like my father, it glided right through my hands, disappearing back into the bottomless well.

Feeling a lump in my throat, I turned away from him.

'Good night, Rocío.'

The sound of the door closing resonated in my heart.

A Man in Uniform

Soon after we arrived in Montréal, neighbors swarmed our apartment, carrying food, secondhand furniture, and kitchen items. Papá bought our beds, night tables, and desks. An old seamstress, Adeline, who lived two floors above us, gave Mamá enough material to make curtains for the entire apartment. Being on the first floor, we had to hang sheets on the windows for privacy, which embarrassed us all except for Papá.

'We have to live within our means,' he would reply when we complained.

So, when Adeline offered to help Mamá make the drapes, we were jubilant. For two weeks, my mother spent most afternoons sewing at Adeline's place.

One day, I went looking for Mamá to ask permission to go with children from our block to the nearest convenience store. I was about to ring the doorbell when Adeline, whom I hadn't yet met, opened the door. I took one step back upon seeing her. She was a short woman with a hunchback and deep wrinkles on her face.

'Mamá?' I asked.

In a hoarse voice, she invited me inside. 'Oui, oui, entre.'

The nasty smell of burned tobacco was overwhelming, so I took advantage of the breeze that came from an open window, taking a couple of deep breaths. We went to a room with two sewing machines, a table, an ironing board, and one large container filled with cutout material. Mamá was bent over the table, tacking the hem of a bright purple flowery fabric. I touched the colorful material, hoping deep inside it wasn't our new drapes.

'Mamá, can I go with some neighborhood kids to the store?'

'What for?' she asked, keeping her eyes fixed on her project.

'I think they are going to buy candy or something.'

'No. You know you aren't allowed to eat candy or go places without supervision.'

I insisted for a few minutes, but I could not change her mind. On my way out, Adeline placed a chocolate cookie in a napkin and then dropped it inside my pocket.

Once we were by the door, she smiled and, baring her stained teeth, said, 'Au revoir.'

I walked back home, eating the crunchy cookie and wondering how my mother could stand the stench of Adeline's apartment. When a light breeze blew a loose bit of hair across my face, the smell of smoke came back.

That afternoon, when I asked Mamá if the smell bothered her, she responded, 'She is a good friend. She gave me the material for the drapes. I know she smokes, and that she isn't pretty. But you overlook those things because she is a nice person. Plus, if I don't accept her help now, we are going to have to wait a long time until we have enough money to have the drapes made.'

'What's the rush?'

Mamá rocked back and forth on her heels.

'I want our place to feel like home.'

I understood the real reason she was so adamant about making our place comfortable and preparing Papá's favorite meals was to entice him to spend more time with us. Suddenly, the memory of his box with the uniform and boots flashed in my head. I pressed my lips tightly together to stop myself from screaming.

He is training for war, and he might leave us. I'm sorry, Mamá. I'm sorry I didn't tell you before, but I couldn't betray Papá.

I feared she would notice my trembling, so I inhaled a shallow breath.

'You look like you've seen a ghost.' Mamá held me by my arm.

'I'm fine,' I said as I struggled for another breath.

Then I went to my room with a heavy feeling in my stomach.

Mamá brought and hung the curtains two weeks later. Then she closed the dining room drapes to show me.

'I know that the purple is bold, but it is better than nothing.' She stood back proudly to admire her work. 'What do you think?'

The hideous large flowers seemed as though they were coming towards me all at once. My worst fear was that they would scare Liliana, and then I'd have to sleep with her again.

'They look good, but it's better to keep them open during the day,' I said, hoping that at night they would look less frightening.

'That's a good idea.' Mamá opened them back up.

That evening, she set the dining table with silverware and glasses. She had made a customized *ajiaco*.

'The soup doesn't taste exactly like Lola's,' she announced, 'because I couldn't find all the spices I needed, but it tastes pretty good.'

She gave each of us a bowl of the steamy chicken soup. As side dishes, she served rice and salad. After a long afternoon playing outside, we were famished, so my siblings and I grabbed our spoons and began eating. The loud ring of the phone scared us all.

'I'll get it,' I said.

'I'll get it!' Orlando shouted.

'No, I'll get it. You both finish your dinner.' Our mother walked to the kitchen and picked up the wall phone. 'Hi, honey,' Mamá said with a beaming face, but then frowned. 'Why not?' She focused for a while, then muttered, 'Hm…

Don't worry. I understand. I'll tell the kids.' She dropped her chin to her chest, hung up the receiver, and came back to the table.

'Who was it?' asked Liliana.

'Your papá. He said he will not be home for dinner, because he has to stay late at work.'

'This late?' Jaime tapped the table with his fork.

Mamá looked away.

'Well, doctors take care of patients during the day, but sometimes also at night. Anyway, he sends you all a kiss.'

We finished our dinner mostly in silence. I kept looking at the door, hoping that my father would come home, but he never did. Mamá smiled throughout the evening, but we all knew how disappointed she was. Despite her attempts to make a home, my father was still working long hours, often coming home after everyone was already asleep.

That night, Mamá came into our room and, kneeling on the floor, said to Liliana and me, 'You know that we each have an angel who protects and helps us during difficult times?'

'An angel?' Liliana questioned her.

'Who is my angel?' I asked, astounded to learn that I had an angel of my own.

'God sends angels to protect children, but we don't know who they are.'

'How do you know they are with you?' I asked.

'Well, that is why you pray, so that they can hear you and protect you. And tonight, I'm going to teach you a prayer. Let's all put our hands together—'

'Papá doesn't believe in God,' I interrupted.

'He does. He just doesn't like organized religion. Besides, he is not here. It's just us,' Mother began.

Angel of God,
My guardian dear,
Don't forsake me
Ever this night and day.
Be at my side
Until I am in the arms
Of Jesus, Joseph, and Mary.
Saint Joseph, pray for us. Amen.

Papá's late work nights became a rule instead of the exception. And the more he stayed away, the more my mother tried to beautify the apartment and the more hours she spent in the kitchen preparing special meals. It upset me she never confronted him, and he never explained exactly what he was doing. I tried sometimes to ignore what was happening to our family.

A massive headache woke me up one cool night. My eyes felt heavy, and my body shook with chills. I got up to call my parents when I noticed that the front door to the apartment was open. Outside, Papá was in his car, changing his shirt. Standing next to the driver's open window Mamá stood in her bathrobe. 'So now you are a soldier?' she said. 'Is that what you've become?'

'Shh… shh… let's go in the house,' he said, and rolled up the window. Then he got out of the car, wearing a scrubs shirt and military pants.

Feverish, and with my heart beating loud in my chest, I walked back to my bedroom where I gagged and then threw up. My parents walked inside to find me standing in a pool of vomit.

'Oh, no. Rocío, what's going on?' Mamá lifted my hair off my face.

Papá placed the change of clothes he was holding and the car keys on the coffee table in the hallway.

'I'll take care of her. Come with me, Rocío.' He walked me into the living room, where I collapsed on the couch. He turned the lights on. After checking my throat, he said, 'Your tonsils are very swollen and you have a fever. I will start you on antibiotics and give you pain medication. So sorry you are not feeling well.'

When I cleaned up and took the medication, I went back to bed. Between feverish nightmares, I woke up to my parents arguing in their room.

In a deep voice, Papá warned, 'For your own safety, it is better if you don't know anything.'

'What about you? Are you in danger?' Mamá cried.

'Do not worry about me. I can take care of myself.'

'Communism is not the solution; you should know that. The Soviet Union and Cuba have repressive governments.'

Cuba, that country, I thought to myself, *the country mentioned in the newspaper.*

'And what about the U.S.? Even their hospitals were segregated into black and white until last year.'

'But things are changing in the States,' she insisted.

'You are going to have to trust me.'

'How can I do that if I don't know what you are doing?'

'We should continue this conversation another day. Right now, I am going to check Rocío.' I heard him come into my bedroom, so I turned to one side and closed my eyes. But he knew I was awake. 'Rocío, how do you feel?'

I felt his touch on my forehead.

I whispered, 'My throat hurts.'

'You are not hot anymore, which is great,' he said. 'I will get you some salt water so you can gargle.'

He left and then came back carrying a glass. He helped me to the bathroom sink and asked me to gargle with warm salt water. The water burned my throat and made me gag, but Papá didn't let me stop until I had finished gargling the solution. Once I was lying down again, he pulled a chair next to my bed and sat on it. The moonlight illuminated his tense expression. 'Did you hear us talking?'

A knot filled with sadness stopped me from speaking, so I nodded.

'You are only a child; you should not have to hear your parents bickering.'

I tried to hold my tears back but couldn't. They rolled onto one side of my face.

'All you need to know is that I love you all.'

Papá walked out of the room. A minute later, the sound of the front door closing made me jump.

He is leaving.

I sprinted to the window. On the sidewalk, he was sitting with his head in his hands, sobbing. The man I was so proud of, the man I admired, the respected physician, was broken. It seemed as though something deep inside of him was tearing him apart.

Dark, rounded clouds flooded the sky, blocking all trace of the moonlight; only my father's silhouette was left. Saddened by his despair, I lay back on my bed, wishing that somehow, I could help him.

'Rocío, I'm afraid,' my sister murmured.

She didn't mention the monsters as she usually did, nor the curtains, so I assumed that she, too, had overheard our parents' quarrel.

'Me too,' I said, climbing into her bed.

Silence is a Crime Against Humanity

Just like our lives, that year the weather in Canada was unpredictable and harsh. It was late February 1961 when the freezing rain and strong winds knocked out the power for a few days. Heavy snowfall covered the cars, and the city stood still. As soon as the weather finally eased, Mamá and the four of us toddled through heavy snow to the grocery store. On our way home, we followed our mother, who was carrying the groceries, when we realized that little four-year-old Orlando was gone. Panic-stricken, Mamá dropped the bags and began screaming and calling out for him. Liliana, Jaime, and I dove into nearby snowbanks in search of our brother, but he wasn't there. Over the howling wind, Mamá kept screaming for help and calling Orlando's name. But there was no sign of him.

'Check for footsteps,' Mamá told us as she traced her steps back towards the store. 'Let's go back the same way we came. Hurry! He could suffocate.'

Like frantic windshield wipers, her arms brushed the surrounding snow. She was now wailing. When Jaime heard our mother's desperate plea, he puckered his lips, and pee dripped from his trousers, turning the snow under him yellow.

'Jaime, get a hold of yourself,' I snarled. 'Help us look for Orlando!'

He nodded. The pee soon froze on his pants, so he walked behind Liliana and me, dragging his stiff legs. Frantic, Mamá kept searching without turning back to look at the rest of us.

Minutes that seemed like an eternity went by, but still, there was no sign of Orlando. The snow was deep, and Orlando was so small that I worried the snow had swallowed him.

I was on the brink of tears when my mother yelled, 'Here!'

She threw herself into waist-deep snow, landing next to a tree trunk.

'It's not him.' She moaned, then began screaming again. 'Oh, my God. Help!'

Her voice echoed through the deserted street. The freezing cold was keeping everyone away.

Liliana and I continue to dive into snowbanks, hoping to find our brother. Jaime stood on the trail we had made, hugging himself in an attempt to stay warm.

Then, with slush all over her face, Mamá shouted, 'Here!'

She grabbed Orlando by an arm and pulled him out of a snowbank. He gasped for air, then let out a loud howl.

'Why didn't you call for help?' Mamá embraced my brother.

Orlando's round face was flushed beet red and his breathing quick.

'I tried, but you didn't hear me. I was so cold and afraid…'

News articles had flooded the papers with reports of children killed by snowplows and warned parents of the dangers of winter. At home, Mamá prohibited my brothers, sister, and me from playing or even walking in heavy snow. She also forbade us from telling Papá that we had lost Orlando.

That night, Papá didn't even come home until the moon was up in the sky and the house was quiet. I woke up when I heard his car idling in front of our place. I knew he was probably changing from his soldier clothes into his scrubs. He was training for something. I knew this now. I was almost twelve years old.

He could hide it from my siblings, but not from me. My chest heaved with anger. I thought about the prayer Mamá had taught us a while back. I couldn't remember all the words, so I whispered my own made-up prayer,
'Guardian Angel, please tell God to make Papá come back to us.'

The days were so cold that even with mittens, our hands went numb. So, every morning, Mamá boiled eggs, which we used as hand warmers on our way to our new school, École primaire Mont-Royal.
At lunchtime, we ate the eggs, so there was little to keep us warm on our way back home. One icy afternoon, Liliana, Jaime, and Orlando led the way back home. My friend, Jocelyne, and I strolled behind them.
Jocelyne was in my class and lived nearby. She was about my height, with bouncy hair and a laughing gaze. She often invited Liliana and me to her apartment to play with her colorful yo-yos and hula-hoops. Jocelyne always won, but we didn't mind. We were happy just to share her toys, as we had so few of our own.
That day, the sky was gray, and the freezing wind whipped us as we strolled along. It was difficult to talk with scarfs tied around our faces. Suddenly, my throat felt itchy, followed by watery, burning eyes. I increased the pace as we walked through the alleys. Some were so narrow, my heart beat fast just imagining that the brick buildings were closing in, leaving us trapped in the middle.
When we arrived at home, Liliana and my brothers went into our apartment. I stood by the door and watched Jocelyne cross the street and run up the stairs to her place. She lived with her family on the third floor of a newer building right across from ours. Even though we were from different countries, it felt like we had always known each other.
Early on, Liliana, Jocelyne, and I created our own sign language mixed with French words. To hula-hoop, we moved our waist in a circular motion and said, 'Jouons.' To go to Jocelyne's place, we pointed at her and said, 'Chez toi.' Liliana or I tapped our chest to indicate we wanted to go to our apartment. To go outside, we signaled with two thumbs up. After a while, we became so proficient at our made-up language that we could speak in front of others without them realizing what we were doing.

Inside our apartment, I found Mamá and Madame Adeline having tea in the dining room. The two women stopped talking as soon as they saw me. Mamá wiped her tears away, and Adeline quickly stood up in front of my mother. In her limited English, she tried to tell me they were busy and asked me to join Liliana, who had gone to our bedroom.

I mumbled in a scratchy voice, 'But I don't feel—'

Mamá moved from behind Adeline and embraced me. 'Go to your room, and I'll check on you in a few minutes.'

My body was aching, and my head was throbbing, so I nodded.

In the bedroom, Liliana was sitting on the floor with the contents of her backpack spread around her. I lay on my bed, wishing Papá was there. I fell asleep but, between dreams, Mamá came in, helped me take medication and then left. It was impossible to open my eyes to see what Liliana was doing, but that seemed to make the headache worse. So, I growled at her.

'Turn the light off, now.'

'Fine, but you don't have to be so mean.'

'What's going on?' Papá walked in.

'Rocío is sick,' announced Liliana.

'I heard, but why are you arguing with her?'

'She—' Liliana started to explain, but Papá interrupted her.

'Girls, girls…' He took a deep breath, then said, 'I am only going to say this once, so listen carefully. You should never, ever fight with your siblings. You are the oldest, so I expect you two to be excellent role models. And not only that, but you also need to learn to take care of one another. Promise me you will always do this.'

I blocked the light with one arm, then sat up in my bed.

'Yes, Papá.'

'Good, now let me see what is going on.'

Papá checked my throat and then pressed on both sides of my neck. He sat beside me and held my hand. 'Your mamá already gave you medication, but I do not like the fact that you have had recurring tonsillitis.'

He told me that surgery was my only option. When I complained, hoping he would be the one operating on me, he assured me that his friend, who was a renowned surgeon, would perform the procedure.

'But I want *you* to be my doctor,' I insisted, thinking about the time when he held me in his arms and took the needle out of my foot. Even though I was in pain, just being with him had made me feel better.

'Look, Rocío…' He sighed. 'I need you to be strong and healthy, and to do that, you must always be brave. Life is not easy. I will discuss this with your mamá and the pediatrician, but my recommendation is to do a tonsillectomy. You should also know that I am not allowed to perform surgeries on my own family.'

He kissed my sister and me then walked out of the room. Like a caged bird, Liliana paced about the room. She kept opening and closing drawers, which made my headache worse.

'What are you doing?' I barked.

'I can't find…' she mumbled something I couldn't understand.

'It's too late. Go to bed.'

'Can I sleep with you?' she asked, with tears glistening in her eyes.

'Why don't you sleep in your own bed?'

She let her arms dangle and looked down. 'I don't like it when Papá talks like that.'

'Like what?'

'You know… it's like he forgets we are children.'

One way or another, we both felt Papá was acting differently, and that scared us. He was acting strange, he was using words as if we were already grown-ups, words you would find in a letter sent by someone from far away, someone you didn't expect to see for a long time.

'I know.'

Liliana stood by my bed in her flannel nightgown, waiting.

'All right, but stay on your side because I'm sick.'

She didn't. She scooted over, little by little until she was beside me.

The laughter of children woke me up the next morning. I stood on tiptoes to see out the frosty window. Like a winter mirror, the sleet had transformed the pavement into a glassy ice-skating rink. My siblings and Jocelyne were skating in a line, holding onto each other's waists. At the end of the street, the chain of skaters circled around and went back. Jocelyne, like a skilled ballet dancer, led the line. Soon, other children joined them. Before they passed by my window, Jocelyne waved to the others to stop. She then left the group and looked at me through the window, motioning for me to come out. I touched my head and neck. She etched on the frosty window, *malade?* I nodded. She placed her hand on her heart and left. I also wanted to ice-skate, but my throat was still sore.

I got up and went to the kitchen to look for my parents. They were having coffee and rolls.

'Good morning.' Papá stood up and hugged me.

'How are you?' Mamá said with a faint smile.

'Not good.'

'I need to clean your tonsils.'

My mother went to the kitchen cabinet and brought back a small bottle with a purple liquid in it.

'That works?' I asked.

'Go with your mamá; home remedies can be helpful too.' Papá touched my hair.

We went to the bathroom where she had a pair of scissors with cotton wrapped around the blades. After dipping the cotton into the purple liquid, she cleaned my tonsils, making me gag.

'Take a shower and then come back and eat something,' she said, leaving me there.

I didn't feel like eating. Even the thought of swallowing was painful, so after I showered, I dressed in comfortable clothes and went back to bed.

The distant winter sun woke me up. I stayed still in bed until I heard my parents speaking in their room. They were discussing removing my tonsils. In the end, they both agreed I needed the surgery. However, Mamá objected to having my siblings' tonsils removed too. 'But they hardly ever get sick,' she said.

'But they could,' he insisted.

'I don't know. It seems crazy to me, but you are the doctor.'

No one spoke for a minute or two.

Then Mamá said, 'By the way, you received a letter from Colonel Moncayo.'

At the colonel's name, I stood up and moved into the hallway. My parents' bedroom door was ajar so I could see in. Mamá pulled a letter out from a drawer and handed it to my father.

'How long have you had this?' He scratched his head.

'A few days. I'm sorry. I forgot to give it to you.' She looked away.

He took the letter, folded it in half, and pushed it inside his pocket.

'I'd like to know what he wants.' She tensed. 'I didn't open it, but I could have.'

With the back of his hand, Papá wiped the sweat off his forehead and said, 'The less you know, the better.'

'Why? I'm your wife and I need to know what's going on. Where do you go at night, dressed like some soldier?'

'Please do not call me a soldier.'

'Then who *are* you?' Her voice was breaking.

'Please calm down.'

'I don't want to calm down. I'm afraid. Why are you doing this to us?'

'Sit, please. We can discuss this like two rational adults.' He tapped the side of the bed next to him and sighed.

She twisted her mouth to one side, then sat.

'I will always protect you and the children,' Papá said.

'But what about you?' Mamá insisted.

'Please don't get emotional.' Papá stood up. 'The world is changing, and we can either be part of the change or maintain the status quo. Mandela, King, and even Castro have chosen to fight their oppressors.'

That name again, Castro, and now more names, Mandela and King. Who are they?

My mother jumped off the bed. 'Castro is a dictator and keeps his people prisoners. Why don't you try protesting or writing to legislators, like most political people do?'

'But history has taught us that this does not work. Mandela's years of nonviolent protests resulted in very little progress for his country. He has been arrested and his protesters killed. King seems to be following a similar path in the U.S. But who knows where he will end up?' Papá shook his head.

'What are you trying to tell me about this? That communism is the magic wand. Communists are *bad*, you must realize this?'

'That is propaganda promoted by the U.S. I've told you again and again that they have everyone convinced that communism is evil so they can keep control over our countries. Why can't you see that?' Papá's voice was low.

'But look what happened to the Cubans. Many of them lost their land, and the same thing could happen to my family in Colombia. Do you think that is fair?'

'All I know is that uninformed people follow their leaders like sheep.'

'I'm not *ignorant*.' Mamá sobbed.

'I did not say that.'

I froze. Then, as if someone had squeezed the air out of my lungs, I gasped for air. My parents must have heard me because they hurried out of their room.

'Rocío?' Papá tried to touch my arm, but I pulled away from him. Mamá was about to say something when air filled my lungs again, my stomach became tight, and then I began choking on my vomit.

After that day, I never heard my parents fighting again. Instead, at night, an eerie silence ensnared our apartment. Like the mourning widow's black veil, silence became a disguise for fear, sorrow, and the unknown.

That same year, in late summer, my siblings and I had our tonsils removed. While at the hospital, Papá came into our room and drew the shades to let the morning sunlight in.

'How are my girls feeling today?'

I wanted to respond, but I felt as though my throat had been scraped raw, so no sound came out of my mouth. Liliana let out a loud moan.

'I know you have some discomfort, but the surgeries were successful. You will be well soon.'

Someone knocked on the door and a round-faced, cheerful nurse came in carrying a tray.

'Good morning. This is the best part. You get to eat ice cream.' She placed a bowl on each of our rolling over-bed tables. 'But first you need to take this pill.' She handed both Liliana and me a small paper cup with a capsule in it and a glass of water. 'Now, I'll leave you with Dr. Velásquez. Enjoy your treat.'

My mouth watered just thinking about the ice cream, a luxury we never had at home. With each bite, the cold vanilla felt like a numbing ointment on my raw throat. Not only was it healing, but also delicious.

Papá glanced at his watch. 'I will check on you later, but now I have to go.' He kissed our foreheads and stepped out of the room. It surprised me he didn't try to stop us from eating ice cream.

My heart ached when he left. But when he was standing in the hallway speaking to Dr. Torres, I shivered. They first shook hands and then patted each other's backs. I couldn't hear what they were saying, but they were both nodding. They talked for a while longer. By the time they left, my ice cream had melted away.

I wanted to be an adult so I could be part of my father's grown-up world. I wanted to know why he felt so comfortable with his friend and so lost around my mother. I wanted to learn what he knew about the world and why it mattered so much to him. Most importantly, I wanted to know if he really cared about us. I felt weak, so I closed my eyes.

Apparently, the pain medication had eased Liliana's discomfort, because she asked, 'Who is he?' I glanced at her and signaled, touching my head and showing the palms of my hands.

You don't know? She shook her head.

'Torres.'

Liliana signaled, showing the palm of one of her hands.

Why?

'Don't tell Mamá,' I croaked.

Mamá walked in at that moment. 'How are my girls feeling?' She gazed at us with a tight-lipped smile. We didn't respond. 'Rocío, you didn't finish your ice cream. I thought you would love it.' She took my bowl and placed it on the table.

Mamá's dress seemed two sizes too big for her. She ate very little lately. Sometimes she threw her entire meal in the garbage. Madame Adeline would make up excuses for my mother's flushed face and swollen eyes.

'She has been cutting onions.' Or 'An eyelash is stuck in her eye.'

I knew she was lying, but I pretended I believed her. It was easier for me. I didn't want to accept that my mother was suffering.

As if I were waking up from a dream, it startled me when Mamá asked, 'Have you seen your papá?'

I looked at Liliana and touched my lips. A hint to shut up, but it was too late.

'Torres,' Liliana said.

Mamá snarled, 'That man is here?'

Once more, I touched my lips so Liliana wouldn't respond. We both shrugged.

'I have to check on the boys.' Mamá stormed out of the room.

Later that night, my dry mouth woke me up. Under the dim light, I saw my father once more sleeping on a small folding cot by my bed, his long legs dangling to one side.

The following year, long after we healed, Papá took my siblings and me to a park. We packed sandwiches and took a ride. A few miles in, he rolled down the window as we drove through a scenic area; rolling hills topped with large pine trees were visible under the cloudy sky.

'Fall is so beautiful here. See all those maple trees?' He pointed ahead. Like honor guards, orangish and honey-colored maple trees appeared. They stood on each side of the two-mile boulevard. A swarm of twirling leaves followed us as we drove down the long road.

In awe, we looked at the colorful scenery for some time until Orlando asked, 'Why didn't Mamá come?'

Papá tapped the steering wheel with one hand. 'She wanted to stay at home.'

Liliana crossed her arms on her chest, our gesture that Mamá was angry.

'Look, we are here. This is the park where I used to come before you arrived. I love watching the ducks.' Papá parked the car near a wooden sign that had the words Lac aux Castors carved on it. 'This is Lake Beaver.' He got out of the car, and we followed him.

Far in the distance was a group of ducks swimming in the calm waters of the lake. Some other ducks were resting on a rock. Orlando and Jaime ran to the shore. Our father held my hand and Liliana's, and together we ran after my brothers.

'Don't get wet!' he warned.

My brothers eased their pace and then plopped down by the shore of the lake. Papá, my sister, and I joined them.

'See the ducks? The ones that have bright green heads, brown chests, and blue patches under their wings, they are males. And the brown ones are females.' Two ducks that were in the water tipped down, pointing their tails high into the air as they submerged their heads. 'They are fishing.'

The loud sound of hundreds of honking geese made us all look up. In a V shape, the birds crossed the steely gray sky.

'Where are they going?' Jaime asked, as he pointed at them.

'South. Many birds fly long distances in search of warmer climates. And like the geese, sometime soon, we will go back home.'

'To Colombia?' I asked, thrilled that we might see our grandparents.

Papá nodded, and we began showering him with questions.

'We will discuss this later at home. Now let's go and find a rowboat.'

We spent an hour or so taking turns rowing, Jaime pushing us to go faster than the other boats, while Orlando pouted that he wanted to go back home. When Liliana and I paddled, we moved slowly, but we were synchronized. Every so often, we looked at one another. I realized our father was trying to distract us instead of answering our questions. And I had the feeling Liliana also knew what he was doing.

Papá sang different songs, trying to lighten the mood. We only ate some of our sandwiches. No one appeared to be hungry. We tried to make the best of our outing, but after lunch, it became clear we wanted to go back home. My siblings and I missed Mamá. When the sky darkened, we were happy to leave. On our way to the car, large drops of rain showered us. Once inside, Papá gave us the towels Mamá had packed in the trunk. My brothers and sister sat in the back, and I rode in the front.

When the rain intensified, Orlando sniffled.

'Orlando, we will be fine. Do not worry.' Papá glanced at my brother through the rear-view mirror.

'We could turn the radio on and listen to some music,' I said.

Papá turned the knob to one side, powering the radio.

We heard a male commentator say, 'Typhoon Freda is pounding the British Columbian coast—'

Papá interrupted the news and tuned into another station with classical music. My siblings didn't understand what we had briefly heard, but I did. I knew British Columbia was on the other side of the country, yet cyclones made my heart beat fast. It beat even faster as I imagined how upset Mamá would be when she found out about Papá's plans to move back to Colombia. I was confident she had no knowledge of it.

A Forced Separation

Mamá had a pile of clothes by her side and was ironing when we arrived home. Liliana, my brothers, and I walked in, drying ourselves with our towels. 'Oh my, you're all wet.' She put the iron down. 'Where is your papá?'

'He's unloading the car.'

'Go clean up. I'll make hot chocolate.'

Jaime looked at me and raised his eyebrows. Apparently, I wasn't the only one worried about a possible quarrel between our parents.

'Why are you all still standing there? Go take a shower.' Mamá gestured to the bathroom.

'Yes, Mamá,' Jaime and Orlando responded in chorus as they ran to the bathroom.

Clinging to Mamá, Liliana mumbled, 'Papá said—' I placed my index finger against my lips, but it was too late, 'we are going back to Colombia. That's good, right?'

The color drained from Mamá's face. She inspected the room as though she were looking for a way to escape and took a deep breath. The panic seemed to leave her, and only sadness flowed throughout her thin and limp body. She didn't storm out of the room. There were no piercing stares, no frown or furrowed brow. Instead, she stood still, like a wounded bird.

I wanted to hug her and tell her I loved her, but my feet wouldn't move. I wanted to tell her that when she had thought she was alone, I had watched her sob. Liliana's apologetic look bored into me. With my hands, I made a large O, our hand signal for big mouth. She was about to signal something back to me when Papá came into the living room. He had left the picnic basket on the kitchen counter.

'Girls, go take a shower.'

Liliana and I darted to our room and closed the door. I was the first one in the shower. I wanted the warm water to wash away that afternoon. Here was, at last, the opportunity to be with my grandparents again, so why was I unhappy?

'Rocío, it's my turn,' Liliana said, and rushed me out of the bathroom.

The loud bang of the front door made me jerk. I peered out the window, and under the dim streetlight Papá had hunched over in despair. From my parents' room, I could hear my mother sniffling. I didn't want to know. I didn't want to hear.

Weeks went by and no one mentioned the move. But then, one cold day when the snow had turned into slush and the air smelled of winter, my father asked all of us to come to the family room. I was the last one to join the group. My parents were sitting on the sofa. I knew something was wrong when I saw Mamá's slumped shoulders and defeated expression.

Papá stood up. 'Kids, please sit next to your mamá. I need to tell you something.'

Orlando sat on Mamá's lap. Jaime looked at me, but I turned away, feeling tears prick my eyes. So, he shrugged his shoulders and sat by our mother. Liliana sat on the opposite side.

'Rocío, please join your mamá.' Papá said.

I shook my head no.

'All right, then. You can stand if that is what you prefer.' Papá cleared his throat. 'It is time to go back to Colombia.'

'Yay! I want to see Grandpa and Grandma.' Liliana shrieked.

My eyes burned with sadness. 'Are you coming with us?'

Papá had an empty stare.

'I love you all, but I will not be traveling with you. I still have unfinished business here. I will join you later.'

'What business?' I challenged. Only the sounds of the street echoed in our place. We became a still picture, paralyzed. Since he didn't respond, I insisted, 'Why? When?'

'I cannot tell you what I am doing or when this will happen.' He touched his chin. 'I don't know.'

Each word felt like a stab, like the knitting needle in my foot, only this time I felt it in my chest.

'Why can't you come with us?' Jaime asked.

Papá stopped walking and fixed his sharp gaze on the wall across from him. 'Because I have many things to do.'

Flushed with anger, I thought of the time when he'd left us in Chicago. Didn't he understand how lost we were without him? Had he forgotten what Mamá had done to get us into Canada? Did he even care about how we felt when we watched our mother being escorted to the police station like a criminal? How she had to leave us on the train alone, to be cared for by strangers?

I glanced at my mother, hoping she would confront him and force him to come with us, but she didn't look up. Her empty stare fixed on Orlando's small tractor. Now, I was annoyed at my mother, so I lay down on the other couch.

My father said many things that afternoon. He asked Jaime to be the man of the family until he got back. Then he turned to Orlando and told him to behave and to be obedient. He patted Liliana and me on the head. 'Do well in school and also help your mamá.'

Soon, his voice faded away, so I closed my eyes. It felt as if I were caught in a nightmare, one of those in which you fall into a bottomless hole, tumbling down so fast you feel your heart is going to stop beating. However, no matter what I did, I couldn't wake up from this one. When I finally opened my eyes again, everyone was gone. They must have thought I was sleeping. Perhaps I was. I didn't know. I felt nauseous, so I went outside for some fresh air. Up in the sky, only remnants of the whitish sun were visible behind the thick cloud cover.

When the cold air filled my lungs, I went to Jocelyne's place. I was about to ring the doorbell when I heard someone playing the piano. I peeked through the window and saw Jocelyne sitting on the edge of the piano stool with her eyes shut. Her fingers moved across the keys with the elegance and precision of a maestro. Astounded, I sat on the floor by the door. The softness of the melody made me forget all about our moving back to South America. All I could think of was the music. I heard her play one of Chopin's works. I recognized the piece because my parents listened to it often in Chicago; Mamá had mended clothes while it played and my father read.

Jocelyne's mother saw me, so she invited me in. Jocelyne was now playing a piece I didn't know. She continued the solo, with her eyes closed, unaware of us. Her mother brought me a chair and smiled before going back to the kitchen. It was possible that Jocelyne had told her about my family problems, or maybe she had seen it in my eyes. Whatever it was, she seemed to know I was distraught. A few minutes later, she came back swaying to the music and carrying a tray with two glasses of milk and homemade *sablés,* a type of biscuit. She hugged me and left again.

Listening to my best friend's private recital made me think about how much music had been part of our lives. I recalled the many afternoons in our apartment in Bogotá when Papá's friends played the guitar while he sang songs like *Perfidia, Solamente una vez* or *Bésame mucho* and others. Many times, he played the harmonica. Long car rides were less tedious when our whole family sang. But now sorrow, like rust, was, little by little, eating us all away. We had left the record player behind in Chicago. Papá didn't sing anymore. He didn't even have time to read to us anymore. His dinner plate was always set but often left untouched.

A few weeks later, we arrived at the train station. The bitter wind lashed us as we walked from the parking lot to the main building, each one of us, except Orlando, carrying a bag. Papá toted Orlando's bag and a duffle bag. The station was overflowing with people wearing heavy coats and hurrying in different directions. On the loudspeaker, a man's brisk voice, announcing departures and arrivals, resonated across the halls. We stood behind Papá while he purchased the train tickets to New York, where we would take a flight to Colombia. Once we had the tickets, we walked along looking for the correct platform. My mother, brothers, and sister were ahead of my father and me. Whistles were blowing. Steam puffing over the trains, forming enormous clouds. A damp smell filled the air.

When we arrived at an awaiting train, my father put the bags down. 'Here we are.'

I dropped my bag. My nightmare had come true. We were leaving. I would probably never see Jocelyne again. My legs felt weak, and I gasped for air. There were so many things I wanted to tell my father, but the words got caught in my throat, so I embraced him and cried, leaving his coat wet. Soon after, I felt my siblings' arms over mine, around our father. We all sobbed.

He squatted and hugged us. 'Don't you ever forget you are my ducklings and that I love you. I am proud of you. Take care of one another as well as your mamá,' he said as he carefully peeled us off him, one by one.

Mamá stood still, her bag and purse tight against her body. Her gaze wandered as if she wasn't part of that scene. When Papá saw her, his voice broke, 'But now you need to go.'

A shrill, loud whistle startled me. Papà helped us board the train. Mamá was last. I sat next to the window through which I could see my parents. Papá hugged Mamá, and bending down, he buried his head in her neck. He said something, but with the racket inside the car, it was difficult to hear. He held her hand and helped her board the train. Once inside, my mother didn't turn back to look at him.

Papá got down onto the platform, where he stood still. Like pools, his dark eyes had a glassy shine I hadn't seen before. I thought he was going to weep, but he didn't. He put his hands inside his pockets. Frozen.

Inside the train, my mother was also standing. Suddenly, as the train shuddered, she turned around towards him and began banging on the window. When he finally looked at her, my mother sobbed. She held her left hand opened, as if it were a writing pad, and with her right hand, she pretended to write.

Shouting, she pleaded, 'Please write, please write, please write.'

The train moved. Papá nodded a few times, then dropped his head. He looked almost too still to be breathing and remained like that until he became a dot in the distance. Mamá kept making the same writing signs until he vanished from view. At that point, she sat in her seat, took her hat off and covered her anguished face with her hands. The four of us sat in our seats. Liliana was hugging George, the doll Papá had given her for her birthday, and my two brothers held their toy cars. I pressed my book, *Le Petit Prince*, keeping it tight inside my hands.

Fusagasugá

Bogotá received us with sunshine and scarce clouds. At the airport gate, my grandparents embraced my siblings and me. When they saw Mamá, they let go of us and, weeping, went to her side. Grandma covered her mouth with one hand.

'My poor daughter.' She wept.

From then on, she wouldn't stop talking about Mamá's unhealthy weight. It wasn't until we were crammed into Grandpa's station wagon that my mother changed the subject.

'So, how is it to be retired?' she asked, smiling.

During our two-hour trip, Grandma told us about how Lola had left with her young son to take care of her elderly mother. Grandma's voice became quiet when she confessed how much she missed her. Soon after Lola's departure, my grandparents had sold their Victorian-style home in El Nogal in Bogotá and moved to the small town of Fusagasugá. Fusa, as it is commonly called, nestled in the central Andean region of the country.

Between 'Oh no!' and 'Ayayay!' my siblings and I lamented not being able to go back to their grand house and our apartment.

Grandma consoled us when she told us she had a Labrador called Bella. My heart raced with anticipation when I thought of Catia and Nala.

Now we have enough space so that they can live with us.

I turned to my grandmother, who was sitting next to me on the front seat, and grinning with hope, I asked, 'Do you know anything about my dogs?'

Grandma hesitated, then placed her hand on my hand. 'I do, sweetheart.'

'What?'

'Well, Colonel Moncayo called us a while ago and said that Nala never recovered from her broken paw.'

'What happened?'

'She passed.'

'And Catia?' I almost howled.

'We don't know. The colonel moved, and no one knows where he went.'

I pulled my hand from under my grandmother's.

She tried to make me feel better by continuing to describe their property, our new home.

'It has fruit trees, lots of ducks in the lake, and a pool.'

But I had stopped listening. My dog had died, and Papá wasn't here to help me find Catia. I wanted to cry, but I couldn't. My mother seemed to have used up all the tears in the world, leaving nothing for the rest of us. And for what? My father still chose whatever business he was talking about over us. Whatever that business was. No number of tears could change that. I felt dizzy, so I focused far into the distance.

For almost five years, I had longed to return to Colombia so that I could be with my grandparents, but nothing seemed the same anymore. Or perhaps *I* had changed. I felt I didn't belong anywhere anymore, the U.S., Canada, and now not even Colombia. My home. It felt strange to hear everyone speaking Spanish again.

The busy morning traffic brought in the smell of fumes left by passing cars. The sound of horns, squeaky brakes, and machines breaking concrete reminded me of downtown Chicago. Bogotá may not have had a great lake like the windy city, but it had dramatic mountains overlooking the great savanna. Cotton-like clouds with bright sunrays dancing among them hovered over the peaks of the striking hills.

On the outskirts of the city, scattered barrios with brick homes came into view. Soon after, we began descending the Andes. An hour later, the warm breeze brought a fresh aroma of eucalyptus. Large trees and colorful plants adorned the hills. We passed through several small towns and drove by roadside stands with street vendors waiting for travelers to stop.

'This is Fusa,' Grandma announced as we drove down the main street of the last town. On one side, a church towered over its front steps. Across from it, there was a crowded plaza with people and food stands. 'That is the Church of Our Lady of Bethlehem,' she said.

Grandpa Miguel chuckled. 'Not that we've ever seen the inside.'

'Ignore your grandfather's jokes.' She rolled her eyes and continued, 'I'm enjoying the weather very much, but there is a lot of poverty here.'

I had noticed the groups of sad-looking children who stood on the street corners with baskets strapped to their necks, selling candy and other sweets. Two-wheeled horse carts shared the narrow streets with cars. Pedestrians wearing Sunday clothes maneuvered across the streets, avoiding the traffic. Small buildings with businesses on the first floor lined the main street. After we left the town, we kept descending for another fifteen minutes until we reached our grandparents' country home.

The gardener, don Rogelio, and his wife, Avelina, were waiting for us. Next to them, a playful Labrador wagged her tail. Don Rogelio took his straw hat off and, bowing, opened the gate for our car to enter. Like a Gaucho, his white shirt shone in contrast to his leathery, dark skin. He wore high boots and loose trousers. Aside from comfort, I learned that his loose attire also served to hide his wooden leg. A machete hung on one side of his belt.

Liliana, Orlando, and Jaime begged Grandpa to stop the car. When he did, they got out, pushing one another to be the first to pet Bella. Still thinking about my dogs, I stayed in the car until we reached my grandparents' house.

The loud sound of splashing water caught my attention so, once I got out, I walked to a water fountain by the front garden. On top of it, there was a tilted terracotta pitcher that served as a spout. A colorful flower from a nearby bush had fallen into the main water basin.

I was about to touch it when I heard my grandmother say, 'I love hibiscus, don't you? They are all over the property.' She smiled and went into the house. I turned around. As if someone had opened the curtain to the stage, I saw for the first time this lovely place. The pain of losing my dogs subsided. A massive rock fence surrounded the ten-acre property. In front of my grandparents' home lay a cobblestone path leading from the Spanish-style house to the large metal gate we'd come through off the main road. Sprinkled around the property were guava, mango, avocado, and guamo trees. Guamos were tall, branchy trees, which protected coffee plants from the sun. The fruit looked like large peapods. I had never seen one, so I went and plucked the soft fruit and ate it. The white skin surrounding the brown pit had a pleasant, sweet flavor.

The swimming pool sat on a hill in the northern part of the property. From there, I could see my grandparents' house. It was right at the center of the estate. On the right side of the main house was a small cottage belonging to Grandma's younger uncle, Mario. On the opposite side was a small lake surrounded by willow trees, like candles on a cake. Behind my grandparents' home stood don Rogelio and Avelina's two-room house, the one my grandma called the elves' home.

We didn't get to choose our rooms this time. At the front of the house were my grandparents' and the guest rooms. Grandma had reserved the back three-quarters for us. Mamá took the one in the middle, and she gave my brothers the one that faced the lake, and Liliana and me, the one that faced the pool. We had our own family suite within the spacious house.

No one mentioned Papá for weeks. I assumed it was because everyone was still upset with him. I certainly was. Other times, however, I missed him dearly. Either way, I felt a surge of happiness by thinking one day he would finish whatever was keeping him away and join the family again.

One warm afternoon, Grandpa came back from town holding a stack of papers. We were sitting on the porch, drinking cold *aguapanela*, sugar cane water with lemon, when he came in. He tripped on a step but somehow avoided the fall. The pile of papers he was carrying, however, fell to the ground. A gust of wind came in, making single sheets spin in the air. In an attempt to help our grandfather, Liliana and I ran after his papers. I caught an old newspaper. The headline read, *The Bay of Pigs Failure - What Is Next?* I took the newspaper and hid it under my dress. I handed Grandpa the other papers.

'Thanks, Rocío.'

Before I could ask Grandpa why he had an article in English if he didn't speak the language, he said, 'Oh look! Over there. You received a letter.' He pointed to an envelope on the floor near a coffee table.

I rushed to pick up the envelope, but Liliana grabbed it. I rubbed my hands, trying to guess whom the letter was from, Papá or maybe Jocelyne?

As I extended my hand, Liliana quickly placed the letter behind her back.

'Give me my letter.'

'Maybe it's for me too.'

'No. I saw my name.'

Liliana frowned and then handed me the letter.

It was Jocelyne's writing.

'Can I read it too?' Liliana crossed her arms.

'Fine.'

Liliana followed me to a boulder with a flat top that was on one side of the pool. The envelope had been opened. I knew Grandpa had been inspecting all mail to see if it had something to do with my father, which, unbeknown to him, it did. Whatever happened, I was thrilled to have news from my friend. My sister and I sat on the large rock while I read the letter from Jocelyne aloud.

February 16, 1963

Chère Rocío,

I hope you had a good flight back to Colombia. I miss you very much. The weather is worse than when you were here, so we have to stay inside. Whenever I play Nocturne, I think of you, because I know you like it so much. School is not the same without you and Liliana. Most days I walk by myself. I want to let you know that your dad moved out, and your apartment is empty. The day he took you to the train station, I saw him walk into your place. I could be wrong, but he looked like he was crying. One day my mother asked him what he was doing with the furniture and all your things, and he said he was donating them. Then he left, and we didn't see him again.

A few weeks after your dad left, a couple of policemen came to our place asking questions about him. I don't know what they wanted, because my parents made me go to my room.

Is he back in Colombia with you?

It took me a long time to write this letter because my English is not so good. My English teacher helped me. One day, I want to go and see you. Say hello to Liliana and your family.

Love,
Jocelyne

P.S. I hope you had a good 13th birthday!

'She remembered your birthday, which is nice. But Papá is not here.' Liliana hunched over.

I folded the letter.

'We should tell Mamá.'

'No. Do you want her to be upset?'

Liliana shook her head. We walked back to the house, both of us dealing with a storm of feelings and thoughts. Once we arrived, Liliana went to our bedroom, and I went to the bathroom to read about the *Bay of Pigs*. I read two full pages of the newspaper, I read it twice over and took it all in. The Bay of Pigs was a failed attempt by the U.S. to overthrow the Cuban government in April 1961. The operation involved a C.I.A. backed invasion of Cuba by a group of Cuban exiles, but it was met with strong resistance from the Cuban military. It was a disaster, with most of the invaders either killed or captured. The newspaper told us the Bay of Pigs invasion was a major embarrassment for the U.S. and further fueled tensions between the U.S. and Cuba, ultimately leading to the Cuban Missile Crisis.

The Cuban Missile Crisis was a political and military standoff between the U.S. and the Soviet Union. The crisis was triggered by the deployment of Soviet missiles in Cuba which the U.S. government deemed as a threat to national security and demanded that the missiles be removed and imposed a naval quarantine on Cuba. The crisis was resolved after a tense 13-day negotiation, which included the removal of U.S. missiles from Turkey and a pledge by the U.S. not to invade Cuba.

I was staggered. The two countries had nearly gone to war over the crisis. We were days away from a nuclear holocaust which was bad enough, but all I could think of was Papá's interest.

Why, oh why is Papá mixed up with Cuba and the man called Castro? Papá is Colombian.

I slipped into the kitchen for a glass of water. I found Grandpa and Mario sipping coffee in the interior garden, as they did every afternoon. Grandpa was a boisterous ex-army captain. Mario wore a French beret, and people called him El intellectual.

'The country is infested with insurgents,' Grandpa said.

'Yes, and it's Castro's doing. He has not only taken over Cuba but pretty soon other countries as well,' Mario responded.

'Jaime is a revolutionary.'

I came to a halt when I heard my father's name. My throat closed, and I gasped for air. I took two steps back and hid behind the door.

Mario fixed his glasses. 'Well, we all knew he had his leftist ideas. I can understand how a young man can become a rebel. I'm not very fond of imperialist governments either.' Mario took a sip of coffee.

'You call yourself a liberal, but I think that deep inside, you are also a communist.'

'I'm not. I just don't like it when the rich take advantage of the poor.'

'Of course. But Jaime… abandoning his family because he wants to save the world? Unforgivable.'

Mario nodded.

Did my family hate my father? Because he was a revolutionary, a soldier, just like Mamá had called him so many times? I didn't know what an insurgent did, but somehow it frightened me.

How was it that the people I loved the most were at odds with one another? I went back to the boulder. The water in the pool shone with the sun as small ripples played with the wind. Part of me wanted to confront the adults in my family and demand they tell me everything they knew about Papá. But the fear of learning he was doing something wrong was greater than my desire to know the truth. As I had done before, I didn't ask anyone.

Dreams Never Come True

In this dream, I was standing at the intersection of an unpaved road when I noticed two bright lights rapidly approaching. I blinked several times, trying to make sense of what was happening, but the thick fog made the shapes blurry. I tried to move my feet but couldn't. Looking down, I saw only gravel. In a desperate attempt to see what was in front of me, I rubbed my eyes, but still couldn't make out much of anything. The lights became brighter as they advanced toward me. I saw a car, then heard a loud scream. When I looked, my mother was standing in front of me. Then she faded away. I threw myself to the ground, searching for her under the car. My mother's inert body was under Grandpa's station wagon. I shouted 'Mamá!' so loudly that I woke up.

As it did every morning, the aroma of fresh-brewed coffee lingered in the air of my grandparents' home. Outside, the sun was shining. Rebecca, the macaw, repeated over and over, 'Quiero cacao.' Hot chocolate was the old, colorful bird's favorite treat of the day.

Still anxious after the dream, I stumbled out of bed. Next to the window was Liliana's empty bed. I walked around the house, searching for Mamá, but all the rooms were deserted. I peered into my mother's room, but she wasn't there. On top of the freshly ironed bedspread lay pieces of colored material, spools of thread, and a pair of scissors. The Singer sewing machine was open as if she'd been sewing. On one side of it, there was a small, tomato-like pincushion overflowing with round, colored headpins. Next to her room, my brothers' room was also empty, and someone had already made their twin beds. I went to the front of the house, searching for my grandparents. Their bed was made, dressed with a knitted bedcover. Grandma's slippers were tucked delicately underneath. Across from them was the mahogany vanity I loved, with a large oval mirror and matching stool, but my mother was not sitting there either, as she sometimes did. Where was she? The morning breeze drifting in from the hallway window suddenly brushed my hair. I felt cold.

I found her near the kitchen window, and I let out a sigh of relief. Mamá was wearing my favorite amber-colored summer dress. A twisted bun held her long hair. I ran and embraced her as I recounted my nightmare. When I finished, she unwrapped my arms.

'My dear Rocío, don't be upset. Dreams never come true.'

She then told me she would be the only driver in the house because my grandparents and Mario were going to New York. That meant she would be safe inside the car. She pulled a loose strand of her auburn hair away from her face. I looked straight into my mother's eyes. Freckles covered her childlike face. This is why Papá addressed the early letters he sent to her with, 'My dear *Pecosa*.' I lowered my gaze. Mamá held my hand and walked me to the dining room where coffee with milk and fresh-baked rolls were waiting.

Liliana came in then, still wearing her pajamas. Her shiny hair was uncombed. 'Where's George, my doll?'

'Girls, eat your breakfast, then go to the pool with your brothers and I will look for George,' said my mother, kissing my forehead. When I lingered, still clinging to her, she insisted, 'Go on.'

Hoping to forget the chilling nightmare, I let go and went with Liliana to the front porch. 'Orlando, Jaime,' I called. 'Let's go to the pool.'

They came running from behind the house.

'I want to go.' Jaime jumped with excitement.

'I don't want to. I want to go with Mamá.'

Orlando, only seven years old, stood erect, like a grown man. He had Papá's darting eyes with curly eyelashes and rounded cheeks littered with tiny freckles.

'Come on, don't be such a baby.' Jaime wrinkled his nose, mocking him.

'I don't want to.' Orlando frowned and went looking for Mamá.

Outside, Jaime, Liliana and I found our grandparents standing next to a taxi. The driver was packing their bags into the trunk of the car. I didn't want them to go to New York. I wanted to tell them to cancel their trip and protect my mother, but I didn't. They were looking forward to visiting relatives. My nightmare wasn't going to change their plans. Jaime and Liliana kissed them goodbye and headed off to the pool. I kissed Grandpa and then embraced Grandma. Somehow, she knew what I was thinking, because she held my hands and said, 'You'll be okay.' Then she kissed me and got into the taxi. They drove away.

At the pool, Jaime said he had forgotten something and ran back down the hill. Later, he came back holding a squawking duck. The animal was furiously trying to get away. Jaime gripped the frightened bird against his scrawny body until he reached the pool. There, he threw the duck into the air. The bird flew away then dove into the tranquil waters of the lake. This wasn't my brother's only pastime involving animals. Don Rogelio and Avelina's son, Benjamin, made bets to see who could swallow the most live fish. The boys used a strainer attached to a long, wooden pole to scoop tiny, black fish from the lake. They held the fish by their tails as the animals moved uncontrollably. The boys swallowed the fish one by one until they began salivating and their mouths filled with bile. Jaime later confessed that feeling the fish flapping down his esophagus made him puke.

Now, Jaime tried unsuccessfully to catch the duck, eventually giving up and deciding instead to look for frogs in the banana plants that surrounded the pool but finding none. Tired of pursuing animals, he finally joined Liliana and me. With every dive into the cool water, I slowly washed away the memory of the horrific nightmare and eventually forgot about it. We spent the morning swimming and playing tag. We also challenged one another to see who could stay underwater the longest, who could swim the fastest, and who could dive the deepest. Jaime won all of them. At lunchtime, I went to the house and brought back food that we ate by the side of the pool. All afternoon we swam and invented games.

The sun was setting when we heard a commotion coming from the main house. Avelina and don Rogelio were screaming and calling our names. Jaime, Liliana, and I ran all the way from the pool to the house to see what was happening. Suddenly, snippets of the nightmare came rushing through my mind. When we arrived at the front driveway, we could see that Grandpa's station wagon had crashed against the stone water fountain.

I threw myself on the ground and looked under the car. And just as in my dream, Mamá was lying on her back.

No, no, no.

Her face was next to the tire, so I couldn't see it. All I could see were her bloody, limp legs and shoeless feet.

'Mamá, Mamá!' I began gagging on saliva. The anguish I felt the night before returned. My mother was under the car. And somehow, I knew it was my fault for dreaming it.

'Don't cry. I'm okay,' Mamá murmured.

But I didn't believe her. I couldn't. How could she be okay? My world was ending. My father had abandoned us, and now I was losing my mother. I tried to touch her legs.

Avelina said, 'Don't touch her. Rogelio is getting the jack so he can lift the car and get her out. We don't know how hurt she is.'

Sobbing coming from inside the car made me jump like a spring. I stood up and went to the driver's side door, where I found Orlando inside, sitting in the driver's seat.

'Mamá told me to do it. The car wouldn't start, so Mamá told me to hold the pedal while she tried to fix it.' He was in tears.

I peeled his small fingers from the steering wheel and helped him out of the car. Liliana ran to the house and came back with a rubber hot water bottle that Mamá sometimes used for muscle pain. Jaime sat on the porch stairs, staring at his feet. Like a broken film projected onto a fast-moving carousel, my thoughts were spinning when I saw a gray Willys Jeep drive onto our property. 'I was on my way into town when I heard the screaming,' said don Pascal, our neighbor.

'Help me with this?' don Rogelio pleaded, kneeling, and then he and don Pascal were lifting the station wagon with a jack. But the higher they raised the car, the louder Mamá screamed.

'You're hurting Mamá!' I screamed, pulling on don Rogelio's arm as hard as I could. 'Stop! Can't you see that this is not working?'

Don Rogelio pulled his arm away and said, 'Her hair is tangled around the chassis.'

Avelina ran into the house and returned with the kitchen scissors, which she gave to Rogelio. The men lowered the station wagon and don Rogelio cut my mother's hair, releasing her from the car.

I felt faint as her auburn curls, the hair Papá loved, the hair we all loved, landed on the cobblestones, and the next thing I knew, I was wakening up on the moist grass.

Next to the crashed car, Mamá was shaking, trying to stand.

'See? I am okay, please don't cry, my children,' she said.

My siblings huddled around her. Don Pascal separated us from our mother, one at a time, repeating, 'I need to take your mamá to the hospital now.'

Orlando slumped, still feeling guilty for releasing the brake.

'If something happens to Mamá, I'll die too,' he said.

My sister and I tried to console him. Jaime sat on the steps of the front porch. Liliana, Orlando, and I joined our brother. We watched our mother being carried into the jeep. My nightmare had become real; I had made this happen. The station wagon had run over Mamá, and now she was hurt. Badly. We watched don Pascal's jeep disappear into the distance with our mother in it. In despair, we stayed on the stairs until late that evening. Avelina and don Rogelio couldn't convince us to go inside. It seemed as if we were hoping Mamá would come back home that night. But she didn't. Like a spotlight on a tragic scene, all that was left was the bright moon illuminating the sky.

Dusk of Fire

After the accident, the days in our remote village seemed longer than ever before. Without Mamá and my grandparents, I felt lost. Even though our mother had survived the accident, the doctor kept her at the hospital because she had been seriously injured. We were not expecting our grandparents to be back until the following month. Hence, as each day waned, I often stood by the dining-room window, like we used to do before they left, and watched the dramatic and colorful sunsets. Some say the name Fusagasugá means *mujer que se esconde detrás de la montaña* or woman who hides behind the mountain. Grandma disagreed. She had argued that in the indigenous language, Sutagao, Fusagasugá meant *atardecer de fuego* or dusk of fire. Regardless of who was correct, the magical sight of an incandescent scarlet sphere setting behind the Andes, was captivating.

During the day, I took care of my siblings. Liliana stopped speaking in public. She rarely even spoke at home. If she did, it was to ask for something. She and I continued speaking our sign language, but only when we didn't want others to understand. At almost nine years old, she spent endless hours dressing her dolls, making beds for them, and mumbling with imaginary friends.

Orlando cried for no reason, and Jaime often got himself into trouble. One warm day, he went fishing with Benjamin. When the boys came back home, Jaime had a fishing hook dangling from his left hand. I tried pulling it out with a pair of pliers, but he growled at every jerk. 'What are you doing?' he screamed.

'I'm trying to take it out. At least it is on the other hand. Not the one you squished through the wringer.'

Frustrated, I grabbed his arm and dragged him into the kitchen. Avelina stood at the counter, cutting up fresh vegetables for the traditional midday soup. With both Mamá and Grandma gone, she had the added task of keeping an eye on us.

'Please watch Orlando and Liliana. I am taking Jaime to the hospital in town,' I said.

The woman frowned, then mumbled something I didn't understand. I interrupted her. I repeated the orders I'd heard Grandma give Avelina and the other servants before.

'That will be all. I have everything under control, thank you very much.'

I dismissed her by nodding my head, turned around, and, pulling Jaime with me, walked away.

'But niña, Rocío, I don't think you should go without an adult,' she begged.

I led Jaime outside with his good hand and didn't look back. We walked for what seemed like hours under the scorching sun. The paved road felt like a gigantic aluminum plate under our sticky shoes. Jaime walked slowly. I was angry with him but thought that perhaps going to the hospital was not all that bad. We could see Mamá while we were there. A shimmer of delight relieved my aching heart.

We arrived at the bus stop, sweaty and exhausted. To make matters worse, my heart pounded in my ears when I realized that my small handbag was empty. I had forgotten to ask Avelina for the money Mamá left at home for emergencies. We couldn't go back home, and it was too far to walk to the hospital, so getting a ride was our only option. I waved to the driver of a large commuter bus to stop.

'Where are you kids going?' he asked.

'We need to go to the hospital, but we don't have money. Can you take us?' I pleaded.

'No money, no ride,' he snapped as he closed the door.

Quickly, I lifted Jaime's hand and pointed at the hook. The driver twisted his mouth to one side and signaled for us to get on.

The bus was overflowing with people, so we stood, swinging back and forth. With every gear change, Jaime tightened his lips while pressing his left hand against his chest. I didn't mind the crowded bus, although the smell was rancid. It smelled like carnival, the circus that came to town for the fair every year.

Farmers were carrying animals on their way to the market. The powerful odor of animal waste mixed with wet hay and food was revolting.

Everyone seemed to be in a hurry at the hospital. Tired of waiting, I grabbed a nurse's arm and didn't let go until she looked at us.

'What do you want, girl?' she snarled.

'Look at my brother's hand.'

'It hurts,' Jaime muttered.

His brown eyes seemed larger than ever before, though he didn't cry. He had stopped crying at four years old when, one Sunday morning, he came into the house with teary eyes and a gash on one leg. Papá had lifted Jaime and sat him on the dining table.

'My boy, you need to be strong because men don't cry,' he said, cleaning my brother's leg.

Jaime rubbed his eyes and sat quietly while Papá gave him a shot and stitched his wound.

'Oh dear,' the nurse said, and rushed us to a waiting room.

The minute we sat down, an E.R. doctor came in. The man lowered his glasses over his straight nose and cleared his throat. I hurriedly recounted what I thought had happened to my brother.

'Where are your parents?' questioned the doctor.

I explained that our mother was there, in the hospital. In a voice that didn't sound like mine, I choked out a lie that our father was on a business trip.

'Okay. Wait here, please,' he said to me, and signaled for Jaime to follow him into an examination room.

I sat on a small chair alone now in the waiting room, worried about my brother, disappointed at Papá for not being there and sorry for Mamá. I closed my eyes. The potent smell of disinfectant brought me back to our last visit to the Saint-Luc hospital in Montréal, where Papá was a surgeon. I had been so disappointed to see the bare wall of his office. No pictures of us, not even the one with the handmade frame I had given him for Father's Day. The E.R. doctor startled me, pulling me away from what were now distant memories.

'Your brother will be fine,' he said.

Jaime dropped his gaze to the bandage. The doctor had clearly removed the hook.

'Thank you, but I don't have money to pay you,' I apologized.

'No problem, just stay out of trouble.'

The doctor gave each of us a pat on the back and walked away. Jaime and I went to see the receptionist at the hospital.

'We want to see Mamá,' Jaime said.

'Who is your mamá?' the woman asked.

'Her name is Cecilia Velásquez,' I answered.

The receptionist skimmed a long list she had on her desk. She then rolled her eyes and warned, 'You are not allowed to visit patients without an adult. Where is your papá?'

'On his way,' I blurted. 'Please let us in. We're worried about her.'

'She's in 232. The stairs are on that side of the building,' the woman huffed, pointing to her left. 'Yes, and tell your papá that after this, he has to accompany you at all times.'

Green and brown bruises covered Mamá's youthful face. Her left leg was in a cast, and her left arm was in a splint.

'My babies, so nice to see you. How did you get here? And what happened to you, Jaime?'

He described his fishing ordeal while Mamá stared at him with tired eyes. She tried to hug him but abandoned the attempt with a loud moan and rested her hands on her broken ribs. Mamá didn't speak much after that. She mostly listened to our many stories. Finally, she held our hands and kissed them softly. 'I don't know when I'll get back home. I hope soon… in the meantime, please take care of yourselves and be good. Get some money out of my purse, Jaime, and take the bus home.'

When we got to the bus station, I asked Jaime for the money.

'I don't have the money.' He had insisted on putting the bills in his jeans' back pocket.

'What do you mean, you don't have the money? Where is it?'

'I don't know. It fell out, I guess. The money was in this pocket.' Jaime pulled his right pocket inside out. 'What are we going to do now? We should go back and ask Mamá for more money.'

'No.' All I could think of was Mamá's distraught look. Defeated. 'Let's take a shortcut over the mountains. It is better than riding the crowded bus. You can see all kinds of animals you have never seen,' I said with forced cheer.

There was a moment of hesitation, but Jaime agreed. On the way home, he ran, tossed rocks into the air and tortured insects. I walked slower than ever before. It was as if life itself had become heavy. What had happened to our family? Papá was gone, Mamá was hurt while my siblings and I roamed around the countryside like lost waifs.

My ruminating came to a halt when I noticed two bulls near a tree glaring at us. Suddenly, they began huffing and puffing through their noses, their heads low, shoulders hunched, and necks curved. They then began pawing with their forefeet, sending dust back.

'Run!' I shouted.

We ran as fast as we could for about a block, but the bulls were closing on us. Holding my brother's left hand high so the bandage wouldn't get wet, we jumped into the nearby Cuja River. Large, slippery rocks bounced us, throwing us to one side. A long tree branch came to our rescue before the current swept us away. I held on to it with one hand, and with the other, I held my brother. The cold water chilled my bones. Jaime's hair fell limp onto his forehead, and his eyes flickered with fear.

'We're okay. It's okay. Let's wait here until they leave.'

The two beasts halted by the riverbank, creating a cloud of dust. They glowered at us with their large, slanted eyes, chests high and huffing. They paced for a while, then left. We got out of the water, still shivering, and sat on a boulder which had been warmed by the sun.

'What did you do to make them so angry?' I snapped at Jaime.

'Nothing. I was just waving a stick. You were spaced out, and I was bored.'

'Yes, but you didn't have to provoke the bulls, did you? You could have gotten us killed.'

We walked for a couple of hours. The sun was setting when we arrived home. Avelina came out to welcome us.

'Are you hungry?' she asked, holding a plate of food.

We both shook our heads.

'How did it go? How is niño Jaime's hand?' She touched his arm.

'He's fine.'

'Did you get to see your mamá?'

'She is getting better,' I responded. 'Thanks for making our dinner, but we are tired.'

Jaime and I each took a glass of lemonade from the dining table and went to our own rooms.

A Letter to Jocelyne

A few days after my grandparents returned home, Grandpa finally brought my mother back from the hospital. The six weeks she had been away had seemed like months. We were jubilant to have her back. That evening, to celebrate, Avelina cooked lentil, carrots, and potato soup. Just like Lola used to do, she served it with rice and coriander on the side. Once we were seated at the table, Grandma scooped some hot broth, tasted it, and said, 'Very good.' We followed her lead and began eating.

'Cecilia, I still don't understand why is it that you didn't let us know about the accident. We would have come back right away.' Grandma shook her head.

Mamá took a sip of guava juice. 'I didn't want to ruin your vacation.'

'But... kids, that is crazy. Why would you do that?'

Grandma looked at the four of us. Everyone continued eating, avoiding her concerned stare. We hadn't told our grandparents about Jaime's ordeal with the fishing hook or about our encounter with the bulls. Neither had we told anyone what happened that day when Avelina was in town grocery shopping. The four of us had decided we were tired of eating the same fruit, so we'd climbed the neighbor's fence and were stealing oranges when two Dobermans chased us out. Scratched and bruised, we went back home, and swore each other to secrecy.

'Well, Avelina was an angel. She watched them while I was at the hospital,' Mother reminded everyone.

Grandma called Avelina her right hand. A woman of short stature, Avelina briskly moved around the house, cleaning and cooking. In the afternoons, she washed clothes in a cement wash sink. Later, she set the soaped whites on the lawn until they became bluish. She argued that there was no better bleach than the grass and the sun. Buried in an avalanche of clothes, she spent the evenings ironing and watching soap operas.

'She is wonderful, but I still miss Lola. Lola was with us so long, she became like family. I heard that Rodrigo is now a very studious boy.' Grandma sighed.

'I still don't understand why Orlando was in the car. He is a child,' Grandpa said. Orlando gazed at me, his bottom lip quivering. I grabbed his hand.

'Papá!' My mother fixed her piercing eyes on Grandpa. 'It wasn't his fault. I asked him to do it.'

'I'm just saying—'

Our mother interrupted, 'Kids, if you are finished eating, you should go and do your homework.'

As if it were recess time, the four of us sprung out of our seats. We went to our rooms to study. After I was done, I was walking towards the kitchen to get a glass of water when I overheard voices in the dining room.

'You should divorce Jaime,' Grandma said. 'He won't be back, and you need a father for your children.'

I panicked.

Divorce?

To hear better, I leaned on the hallway wall near the dining room where Mamá, my grandparents, and Mario were drinking tea.

Mamá fought back.

'I love him, and I know he loves me too. You know he sends money and vitamins, right? He'll come back. I know he will.'

Grandpa cleared his throat. 'I wouldn't count on that.'

Mario joined in. 'I know this is none of my business, but Jaime is a good man. Our country is in chaos, and he is trying to do something about it. Not that I agree with his methods—'

Grandpa interjected with a chuckle. 'Ay, Mario, don't deny it. You are a socialist at heart.'

'Please. Don't say anything about Jaime in front of the children,' Mamá begged.

I stormed into the dining room. The table was clear. From the laundry room, the sound of squeaky violins followed by a series of short drum strokes and a woman's voice were coming from Avelina's TV.

'Why aren't you in bed?' asked Mamá.

'I was thirsty.' I stared at them, one by one. As if they were in trouble, they all looked away.

'Rocío, get some water and go to bed,' Mamá said. 'It's late and you have school tomorrow. I'll be going to bed soon too.'

'I can't sleep.'

'Why not?' Mamá squinted.

I inhaled and challenged my mother. 'What are you talking about?'

She fixed her eyes on Grandma's and said, 'Grown-up stuff.'

Grandma pushed her chair back and said, 'We should all rest.'

'I'll help you.' Grandpa held Mamá's arm, and they left the dining room. I trailed behind, frustrated because the grown-ups kept all matters regarding my father hidden from me. We stopped in the hallway. My siblings were asleep.

'I'll talk with Jaime tomorrow. Apparently, he hasn't been turning in any work at school,' Mamá said, and sighed. 'You know about this, Rocío?' Still consumed by what I'd heard, I shrugged.

'The two of you go rest. Tomorrow is another day,' said Grandpa. After kissing me on the cheek, he walked my mother to her room.

'Good night, Rocío.'

'Good night, Mamá.'

I couldn't sleep. I had to do something to bring my father home before it was too late. So, I sat at my desk and wrote a letter to Jocelyne.

November 22, 1963

Chère amie,

I haven't heard from you for a long time. In your last letter, you said that you were traveling to Toronto for a recital. I wish I could have been there. I am sure it was beautiful. Please write soon and tell me all about it. I feel better now that Mamá is back. My grandparents brought her home from the hospital a few days ago. She walks slowly and looks sad, but she is recuperating.

We are back in school, but we don't like it. Mamá said that when we get more money, she will send us to private schools. The sad part is that Papá still hasn't arrived. I feel that if I don't do something fast, my parents will get a divorce or something. Please help me and let me know if you hear or see anything about my father.

Mamá doesn't want me to write to you. It isn't that she doesn't like you. I think she just wants to forget everything bad that happened to us in Montréal. So, you need to promise me that you won't tell anyone about this, because I can get in trouble.

Au revoir, mon ami,
Rocío

I folded the letter and placed it in the envelope I had pulled out of my desk. I glued the flap and addressed it. Then I hid it under the mattress. I had to find a way to send it to Jocelyne without my mother or my grandparents knowing, because they didn't want me to inquire about Papá.

I stayed awake for some time longer, listening to frogs croaking and crickets chirping. I tried to visualize Jocelyne's and Papá's faces, to hear their laughter, or to remember special moments I had spent with them, but the memories were slowly fading away, like those of Sam, the friend I once had. Papá had to come back, and soon, before it was too late. I had to tell him about Mamá's accident. I thought that if he was worried about us, he'd come home.

After school the next day, I went to Mario's cottage carrying my math book and knocked on the door. 'Who is it?' he yelled from inside.

'It's me, Rocío,' I whispered.

I didn't want Mamá or my grandparents to know I was at his house inquiring about my father. They would be upset and more likely to stop me from visiting the old man.

'Who?' Mario opened the door. He was wearing a beret and had a paintbrush in one hand. 'Why don't you speak up? I'm getting old and can't hear as well as I did before.'

'I... just—'

'Come in. What is that book for?'

I had never been inside Mario's cottage before. Life-size paintings of nude women were painted on the walls. I chuckled to see so many of them.

'Did you paint these?'

'Yes, I did. Why are you giggling? This is art.' He scowled. 'Only ignorant people don't appreciate real art.'

My lips were pressed together, then I said, 'I'm sorry.'

I wanted to run away but decided to stay. I had no option. Mario was the only one that could help me bring Papá home. His voice softened when he noticed I was blushing.

'Come, girl, I'll show you.'

I let out a deep breath of relief.

'This one I call The Birth of Venus. Sandro Botticelli painted the original. It had angels. But I don't like them because I'm not religious.'

The concept of a naked woman standing on a gigantic seashell seemed rather odd, but I liked that she had a youthful tenderness in her gaze.

'Mamá taught me to pray to my guardian angel.'

'Your mamá is sweet, but she is a little naïve.'

I liked angels, but I wasn't about to start an argument with Mario. I had watched him pull out the encyclopedia and debate with my grandfather about practically everything. Proud, he would walk away when he could prove he was correct.

After we completed the tour, he wiped his brush with a towel and put it inside a glass with some sort of gasoline-like, smelly liquid.

'Mario, I wanted to ask you for a favor.'

'Yes, what is it?'

'Would you take this letter to town and mail it for me?'

'And why don't you give it to your grandfather to mail?'

'It's for my friend Jocelyne in Canada.'

'Hm... I see. You don't want to tell them you are writing to her?' He gazed at me.

'Well—'

'Come on. Tell me what's going on.'

'See, I want to know what my father is doing and where he is, but no one wants to tell me anything. I could ask Mamá, but I don't want to upset her.'

'She made us promise we wouldn't speak to you about your papá.'

'Why not?'

'That is what she wants, and I have to respect that.'

I began walking to the main door, discouragement weighing me down.

'Wait, but she didn't say I couldn't mail a letter for you.'

I hugged him, bubbling with happiness. The smell of his spicy cologne tickled my nose.

'Thank you.'

I pulled out the letter from inside my math book and gave it to him. Mario was my accomplice in my correspondence with Jocelyne.

Collaborating with Castro

One warm afternoon, we were drinking fresh guava juice on the porch when we saw don Rogelio open the gate of the property to let a taxi in. My grandparents came outside and, with unusual enthusiasm, welcomed Papá's college friend, Dr. Carlos Arango, a bushy-browed, middle-aged man with thick bifocals resting on the tip of his nose. I had heard his name before, but I didn't remember ever seeing him.

Grandma rushed to show him to Mamá's room and asked my brothers, sister, and me not to disturb them. My siblings went to the pool, but I stayed back. I sat outside my mother's room, next to an open window, eavesdropping.

'Hi Cecilia, how are you?' I heard the man say.

'Not well. I think my parents told you I had an accident.'

'Yes, I heard. But this happened three months ago, correct? Your body is healed, but I understand you don't want to move on. Look at you. You are usually so energetic. You look sluggish and pale now. I know Jaime is gone. And God knows what he is going to do next, but you have four children, for God's sake! You have no choice but to make a life for them and for yourself.'

'What do you know about Jaime?' asked my mother.

'As you perhaps know, he's on the front page of every newspaper. They're accusing him of collaborating with Castro. You know how much I care about Jaime. He is a man of integrity and great dedication. But the police are looking for him. Even the C.I.A. is involved. This is not good. I suggest you get on with your life. None of this is new to him, you know that. He's been involved in politics since we were in medical school.'

I peeked in and saw Mamá covering her face with her hands as she sighed and said, 'I know what I have to do. What do I tell the children:'

I wanted to scream at her, *Tell us the truth.*

'Tell them he's gone. They wouldn't understand what their papá is doing, anyway. Plus, if the authorities think you are supporting your husband, it can be dangerous for you. They can put you in jail. They could take your children from you.'

Cold with fear, I sobbed quietly so my mother and Dr. Arango wouldn't hear me.

'But please tell me what the truth *is*.' Mamá begged. 'Tell me everything you know about Jaime.'

I wiped my tears when I heard this and got closer to the window.

'Well, it's a long story, but I guess it's time for you to know,' he muttered. 'He has been supporting the Cuban revolution since the beginning... probably since 1954.'

'Wow. Rocío and Liliana were already born.'

Dr. Arango continued, 'In 1955, he met with Castro in Cuba.'

Suddenly, I remembered the conversation between Grandpa and Mario about my father and his involvement with the guerrilla movement. Like a spring, I jumped up. I wanted to question the doctor. No, I couldn't. They couldn't know I was listening. I sat back down.

Mamá raised her voice, 'Wait. I don't understand; Jaime did this *after* he completed his work in Puerto López? So, that's why he stayed behind and sent us back to Bogotá.'

'Yes. As a matter of fact, Batista's army imprisoned him soon after he arrived in La Habana, but he escaped. After a few days, he came back to Colombia.'

I didn't care who Castro and Batista were, but Papá in prison?

All I could hear was Mamá's heavy breathing.

'Remember that in 1958, he told you he had been admitted to the University of Chicago for general surgery? Well, he had not been admitted yet. He used this as an excuse to go back to Cuba. He joined Castro in Cuba the guerrilla base in the Sierra Maestra. I was told he treated wounded fighters, but the real reason he was there was to learn from Castro. Once he found out he had received the scholarship from the University of Chicago, he left Cuba and went to the United States. You and the children arrived in Chicago a few months later.'

'I'm an idiot. I cannot believe I didn't know any of this,' Mamá said, her voice breaking.

'Maybe he was trying to protect you and the kids. I'm sorry, but there's more. Jaime is helping coordinate the underground communist movement in Latin America. And now he is back in Colombia. He is one of those who wants to make the Andes the Sierra Maestra of South America. Men like Che and Jaime think they can win the war with the support of the peasants and by hiding in the Andes.'

'I don't know what to say. You think you know your husband, but I had no idea to what extent he has been involved,' exclaimed Mamá.

I peeked again and saw her staring at the floor. She moved her head from side to side in disbelief.

Dr. Arango cleared his throat. 'As I said, you need to move on, for your children's sake, so go to work or do something. Jaime is like a brother to me; therefore, I feel as though you are all part of my family. So please, let me know if you need anything.'

He stood up, kissed her on the cheek, and walked out of the room. I pretended I was coming back from the pool and went to the front of the house. My grandparents were standing by the main door. The doctor whispered something to them and then left in the awaiting taxi.

I needed time to understand what Dr. Arango had just said about my father. I needed to convince myself that Papá was simply working on some sort of international project. Perhaps he loved us, but simply wasn't able to come home.

Suddenly, the smell of coffee reminded me of Mario's afternoon treat. I needed an excuse to go see him. I went to the kitchen and had Avelina pour hot, foamy milk and coffee into a cup. 'Be careful, don't burn yourself,' she said.

I held the tray tight all the way to Mario's cottage. My heart was racing out of control. When I arrived, I placed the tray on the ground and knocked several times. 'Mario, are you there?'

No answer.

'Mario.' I knocked harder.

'Coming, coming.' Mario opened the door, half asleep. 'Don't you know I take an afternoon nap?'

'I'm sorry. I thought you were ready for your coffee.' I picked up the tray.

'I wasn't... what do you want?'

When his forehead wrinkled, I said, 'I... I wanted to—'

'This better be important.'

He showed me in. He then took the tray and put it on the side table. I told him everything the doctor had said, hoping he would help me understand my father's actions and why Papá's cause was more important than us. Mario took the coffee cup in his hands and closed his eyes as if hypnotized by its aroma. Then he looked at me, sipping his drink.

'You know that eavesdropping is unacceptable. People need privacy.'

I was surprised to be scolded.

'I know. I am sorry, but I had to know what's going on.'

'Well, I suppose I can understand that.' He rubbed his bald head. 'Look, you're a smart girl, and like your mamá, you are just going to have to accept that he is gone for good.'

Tears made my vision blurry, so I wiped them away with my hands. Mario held my arm and walked me to his study.

'Sit down, my dear child.' I did. 'First, let's talk about Jocelyne's last letter,' he said. 'I don't know how long I'll be able to keep this from your grandfather. Every time I pick up a letter for you, he gives me a nudge and calls me a dog. Can you imagine? He thinks I have a girlfriend.'

Impatient, I fidgeted.

'With my limited French, I've been translating an article that Jocelyne sent you. Rassemblement pour l'indépendance nationale is a group of people pushing for the independence of Québec from Canada. Apparently, your papá is supporting that group too. And Jocelyne's parents are against that movement. That is why they forbade her from keeping in touch with you.'

'What article? What are you talking about?'

'I'm sorry. I had to open the letter because your grandfather was watching me, so I had to pretend it was mine. Then I became interested.' Mario cleared his throat.

I didn't worry about Jocelyne. I knew she wouldn't stop writing. I wasn't interested in what was happening in Québec. My only goal was to find Papá.

'Does **Papá** still have a job in Canada?' I asked.

'That kind of work doesn't mean he has a job. You are as naïve as your mamá.' Mario opened his eyes wide. 'What's going on in Canada is not our problem.

What happens in Colombia is. One issue here is the social classes. The wealthy want to maintain the status quo.'

'Status quo?'

Mario shook his head.

'All right, let me give you an example. Avelina's mother was a servant. Avelina is a maid, and her daughter, if she had one, would eventually be a maid too. It is very difficult for the poor to go to college and to buy property.'

'That's not fair.'

'I agree. And we need to do something about it, but it's not going to be easy. Your **papá** believes that the current political system must change in order to eliminate the social classes. To do this, the new government would have to control most everything in the country, including education, properties, and so on. Don't get me wrong, your **papá** is very smart, but he is an idealist.' Mario buttoned his sweater. Then he stopped and put on his smock. 'The light is perfect. Can I paint you?'

I thought it was a little odd for him to paint me in the middle of the conversation, but agreed so that he would explain to me all that he had just said about my father.

He began painting and talked on and on. I only understood a little of what he was saying. Eventually, I stopped listening. All I could think of was how to bring **Papá** back home. Whatever he was doing or whom he was helping wasn't important to me. I just wanted him with us again. But I couldn't tell anyone, not even Mario. Apparently, they all agreed he was gone for good.

'Come see this,' he said.

I was so deep into my thoughts I forgot Mario was sketching my face on a canvas.

'You drew me?'

'Well, yes. And you are going to have to come back so I can finish it. If you aren't going to let me sleep, and you keep asking me questions, then you need to work as a model for me. I've only painted grown women's faces. Yours is unique: large, curved forehead, high cheekbones, and square chin.' He tilted his head to one side, squinting at the sketch. 'Interesting. You seem indifferent in this portrait.'

No one had ever drawn me before. So, I jumped off my seat and went to look at it. The portrait of an older girl with short, wavy hair and an empty gaze stared at me. Mario was right. The girl appeared distant, almost uninterested. Perhaps I was just tired of fighting, hoping others could help me bring Papá back. Suddenly, chills went through me when I thought that perhaps I, too, was giving up on him.

'I've got to go.'

'Do you like my sketch?'

'I do. Thanks,' I lied.

It scared me.

I don't recognize myself anymore.

The Meeting

After Dr. Arango's visit, our mother went back to her old self. She painted rooms, changed blinds, and fixed and lacquered furniture. One evening, the lights went off, followed by the smell of smoke. We all rushed to see what was happening and found Mamá putting out a small fire.

Grandpa pointed his flashlight at her and said, 'Caramba Cecilia, are you planning to burn the house down?'

Her posture stiffened as she explained that she was trying to change the plug on the iron. Grandpa shook his head and demanded she leaves all electrical related work to him. Grandma offered to hire a handyman to assist with her many projects, but she refused. Sometimes we'd come home from school to find our mother up on a ladder with her hair and face spotted by paint, or she'd be drilling nails in the cement walls to hang pictures. Other days, she'd stay up at night sewing. '

'Follow the noise and you'll find your mamá,' Grandpa smirked.

This went on for many months.

When Fusa's springlike weather turned humid, we had another surprise. My siblings and I were helping Grandma water her many orchids when we saw Grandpa clutching a letter. Usually, when he arrived, he greeted my brothers, my sister, and me by calling us funny names or tickling us, but this time was different. He didn't say anything. He simply handed the envelope to Grandma, who instantly took it to Mamá.

'Who is it from?' I asked.

No one responded.

It wasn't until after dinner that our mother pointed with her chin and said, 'Kids, follow me to my room.' There, she pulled a letter out of her nightstand.

Rolling it back and forth with nervous hands, she announced, 'Mamá Sarai…
your papá's mother… Grandma Sarai, you do remember her, right?'

We nodded.

'She has invited you to stay at her home in Barranquilla.' She paused, then
continued, 'But you should know that you would be going alone.'

'I don't want to go,' Orlando said.

'I don't want to either,' chorused Liliana and Jaime.

Jaime placed his hands in his pocket. 'I hate Papá and his family.'

With darting eyes, Mamá snarled, 'What are you saying? Don't you ever say
you hate your papá!'

'Why isn't he here with us?' I grumbled.

'He has things he must do,' she said, looking away. 'And you, Jaime, you
remember that he spent hours in the operating room reconstructing your hand?'

Jaime twisted his mouth to one side. 'Nope.'

'It took your papá many hours to put your hand back together. See, you don't
even have a scar.' Mamá touched Jaime's hand.

'I thought Papá was not allowed to operate on his own family,' I said.

'I wasn't supposed to tell anyone, but your papá pleaded with the director to
let him do the surgery. The man made an exception that day because he thought
your papá was the most qualified surgeon for the job.'

'What has he done for us lately?' Liliana challenged. 'Why aren't you mad at
him? He left you too, you know.'

Mamá's face drained of color, replaced by fury, and she raised her hand to
strike Liliana. I held my breath. Liliana squinted. But then Mamá stopped, and
her eyes overflowed with tears. She gently brushed my sister's face.

'I'm sorry. It's just that your papá is my life,' she uttered as she collapsed onto
a small sofa.

A wave of relief poured over me.

It isn't too late, I thought. *I can still reunite my parents.*

'Then call him and make him come back,' I said.

Mamá shook her head. 'He cannot come.'

'I heard what Dr. Arango told you about Papá. Why can't you tell us what he
is doing? Don't you think that if we understood, we wouldn't be upset with
him? Why is he working with Castro? Is he in trouble?'

'I don't want to talk about him,' Jaime said.

'When you grow up, you will learn more about what is going on in this country.
For now, you are just going to have to trust me,' said Mamá.

I felt rage tearing through my body. My brothers and sister sat on the floor, staring at me.

And then, as if nothing had occurred, Mamá continued, 'It is important that you go and visit your other grandmother. She loves you too. What do you say?' With tight lips, Jaime gazed at me, then jumped up and walked towards the window.

Liliana squealed, 'But—'

I made eye contact with her and crossed my fingers, our special hand signal for *stop*.

The flight from Bogotá to Barranquilla was short and bumpy. Through the window, I could see the Andean mountains like a massive snake winding across heavily vegetated plains. Scarce tiny towns were also visible below. An hour into the flight, the airplane turned around and descended. The Andes slowly faded away. Pearl-like sandy beaches, splashed by the aqua-blue Atlantic Ocean, now dominated the landscape. Liliana squeezed in next to me. The boys fell asleep and didn't waken until the airplane landed with a brisk thump. Once the plane stopped, passengers jumped out of their seats and began disembarking. A gust of heavy, hot air filled the cabin. My short hair quickly became completely out of control. I would have given anything to have Jaime's straight and soft hair or Mamá's bouncy red curls.

A stewardess startled us when she approached us with raised eyebrows and asked, 'Kids, aren't you getting off the plane?' Without waiting for a response, she grabbed our carry-on bags and walked us to the house-like building they called an airport.

Two skinny girls giggled when they saw my siblings and me. The taller of the two pointed at us and said, 'How cute, *twins* and boys with *shorts*.'

Mamá had made Liliana and me two identical lavender pastel dresses with fabric she had found on sale. Orlando was going through a growth spurt, so she had cut my brother's pants and convinced him that shorts were in style. We knew that our father's packages with vitamins and checks had become less frequent, so we didn't complain.

We followed the stewardess until we exited the building. Grandma Sarai's silvery head towered over the large and noisy crowd of people waiting for passengers outside the luggage area. We wriggled through the river of people until we reached her. The stewardess handed our grandmother our documents, had her sign a form, and left. Our grandmother's light linen dress and leather-

164

heeled sandals made her look taller than I remembered. I hadn't seen her for over six years. She hugged and kissed my siblings and me. She then rushed us to a black taxi.

'Please take us home, Leonel,' she said.

The driver, Leonel, was a heavyset, bearded man who spoke with a funny accent. He mumbled something about the warm weather as he opened the door for us. He drove fast and kept looking in the rearview mirror. His bear-like hands were tightly wrapped around the steering wheel. A scar ran across the back of his hairy right hand. He looked familiar, but I couldn't remember where I had seen him before. Grandma Sarai didn't seem to mind Leonel's erratic driving.

Instead, she looked back at us and said, 'I'm so glad you are all here. I hope you can stay with me for a long, long time.'

We didn't respond. Meanwhile, the driver kept looking in the rearview mirror. We drove for about twenty minutes until we arrived in a neighborhood with large houses surrounded by elaborate, colorful gardens and brown-orange clay rooftops. Grandma Sarai's house was across from the Prado Park. I was mulling over a dreamlike memory of Papá chasing us at this park. I could almost hear his deep, infectious laughter when Carmiña, the maid, opened the door. She hugged each one of us tightly. Her dark skin seemed even darker in contrast to her white starched maid's uniform. I recalled the house, but now it seemed smaller. The shiny, taupe tiles gave the floor a wet and fresh look. The large windows were open, and the silk like drapes flapped like butterfly wings in slow motion. Grandma Sarai showed us to our rooms. From my closet, she pulled several beige and white sets of clothes and shoes she had bought for us. 'I like your dress,' she said, as she made me twirl around. 'But while you are here, wear only these clothes. They are more appropriate for this coastal weather. Plus, I want everyone in our family to meet Jaime's children, and I want you all to look nice.'

She sighed, gazing at my homemade dress with her deep blue eyes. She then turned around and walked away, leaving me standing and holding my small suitcase filled with clothes I was not allowed to wear.

In those first weeks, Leonel drove us in his car, which had multiple dents on the fender. Every time I got in, I cringed, wondering what he had done to smash his car so many times. No one else seemed to mind, so I didn't say anything.

Our grandmother was too busy taking us to visit relatives. My sister and brothers giggled, looking forward to spending time with our cousins. Rita was my favorite aunt because she reminded me of Papá. Her perfectly aligned posture and long legs made her look poised and confident.

One day I asked her, 'Why can't we walk to people's homes like we did before? Why do we always have to go in that black taxi with that man?'

She looked to one side, then the other.

'You'll be fourteen years old soon, so you should understand that your papá is only trying to protect you.'

'Protect me from what?' I responded, irritated that no one would give me a straight answer.

She held my hand.

'You'll find out when you get older. For now, you must do as we say. That's what your papá wants, and that should be enough for you.'

My voice cracked. 'Is that why we are not allowed to go to the park?'

'Yes, my dear Rocío, there are people out there who don't agree with your papá's views.'

'What views? Where is he anyway? Do you know?'

'I can't say anything more.'

Letting go of her hand, I made my way to my room. I spent the rest of the evening looking out the window into the clear sky, thinking how I envied the stars. I wished I could be one of them and disappear into the quiet sky.

Grandma Sarai walked into my room the following morning.

'Rocío, it's late, and I have to run some errands. Please take care of your brothers and sister. Carmiña went to the market, but she should be back soon.'

I had no desire to babysit. I wanted to stay in bed and not see anyone. That day, I didn't play. I just watched my brothers and sister. Liliana searched every drawer in the house. Jaime and Orlando were more difficult. Jaime hid Orlando's toy cars and stepped on the miniature cities he had built. Orlando chased Jaime, threatening to punch him, but most of the time, Jaime got away. They called each other girl's names and spoke with high-pitched voices, imitating one another.

I was about to scream at my brothers when my stomach hurt; then I began salivating. I gagged as I dashed to the bathroom but didn't get to the toilet on time. Like an explosive lava stream, vomit covered the floor of the small room. My head was spinning, so I lay on my bed and closed my eyes for a while. When the nausea finally ceased, I peeled myself off my bed, rinsed my mouth, and cleaned the floor. I looked at myself in the mirror and was surprised to see my colorless complexion.

I miss Mamá so much. We have never been apart. What if I don't ever see her again? A chilling sweat coated my body.

Dusk had fallen when Grandma Sarai asked us to the dining room. Orlando skipped in, hoping to receive a gift. Liliana, Jaime and I, on the other hand, dragged our heels, perhaps we were all missing Mamá. The menorah stood vigilant in the front window near the main door. Next to it, three candles waited to be lit. Assorted dishes with sweet cheese pancakes, hot fried *buñuelos*, and patties de *espinaca* were on the table.

'Isn't this wonderful?'

We all nodded.

'Today, I have a special gift for you. Go to my room. You'll find it there.'

In Grandma Sarai's bedroom, I found Papá sitting in a wooden rocking chair. My legs felt flaccid and my heart pounded. I bit my lip and blinked tears from my eyes. It had been two years since we had seen our father. Liliana ran to him and hung from his neck as he embraced her.

Orlando yelled, 'Papi!' and also ran to him.

Jaime dropped his head to his chest. I stood by the door, blinking, not sure if this was all real. Papá was slimmer. A few silvery strands of hair brushed his sideburns. Faint lines framed his clear brown eyes. He was the same, but different too. He smiled and extended his arms for Jaime and me to go to him. We didn't.

When he realized we were not coming, he got up and hugged me, lifting me off my feet. I wanted to cry but couldn't. It was as if my tears had dried up. For a long time, I had been rehearsing questions I wanted to ask him. What was his business with the law? Why did he leave, breaking our mother's heart? Did he still love us? I despised him, but was delighted to see him at the same time. But now that he was holding me, I had nothing to say.

Papá put me down and walked over to Jaime, giving him a great bear hug. My brother froze, fixing his eyes on mine. My father then went back to the chair where he sat. A prolonged silence enveloped the room. We turned to stone.

How could he hurt my brothers? My sister? My mother? Why couldn't I just scream at him? And why couldn't I tell him to go away and leave us alone?

I am just like Mamá.

Like a sail on a windless day, I felt limp.

Our father broke the painful silence by asking us about school. Liliana was the first one to respond.

'Rocío gets sick at school. She even got sick here. She didn't tell anyone, but I noticed that she was cleaning the bathroom.'

'Well, we need to fix this,' assured Papá.

I fought back.

'Liliana doesn't speak at school. It is as if when we go out, she becomes mute.'

'Is that so?' Papá rubbed his chin.

Orlando chipped in, 'Jaime fights every day and comes home with ripped clothes and bruises. He lost his books a couple of times and argues with Mamá.'

'Jaime, we will discuss this issue too.'

Pretty soon, we were all sharing our school and family experiences with our father, although all he did was nod.

'Mamá had a bad car accident and was in the hospital for a long time.' I wanted to scare him, but nothing phased him.

'She is fine now, correct?' He kept nodding.

'But she almost died,' I wailed, hoping he would reconsider and come back.

'I am so sorry she was hurt.'

'Why aren't you with us?' protested Jaime.

'If you had been with us, Mamá wouldn't have had the accident,' I challenged him.

Papá stood and picked up a glass of water from the night table. He mulled in silence while sipping the water.

Then he responded, 'I have a job to do. I have to take care of *all* the children in Colombia. You are not my only children. Poor children also need my help. I know that you are young, and you might not know what is going on in this country, but there are a lot of people who don't have homes, access to education, or even medical care. I am working diligently to make this a better country for all. And I hope that if something happens to me, you will continue my work. With courage, you need to fight against the exploitation of the poor.'

'What's exploitation?' Liliana played with her hands.

I screeched, 'What do you mean if something happens to you? Are you sick?'

'Exploitation is when people take advantage of others. And no, I am not sick.'

'Can we come?' pleaded Liliana.

'Yes,' he said, beaming. 'That is what I want to tell you. We will be moving to Russia soon.'

Russia?

All I knew about Russia was what Grandma Emilia taught me while spending long summer days reading *Doctor Zhivago*. Tsars, war, and love. Somehow, the lives of these monarchs fascinated her.

'And Mamá too?' I asked.

We could have a place like the one we had in Canada, a warm home where we could hide from the dark and icy days.

Scratching his head, he muttered, 'No, Rocío. Your mamá can't come. It would be just the five of us.'

'Why can't Mamá come?'

'You will go to a boarding school. That means that you will live at the school. I will be in Russia, too, but I will be traveling. There would be nothing for your mamá to do there. I will come and see you when I can.'

We all shook our heads. 'No. No.'

'If you don't like Russia, how about France? I will be there too.'

Again, we shook our heads.

'Can't you live with *us*?' asked Orlando, crossing his arms.

'No. As I said, I have to travel a lot for work, but let's talk about this some other time,' concluded Papá.

Travel a lot. I repeated in my mind.

Wasn't that what he had been doing all along? That meant we would never see him.

'So, you expect us to go to Russia and be alone? Because you aren't going to be there... and leave Mamá?' I said, tightening my lips feeling crushed inside by indifference. 'She almost died twice, when we left Montréal and when the car ran over her.'

Papá bent down and gazed at us.

'I have never left you. We all came back at different times. But I have always watched over you.'

'How can you do that if you aren't there?' I asked.

'Look, why don't we discuss this matter later? For now, let's try to spend some time together.'

It was always the same. The conversations with the adults ended before they responded to our questions. We didn't insist, because perhaps deep inside, it was better not to know.

At dinnertime, Grandma Sarai asked father to lead us in prayer.

'Mamá, you know I am not religious,' he said.

'But it's Hanukkah.' Grandma Sarai's face tensed, then said a prayer herself, almost as if ignoring she'd ever asked him the question. Like me, like Mamá, she too could not confront my father.

Grandma Sarai's smile didn't return to her face until Carmiña walked in with a platter of her famous *bollos limpios*, corn butter rolls, our father's childhood treat. After dinner, Orlando showed Papá the small cars Grandma Emilia and Grandpa Miguel had brought him from their trip. Jaime said little, but followed our father everywhere he went. Liliana carried George, her doll, and also followed him. Later we played Parcheesi. Papá said it was a game adapted from a traditional Indian game. Papá and Orlando were one team. Liliana, Jaime, and I played independently with our own set of pieces. I was winning, but Liliana caught up to me, and in the end, she won. Jaime was sent back several times and had to begin all over. Laughing and fidgety, he kept forgetting which ones were his pieces. Jaime came in third, and Orlando and

Papá last. Fixing his eyes on the board while panting, Orlando suddenly brushed the pieces off the table.

'Orlando, what's the matter?' scolded Papá, as he looked down. With wide-open eyes, Papá enunciated each word. 'Men face their problems and learn from them. Then, they make sure they do better the next time around.'

He became pensive. No one spoke. My siblings and I gazed at one another. I didn't want to upset Papá because he might leave again. When Papá finally patted Orlando on the back, we all let out a loud sigh.

That evening, I couldn't take my eyes off my father. A broad-shouldered man, he filled the room with his deep voice. I noticed that his hands had changed. They were now dry. They reminded me of Dr. Torres's hands. But that night, I wasn't troubled about what was keeping us apart. All I could feel was a floating sensation of happiness.

Finally, we have him back, I thought, but didn't say anything.

When it was bedtime, Papá tucked Liliana, Jaime, and Orlando in bed.

I heard him tell Orlando, 'Men fight for a cause to protect or help others not to prove they are strong or better than others.'

The faint glow of the moon shone behind thin blinds, casting an elongated shadow of the wooden armoire on the floor. I was about to push the covers off because it was warm when Papá came in and sat on my bed next to me.

Hunching over, he sighed. 'I understand that you eat very little and that you get sick often.'

I wanted to make him aware of how hard life had been living without him, but before I could reply, he continued, 'I will send vitamins so that you will stay healthy. Once you are in Russia, you will receive excellent health care.'

'We don't need vitamins. All we need is for you to be with us,' I sniveled.

He gazed at me for a moment. My heart began beating fast at the thought that he might reconsider.

'I cannot do that. At least not now. This is why I need you to be there for your brothers and sister. I know that this is a lot to ask from someone as young as you are. This is the responsibility of the adults, but do not let these things frustrate you. People fall into one of two categories when facing adversity:

they either rise above their challenges, or they let the difficulties overwhelm them. You have to stay strong, for yourself and for me.'

'Why are you doing this? We are just children. I heard you tell Orlando that we should fight for a cause. What type of *cause* are you talking about?'

I wanted to make him aware that I knew the authorities were after him. I was hoping at one point he would confide in me and tell me all about his involvement with the communists.

'Well, we have to set goals in life and work hard to achieve those goals.'

I raised my voice, 'If you don't come back, Mamá will divorce you.'

Papá closed his eyes and rubbed his head for a while. Anxious, I held my hands tight. He didn't respond to my comment. Instead, he forewarned me that there were going to be some more changes in our lives. I sat up in my bed.

'More changes? What do you mean? I just want us to be a family again. What happened? Why did you send us back to Colombia, and where did you go? You should come back with us.'

'That cannot happen… I am busy, and you have to go to school. There are things I am dealing with that you would not understand now, but one day you will.'

My throat tightened. I would have understood practically anything if someone had taken the time to explain it to me, but no one did, not even him.

Papá got off the bed and dropped to his knees.

'Rocío, please speak with your siblings. I know they listen to you and maybe you can convince them it is best for all of you to go to school in Russia. It would be safer for you there. I will join you later, I promise.'

The thought of being apart from my mother was unbearable. Her heart was already broken, the car accident, and now… losing us too? I knew that would've been too much for her to bear.

'We are safe where we are,' I said.

My father stood with a downcast gaze. I wanted to scream at him, but no sound came out. I covered my face with both hands. Papá kissed my forehead and left the room. I stayed in bed. Numb. Looking at the door, hoping he would come back, I fell into a fitful sleep.

When the summer sun broke, I woke, dripping in sweat. In my dream, I had seen blood on Papá's face. Frightened, I rushed to his side to help him, but when I got near him, he faded away.

My heart was still racing when I woke. So, I sat upright in bed. I was angry with Papá, but the fear that something terrible could happen to him made my chest hurt. I sprung to my feet and raced to his room. His bed was unmade. A wet towel hung from the metal chair where the previous day had sat his old maroon suitcase.

'Papá! Papá! Papá!' I screamed as I dashed into the hallway.

Grandma Sarai came out of her room, startled and sleepy. 'What is all that racket?' she asked.

'Where is Papá? I can't find him.' I gasped.

My grandmother pulled me towards her with long, delicate hands and held me against her bony chest.

'He is gone,' she whispered. 'He had to go back to work, but he loves you very much.'

I had lost my father again. I had to let him know about my nightmare, about the blood on his face, but I couldn't now. Sitting on the cool tile floor with my head sunk into my crisscrossed legs, I stayed there for hours, weeping.

After he left, there was little our grandmother could do to console us. Liliana retreated, playing with her dolls and invisible friends. Jaime and Orlando fought constantly. I stayed in my bedroom. I felt like I was tumbling down into an empty, dark, and bottomless well.

Profound Truths are Found in the
Quietest of Whispers

A few days after Papá left, the sun was setting when I looked out my bedroom window and saw Aunt Rita, my father's older sister, arrive in the black taxi. Leonel helped her out and handed her a bag from the trunk. Aunt Rita's cotton dress and summer sandals gave her the appearance of a model with long legs. She looked at me, then smiled. 'Your papá sent you these gifts. The ball is for your brothers, and the castanets are for you and Liliana.' She handed me a paper bag.

'Papá sent us gifts! Is he here?' I said, thinking he had come back.

'No, he's not. I am sorry.'

I peeked outside. My heart ached when I saw my aunt was telling the truth. He wasn't there. Like a phantom, Papá, in one way or another, came into our lives for brief moments, only to disappear later, leaving no trace.

When I showed Liliana the castanets, she looked at them, then grunted, 'I don't want them.'

She passed them to me. Jaime and Orlando took the ball and went to the back patio to play soccer. My initial disappointment eased when I thought that perhaps one day, I could play castanets while Jocelyne played the piano in a recital together at the National Theater, Teatro Colón. Maybe then, Papá would come back and be proud of me. I had wanted a pair like this for so long. How did he know? I had asked my mother to buy some for my birthday, but she said she couldn't afford them. Now, I put my thumbs through the loops and began tapping one finger at a time.

I practiced playing different songs. I wore my grandmother's long, silky skirts and old high heels. At the beginning, my family enjoyed my amateur home performances. However, when they realized that the novelty wasn't wearing off, fewer people came to my shows until one day, no one did. My siblings made all sorts of excuses. Carmiña complained she had too much work to do, and Grandma Sarai often retired to her room, explaining that she needed a nap. I was upset at first but then realized that I was just as happy dancing and playing the castanets by myself in my room, pretending that my father was there watching my show.

One evening, Aunt Rita joined us for dinner.
After we finished eating, she said, 'Would you like to hear the story about how your papá discovered he was going to be a doctor?'
With a loud cheer, my siblings and I said, 'Yes.'
We sat outside in the backyard, sipping lemonade.
'He was a very studious boy, but at home, he was sometimes a troublemaker,' began Aunt Rita with a frown on her face. Then she laughed as she looked away, shaking her head. 'One day, Grandma Sarai found a dead frog outside in the backyard. She noticed that the belly of the animal had been sliced. She was flabbergasted to see the guts spilling out of the animal, so she asked her children if they knew anything about such a horrific act. No one knew. A few days later, she walked into the patio and saw your Uncle Oscar holding a small, gray mouse with both hands while your papá slit its round, small belly open with a razor blade. Grandma Sarai stood by the kitchen door, terrified by the sight. "What are you doing?" she shouted.'
Aunt Rita finished her lemonade and licked her lips. My brothers, sister, and I listened to the story. A couple of times, my siblings' mouths dropped open. This was the first time we'd heard that our father had been mischievous and even cruel. No one moved.
Aunt Rita continued, 'Carmiña, your two aunts, and I burst out of the house to see what the uproar was about. We found Grandma Sarai screaming hysterically, flapping her arms at the two boys. We were all young. Your papá was the oldest boy, but he was only eight years old. He excused his actions by telling your grandmother that he wasn't going to kill the mouse. He had a plan. He was responsible for cutting the animal open so that they could see what was inside of it. Uncle Oscar's job was to sew the animal back up so it wouldn't die.'
'Papá was just like Jaime. Did he like to torture animals?' I asked.
'No. Let me tell you the rest of the story,' Aunt Rita said. 'Grandma Sarai grabbed both boys by their hands and stormed out into the street. They went to see the rabbi, who made them promise not to do it again.'
'So, were they in trouble?' asked Orlando.
'Yes, they were,' Aunt Rita said. 'Three years later, Grandma Sarai thought that your papá had been redeemed, but she was stunned yet again. Carmiña

was sweeping the house when from under his bed rolled out a bag filled with human bones. Grandma Sarai's skin turned colorless. 'What is this? Is my son going to be a criminal?' Her rage was even worse when she questioned him. Instead of repenting as she expected, he confronted her.

'He fixed his eyes on hers and said, 'These bones are mine. I found them in an empty lot where workers of a building company were excavating, so now they are *mine*.' He grabbed the bag and walked away. 'No, they are not yours. They belong to dead people, and we are taking them back to where they belong!' Grandma Sarai yelled.

'That day, my grandfather came home from work and found out what had happened. He was furious, so he took his belt off and whipped your papá's back until he said he was sorry and returned the bag of bones. No one knew what happened to the bag after that day. Grandma Sarai found out years later that Carmiña had hidden it in her room so your papá could study them. When he turned twelve years old, the family finally understood his passion for bones and organs. One day, he went with his Aunt Aura to see the doctor. After they left the doctor's office, your papá said to her, "I want to do what that man does. I want to cure people."'

That night I dreamed of watching my father surrounded by books, medicine boxes, syringes, and people. I looked down and saw the white shoe streaks my father had left on the hardwood floor. I tried getting to him, but the harder I tried, the farther away he appeared to be.

The echoing ring of the old phone woke me up. Curious, I leaped out of bed and toddled to the bedroom door. I was about to turn the doorknob when I heard Grandma Sarai say, 'Hi, Cecilia.'

Hearing my mother's name made tears spring from my eyes. I missed her so much.

'Yes, the children are asleep,' continued my grandmother, followed by what seemed a monologue by my mother, but I couldn't hear how she was responding.

Then my grandmother said, 'No, for now, they must stay.' She paused to listen, and then said, 'I know they are your children, but they are Jaime's children, too, and he wants to see them again.' Another pause. 'No need to cry. You will be able to pick them up soon, but not now.'

Mamá is upset.

I covered my mouth with one hand so my grandmother wouldn't hear me weeping.

'You can think whatever you want, but you cannot have them, not right now.' My grandmother hung up.

I looked through the keyhole and saw Grandma Sarai sitting on a chair next to the sculptured phone table. Her long beige nightgown hung from her fragile body. Shoulder-length, silvery curls fell to one side of her face. With her gaze fixed on the floor, she lifted the receiver and dialed a number. Her whispers were barely audible.

'Hi, dear. She called, and she is in town. She wants the children back now.' Grandma Sarai paused. 'I told her you wanted to see them again. That is correct, right?' She paused. 'I don't think you should take them out of the country without her permission.'

With my ear pressed against the keyhole, I desperately tried to listen to what my father was saying to her, but all I heard was my grandmother's voice.

'I think we must change the plan. They should be out of here tomorrow. I fear she will come for them and take them with her.'

Is Papá going to kidnap us? I felt faint.

'I will pack their suitcases,' she said. 'In Russia? There are excellent schools here too, you know?' Pause. 'But those are your political views, not ours.' Another pause. 'You will have the opportunity to ask them again as soon as you see them. Be careful,' she cautioned as she hung up.

With my heart pounding, I tiptoed back to my bed. I tried to make sense of what I had just heard. There was so much I didn't know.

Mamá is here? And why can't she see us? Where are we going with our father? To Russia?

These questions were racing around in my mind when I heard Grandma Sarai come into my room. I stayed still. Quietly, she scooped clothes from every drawer. When she finished, she left, closing the door behind her. Then I heard her heeled slippers clicking inside my siblings' rooms.

I wanted to confront my grandmother and ask her to tell me the truth about Papá's plan. The thought of him taking us away from my mother made me sick. I stayed in bed, motionless, wondering what to do. But the sound of an automobile approaching made me jerk. I got up and moved the curtain to one side, and saw a car parked in front of the house. The faint glow of the streetlight revealed the unmistakable stocky silhouette of Leonel González.

Why is he here if it is still dark outside?

A chilly wave of sorrow swept through my body. Taking a deep breath, I peeked through the keyhole once more and saw four small suitcases lined up by the main door. I jumped back into bed. A while later, Grandma Sarai closed her bedroom door. I held on to my pillow tight and cried myself to sleep.

I woke, gasping for air, when I felt a hand over my mouth. Instinctively, I grabbed what seemed like someone's forearm. I was ready to scream when I saw Carmiña's very white teeth.

She whispered, 'I'm going to move my hand. Don't say a word. You need to get dressed and come with me. Your mamá is waiting for you. You must leave before the sun comes up.'

I sat on the bed, quietly sobbing. 'I guess this means that I will never see Papá again?'

'You will, but not now,' said Carmiña.

She handed me my clothes. After I dressed, she held my hand as we crossed the dining room, then the kitchen, and finally exited through the back door. I saw Mamá standing near don Pascal's jeep. I let Carmiña's hand go and ran to her.

She hugged me and said, 'We will be fine.'

How can we be fine? It all seems to get worse and worse. Now we are running away from Papá. I will probably never see him again.

I held my breath, hoping to disguise my fear. That was when I looked at my mother. Her wavy hair was uncombed. Dark shadows cast by her swollen eyes made her seem ill. I felt sorry for her. I felt sorry for myself. I felt sorry for all of us.

'Carmiña, would you like me to help you bring out the other kids?' Mamá asked.

'No, we don't want to wake doña Sarai. I know how to walk around in the dark in this house,' she said before going back inside.

Not much later, she came out carrying one brother, then the other, putting them half asleep in the back seat of the jeep. She then came back with Liliana, who was carrying her doll. My sister and I joined our brothers. Carmiña went back inside one more time and, moments later, brought out our bags, which she handed to don Pascal.

Mamá hugged her and said, 'Thank you, *que Dios te bendiga.*'

'I would do anything for Dr. Jaime. But this time, I think he is wrong. These kids are like my own grandchildren, and they should be with their mother,' Carmiña said, wiping her tears with her hands.

Mamá embraced her again. 'Are you all right?'

'I don't know what he is thinking… to take them so far away. For what? To be alone?' Carmiña shook her head.

'It is almost dawn,' don Pascal said, 'and we need to be at the airport.'

My mother jumped in the front, next to him, and waved goodbye to Carmiña. She waved back as she rubbed her heavy-lidded eyes and said, '*Adiós, mis niños.*'

Don Pascal stepped on the gas pedal, driving us away. Carmiña clenched her fists against her chest. Pretty soon, she faded away into the distance.

'What is going on, Mamá?' I asked.

'All you need to know for now is that Carmiña raised your papá, and she loves you; this is why she must receive many blessings. She was good to him, and now she has been good to you.'

Don Pascal interrupted us. 'There is a taxi following us.'

I looked back, and indeed, there was a taxi approaching fast.

'I know who he is. It's Grandma Sarai's driver,' I said.

'How do you know?' Mamá asked.

Don Pascal turned into a brightly lit commercial street, allowing me to see the car. It had a large dent on the front bumper.

'I recognize the car. Please believe me,' I said.

'I believe her. Forget the airport. We can't go there because they will find us,' urged my mother. 'We will drive back with you to my parents' home.'

'Driving from the coast back to Fusagasugá is difficult, you know that? You flew here, but I just made the trip, and it is exhausting and long,' warned don Pascal.

'It doesn't matter; we have to do it, or I'll lose my children,' Mamá said.

'Okay, whatever you want, Señora. But I hope you understand it is not going to be easy with four kids.'

The taxi stayed close to us for a while until don Pascal made a sharp turn, almost tossing us all out of the jeep. Now my siblings were awake, and Orlando was clenching my mother's hand. Two blocks later, after I thought we had lost Leonel González, I turned around and saw a pair of car lights approaching.

I said, 'He is getting closer to us.'

The chase continued through neighborhoods and city streets. Once we left the city lights behind and drove on unpaved streets.

Mamá asked, 'Can't you go faster?'

Don Pascal didn't respond. He made another sharp turn, this time south. After driving on a gravel road for some time, we arrived at a dead end. He looked around for a way out, then told us to hang on as he drove into a banana plantation that was in front of us, flattening young banana plants like a bulldozer. Leonel González kept the pursuit, dragging plants along until his car stalled. Long, arching leaves saturated with dewdrops were now slapping the jeep. They seemed almost angry at us. For a moment there was relief, then suddenly, we were driving down a steep hill. We were screaming. The next thing I remember was the jeep hitting a tree. The impact threw Jaime and two of the suitcases out of the car into heavy vegetation. We sat for a few seconds. Shocked.

My mother jumped out, screaming, 'Jaime. Jaime!'

Don Pascal hauled Liliana, Orlando, and me out of the car. We stared at each other.

I squinted and saw Mamá kneeling on the ground, lifting my brother into her arms. Soft rays of light were now breaking across the horizon, burning away the fog. I noticed that his right leg was badly scraped. We sat on a small grassy area while Mamá cleaned Jaime's bloody gashes with water from don Pascal's water bottle. We said little. Don Pascal finally got up. He was a man of middle stature with chalky brown skin.

His sunken, wary eyes twinkled as he said, 'I think we are all okay. I need to see if the car still works.'

He jumped into the old Willys and put it in reverse. We clapped with joy as soon as we saw the car move, dragging the bumper along.

'I'm going to tie the bumper with this rope, and then we can go home,' said don Pascal. A strong breeze suddenly made the yellow flowers that were near me spin around on their stems like mini wind spinners. It was then when I remembered my castanets.

'Oh no. I forgot my castanets,' I squealed.

'We can't go back to your grandmother's house. They'll take you away from me. I'll try to buy you another pair,' Mamá said.

'I don't want another pair,' I snapped. Then I felt my voice break: 'I want the ones Papá gave me.'

When I turned around, I saw my mother holding Orlando on her lap. Jaime and Liliana were next to her, one on each side. Jaime was covering his right leg with a bloodstained handkerchief. Mamá's tousled hair and furrowed brows made her look years older.

Look at us. We are nothing but fugitives, all of us, including Papá. How can he expect me to look after our family? Isn't that his job? My stomach suddenly contracted. I swallowed several times so that I wouldn't get sick.

Don Pascal handed me a rag and a metal container. When I finally stopped feeling ill, I sat on the ground, drenched in sweat.

'Excuse me, Señora Cecilia, but how do you know they will not look for us in Fusa?'

'Don't forget, Grandpa Miguel is a well-known ex-military officer,' Mamá said. 'They would have the entire army after them if they got near us.'

'All right, then let's go,' ordered don Pascal. 'We can't waste any more time.'

Without questioning, we jumped in the jeep and left.

Don Pascal was right. The trip back to Fusagasugá was long and exhausting. At first, the weather was humid and hot, but as we climbed over the easternmost Andean range, the weather became unbearably cold and foggy. Don Pascal stopped and placed the soft top over the jeep, but it had so many rips that it was useless. After an hour of driving in the cold, we found a peasant woman selling wool blankets by the roadside. Mamá bought four, and we shared, but we couldn't stop shivering. The rattling of the loose bumper was so loud it was difficult to understand what was being said. We stopped only to eat and sleep, both inside the jeep.

Two days later, we passed Bogotá. We drove for what seemed like hours, plowing through busy streets of early rush hour. We finally left La Sabana, which many called the high plateau, close to midmorning. After some time, we descended the mountain. The warm breeze greeted us. Large trees and colorful plants dressed the small hills around us. The ordeal was over.

Grandma Emilia, Grandpa Miguel, Mario, and Bella were waiting for us by the large metal gates. The Labrador barked and wagged her tail as don Pascal helped us out of the car. We celebrated our return. No one mentioned anything about Papá and his family. The only thing we talked about after dinner was our journey back from the coast.

My grandparents and Mario waited until we went to bed to ask Mamá about our exodus. I returned to the dining room hoping to find one of my notebooks, and that's when I overheard my mother recounting our escape. In distress, I listened behind the open door. Apparently, Carmiña had called Mamá to warn her that Papá was going to take us outside of the country. She had urged her to take us back home as soon as possible. Carmiña also confessed that she loved him and felt terrible for betraying him but, she felt that we'd be better off with our mother than alone in a boarding school in another country. At the end of the conversation, my mother asked my grandparents never to mention a word about our father to us. My hope of getting my parents back together was gone, like my castanets, like Papá. With it all, a part of me had died.

I went to my bedroom and prayed to my guardian angel for him and for us.

Life in Fusa

Months went by without news from Papá. Life in Fusa went on like *salpicón*, a Colombian beverage, a medley of orange and melon juice; each sip filled with surprises. You never knew what was coming next, sweet or sour.

On a rainy day in 1965, I found our uniforms neatly folded on my bed, two white cotton blouses and two blue skirts, and underneath the bed were two pairs of black leather shoes.

'It is time to go back to school. I left your clothes on Rocío's bed,' my mother said to Liliana and me as she peeked into our room.

I could only recall scattered pictures of our first school back in Colombia. We had been out of the country for over five years, and even though our parents spoke to us in Spanish, our language skills in Spanish were two years below grade level. This made it challenging for all of us to do well in school. I could speak three languages, all at different levels, and none of them proficiently. A sense of not belonging followed me everywhere I went.

'Thanks,' was all I said.

Since our escape from Papá, my mother evaded all conversations related to him and to our past life. As a result, I learned to refrain from sharing my feelings. The only person I felt comfortable speaking with was Mario, so one Sunday afternoon, I went to visit him. We had been told not to bother him because he was ill with pneumonia, but I went anyway. A nurse was leaving when I arrived.

'How is he?' I asked.

'Not well. But I can assure you that the old, stubborn man will not go without a fight. If I were you, I'd stay away from him. He may still be contagious, plus he's in a bad mood.'

The heavyset nurse wrinkled her nose.

I went into his house and closed the door behind me. The welcoming living room had a corner table with books and a radio on it. A plush couch and an armchair were on the opposite wall. In the middle, brightening the room, was the colorful rug where I had often sat while Mario read poems by Burgos, Mistral, and Neruda. The neatly kept dining room and kitchen were on one side of the living room. Mario's studio was on the opposite side. It looked like it had been untouched for some time.

A wall-to-wall window let a timid sun into Mario's workshop. Outside, the rain had ceased. Small, crystal-like raindrops hung on the large, heart-shaped leaves of the nearby bushes. Aside from orchids, Grandma Emilia spent a large portion of her day tending to these dramatic shrubs she called Elephant's Ears. Inside the room, a blank canvas sat on an easel. Four unfinished paintings were on the floor, leaning against Mario's bookshelves. On the other side of the window was a drawer-filled cabinet. On top of it, there were several glass jars with brushes, a box with pencils, and a container with pieces of drawing charcoal. His stained smock lay on the back of a chair. In the middle of the room was a wooden table packed with carefully organized art supplies. With my heart racing, I went to the bookshelves and searched for newspapers or any document that might give me a clue as to the whereabouts of my father. No one left newspapers around our house where my siblings and I could read them. The only TV we had in the house was always restricted unless there was adult supervision.

I found a paper tucked in between two books.

The headlines screamed out: **Dr. Velásquez, FARC, Communism, and Violence.**

My heart pounded inside my chest as I read on.

'The Doctor,' as he is known, left Canada to organize the Guerrilla Solidarity Movement in Latin America. He has joined forces with Manuel Marulanda, the founder of las FARC.

This confirmed what Papá's friend, who visited Mamá after the accident, had said about him. Worse, I recognized Marulanda as the farmworker who was standing near my father. The photo in the newspaper was blurry, but I could tell he was the same person who had come one day to visit Papá. That day, Colonel Moncayo also brought another man whose name I couldn't remember. A few moments after, it came to me, the name Leonel, Grandma Sarai's driver. Perhaps he had been the one who had thanked Papá for saving his hand. I didn't remember him, because I was too young when I met him or perhaps I had forgotten. All that was important to me back then was that the three visitors had brought Nala and Catia, my dogs. It all made sense; Papá had been involved in the movement since I was a little girl.

All of this was too much for me to bear. I placed my hands over my head, trying not to think about him, and accidentally dropped a metal box Mario had left on one shelf, scattering oil paint tubes all over the tile floor.

'Who's there?' Mario's infirm, gruff voice made me halt.

'It's just me,' the words croaked out of my throat.

'Who? Speak up. Get in here.'

I kneeled on the floor and immediately picked up the paints, placing the tubes in the metal box, setting the container back on the shelf, and tucking the article between the books.

'I'm coming.' Walking down the hallway, I found his room. 'I'm sorry I didn't bring you coffee. They say it's not good for you.'

'Ha, I'll never stop drinking coffee. I don't care what that doctor says. He's a quack anyway. And open the curtains. That nurse is an imbecile.' He coughed. 'I told her I don't want to sleep.'

I pulled the heavy drapes to one side, letting the sunshine stream into the dark room. Mario lay on his bed, the sheet pulled up to his chest. His bald head shone with the light. A few gray hairs peeked from behind his ear.

'Are you sick?'

Mario rubbed his forehead. 'You sneak into my house, you rummage through my things, and then ask me ridiculous questions?'

'I'm sorry, I wanted to see you.'

'What do you want?'

'The newspaper—' I mumbled.

'What? Speak up.' He coughed again.

'How are you?' I said to change the subject.

The fact that I hadn't been able to reunite my parents saddened me. But perhaps my mother was right; maybe it was best not to know anything about Papá. At least not for now. All I needed was a new plan.

'As you see, not well. But what else do you want?'

'I haven't heard from Jocelyne in a long time.'

Wheezing, he sat up in bed. 'She is probably busy.'

'It's not like her.' Tears filled my eyes.

Mario looked at me, and his expression softened. 'If you want to know about your papá, come back another day.' He blew his nose.

'I will.'

'Open the window. That damn nurse wants to suffocate me.'

I cracked the window open. A gust of wind ruffled a stack of papers he had on his night table. Mario turned and looked at the papers. In that instant, I sensed he was hiding something from me.

'Do you have a letter for me?'

'No.' Mario coughed again.

Propelled by rising anger, I pulled the drawer open, and that's when I saw my father's neat handwriting on an envelope. I grabbed the letter.

'How long have you had this letter?' I roared, my face burning with sheer fury.

'What letter?'

'This one, of course.' I waved the envelope in the air. 'Tell me, how long have you had it?'

'Weeks.' Mario covered his face with his hands. 'Girl, you give me a headache.'

No wonder we hadn't heard from our father since we left Barranquilla; Mario had been hiding our letters. I sat on the floor and opened it.

January 6, 1965

My dear Rocío,

Please read this letter to your brothers and sister. I love you and think of you all the time, specifically when I see children playing or when I see them walking to school. I hope your appetite has improved and that you have stopped getting nauseous. Every time you eat, think of me and remember that you are always in my heart. If there is something that is bothering you, let me know what it is. Write a letter and send it to Grandma Sarai. I will do whatever I can to fix it. A few weeks ago, I received a letter from you and Liliana, which made me very happy. Let me know how your brothers and sister are doing. I will send some money to your mamá so that she can give each of you a few pesos. Please write and tell me how you are doing at school. Education is very important, especially since we live in a society that values you for what you know. Learn to love books. Someone like you, who is intelligent and kind, will walk through life leaving a luminous wake, and in doing so, you will be a model to others. Imagine the satisfaction you can bring to those of us who love you!

All right, my dear Rocío, give a kiss to my other ducklings. Receive my love, your papá who thinks of you.

Papá

I stood up, crinkling the letter in my hands. A whirlwind of emotions, feeling my father so close yet so removed, were spinning inside of me.

'Your grandfather told me to get rid of it, but I was saving it for you.'

I closed my eyes to stop myself from screaming at Mario.

Liar. I don't believe you anymore.

When I opened my eyes, he had turned his back on me. The weight of disappointment and betrayal hovered over me as I walked back to the main house. I was angry at my family for keeping me away from my father. I was furious at Mario. The only person I could trust was now keeping information about Papá from me. And Papá's letter made no sense. No mention of Russia. The authorities were after him, and he had written a letter as if he were on a business trip and would soon come back home. How could he expect me to be healthy and do well in school if he wasn't around to do his job? How could he fix my problems if he wasn't here?

When I got home, I went to my room and hid the letter inside the notebook I was using as a diary. I waited until Liliana was asleep to write a letter to my father. I didn't want to tell her yet that he had written. She blushed every time she withheld something from Mamá, which gave her away. First, I needed a plan; then I would recruit her.

I wrote, *Dear Papá,* then tapped the notebook with the pencil for some time, unsure what to write. After staring at the blank page, I closed the notebook and put it back on the night table together with the pencil.

'Now,' Liliana squeaked, pulling me away from my thoughts, 'turn the light off!'

I did. When I closed my eyes, the nightmare I had had in Barranquilla flashed in my head. Blood dripped down on one side of Papá's face.

That's it. I need to protect Papá so that he won't get hurt.

I had to go back to Mario's house and try to unveil the colossal puzzle Papá had left us. It felt like the only way to bring him home.

The sun was rising when I heard my mother say, 'You can't be late for school.' Liliana and I stretched in bed. My eyes felt heavy. The night before, I had spent many hours thinking about ways I could make my father come home, pretend I was sick, hide for days so my parents would have to look for me, or escape from Mamá and go back to Barranquilla so Grandma Sarai would bring Papá to me. But in the end, nothing seemed like a good idea. All these plans would have devastated my mother. Tossing and turning, I had eventually fallen asleep.

It wasn't until we heard Mamá scream again, 'You'll be in trouble if you don't hurry.'

At that, my sister and I jumped out of bed, got dressed, and hurried to the dining room carrying our bookbags. Jaime and Orlando were already at the table, drinking milk. The sweet aroma of fresh-brewed coffee and baked bread hung in the air.

'Niña Rocío, this is for you,' Avelina said, as she placed the cup on the saucer in front of me. 'And this is yours, niña Liliana.' She poured hot milk into Liliana's cup.

Liliana twisted her mouth to one side.

'I can't wait to turn fourteen so that I can drink coffee too.'

I smiled, glad to see that each day she was speaking more and more, even if it was to complain. Smiling, I thought of the time I found her trying on one of my bras, stuffing the empty cups with toilet paper. Her skinny body still resembled that of a boy. No hips or chest. When I opened the door, she quickly slipped it off. I pretended I hadn't seen what she was doing. 'A few more years and you'll be wearing one of your own,' I had reassured her.

'Don't tease me. I wasn't doing anything,' she had said before storming out of the bathroom.

Avelina left a basket of steaming rolls on the table and went back to the kitchen. We all looked forward to her *mogollitas*, the round wheat bran rolls she had made. When we finished breakfast, we grabbed our bags and ran to the car where Grandpa Miguel was waiting for us.

'Get in, get in, monsters.' He opened the rear doors for us. Motioning to the car, he said, 'How do you like my car? It's a classic.'

'Nice. But what happened to your station wagon?' I asked.

'Since your mother's accident, I haven't cared much for that car.'

Grandpa got into the driver's seat. Liliana and I sat in the back. Jaime and Orlando jumped in front. Grandpa drove us off the property and onto the road that would take us to the main highway. He drove proudly, his left arm resting on the open window frame while he steered the wheel with his right hand. Along the road, farmers waved to him as they greeted him.

'Capitan Díaz!'

Our grandfather touched the tip of his fedora in a salute, then muttered back funny greetings that the farmers couldn't hear.

'Hello, flat nose. Hello, shorty. Hello, lady who doesn't shut up.' He chuckled, making my brothers giggle.

Liliana and I were preoccupied because the cushions in the back seat were old and had sunk low.

'Grandpa, we can't see out the window.'

Orlando and Jaime turned around and, pointing at us, cracked up. Suddenly, the interior of the car smelled like exhaust fumes. We coughed and coughed until we were all laughing out of control.

'Don't make fun of my car; it's a collectible. Keep laughing, and you are all going to have to walk to school,' Grandpa scolded us, but in the rearview mirror, I could see a smirk on his face.

By the time we reached the main highway, Liliana and I had discovered that if we kneeled on our seats, holding on to the backrest, we could see outside. And soon, the scent of morning dew evaporating from the lush vegetation replaced the smell of burned gasoline.

'Did you know that I bought my first car when your mamá was a small girl?'

'What did you do before then? How did you go anywhere?' Jaime said.

'We walked, or I rode my bike. But then one day, I bought a 1936 Ford Sedan. I was the first one to own a car in our neighborhood. All our neighbors came to touch the car and to check the tracks the tires had left on the road.' Grandpa handed his wallet to Jaime. 'Open it up and check out my driver's license. It's number three.'

Grandpa must have been distracted as he told us this story, because he didn't see the commuter bus coming to the intersection where the bus had the right of way. I tried to warn him, but it was too late. Grandpa didn't stop. A violent impact followed the loud screeching of tires. Liliana and I flew over our brothers, landing headfirst in the front seat, our skirts flipped over our heads. After we had untangled the human knot, we helped Orlando and Jaime back into their seats. The boys were stunned but not hurt. Our bodies had shielded them.

'Are you all right?' Grandpa stared at us with fearful eyes. He had a couple of bumps and a cut on his forehead.

'I think so.' Jaime straightened his shirt and combed his hair with his fingers. A burning sensation ramped up my back. 'I think I hit the dashboard.'

'Me too,' Liliana grumbled.

Orlando picked up his math book, which was trapped under Jaime's foot.

'My book. The teacher is going to be upset,' he moaned, wiping the dirt off its cover with his trembling hands.

'Orlando, we almost died, and you're worried about a stupid book?' I snapped.

'Not a word about this to your mamá or grandmother.' Grandpa wiped the blood from his forehead with a handkerchief.

Outside the car, a husky, dark-skinned man screamed at our grandfather, 'Are you crazy? You wrecked my bus.'

'It was your fault—' Grandpa was interrupted when we saw the man's strong hand reach in through the window and grab him by the neck.

'Let him go,' I screamed.

Out of nowhere, two other men opened the passenger doors of our car and pulled my brothers out. My sister and I jumped out after them.

'Do you need to go to the hospital?' asked the younger man.

The four of us held hands and shook our heads.

'We can take you,' offered the older man. He tilted his hat to one side, almost covering his right eye.

'No thanks.' I stood in front of my siblings as they huddled behind me.

I thought of Leonel, Grandma Sarai's taxi driver, and our escape.

Could these also be men who know my father? Is he still trying to take us with him to Russia?

'Don't touch them,' I snarled.

'The hospital is nearby. You need to be checked,' said the older man as he pulled me towards him.

'Leave her alone.'

Somehow Grandpa had gotten away from the irate bus driver who stayed behind, yelling, 'I'm calling the police.'

Around him, there were a few curious bystanders. As Grandpa approached, the older man let go of me.

'We're just trying to help.'

'I know who you are. Tell Jaime to go to hell. The kids aren't going anywhere.'

My heart began pounding in my chest when I heard my father's name.

In tears, I said, 'You know Papá?'

They gazed at one another, then hopped into a nearby jeep and sped away.

'Who were they?' I confronted Grandpa.

'Nobody.'

I barked, 'You know, but won't tell us. Why do you keep so many secrets? I know what you are doing. I found a letter.'

There was a sniffle, so I turned around. My siblings were still huddling together, and Liliana was rubbing her teary eyes.

The bus driver was yelling, 'Come back, you old man. The officer is here.'

Grandpa pulled me to one side, and pressing my arm, he whispered, 'Rocío, you shouldn't be in contact with your papá. That will put all of us in jeopardy. He has gone into hiding, and the entire army is looking for him. They don't like commies.' Grandpa tapped his forehead in frustration. 'And they are killing his supporters.'

Kill? This means they could hurt us all.

I flinched with fear. 'But he is my papá, and I have to protect him.'

'What? That is insane.'

'Sir.' A skinny policeman called to my grandfather.

Before walking to the officer, Grandpa fixed his eyes on mine and said, 'You have no idea what you are talking about. No one can protect him. It's too late.'

Like a dagger, his words pierced through me. I shuddered.

Why can't I protect my father? I could at least tell him about my dream. Perhaps he'll believe me and save himself. I had been right about Mamá.

In silence, I watched as my grandfather walked away.

After studying the scene, the policeman informed him and the bus driver that they would each have to pay for the damages to their own cars. Apparently, they were both at fault. Like our grandfather, the bus driver had some minor bruises on his face. We had been fortunate that the bus was empty. Grandpa had a grin on his face when he noticed his Packard was intact.

'See, my car is like a tank!'

I was still shaking from the accident when we dropped the boys at Nibia, an all-boys school. Grandpa then drove Liliana and me to La Presentación, our new all-girls Catholic school. The steep stairs in front of the red brick building seemed endless. I held Liliana's hand as we walked up. At the top, we were about to ring the doorbell when a nun opened the massive, ornate door.

'You must be the Velásquez students.'

I was still trying to make sense of the conversation I had had with Grandpa about my father, when I heard Liliana reply, 'Yes, we are.'

'Well then, follow me. Mother María is waiting for you.'

Hundreds of girls dressed in uniform just like us were giggling and talking in the hallway. Suddenly, I felt drops of sweat on my forehead.

'No, Rocío, you can't get sick here. Not the first day.' Liliana pulled me into a bathroom. 'Please don't,' she begged, walking me inside a stall.

But before I knew it, I began vomiting with uncontrollable spasms.

I heard someone say, 'How gross! She's one of the new girls.'

Liliana closed the door to my stall.

'Are the Velásquez sisters in here?' I heard the nun calling. 'I lost you. Where did you go?'

'Yes. Sorry, Sister, but Rocío doesn't feel well.'

'What is wrong with her?'

'Nothing. She does this all the time.'

I came out of the stall and cleaned up. 'I'm ready.'

'You look like a ghost.' The nun frowned.

I saw myself in the mirror. The freckles on my cheeks seemed much darker in contrast to my pale skin. My shoulder-length, curly hair was held back with a headband. Part of my bangs had gotten wet when I washed my face and were pasted onto one side of my forehead.

'I'll get you a glass of water,' the nun offered.

The rectory was on the opposite side of the main door. When we arrived, the nun that had accompanied us excused herself and left.

'Come in.' Mother María stood up from her chair and walked towards us. 'I just spoke with your grandfather. I am so glad the accident was not serious,' said the hunchbacked sister. She then directed us to a couple of chairs that were in front of her desk. She moved behind her desk and sat down. 'Velásquez? Any relationship with the famous Dr. Velásquez?' She stared at us.

'No,' my sister and I said in unison.

I felt sick again; this was the first time we had denied knowing our own father. I was staring at my shoes when I saw Liliana cross her legs. This was our signal for *we had to lie, so it doesn't count*. However, I still felt bad about denying my father, the person I loved so dearly and missed so much. On the other hand, we had no choice. We were tired of people looking at us, questioning us, distrustful after learning our last name.

'Hmm.' Seeming unconvinced, she continued, 'All right. We have a parents' night in a few months. Will you sing a song in English or French?'

I was going to say no, but Mother María interrupted me.

'No buts, please. I know you speak English and some French because your mother told me. So, I can count on you, right?'

I laid my right hand over my left hand, the hand signal for *we have no choice*. Liliana understood. 'What song?' she asked.

'You decide.' The nun stood up and shook our hands. 'Sister Cecilia will walk you to your classrooms now.'

The nun who had shown us around earlier was by the door, holding a glass of water. I drank it. The cool water felt soothing in my empty stomach. When I was finished, I thanked her and handed the empty glass back to her. She then walked Liliana and me to our classrooms.

All eyes followed my every move as I entered the classroom. It felt the same each time we changed schools. Sister Teresa raised her bushy eyebrows when she read my name aloud. 'Rocío Velásquez? Any relationship to—'

I interrupted, 'No.'

The girls in the class whispered and giggled.

'No talking in class,' Sister Teresa admonished. 'You are late.'

'I'm sorry. We had a car accident.'

The silence in the room and staring eyes brought back the light-headed sensation I had felt earlier in the bathroom. Like Papá had taught me once, I inhaled, and when my lungs were full of air, I slowly let the air out.

'Thank God you are okay.'

The sister showed me to my desk before resuming the lesson.

I spent the rest of the day thinking about what had happened that morning. My grandfather had been driving like he was the only one on the road. Even worse, he seemed preoccupied with his car rather than concerned about us. And the men who pulled my brothers out of the car knew Papá? Were they going to kidnap us and take us to Papá as Grandpa claimed?

Wait! Maybe *Papá is nearby and I can talk to him.*

Sister Teresa startled me. 'You've been very pensive today. It is time to go home.'

When I looked around the room, I realized that all my classmates had left.

'Sorry.'

I ran out of the building and found Liliana waiting for me at the bottom of the stairs. Soon after, Grandpa picked us up. My brothers were in the back seat. On the way home, I felt as though someone were looking at me, so I turned around, and in the distance, I saw a jeep that resembled the one with the two men from that morning following us. When I looked again, they were gone.

Unmasking the Kidnapper's Plot

Our grandfather seemed to have forgotten about the men in the jeep. He was always too busy driving and dodging cars to notice anything else. Angry drivers honked their horns every time he cut in front of them or forgot to make the proper hand signals. Liliana and I worried we would have another accident, but my brothers roared with laughter at every incident, making our grandfather angry. He threatened that if we wouldn't stop mocking him, he would make us get out of the car and walk, though he never did.

Instead, my sister and I stayed glued to the car windows, wary of any car that followed us for too long. One day after school, Liliana and I sat on the last two steps and played jacks as we waited for Grandpa to pick us up. After an hour or so, Liliana took a water container out of her bag, had a sip, and passed it to me.

'I guess Grandpa forgot about us.'

The other students had gone home. The employees from nearby businesses were crowding the streets.

'Yes, he did.'

I was putting the jacks, our favorite game, away inside a plastic bag when I saw the jeep with the two men approaching. My heart raced.

'The jeep,' Liliana screamed and pointed at the car. 'Let's run.'

'No.' I grabbed her by her arm and fixed my eyes on hers.

With her bright, dark eyes wide open, she squealed, 'Why not?'

I looked around to see if I could find Papá, but he was nowhere to be seen. Panic swept over me.

'Let me go. You're hurting me,' said Liliana.

I held on to her arm, trying to figure out what to do. When I tore my eyes away from hers, I saw the driver park the jeep nearby. The older of the two men was sitting in the passenger seat. The younger man got out, leaving the door open.

'Get in, girls, your mamá told us to take you home.'

'I don't know you,' I said.

The driver's hoarse voice demanded, 'Get in, you damn girls.'

Suddenly, the young man grabbed my sister by one arm and pulled her into the jeep. I reached out for her. Struggling, Liliana broke free, pushing the man away. I picked up our bags, and holding hands with my sister, we sprinted away. We crossed streets, wheezing in panic, evading upcoming cars. Liliana yelped at the honking of the angry drivers.

The pair abandoned the car and chased after us. I dropped our bookbags and continued running. After a couple of blocks into the pursuit, we found the main plaza. The crowded streets and the local vendors' stands became an intricate maze we used to hide in.

We darted through narrow passages left between the different merchants' tables and arrived at the food stalls. The smell of roasted beef made me gag, so Liliana pulled me away from the plaza, and we continued running. Two blocks later, we arrived at the Church of Our Lady of Bethlehem. Breathing hard and drenched in sweat, we hid behind one of the enormous open front doors. Neither of us said a word.

Once we thought we were safe, Liliana gazed at me with tears in her eyes and asked, 'Why don't they leave us alone?'

'Papá wants to see us.'

'Papá? They know him?'

'Yes.'

'Then why don't we go with them?'

'Because—'

A firm hand yanked me out from behind the door. The man then pulled my sister out with his other hand.

'Stop running. We don't want to hurt you. Your papá just wants to talk to you. See? He sent this note for you.'

The young man squinted with frustration. The older man was nowhere to be seen. I grabbed the note in Papá's handwriting and began reading.

My dear Rocío,
I hope you and your siblings are doing well. Soon, I will be traveling outside the country and would like to see you before—

'Come on. I'm running out of time,' the man said, exasperated.

I crumbled the letter in my hand.

'If he wants to see us, why doesn't he come to us himself?'

'He can't.'

'I will go then but she has to stay.'

'Are you crazy?' My sister tightened her grip on my arm. And then she began screaming, 'Help. Help. They are trying to kidnap us.'

It suddenly filled the man with rage. He covered her mouth with his hand. Angry, I kicked him so hard in the shin, he let go of her.

Soon, churchgoers and local merchants surrounded us.

'They're trying to kidnap us,' I said.

The man pushed his way through the crowd and escaped. My sister and I embraced. The sound of the police sirens brought a sense of relief, but also of intense sadness. After a long interrogation, in which we denied knowing our pursuers, the officers drove us home. In the car, I desperately searched for Papá's note, but couldn't find it.

'I lost his letter.' I wept.

Liliana leaned back, closed her eyes, and squeezed my hand.

The police officers must have noticed how frail and unhappy we felt, because they talked all the way home. They explained that the Packard's radiator was leaking, so our grandfather had taken it to the mechanic. Even though he was late picking us up, Grandpa had assumed we would wait for him. When he didn't find us, he scooped our brothers up and went home, assuming we were with our mother. When he realized we were not at home, he contacted the police commissioner, who sent his officers looking for us.

After a while, I stopped listening. I let go of my sister's hand, and with my forehead resting on the window, I stared at the sky. The dusk had swallowed the last rays of sun and with it, my hopes of seeing Papá.

Mario's Revelations

When we arrived home after our ordeal, Mamá and our grandparents hurried to meet us at the gate. Bella paced next to them. When she saw Liliana and I get out of the car, she wagged her tail and pushed ahead to welcome us. 'My girls.'

Our mother extended her arms to us. Her sorrowful eyes and splotchy cheeks reminded me of our time in Montréal. So many times, I had walked into the dining room to find her sobbing, her arms over her head, forehead resting on the table. Liliana was right. What had I been thinking? My mother would've been shattered had she lost one of us.

A cascade of hugs and kisses made me realize how much I needed to be held. Mamá's, Grandpa's, and Grandma's faces brightened with relief. The officers pulled our grandfather to the side and said something to him. Sometime later, we waved goodbye to them. We then went and sat on the front porch. The adults had begun questioning us about the pursuers and their intentions when Avelina walked out with a tray. She gave us each a cup of hot *aguapanela* with lemon and hurried back to the kitchen, taking the tray with her. The sweet drink felt soothing to our wearied hearts.

My sister and I told them the same story we had shared with the police. Mamá raised one eyebrow, perhaps doubtful of our version of the story.

'I'm glad you are fine; that is all that matters.'

Our grandparents agreed.

'We lost our books,' I said, changing the conversation so that Mamá wouldn't ask questions about the men.

Mamá inhaled. 'Girls, you know that your papá doesn't always send me money.'

Grandma sipped her *aguapanela*. 'We'll buy the books, right, Miguel?' She gave him a nudge and Grandpa smiled at us.

'Thank you. You are already doing so much for us.' Mamá touched my grandparents' hands, and her cheeks colored red. 'I hope to find work or do something to repay you.'

It surprised me when no one probed further about the incident. Lies used to outrage my parents. It was clear to me now that we knew Papá was gone for

200

good. All he wanted was to take us to Russia so that we would become communist like him. We were hiding from the truth, even Mamá. Or maybe we were pretending because the truth hurt too much.

Avelina came back. 'Dinner is served.'

'Thank you, Avelina.'

Grandma stood up and walked to the dining room. We followed, but I noticed there were only five place settings.

'What about Orlando and Jaime? Where's Mario?'

Mamá took a deep breath. 'Mario is not well yet. Jaime is in trouble, and Orlando's left eye itches. I am concerned about his vision.'

His left eye was often irritated so Mamá treated him with sticky eye creams. She and my brother spent long hours at the doctor's office, but nothing seemed to work for Orlando's eye.

'The doctors here don't know what it is or how to help him, so I called to make an appointment with a specialist at the Barraquer Clinic in Bogotá.' Mamá's face was flushed with anguish.

I had heard that people from around the world traveled to be treated at that clinic.

'That must be expensive. How are we paying for that?'

'We'll see.' Mamá's voice broke.

'I guess we can't expect Papá to pay for it,' I snapped.

A sudden sorrow clouded us as everyone stopped eating and looked at me with wounded eyes.

Liliana came to my rescue when she smirked and asked, 'What did Jaime do this time?'

Avelina began placing the food on the table. *Arroz con pollo*, rice with chicken, and vegetables, which was another of Avelina's specialties. '

'Delicious,' Grandpa said.

Mamá continued, 'The principal took Jaime's notebook away because instead of taking notes, he was drawing rude cartoons of his teachers. I'm so angry at him.'

Grandma Emilia changed the subject.

'Girls, your mamá is going to need your help. As soon as she gets the appointment at the clinic, Rocío, you will go with her and Orlando to Bogotá. Liliana, you will need to help us keep an eye on Jaime. The neighbor complained that he was shooting rocks in the air with his slingshot, and he even hit one worker in the forehead.'

'Why me?' Liliana complained.

My mother rubbed my sister's back. 'Because you are older than him.'

'Is the worker all right?' I asked.

'Yes. But that's another reason why Jaime is grounded. I don't know what I'm going to do with that boy.' Mamá swirled the food around the plate. 'Now, let's speak about something more positive. Mother María sent me a note to let me know you apparently are singing a song in English at a parents' night?'

My sister and I had forgotten about our deal with her. Liliana and I exchanged glances.

'We're singing Jingle Bells,' Liliana said.

I felt Jingle Bells was a stupid, childish song. But then I reconsidered. With all that was happening in our lives, any song would work.

'Sure,' I said. 'That is what we'll do.'

'But that is a Christmas song and it is not Christmas.' Mamá scratched her head.

'No one will know. Plus, we don't know other songs.' I argued.

I was physically and emotionally exhausted. I was glad no one else objected to our song choice. Perhaps because we were all worried about Orlando's eye. It was often red, and he complained of blurry vision. And Jaime had become a problem at school and at home. I had to choose. Papá had left, so my loyalty was with my mother now. I had to help Mamá.

Even though I had decided to support my mother, I still wanted to know about my father's whereabouts. I went to see Mario again, hoping to get a straight answer this time. The door of his house was ajar, so I knocked.

'Mario, are you here?'

'Who is it?'

'It's me, Rocío. Can I come in?'

'What a dumb question. Get in here.'

I found Mario sitting on the couch, reading. He glanced at me with his glasses perched on the tip of his nose. 'You came to visit the old man. What do you want this time?'

'Nothing,' I said apologetically.

'Your grandfather told me about those men. You know they are involved with your papá, right? You can't lie to me.' He took his glasses off, placed the book on a small table, and gazed at me.

'We... we—'

'Don't we, we... me. I know you too well. You should not cover for your papá anymore. Now tell me what really happened.'

Standing up, I recounted the incident while Mario listened. He closed his eyes and put his hands on the quilt covering his legs. He remained still until I finished; then he opened his eyes.

'There is nothing you can do to help him, believe me,' he said, throwing his hands up in frustration.

Crushed by the weight of extreme sadness, I collapsed on the chair next to him. 'Look, I'm sorry, but you need to be pragmatic,' he whispered. 'Your mamá is dealing with a lot, and you are going to have to be by her side. Stop being so idealistic. Like I told you before, you are just like your papá. We can't control others. You can only control yourself. He is going to do whatever he wants, and you can't stop him.'

'Would you at least let me read the newspapers?'

'You are so stubborn.' He stood up. 'Fine, but you stop whatever you are doing. I don't think your mamá can take one more problem. That's a deal?'

'I will,' I lied.

He paused for a second. Then, tilting his head to one side, he sighed.

'Come with me.'

We went to his studio, where he pulled out a couple of books from his library. Behind them, there was a folder with several newspaper articles and other documents. 'What is it you want to know?'

'Where is Papá, and why is everyone after him?'

'Well, first I want you to read this article written by a newspaper reporter who infiltrated a guerrilla camp and who worked with your papá.'

'What do you mean, worked? At a hospital?'

'I don't mean a job. I mean, spent time with him.' Mario paced, rubbing his head as if he were searching for the right words. 'Anyway, this underground publication has a section on your papá. I didn't want to give it to you before because I didn't think you were old enough. But I guess you are a mature girl. I think it will help you answer some of your questions.'

Mario handed me a three-page narrative titled **Marquetalia**.

'What is this?' I asked.

'That was a small territory of the country where armed communist peasants lived. They were like an independent republic within Colombia. That ended last year.'

'How do you know this man is telling the truth?' I challenged Mario.

'Go ahead, read it, you'll see.'

Filled with curiosity and elated that finally, at fifteen, someone was treating me like an adult, I sat on the floor and read the newsprint chronicle.

May 21, 1965

Marquetalia
By Eduardo Alvarado

This is the story of my year assignment as a member of the guerrilla movement in Colombia, which ended in 1964 with Operation Sovereignty. In 1963, I left my family and my job as a journalist in Bogotá and moved to the Republic of Marquetalia. This was a territory that was controlled by communist armed peasants as well as a number of intellectuals and other supporters of the cause. It is important to note that I included in this diary my personal interpretation of the main events and the reactions of those who participated in them. No one can remember in detail what happened in the span of two years. To make sense of some of my notes, which I wrote during highly difficult situations, I later interviewed guerrilla combatants, farmers, and military officers.

The Diary
During my first year as a trainee, I was sent to a guerrilla camp near Marquetalia where I received basic combat and physical training…

I skimmed over the first part of Alvarado's diary and didn't slow down until I found a date, followed by my father's name. When I read, *On January 10, 1964,* I remembered that had been the same year we visited Grandma Sarai during Hanukkah. The same year we had last seen Papá. Heartbroken, I held the paper close to my chest as tears filled my eyes. When I could finally regain my composure, I continued reading.

… seven men, three women, and I, commanded by Dr. Velázquez, hiked a trail deep in the Andes. The doctor was the only one who knew I was a journalist. He argued that the facts were often misconstrued by interest groups and foreign governments in an attempt to eradicate communism in Latin America. My role was to bring to light the truth of the events that were to take place during my stay in this remote area of the country.
We hiked for days on a treacherous trail. On the fourth day, we walked for hours without resting. We finally stopped so that the doctor could study the map. The rest of us sat by a large tree and drank water from our canteens. We watched how a misty blanket covered the green mountains ahead of us. We

were all cold, muddy, and hungry. We had very little food left, and exhaustion
had slowed down our pace.
'We are almost there,' Dr. Velásquez said. He spoke very little during our long
and strenuous four-day hike.
Hours later, the team descended onto a plateau inhabited by a small guerrilla
community. Three armed men were waiting for us.
'Take us to the camp, please,' the doctor said to the receiving party. The
uniformed men asked us if we wanted to rest for a while, but Dr. Velázquez
refused to stop. We drank more water and continued walking until we crossed
a rudimentary village.

'That's definitely Papá!' I exclaimed. 'If we were learning English, or riding
a bike, or had problems at school, he always pushed us. Obstacles to him were
just learning opportunities.'
'See, I told you this man knows your papá.'
Mario walked back to his reading chair. I stayed in his studio, reading. It was
as if someone had opened a heavy shutter into the past, allowing me to take a
glimpse at my father's life without us. Elated, I devoured the rest of the article.
Alvarado described the town of about fifty families. Children ran around the
streets. Cows were being herded in the nearby hills. Plantations of corn
flourishing in the fertile soil. Near the creek, the travelers found a series of
well-guarded brick cabins. Manuel Marulanda, the commandant, came out of
the largest cabin to greet them and invited them to join the others for lunch. A
stuffed pig lay on a wooden table. People walked around it, filling their plates
with rice, vegetables, and pork. Alvarado and the doctor, as everyone called
my father, excused themselves and went to their cabins.

After lunch, the group was called into Marulanda's shack. Alvarado was
introduced as the teacher. That became his nickname. The group welcomed
my father. There was a table filled with medicine. Maps were taped to the
walls. Marulanda warned everyone that there would be an imminent military
attack. They just didn't know exactly when it would happen. A few minutes
later, Ayala, another guerrilla leader, and five others joined the group. Papá

explained that the resistance was fighting other fronts, and that they were the only combatants who had come to support Marulanda and his men.

The men decided all they could do was prepare for the attack while they waited for their informants to confirm the date of the military operation.

Again, I skimmed over Alvarado's diary, searching for more information about Papá.

I was surprised to see how quickly the doctor gained popularity among the locals. When there were confrontations between the leaders and the farmers, the doctor served as a mediator, attaining the trust of everyone in town. The doctor became impatient when he noticed any type of status preferences. He claimed that commanders and combatants should work side by side with equal rights and privileges.

Commandant Ayala, who was a well-trained combatant, and the doctor, who was a natural teacher, became the leading instructors. Both men were committed to the cause and believed that education was key to success. In the morning, the doctor and Ayala taught us defense tactics and key counterattack strategies. We also had intense physical and military training. In these exercises, we learned self-defense, first aid, topography, and navigation skills. In the afternoons, I joined Ayala and the doctor, and we taught reading, math, anthropology, and other subjects. They both spoke several languages, so at the end of the day, I often heard them reading selections to one another in French, English, and Russian.

At night, I spent long hours writing in my cabin under candlelight. The only candle that was lit, aside from mine, was the doctor's. He told us one day that he was incorporating all the guerrilla warfare tactics he had learned with Castro, Che, and other commanders into the book he was writing, Counterinsurgency and Revolutionary War.

Wow, Papá wrote a book! I wondered what it would be about. I didn't understand the title but wanted to read it.

One day, I asked him if I could read the manuscript. The doctor was pleased to share his work with me. It was interesting to find out that the training exercises we were conducting at the camp mirrored those found in the book. According to Doctor Velásquez, it was important to study the enemy's tactics, including how they used disguises to infiltrate the movement. The doctor

confessed he worried about the intense harassment and psychological warfare
used by the enemy to weaken the guerrilla units.

At the first monsoon, the preparation for the inevitable assault came to a halt.
When the rains ceased, 16,000 (the number varies based on who you ask)
Colombian soldiers backed by fighter planes and helicopters swarmed the sky.
Bombs hit the ground, creating large explosions. Highly trained infantry
charged through the fields, firing at everyone in town. Some women and
children, carrying bags of food, rushed their animals to the mountains where
they vanished. The doctor and I searched for survivors among the fallen, which
included fifteen children. With the help of trained medics and others, we picked
up those who were still alive and others suffering from questionable skin
blisters and fled. We did not stop running until we found a small camp.
Astounded, I watched how the doctor's agile hands removed bullets from
combatants and treated those experiencing high fever and blisters caused from
some type of chemical. The only time I saw the doctor lose his composure was
when we buried two young boys who did not survive their wounds. The doctor
and his assistants worked day and night until all the patients were taken care
of.

Proudly, I filled my lungs with air, thinking about what Papá had done. He was
a good man and a brilliant doctor. He supported the farmers like Marulanda,
the man who had come to our house the day the colonel brought my dogs.
However, that pride soon faded away. I wondered if our father knew about
Orlando's eye and Jaime's troubles at school.

With all he is doing, I guess he forgot about us.

Tears burned my eyes as I finished reading.

In the meantime, the combatants who stayed behind resisted the military for
some time. Those who survived later slipped away, leaving no trace. All that
was left was the burning town. Later, the survivors, including the doctor, met

at the First Conference, which some say resulted in the birth of the Revolutionary Armed Forces of Colombia (FARC).

I stumbled to my feet, feeling the weight of my thoughts, and went to find Mario.

'I'm starting to understand what my papá is doing and why they are after him. But doesn't he know that they won't stop looking for him?'

Mario held my hands in his.

'Yes. He knows. And apparently, he doesn't care. Rocío, your father wants to protect the peasants and poor people in general, at all costs. He believes that the government should be committed to social benefits, and that is admirable. But the problem, my dear, is that it's not easy to change a system. He is probably staying away to keep you safe, so let it go.'

Clarity Unveiled

The school year ended with our performance. On our way to the stage, Liliana and I walked by a full-length mirror. When we saw ourselves, we burst out laughing.

'We look like little girls,' Liliana joked.

We were wearing sailor dresses, ankle socks, and white shoes. Our short bangs and tight ponytails, held by a white ribbon, made us look much younger.

Mother María found us on the floor, snorting and wiping the tears from our eyes.

'What's going on here?'

'Nothing.' I stood up. Liliana jumped up too.

'Are you ready to sing?'

'We are.' I elbowed my sister.

I just wanted it to be over. We were singing a ridiculous song, and our attire wasn't any better. We hadn't complained to Mamá because she had spent long evenings hunched over her sewing machine making the dresses.

'And now the Velásquez sisters,' announced Mother María.

The curtains opened, and Liliana and I walked onto the stage. Suddenly, it wasn't funny anymore. The audience went silent as soon as the music blared through the speakers. When they realized the song was in English, people clapped as if we were some sort of prodigies. Even though I knew our voices weren't beautiful as our father's, we did our best. Mesmerized, we used to stop what we were doing every time we heard him singing. His deep voice, in perfect pitch, resonated around the house like a famous singer.

Our audience must have simply been excited because of the newness of English songs. Singing Jingle Bells must have brought back memories of our life in Chicago for Liliana because her joyful gaze turned solemn. I held her hand and sang, wishing Papá was watching.

You should be proud of Liliana. Now she is not only speaking in public but also singing. I spoke to him in my mind.

At the end, we bowed; then embraced each other. No words were needed. We knew why our mood had changed. People stood up and cheered. We curtsied, then the curtains closed. After the end-of-the-year celebration, we went to the ice cream parlor in town.

A few moments later, Mrs. Beltran, the owner, appeared.

'Mrs. Díaz, Captain Díaz, Mrs. Velásquez.' She nodded. 'So, these are the famous Velásquez kids.' She smiled.

We didn't smile back. When she was gone, Jaime asked, 'Why did she say we were famous?'

'I don't know. She's probably just trying to make you feel important,' Mamá said.

Liliana kicked me under the table and made the symbol for Papá, forming a V shape with two fingers. I nodded. It seemed like everyone we met knew about our father. I loved him, but I hated living life in his shadow.

When my brothers were getting restless, a waiter appeared with our popsicles. They made mine with *guanabana*. As I sucked the soursop popsicle, chunks of the whitish fruit dissolved in my mouth, making my jaw tingle. We were enjoying our treat when Orlando began rubbing his eye. Mamá pulled a handkerchief from her purse and gave it to him.

'Please don't touch your eye with your hands. It can make it worse. By the way, Orlando has an appointment in a month with the specialist.' Mamá cleared her throat. 'Rocío, I need you to come with us so that you can help me.'

She told us that my siblings had to stay with our grandparents. Liliana began panting, and Jaime stopped eating his popsicle. When he was about to complain, Mamá embraced him and assured him it would only be for a few days.

I am going to miss them both, I kept my thoughts to myself.

On a cold, early January morning, we took a two-hour bus ride to the Barraquer Clinic, north of Bogotá. When we arrived, we came to a halt when we saw the block-long line that was in front of the building.

'Don't worry.' Mamá held my brother's and my hands tightly. 'The receptionist told me to go to the back of the building.'

'Why?' I asked.

She hesitated. 'Well, people who can't afford to pay go to the back.'

That's where poor people go?

'Papá is a doctor, and we are begging for medical services?' As soon as I finished making that remark, I wished I hadn't said anything.

My mother pressed her lips together, then covered her face with her hands. I wanted to hug her and tell her I was sorry for hurting her, but my body became stiff. So, I waited until she put her hands down.

'I'm sorry, Mamá.'

'I know this is difficult for all of us. But please know that there's nothing wrong with a little help when you need it. Can we go now?'

Orlando and I nodded. We made our way around the line, crossed the gardens, and walked to the other side of the building. Mamá came to a stop when she realized that the line outside the free clinic was even longer.

'Rocío, stay here with your brother. I'm going to tell them I have an appointment.'

I held my brother's hand while Mamá walked to the front of the line. She said something to the pear-shaped man guarding the door. When she finished explaining, the man shook his head and pointed to the back of the line. Mamá argued. The guard raised his hands in frustration and then closed the door. When our mother returned, she mumbled, 'We have to wait.'

The gray clouds hung over the savannah. Our wool coats did not protect us from the chilly wind, so I wrapped my arms around myself. 'Mamá, don't worry. We can wait.'

Orlando touched his eye. 'I'm all right.'

'Please don't rub your eye. It makes it worse.' Mamá embraced my brother.

The sun was in the middle of the sky when we were finally asked into the building. A talkative nurse completed a form with my brother's information. When she was done, she walked us to the doctor's office.

'He'll be in soon.' She left, closing the door behind her.

My legs hurt from standing, so I hurried and sat on a small sofa. Mamá and Orlando joined me.

A slender doctor walked in with a clipboard.

'Mrs. Velásquez? My name is Dr. Fernández.' He shook our hands. 'I apologize for the long wait, but we had a few emergencies.' Then he focused on my brother. 'So, this must be Orlando.'

My brother stood up.

'How old are you?'

'Ten.'

'You are a tall boy. Come sit on this chair so that I can see what is happening.' Dr. Fernández tapped the examination chair that was across from his desk.

After testing my brother's vision and examining both eyes with a circular machine, he asked, 'Ma'am, would you like for the children to wait outside while we discuss the diagnosis?'

'No. They should stay.'

Mamá stood up and extended her arms so that we would be close to her. Orlando and I joined her.

'All right,' he said. 'Orlando has keratoconus. The cornea has gotten thin and has a cone-shaped bulge.'

'So, what can we do?' Mamá asked and kissed my brother's head.

'At this point, the only thing that will work is a cornea transplant.' The doctor raised his eyebrows, staring at Mamá.

Orlando moaned, 'Will it hurt?'

'No. You will be asleep.'

'How much would that cost because—?'

'Doctors' children receive free services.'

Shocked by the doctor's comment, I rubbed my forehead. How did he know my father was a doctor? Was Papá still following us? Mamá must've been asking herself the same question because she grabbed my arm in relief.

'See, he is protecting us,' she whispered.

The doctor continued, 'By the way, on your next appointment day, do not wait in line. Come in through the front door and show this.' He pulled a business card from a drawer and handed it to my mother.

'Thank you, Doctor, God bless you.' She kissed Orlando's head again. 'I've been so worried about him.'

'Tell me your name again,' he said to me, cocking his head.

'Rocío.'

'Rocío, please tell my nurse to take you and your brother to the café to buy you whatever you want. You must be very thirsty and hungry.' He winked at me. 'Your mamá and I need to discuss the treatment.'

I understood that the doctor didn't want to scare my brother with the details of the surgery, so I did what I was told.

'Come on, Orlando,' I said.

My brother and I stepped into the waiting room, where we found the nurse who had checked us in. With her cinnamon-flowing hair, she yakked all the way to the small café, which was on the opposite side of the building. She told us about the many famous people she had met while working at the clinic, making us forget about the surgery. Orlando ate like he hadn't had anything in days. After eating three *empanadas* and drinking two glasses of milk, my brother burped.

'Excuse me.' He wiped his mouth with a napkin.

The nurse smiled. 'Where does the food go? You are all bones.'

That evening, we went back to the room Mamá had rented in the city. There was a double bed, which I shared with her, and a single bed for Orlando. The stale smell of the room was strong, so Mamá kept the top window in our adjacent bathroom open. She waited until Orlando had fallen asleep to tell me all about the surgery. Mamá explained that our first job was to find a donor.

'Who would give a cornea away?' I gasped in disbelief.

'Someone who is about to die.'

'You're telling me we have to go to hospitals looking for people who are almost dead and ask them if they want to donate one of their eyes?'

'Yes.' Mamá took a deep breath. 'I wish there was another way. If Orlando doesn't have the transplant soon, he could lose his vision.' She bit her lip in distress.

'Did you tell the doctor about Papá?'

'No. I have no idea how he knew who we were. Anyway, I'm just relieved we don't have to pay.'

Somehow, I was certain now that Papá already knew about Orlando's condition and had arranged for this. I embraced my mother and didn't say anything despite my suspicion. Outside, the city noises muffled the loud thumping of my anxious heart.

The next day, we set out on one of the scariest journeys we had ever taken. Dressed in our warm coats, we walked to a nearby bakery. The place was swarming with people. We sat at a round table by the window. Outside, a policeman was directing the morning traffic, whistling so loud my ears rang. Mamá bought coffee with milk for us and cold milk for Orlando, with warm rolls for all of us. When we finished, she pulled out a piece of paper, hands trembling.

'These are the hospitals we need to visit.'

'There are so many,' I said.

'That's all right, because we'll work together.' She went on to explain what we were about to do.

Orlando grumbled, 'I don't want someone else's eyeball.'

'Well, if I could give a part of me so that you could see, I would do it.' My mother stroked his back. 'But we don't have any other option. Either you have this surgery, or your eye will get much worse.'

Orlando stopped eating and stared at the street.

Mamá continued, 'The first thing I will do is ask permission. Then I'll speak with the relatives of the patients. You must stay outside the patients' rooms.

Do you understand? Do not go in no matter what.' Her voice rang across the bakery.

After Mamá paid the bill, we walked for ten blocks to the Hospital of La Merced. At reception, she asked to speak with the director. The person was unavailable, so we were sent to his assistant's office, Mr. Amaya. The room was cluttered with papers and boxes.

'Please sit down.' He invited us, indicating three chairs by the door.

Mamá explained the reason for our visit. His wrinkles became more pronounced every time he asked a question. His wide face seemed almost too big for his small mouth.

At the end, he came around his desk and said, 'Look, lady, I'm sorry about the boy's eye, but I can't ask grieving families to give you parts of their loved ones.'

'I didn't ask you to do it. *I* will. All I need from you is a list of patients who will not be around much longer.'

Orlando slouched in his chair.

'I can't do that. I could lose my job.' He went back to his desk and began reading a paper. 'I'm sorry, but I'm busy. You need to go.'

'Please. Help my son.' Mamá stood in front of Mr. Amaya's desk.

'Ma'am. What don't you understand? I'm about to retire, and I cannot lose my pension over this!'

I rushed to his side.

'If something happens to my brother's eye, it is your fault. Look at him.'

Mamá showed Orlando's left eye.

'Please.' She reached for the assistant's hand.

He pulled his hand away from her, shaking his head. She began weeping out of frustration. Orlando and I hugged her.

'Know that I'm doing this only because last year we lost our only daughter. I would've done anything to save her.' The man stared at his desk. Then he looked at us with a piercing stare. 'But if you tell anyone, I'll deny I ever gave you that list. So you write it yourself.' He handed Mamá a blank piece of paper and a pen.

Our mother wiped her face with a handkerchief from her purse and began writing.

The first patient was on the third floor in a room near the elevator.

'Stay here.'

Mamá left us in the hallway while she went into the room. Shortly afterwards, she walked out. A gray-haired woman came after her.

'And you have the nerve to come here and ask for my husband's cornea. What kind of woman are you? Nurse. Nurse.'

'Please, Ma'am, I'm just trying to help my son.'

A nurse came over to see why the woman was screaming. But before she could ask us anything, Mamá grabbed our hands, and we raced back to the first floor. Out of breath, we sat on the steps.

'I'm not going to stop until we find one.'

We took the elevator to the fifth floor. But the same thing happened. An acne-faced woman and an older woman chased Mamá out of the room.

'Please. See, this is my son. And he's just a little boy,' Mamá begged.

The woman didn't scream at my mother but came very close to her and said something I couldn't hear. Mamá covered her face in desperation. When they were gone, she directed us back to the elevator.

For weeks, we walked from hospital to hospital. Every time, angry, grieving relatives asked Mamá to leave and never come back.

One evening, carrying the weight of defeat, Mamá finally said, 'We should go back to Dr. Fernández. I don't know what else to do.'

Emotions spun out of control inside of me: sorrow, anger, and disappointment. It saddened me to see how sluggish my mother had become. At night, she tossed and turned. Orlando had also lost his spark and developed a fear of hospitals. No one seemed to want to help us. Mamá was thrown out of hospital room after hospital room as if she were a delinquent. I felt helpless.

The following morning, we took the bus to the clinic. On our way there, our mother wore a fake smile.

'I know Dr. Fernández will find some other treatment.'

Orlando and I didn't respond. We knew there were no other options. My brother held a small truck in his hands. Every day, he was beginning to look more and more like my father. There was a coldness in his features, square chin, broad forehead, and high cheeks that could frighten people who didn't know him. But inside, he, like Papá, was loving.

But if that were true, and if Papá had somehow intervened, why wasn't he here with us now? Didn't he know how difficult this was for all of us? I thought of Liliana's and Jaime's hurt looks when we drove away to go to the city. I hated being away from them.

The bus came to a screeching halt.

'Let's go,' Mamá said. 'This is our stop.'

At the entrance of the building, Mamá showed the guard the doctor's card. The man opened the door and directed us to the lobby. We had been waiting for half an hour when we heard a car coming to a screeching halt, followed by screaming people.

The three of us jumped out of our seats and rushed outside.

A young woman was kneeling in the middle of the street howling, 'Monique!' Next to her lay the inert body of a young girl.

'I didn't see her,' a taxi driver repeated over and over, stroking his head frantically.

A man in a suit loosened his tie and began directing the traffic away from the accident.

Orlando, shaking with shock, buried his face in Mamá's chest, but she pulled him aside.

'Take Orlando inside the clinic!' Mamá ordered as she ran to the scene of the accident. The traffic had stopped, and people from nearby buildings came out. Once outside of the clinic, our mother dropped to her knees next to the young woman and the little girl's lifeless body. Mamá was weeping as if she, too, had lost her own child. Two policemen arrived at the scene a few moments later. One began interrogating the taxi driver. The other one made a barricade around the accident, then took the place of the man in the suit and continued diverting the cars.

At the same time, two doctors from the clinic ran to the scene. They examined the girl but shook their heads. My mother and the woman embraced each other and cried. A couple of nurses brought a stretcher, placed the limp girl on it, and then covered her body with a white sheet.

The woman and my mother walked behind the stretcher in a funeral-like procession. My brother and I stood by the window until we watched them come in through the front door, Mother following the woman.

Orlando asked between sniffles, 'Where is Mamá going?'

I hugged him until he calmed down. The horrific accident had left us shaken. The mood in the clinic had turned somber.

An hour after the accident, Mamá joined us. Her mascara had worn off. 'Dr. Fernández wants to see us in his office,' she murmured. Our mother put her arms around us, and together we walked back to the west wing of the clinic. The doctor opened the door for us to come in.

'Have a seat, please.'

We entered and sat on the sofa. He reviewed some papers, then turned to Orlando.

'Young man, I know that what happened today is very sad, specifically for the girl's mother. But her mother has donated her organs, and she wants you to have Monique's cornea.'

We were stunned. Orlando put his face in his hands.

Mamá tenderly pulled his hands down.

'She wants you to have it. She said that she feels some comfort knowing that at least a part of her daughter will stay alive. Why don't we pray for Monique and her family?' She began praying, 'Our Father, who art in heaven…'

Orlando mumbled something, resting his head on Mamá's.

I didn't know that prayer, so I listened to our mother's soothing voice.

Dr. Fernández waited until she was finished to say, 'I agree with your mamá. Think of this as a gift.'

An hour later, my brother was taken to the operating room.

Whispers of the Past

A month after Orlando's surgery, we returned home to Fusa. When we arrived, the sun shone, and the leaves danced around in the wind. Don Rogelio opened the gates, and we drove in. Liliana, Jaime, and Bella ran towards us. Once we parked, I jumped out of the taxi, delighted to see my siblings and our dog. My brother leaped into my arms, almost making me fall. Liliana rescued me by embracing both of us. Mamá and Orlando joined in one big hug. Bella gazed at us with her soft puppy-dog eyes. I let go of the others and was petting Bella's back when my grandparents and Mario made their way out of the house.

'Welcome home.' Grandma grinned with delight. 'Come in and have lunch. You must be starving.'

During lunch, Mamá wouldn't stop talking about the surgery. Not only had it been successful, but it also had been free. She didn't mention the fact that Dr. Fernández knew our father was a doctor, nor that she had been yelled at by the patients' relatives. Before we left the city, she'd made us promise we wouldn't tell anyone about it. According to her, if we did, we would upset everyone. So, when Mamá finished recounting her version of the story, Orlando let out an enormous sigh, as if he'd been holding his breath. It was possible that, like our mother, he, too, wanted to forget all about our trip. I, on the other hand, covered my mouth with my fists so that I wouldn't blurt out the rest of the story. I thought everyone should know how brave Mamá was. First, she got us into Canada, and then she fought against all odds to find a donor for my brother. The words tumbled around in my head until Mario excused himself from the table.

'I'll walk with you,' I offered, hoping for a distraction. 'Why are you using that cane?'

'I fell, so your grandma insists I use this idiotic stick.' His sunken cheeks and tired eyes scared me.

'I'm sorry.'

'Don't be sorry. It happens.' He opened the door of his house. 'Your mamá didn't tell us the entire story about the trip, did she?' Mario studied my face.

I shook my head.

'It's all right. We don't need more drama. Unless you want to tell me something?'

I shrugged. I wanted to forget all the drama too.

'All right, tell me, why are you here?'

'I want to talk to you about—'

'You're telling me you missed me?' Mario asked.

Before I could respond, he continued.

'I have something for you,' he said.

My heart began racing when he moved a couple of books and then took an envelope out. He waved it at me.

'It's from Jocelyne. But I must warn you... there is some bad news.'

I tugged at the letter until he released it; then I eagerly began reading.

December 26, 1965

Ma chère soeur,

I am sorry for not writing for a long time, but we have had many problems. My mother became very ill and was hospitalized many times. She had cancer, but in the end, there wasn't anything the doctors could do to help her. She died. I was so sad I stopped going to school for a while. Now, I finally understand how difficult it must be for you to live without one of your parents.

Mon père and I moved to the United States. We live in San José, California, which has better weather than Canada. Also, in Montréal, the problems between the French and the English were getting more difficult every day before we left. After your father left, the police kept coming to our house looking for members of the Front de libération du Québec. It could be that they thought mon père was helping your father and the FLQ. You told me to find out what this group does. Mon père said they want Québec to be independent from Canada. He thinks that they don't like the English Canadians because they treat French people like they are less. The government fights with the FLQ because they attacked some government buildings. It's a long story, but I don't know if I understood all of it. You can also find it in an encyclopedia or ask a teacher. I wish I could help you more.

Believe it or not, I wrote this letter all by myself. I miss many things from Montréal like the food and my friends. But California is nice too. We go to the beach almost every weekend. School is different, but I like it, too, though now I have to learn more English, whether I like it or not.

I hope one day you can come to my house. I think you would like it here. Please write and tell me about you. How is school? Do you like a boy? How is your family?

Gros bisous,
Jocelyne

I held the letter against my chest. She had greeted me with my dear sister. That was exactly how I felt about her. It had been four years since I had seen her. She was my age, also sixteen. Sadness made me feel heavy inside. The last time I went to their house, Jocelyne and I hid so we could watch her mother rhumba around the kitchen while she baked cookies for us. And now that joyful lady was gone. I swallowed because, in a way, Papá, too, was fading away. Only his ghost was left behind.

Mario surprised me.

'I apologize for reading your letters,' he said, 'but with all that is going on with your papá, I just want you to be safe. I must say it always takes me a long time to translate. And by the way, you should know that I am helping because I, too, hated when adults hid things from me.'

Apologetic was not how anyone would describe Mario. Most of the time, he thought he was correct, so I accepted his apology with a light stroke on his forearm.

'What's that long face for? It's sad that she lost her mother, but that's part of life. California sounds like a great place.'

He began placing his books back on the shelf.

'Yes.' I sighed.

One day I will walk the beach with you, my friend.

'You thought she had forgotten about you, but it didn't occur to you she had problems too. See, everyone has problems. Not just you. The world doesn't revolve around you.'

'I know.' I suddenly felt ashamed.

'Anything else?'

'What about Papá?'

I feared he had something to do with the FLQ, and that perhaps that was the reason Jocelyne and her father had to leave Montréal.

'He is gone,' he said. 'Some say he is in the mountains with the guerrillas.' My face must've shown my disappointment, because Mario cheered, 'Come on, girl, you received a letter from your friend. You should be happy.'

Mario went to his living room, sat on his chair, and began reading as if I weren't there. I plopped on the other chair and suddenly felt the urge to tell him the entire story related to Orlando's surgery. I didn't want to break the promise I'd made to Mamá, but I couldn't forget how her hopeful expression tightened out of despair each time she'd been asked to leave a hospital. She always pretended to be fine, but her furrowed forehead showed otherwise. I was proud of her for being so persistent. I needed to share the story with someone. And I trusted Mario, and so I told him.

I didn't know if he was listening, because he put the book down and closed his eyes. When I was finished, he stood up.

'You are lucky to have Cecilia as your mamá. Now, go home and be with your family.'

I got up and embraced him. 'You're also my family.'

Mario kissed my cheek.

'I don't know what I would do without you.' I hugged Mario.

He patted me on the back.

'Go on, that's all the hugs and kisses I can take for one day.'

Then he opened the front door. I hugged him again and left.

Mamá began looking for work soon after Orlando recovered. She was gone all day and came home at night, slipping off her high heels before collapsing on a chair. My grandparents offered to pay for our expenses, but Mamá refused to keep taking money from them. So, she continued searching, but the result was always the same. No work.

One afternoon, the phone rang. Mamá answered it. We turned our heads, trying to listen to find out who was calling.

'Hello. Yes, this is she.' Mamá stood still, squinting as she played with the phone cord. 'I'll be there tomorrow. Nice talking to you too.' Like a schoolgirl, she hung up the phone, then clasped her hands on her chest. 'I have an interview tomorrow.'

'That's great.' Grandma tapped on the sofa next to her. 'Tell us all about it.'

Mamá joined my grandparents on the sofa. My siblings and I were at a small side table, playing Parcheesi. We stopped the game to watch our mother. I had not seen her eyes glow like this for a long time.

'Well, I would be working in the fabric department, La Túnica, helping customers with their sewing inquiries.'

'You'll like that, right, Mamá?' Liliana cheered.

'I would be delighted. Now, I just have to do well in the interview.'

The next day Mamá left with our grandfather soon after breakfast. Her pointy patent leather heels matched her charcoal dress. In contrast with her rosewood lips, her teeth seemed whiter that day. Her eyes sparkled as she waved goodbye to my siblings and me. For hours, Liliana, Orlando, Jaime, and I roamed the grounds of the property, awaiting her return.

Midday, we heard someone honking by the gates. The four of us ran to the entrance of the property. Dropping his machete where he was pruning bushes, don Rogelio trailed behind us. Together with my two brothers, he opened the heavy gates. Grandpa and Mamá were inside the car talking. When they drove in, don Rogelio closed the gates, and my brothers, Liliana, and I followed the car until Grandpa parked it by the house.

'What happened?' I peeked inside the passenger's side.

Mamá got out of the car. She embraced me, then kissed Orlando, who was now standing next to her.

'Let's go inside where we can talk.'

'What did you bring us?' Orlando tugged on our mother's purse.

Liliana and Jaime stared at Mamá with hopeful eyes. Grandpa got out and opened the trunk of the car.

'Kids, help us with the groceries, please.'

Jaime, Liliana, and I did as we were told. Orlando stayed with Mamá.

We had finished placing all the baskets on the kitchen counter when Grandma walked in. She embraced Mamá.

'So, how did it go?'

We all stopped what we were doing. All we could hear was the sound of a barking dog in the distance. Mamá lowered her head. 'They want to hire me.'

'Why are you so sad? That's wonderful news,' Grandma said.

Grandpa scowled. 'Not so wonderful if you knew how meager her salary will be.'

My throat tightened when I saw Mamá's watery gaze.

'It's that bad?' Grandma asked.

Mamá nodded. 'All I would be able to pay for are two school tuitions, not four.'

'Why can't we go to public schools like we have done before?' I suggested.

'You need to be in a place where you are safe, and private schools tend to be stricter about who they allow into the school. More secure. Besides, you'll get a better education.'

'Safe? From Papá?' My voice croaked.

We hadn't seen the men who had tried to kidnap us. But I didn't bring them up in conversation. I thought that would make Mamá even more nervous.

Mamá hesitated. 'It's that… I have no choice.'

After weeks of working in the customer service department of the fabric store and seeing no future in that profession, Mamá called my siblings and me to her room. Somehow, we knew we were not going to like what we were about to hear because we held hands. Our hearts hammered with fear and anticipation. She told us she was moving to Chicago. She planned to live with

226

her brother there, and to work and go to night school. Liliana was going to move in with Mamá's friend, María Raquel, in Bogotá. She and I'd attend the same school, but I'd be the only one living in the dormitories there. My two brothers were staying with our grandparents and continuing with their school.

We complained we didn't want to be separated, nor did we want her to go away, but she insisted she didn't have an option. Our father hadn't sent her money for a while and our schools were expensive. She refused to have our grandparents pay for our expenses and argued that it was her responsibility to support her own family.

Jaime kicked the leg of a chair that was near him, then plopped on the floor. Orlando sniffled.

'But I don't want to,' Liliana squealed.

I, too, sat on the floor, astounded. A year felt like forever and a day. First our father, and now our mother was leaving us. Even worse, I was going to live alone. Words were stuck in my throat, so I just wept. Soon we were all sitting on the floor, and together we mourned our coming separation.

Later that month, on a damp morning, we drove Mamá to the airport. Rain and wind slapped the windows of the old Packard. Crammed inside the car, we sat in silence for a long time. Once we climbed the mountains, the large drops of water turned into hail. It was like thousands of marbles were beating down on the automobile. A while later, the hail finally ceased, and with it, its deafening sound. The sun came out, and the clouds faded away. Only the intense emerald color of the mountains remained. This sudden and drastic change in weather made me think about how my family dealt with my father's abandonment, and now my mother's trip to the USA. It hurt us all, but we weathered the storm. Then we went on as if nothing had happened.

'I wrote a letter to Uncle Mauricio. He knows my plan and is ready to help me,' said Mamá, breaking the silence. 'With your papá gone, this is the best I can do.'

Every time we heard the word papá, we all stiffened, as if a heavy blanket of ice had fallen over us, leaving us immobile.

'We're almost at the airport.' Grandma tried to steer the conversation away from Papá, perhaps noticing that my mother's comment had left us pensive.

I was sitting in the front with my grandparents, so I turned around to ask her again what time her flight took off just to hear her voice.

I am missing her already.

Jaime was by the door, peering off into the distance. Liliana was next to him, embracing her doll. Orlando held Mamá's hand, his head leaning against her arm.

What's going to happen to him when Mamá leaves? Orlando has never been apart from her. I won't even be able to console him. But I kept this question to myself.

At the airport, we walked Mamá to the gate. There, she put on her gloves, which matched the cobalt coat and hat Grandpa had bought for her. With her hair flipped up at the ends and pearl earrings, she had the elegance of a movie star. She hugged each one of us, reassuring us she loved us and would see us as soon as she finished her studies. No one shed a tear.

Once she entered the corridor, we ran to the large window that overlooked the tarmac.

A line of passengers carrying small bags were climbing the portable stairs to the aircraft. Suddenly, we saw Mamá. She stopped, looked up, blew us a kiss, and then stepped inside the airplane. My siblings and I rested our heads against the window until the airplane took off. Only then did Orlando sniffle, and we all followed him. Grandpa and Grandma tried their best to distract us, but they were unsuccessful. My brothers, sister, and I sobbed all the way home.

A few days after Mamá left, Grandpa drove me to La Sierra, an all-girls boarding school in the city. At the gate, he kissed me and drove away. I was on my own. All I had left of my old life was a suitcase and a pillow.

I wanted to scream, *Bring back my mamá! I want to be with Liliana, Jaime, and Orlando. Take me back to my grandparents' home. This is my papá's fault for leaving us. I don't want to be here. Let me go.*

'Hey, move, you're blocking the entrance,' a sassy girl said as she bumped into me.

Lost in a sea of painful thoughts, I tried to keep my composure by clasping my pillow and bag. I didn't move until another girl pushed me.

'Get in line.'

I had no energy to fight back. So, I did what the abrasive girl said. We went to the second floor of the Victorian building. By the door of one of the dormitory rooms was a gray-haired woman recording our names on a piece of paper.

'Your name?'

'Rocío Velásquez.'

'This is your room. Next,' the woman continued.

There were five rows of beds; each row had four beds. On top of each bare mattress, there was a set of sheets and towels. Girls came in carrying large bags, boxes, and pillows. A group of girls who were by the door wore makeup and were talking about boys. A younger girl with long hair pulled me aside.

'Hurry. Let's take the beds by the window,' she said.

She took my pillow and threw it on a bed facing the street.

'You take the best one. I'll take the one next to yours.'

The wooden shutters were open. Across the street, children played in the park with their parents.

'My name is Gabriela,' she said.

'Rocío.' I shook her hand.

The bell rang.

'Hurry up, ladies. You need to be downstairs in five minutes,' said the lady with gray hair.

I had begun making my bed when Gabriela pulled my arm. 'We don't have time. Let's go.' She rushed down the stairs, and I trailed behind her.

It was a brisk but sunny morning. Adjacent to the main patio was a small garden. I thought of Grandma when I touched the reddish jungle blueberry flower. When I was younger, she often asked me to help her water her ornamental plants. She had taught me all about the different parts. I took a deep breath and continued walking. Birds were chirping high in a tree. One small one was bathing in the water fountain, flapping his wings as if he were the ruler of his little oasis.

At the sound of the bell, I hurried to get in line. There were about one hundred of us standing in rows of ten. The principal came out of her office, and like magic, the group was silent. Miss Galán was a tall, middle-aged woman with thick glasses. She welcomed us and then read a list of things we could and could not do.

'You must wear your uniform at all times while you are at school. There is no drinking or smoking allowed. You are not allowed to use makeup or wear high heels at school.'

A chorus of disappointed girls groaned and complained.

'Male visitors are not admitted in this school. I don't care if they are your friends, brothers, or uncles. Your father may visit you, but only if he makes an appointment with me.'

I didn't hear anything else after that.   My heart pounded when I heard the word father. Moments later, I felt a hand on my arm. 'What is your name?' asked Miss Galán.

'Rocío Velásquez,' I responded in a soft voice.

'Did you hear all that I said?'

'Yes, Miss Galán,' I lied.

'Then hurry up and go to the dining hall for breakfast.'

It was then that I noticed that the rest of the girls were gone, and I was the only one left. So, I hurried along. I found the dining hall buzzing with students. The thought of food made me nauseous.

What if I get sick in front of all these people? Liliana is not even here to help me.

Gabriela's high-pitched voice interrupted my thoughts. 'Here.' She showed me her table.

I joined her and five other girls who were sitting with her. Trays with food came and went, but the only thing I did was to pass them to the next person. All I had was a glass of fruit juice. After breakfast, the principal took us new girls for a tour of the school.

The classrooms were large, with hardwood floors. I walked with the group, but somehow, I felt as if I wasn't there. Pretty soon, I stopped hearing what Miss Galán was saying. This was the first time in my life that I had been away from my siblings and my mother; I couldn't stop thinking about what they were doing at home and how they might be feeling. Again, I felt a hand press on my arm. 'Are you paying attention?' asked Miss Galán.

'I am sorry. I was—'

'If you want to stay in this school, you better listen. Go upstairs and unpack.'

After we finished making our beds and putting our clothes away, most girls went back down to the playground to sit in the sun or to play basketball.

'Aren't you coming?' Gabriela asked.

'In a little while,' I said.

Gabriela smiled and then left. I lay on my bed when everyone was gone, staring at the ornate ceiling. Suddenly, a breeze blew in, making me shiver, so I covered myself. A while later, I vaulted out of bed when I sensed someone standing next to me. I looked around the dark room, but no one was there. I then remembered the leather case Mario had given me before I left. When I opened it, a mild, sweet, earthy smell came out of it. Inside was a hardcover diary.

On the first page he had written, *Remember, no one can take your memories away. They are for you to keep.*

Echoes of Home

On the evening of February 26, 1966, I wrote my first diary entry. I was determined to take on the role of memory-keeper as Mario had recommended. It was also an opportunity to understand an adult world I viewed as confusing and, on some occasions, cruel. I thought of the collection of watercolor pieces I had painted at school in Chicago. I had been cast away from my classmates because I didn't speak English but, just like in my diary, my paintings told my story.

All I wanted was to have our family together, but the opposite had happened. Mamá returned to Chicago and the thought of her not coming back made me feel ill. My brothers and grandparents were hours away from my school. The only one I had left was Liliana. Now, I lived in a boarding school with lots of rich and spoiled girls.

Every morning, I stood by the gates and waited for my sister's bus to arrive. Liliana seemed to be fine. She told me that my mother's friend Raquel, treated her well. She also got to play with Raquel's two small children.

When Liliana was at school, we spent every moment we could talking and telling one another about what we had done the night before. Afternoons were difficult for me. I never told her. It wasn't necessary. She knew. She waved goodbye until the bus turned the corner. Once I couldn't see her anymore, I choked up, trying very hard not to weep. I wanted to run after the bus and scream, but I never did.

When I was alone, all I did was read. Books didn't hurt me. Books didn't leave me. They were there when I needed them.

'It's nine o'clock. Good night!' called Miss Rodriguez, the lady with gray hair who had checked us into our rooms that first day.

'Good night, Miss Rodriguez.'

A few girls giggled.

When I closed my diary, I felt better.

I can also write a letter to Jocelyne to tell her everything about school.

I smiled, and in my mind, I thanked Mario. The lights went off. Only a sliver of moonlight filtered through the shutters. Once the room was silent, the solemn night sent me far away into the past. I tossed and turned, thinking about our last night in Fusa. Orlando and Jaime had hovered around Mamá, Liliana, and me while we packed, probably feeling abandoned too. I wished I had said something to them. *I'll be back soon* or *You can come and visit me.* But I couldn't. Mamá said we were going to be apart for a year. Just thinking about being away from family for such a long time left me numb.

A loud snore made me jump. Soon after, the dorm went quiet. Still restless, I opened the shutters, hoping to see a shooting star so that I could make a wish. *Bring my mother back soon.*

Papá found superstitions to be ridiculous and unfounded. But I didn't care anymore about what he thought. He had ripped apart our family and now all I could look forward to was a starry night. The rain lingered; the sky hid behind a thick cloud cover. I wept.

Sometime later, I heard someone else crying, so I perked my head up to see who it was. Gabriela was drying her eyes with the sheet. It hadn't struck me until then that she, too, could be missing her family. I went to her bed and offered her my *ruana*. Gabriela took the shawl and covered herself with it. Silence followed.

The next morning, as soon as the wake-up bell rang, Gabriela came to my bed and handed me the ruana.

'Thanks. It's very soft.'

'My grandma gave it to me before I left.'

'That's nice. My grandmothers have both passed away.'

'I'm sorry.'

Miss Rodriguez marched around the dorm, barking out commands, making sure we were up.

That evening Gabriela waited until everyone was asleep, then tiptoed her way to my bed.

'Are you awake?' she whispered.

'Yes.' I blinked, trying to see her.

'Follow me.'

'Why?'

Gabriela didn't respond. Though only a year younger, she was much shorter than I was. She walked away, carrying a blanket. I took my ruana and followed her.

Under our feet, the old hardwood floor creaked, making us halt at each sound. Other than the sounds we made and the occasional snore, the room was quiet. We left the dorm and went downstairs to the advisor's office. The cozy room had two chairs and a floor lamp. Gabriela turned the light on and then closed the door behind us. Bundled in our wraps, we each took a chair. 'Are you crazy? We can get in trouble if we are caught,' I said.

Gabriela smiled. 'Don't tell me you haven't done anything naughty before.'

She was annoying me.

'I don't know.'

'C'mon tell me a story. I can't sleep. Please… please.' She wiggled in her seat.

'Well, this is kind of ridiculous, but years ago I spied on the nuns at my school in their shower.'

'Why?' Her eyes danced.

'I didn't know if they were real people or not.'

She covered her mouth with one hand, trying to contain the laughter. 'That's funny.'

I smirked.

'Where is your family?' she asked.

I blushed. 'Tell me about yours first.'

'All right. We have a ranch in Puerto López with a lot of cattle.'

I propped myself up in my chair. 'We lived there too!'

It was the same town where Papá had completed his social service program, the same town where the colonel, Marulanda, and other men that Papá called compañeros met at our house in the evenings.

'Oh wow! So, then you know how it is there, such a small town?'

'Yes,' I said. Gabriela had my attention. 'So why did they send you here?'

'My parents wanted my siblings and me to go to schools in the city.'

'What about your parents?'

'They stayed at the ranch with my older brother. I didn't want to leave, but they made me.'

'Is that why you were crying?'

Gabriela nodded. 'They said that this is a good school. Plus, they think it's dangerous to live at the ranch.'

'Why dangerous?'

'My parents say that the guerrillas want rich people like us gone.'

I swallowed.

Were Papá's associates intimidating her family? Was it true that the rich kept others poor?

It was all too confusing for me.

'Do you know what the guerrillas are doing?'

'Not really.' She shrugged her shoulders. 'All I know is that my father said they have to stay behind to protect the ranch.'

Memories of my father treating his patients, visions of him hiking the Andes dressed in fatigues, and the sound of mother's voice screaming at him, 'Soldier' were spinning in my head when Gabriela snapped her fingers at me.

'Hello? Gabriela calling Rocío.'

'What?' I snapped.

'What's wrong?'

'Nothing.'

'You look pale. Are you sick?'

'I'm fine.' I pulled the ruana tightly around my body.

'Your turn. Tell me about your family.'

I was about to get up and leave, go back to my bed, but stopped when I thought of Mario and how I had annoyed him with my many questions, the same way Gabriela was irritating me. My heart filled with warmth just thinking about the many hours he and I had spent together, how patient he was with me, and my constant search for answers.

So, I took a deep breath. 'Well, it's kind of a long story.'

'So what? I'm not sleepy.'

At that point, it was clear she wouldn't let it go.

'My mother is in Chicago, and my brothers stayed with my grandparents. My sister goes to this school.'

'Why isn't she here in the dormitory with you?'

'As I said, it's a long story.'

'What about your father?'

I raised the shawl to my lips. 'I don't want to talk about my father.'

'Why not?'

I was angry, disillusioned, sad, and embarrassed. How could I feel ashamed of my father and miss him so much at the same time?

'Listen, we shouldn't be down here. And I've got to get some sleep. I'll tell you about him another day.'

I went back to the dorm, repeating in my mind, *Embarrassed? Embarrassed?* Perhaps Gabriela noticed how unsettled I had become because she didn't try to stop me. She just trailed along, clutching her blanket.

A month into the school year, I received a package in the mail from Grandma. Nervous, I chewed on my lips, holding the envelope. I didn't want to open it in front of the other girls, so I waited until everyone was asleep. I took the box, sneaked out of the dorm, and went downstairs to the advisor's office. Inside were two envelopes: a small one and a large, heavy one. From the small one, I pulled out a letter in Grandma's handwriting.

My dear Rocío,

I hope you are doing well and enjoying your school. You, Liliana, and your mamá left an enormous void in our lives. We are all trying to adjust, but I confess that not having you around has been very difficult for everyone. The boys do not say much; however, I know that they miss you dearly. The good news is that your mamá called a few weeks back and said she was working hard, and she will begin secretarial school soon.
It breaks my heart to give you sad news, but I think you should know that Mario caught pneumonia again. This time, he had to be hospitalized because he was frail. Unfortunately, there was little the doctors could do to save him. He passed away on February 25th.

I held the letter tight in my hands. That was the same day I had felt someone standing by my bed.

Mario came to see me.

With tears rolling down my face, I continued reading.

He left you this sealed envelope. You two were very close, and I know that his passing will sadden you. I wish I could be with you when you read this letter, but it is hard for us to travel. Your grandpa and I are getting older. He does

not feel comfortable driving at night. Remember that we were fortunate to have had Mario in our lives.
Please write and tell us all about your school.

Love,
Grandma Emilia

It all felt unreal. I could see Mario's firm yet playful eyes. I ripped open the large envelope open, hoping to find a letter from him. Like a feather in the wind, a loose piece of paper flew out, landing by my feet. It was Mario's note:

Rocío, I thought you might find this interesting.
Mario

There were no *goodbyes*, no *I love you* or even *take care of yourself.* That was Mario.
I'll miss you so much. In my mind, I blew him a kiss. He would probably rub it off and tell me not to be sentimental.
I pulled out the rest of the papers. There were newspaper articles, photocopied sections of books, and other various documents. I wanted to read them, but losing Mario had left me immobile and cold inside. So, I stared into the night, thinking about him. The stack of papers suddenly felt heavy, so I dropped it, scattering them all over the floor. I covered myself with the ruana and howled in despair.

Papá: The Enigmatic Puzzle of My Life

The next morning, during recess, I pulled Liliana aside and told her about Mario.

'Oh my God, I can't believe it.' She embraced me. 'How are you?'

'I'm fine now, but it's difficult.'

'Sorry, Rocío.' She hugged me again. 'He's an angel now.'

Just picturing Mario with angel wings and floating on a cloud made me chuckle.

'An angel? I don't know about that.'

Liliana raised her eyebrows. 'He was nice to you.'

'Yea. He sent me some documents, and now he is gone. I'll never get to talk to him again.'

I felt as though I had been climbing a slippery hill, and when I was about to reach the crest, my partner had let go of me, sending me back down to its base. Fatigued, I took a deep breath. 'I'll never figure out where Papá is now.'

'Mario was helping you find Papá?' asked Liliana.

I nodded.

'Would you tell me what's in Mario's papers, please?' she said.

'I don't know if that is such a good idea.'

Each time I shared something new about our father with Liliana, she bombarded me with questions I couldn't answer.

'Why not? He's my papá too.'

'I know, but the articles are difficult to understand, even for me.'

Liliana held my hand. There was a sense of fear in her face I hadn't seen before. Like me, I knew she was afraid to lose Papá altogether. Very seldom did we use our hand language anymore. There was no need. We knew what the other one was thinking. I bit my lip, wishing I could give her hope.

'All right, I'll share them with you, but you can't tell anyone. Don't mention Papá or anything.' It pained me to see my sister broken like this.

'Why? Mamá didn't say anything about denying that we were Papá's kids.' She exhaled.

'Because you know how people are. You have seen their weird look when we tell them that our last name is Velásquez. They gossip, plus we could have problems at school.'

'Do you think Miss Galán would expel us?'

'I don't know, but it's better not to say anything.'

'I won't.' Liliana raised her shoulders. 'But why was Mario helping you?'

'I think it's because he cared for me.' The wind brought the scent of eucalyptus, reminding me of Mario's home. 'And I loved him too.'

'He was grouchy.'

'I know, but inside he was different.'

We both flinched at the sound of the bell.

'I'll see you at the gates.' I patted Liliana on the back.

'See you.' She walked away.

As soon as my sister's bus left, I retreated to the library, hoping not to be interrupted. The previous night, I had scanned other articles with a flashlight. There were photocopies of pages of history books, and magazine and newspaper clippings on world events with headlines like: **Soviets' Moon Landing, Anti-Vietnam Protests, The C.I.A. Behind the Assassination of Jorge Eliécer Gaitán?** and **Camilo Torres, Sociologist and Reformer, Dies in Combat.** Was Mario trying to help me understand the circumstances of Papá's actions? Did he want to justify Papá's commitment to his cause? And, if so, why? And why not just come out and explain it all to me in a letter?

It was true Papá was an enigma to me. But if Mario was trying to explain why my father had left to make me forgive him, he had misjudged me. Reading all those reports would not help me understand his absence. He had virtually abandoned me at a school. My mother was gone, my brothers were far away, and even Liliana did not live with me, and it was all Papá's fault. There was nothing I could find in those papers to change that. So, I left most of them in the box, though there was one I couldn't ignore.

I opened the math book where I had inserted a single article the previous night. It was written by the same reporter who had infiltrated one of the guerrilla settlements. The man who later helped my father carry the injured out of Marquetalia, the town under military attack.

February 1, 1966

Valledupar Lost a Visionary
By Eduardo Alvarado

Doctor Velásquez made one last attempt to change the medical system from within before vanishing. Velásquez and a group of physicians founded the Sarai Clinic in Valledupar. The clinic became the main health center in the region only a few months after it began operating. The medical board soon noticed that Doctor Velásquez charged his patients' fees on an income-based scale. Sometimes he performed long and complicated surgeries in exchange for only a bag of oranges or a chicken.

I thought of the many times patients wearing worn-out shoes and tattered clothes came to the infirmary asking for Papá's help. After thanking him, many people confessed they didn't have money to pay for their medicine. Still, no one left untreated. He kept a reserve of medication in the infirmary for these cases. At first, Mamá argued that his salary wasn't enough to buy prescription drugs for others, but she gave up after she realized Papá wasn't about to stop. Proud to be his daughter, I sat up straight and continued reading.

When the other physicians confronted him about his billing practices, he became outraged. He demanded that all the doctors in the clinic use his pay scale. 'The mission statement makes it clear that the main goal of the clinic is to serve all people,' argued the doctor at a meeting with his colleagues. The medical board revolted and refused to follow his orders. To complicate matters even further, informants confirmed that he was using the clinic for political meetings. Eventually, Doctor Velásquez encountered so much resistance from the rest of the medical staff that he left.

Immediately after, pistoleros flooded the city. These armed civilians, privately hired, now roam around, killing anyone suspected of being a revolutionary.

Gabriela came and sat next to me. I quickly shut my book.

'What are you doing?'

'Nothing,' I snapped, still distraught about what I had just learned.

Inside, I was screaming, *Stop, Papá! Stop or they'll kill you!*

'Math?' Gabriela brushed her fingers over the cover of my textbook.

'Yes, *math*.' I pulled the book towards me. 'What do you need?'

'I'm bored.'

'Do your homework.'

'I'm done.'

'I've got to study.' Glaring at her, I hoped she'd leave me alone.

'Can I stay here?' she pleaded.

'Nope.'

I needed time to finish the article. To think about Papá, about what Mario was trying to tell me. I took a deep breath, crossed my arms, and waited for Gabriela to leave. But she didn't. Instead, she lowered her head.

'I'm sorry, but this is not a good time.' My voice was soft now, trying to help her understand that I just wanted to be alone.

'I'm homesick,' she said.

I hated when she looked at me with longing eyes.

'Fine,' I said. My body stiffened. 'Come with me. I have to study the Colombian map.'

If she wasn't going to leave, she could at least help me.

'I thought you were studying math,' she said.

'I need to find something.'

'What are you looking for?' she asked.

'Valledupar. It's for a geography assignment,' I lied.

I wanted to know where Papá had last been seen. We stood next to a map of Colombia.

'Look, it's up there.' Gabriela pointed to a northeastern spot. Then, together, we read the encyclopedia. It was an agricultural region and one of the major music centers in the country, but there wasn't anything in Valledupar I could link to my father. The desire to find him or even simply learn more about his whereabouts filled my heart with hope. But it was always the same, dead ends everywhere.

Gabriela found my fake assignment boring and finally left me alone. I stayed, grappling with my thoughts. I agreed with Mario; Papá had given his life to helping others, knowing that his own life was at risk. And perhaps there wasn't anything I could do to help him. I banged the library table with my fist. I didn't want to chase after him anymore. Tracing Papá's moves was more difficult than following the wake of a sailboat at sea under unpredictable winds.

All students, except for me, went home for Easter week. Liliana stayed with Máma's friend. The immense silence of the dormitory became my companion and the library, a window to the world. Saturday morning, I was in the garden reading when Miss Galán came and sat next to me.

'What are you reading?'

'One of my grandma's novels.' I showed her the cover.

'Jorge Isaacs wrote it a century ago. You know that, right?'

'Yes.'

'I am sorry you didn't get to go home for the holiday.'

I shrugged and looked away.

'Would you like to have lunch with me?' Her eyes danced behind her thick glasses.

'Well... thanks, but I don't want to bother you. You are so busy.'

'I'd be pleased if you'd join me. It's not fun to eat alone anyway.'

'I will. Thank you.'

'Meet me at noon at my quarters.'

In the third-floor hallway, Miss Galán was waiting for me.

'Come in,' she said, ushering me into her private dining room.

A round table surrounded by four chairs sat in the middle of the room. Dressing the table, a white starched tablecloth gave the room a fresh look. A sense of warmth filled my senses when I remembered Avelina and how adamant she was about keeping her whites impeccable.

'Do you like my plants?' Miss Galán stood up.

She had scattered small plants around the dining room.

'They smell so good,' I said.

'It comes from those purple flowers by the window. Lavender.'

'You have so many.'

'I grow them here. Then the gardener transplants them outside. See those bushes out in the yard?' She opened the window.

Like colorful snowflakes, violet- and rose-colored flowers covered the large bushes bordering the back of the building.

'My grandmother loves flowers too.' I pictured Grandma caring for her orchids.

Miss Galán sat at the table.

'Join me.' After we sat down, she fixed on me with her dark eyes. 'So, tell me about your family.'

I felt the blood burn inside my face.

'Do you have siblings?'

'I have two brothers and a sister, Liliana.' I held my breath, trying not to show how much I missed them.

'I know Liliana. She has freckles like you.' Miss Galán smiled.

'My brothers live in Fusa with my grandparents.'

'And your parents?'

'Mamá is in Chicago, working.'

Silence lingered.

She finally said, 'I remember now.' Then, looking at me with curious eyes, she continued, 'It has been brought to my attention that you might be related to Doctor Velásquez?'

'No.' The word burst out of me, surprising us both.

Inside I was screaming, *Papá is gone! Why do I have to always feel like I'm being watched all the time, the men in Fusa, friends, teachers? Leave me alone!*

I wanted to ask her who exactly was inquiring about my relationship with Papá, but then I'd be admitting that we were related, so I desisted.

'Interesting.' She rubbed her chin. 'I thought… Look, you do not have to tell me anything you don't want to. But know that if you change your mind, I am here for you.'

The maid came in at that moment, holding a metal tray.

'Two *ajiacos* and two guava juices.' She placed the plates on the table, then the silverware. 'Anything else?'

'That is all, thank you.' Miss Galán nodded.

When the woman was gone, I tried to make up for my abrupt reaction.

'I love chicken soup.'

'I do too. Please eat.'

I stirred the soup, wishing I were invisible so that I could run away without being noticed.

'I thought you said you liked it.' Miss Galán peeked at my full plate.

'I do. It's just a little hot.'

'I've seen you have become friends with Gabriela Gonzáles. She is a fine girl, and so is her family.'

'Yes, she is.'

'You might want to join the basketball team. You'd like it. And you can make even more new friends.'

'I don't know. I wish I could swim instead.'

Memories of my brothers, sister, and I playing tag in my grandparents' pool flashed through my mind like a distant movie.

'Well, perhaps you could try something new. That's how we grow.' Her face shone. When we finished eating, she said, 'As I said before, you know you can always come and talk to me, right?'

I felt her gaze go right through me.

She knows he is my father. But why is she asking me, then? What does she want? I couldn't trust anyone.

I checked my nails, trying to hide my discomfort.

'Thanks.' I was glad she didn't keep interrogating me.

All I wanted was to be me, without a past, without a well-known last name.

Sunday afternoon, at the end of Easter break, I heard girls chatting and laughing outside. I peeked out the window, adrenaline rushing through me. It had been a lonely week, and I couldn't wait to see Gabriela again. There was a line of cars idling in front of the school. Impatient drivers waiting to drive up to the gates and drop off the students. Almost everyone exiting the cars carried some type of bag. Maybe cookies or candy their parents had bought for them?

If my parents were here, what would they give me? Sweets? No, perhaps dried fruit or even a box of coloring pencils?

Happiness glowed inside me just thinking that one day I could draw again.

'Coloring pencils are expensive.' I could still hear Mamá's voice before she left. 'I'll send money soon so that you can buy some.'

A car honked in the distance, and through my window, I saw a well-polished automobile. The driver jumped out of the vehicle and opened the back door for Gabriela. With the grace of a gazelle, she stepped out of the car. Her colorful blouse and jeans made her seem older. Something about her had changed.

From the other side of the car came a tall, young man. His shoulder-length, brown hair, boots, wide belt, hip-high jeans, and a cotton shirt with rolled-up sleeves made him appear as if he had just jumped out of a western movie. I stared. Captivated. When he looked up at me, catching me watching him, I moved away. I leaned against the wall and waited until I caught my breath.

Who is he? Is that her friend? A boyfriend?

I glanced out once more. The young man was kissing Gabriela on the cheek. Then he looked my way again. This time I didn't hide. I pretended to be waiting for someone, but my heart was thumping with excitement. Girls were coming up, so I ran down the stairs to greet Gabriela. When I arrived at the gates, the young man and his chauffeur were driving away.

'Rocío!' Gabriela dropped her bag, and we embraced.

'Is this new?' I touched her silky blouse.

'Yes.'

'It's so pretty.'

'Much better than our gray uniform, right?'

We both laughed.

'Can I help?' I asked.

'No thanks. But come with me. I have something to tell you.'

Once Gabriela had unpacked, we walked out to the garden.

'Something incredible happened,' she said, pulling me over to a bench. 'With a boy.'

'What?' I asked.

'I met this guy, Luis. He's my brother's friend. Much older than me, but he is sooo cute.'

'Was that him in the car with you?'

'No, silly. That's my brother. Did you see us?'

'Yes, I was waiting for you.'

'Ricardo, my brother, is nineteen. But sometimes he acts like my father. I hate that.' She twisted her mouth to one side.

'He seems nice,' I said, feeling jittery with adrenaline. 'I saw him drop you off.'

'Wow, you're blushing!' Gabriela smiled.

'I'm not.' I touched my face. 'I think I'm just warm. But tell me about your friend.'

Gabriela looked at me with probing eyes, then continued, 'Let me tell you what happened. Luis was waiting for Ricardo, so we talked. I mean, he actually did most of the talking. I just listened. It was like I couldn't take my eyes off him. You know?'

'I know.'

'Why are you smiling?'

'I'm just happy for you.'

That afternoon, Gabriela confessed she was glad to be back at school. Apparently, her parents were arguing more often at home. One day, her parents were in the middle of a screaming match when Ricardo intervened. Their father became outraged. Gabriela heard her brother yell at their father that it wasn't a good idea to hire pistoleros to protect them from the guerrillas.

'Pistoleros are hired to *kill* guerrillas,' I said, digging my nails into the palm of my hands. Had her father sent Gabriela to this school so she could spy on me? Did Miss Galán know anything about it?

'Are you okay? You look pale.'

'I'm fine,' I mumbled.

'Good.' Unsure if I was being truthful, she forced a smile, then continued, 'My father and brother fight all the time. Father says that the university where my brother is going is poisoning his head with socialist ideas.'

Could I ever be with Ricardo, knowing that I could put my father in danger? Plus, Ricardo's father would probably hate me. I began hyperventilating.

'I think it's something I ate.'

Words pounded inside my ears, *I don't want to be Rocío Valásquez anymore.*

Homecoming: Embracing the Familiar

During the two months following the spring break, I practically lived in the library preparing for finals. One day, Miss Galán walked into the area where I was studying and tapped her pen on my table.

'Rocío, would you please see me in my office in ten minutes?'

'Yes, ma'am.'

My body tensed. Memories of my parents, siblings, and grandparents spun in my head.

I can't handle more bad news.

Mario's passing still brought tears to my eyes. I gathered my things quickly, hoping to follow her, but by the time I was ready, she had gone. The door of her office was closed, but I could hear Miss Galán speaking on the phone.

'I'll see you soon, Mr. Díaz.'

When I heard my grandparents' last name, I knocked on the door.

'Come in.' Inside, she was hanging up the receiver. 'Please, sit down.' She lowered her glasses and gazed at me. 'How are you, Rocío?'

'I'm fine.' I placed my schoolbag on the floor next to her desk.

For some reason, I felt the sudden desire to run. But I kept standing, waiting for her to tell me what was going on.

'I have good news. Your grandfather is going to pick you up and take you home for the midyear break.'

'Really?' I asked in disbelief. 'What about Liliana?'

'He said, "the girls" therefore, I am assuming she is going too.'

I was bursting with excitement. 'When?'

'This coming Friday. He will be here with the rest of the parents. So, be ready at three o'clock.'

'Thank you. Thank you.' I leaped up with happiness.

'I'm glad for you. But there is something else. Please sit, this will not take long.' The principal cleared her throat. 'As I mentioned before, there are a couple of parents who have approached me, concerned about your relationship with Doctor Velásquez. I assured them you are not related. You probably know that our country has been highjacked by extremist groups and those fighting

250

the rebels. And I am not about to let politics take over this school. I am here to protect all students and that includes you and Liliana.'

With my heart hammering in my ears, I remained quiet. I didn't want to cause any trouble for the principal.

She continued, 'Anyway, I suggest you don't discuss your family affairs with other students.'

'But what do they want?' I finally had the energy to ask.

Those nosy parents probably want us expelled as an act of reprisal for my father's involvement with revolutionary groups, the same groups who were fighting against them, those wealthy families. As if someone were pouring ice water down my back, I shivered.

'I don't know. They are probably trying to keep their children away from anyone who could influence them... politically. But don't worry. I will continue to deny you have anything to do with him. You should do the same thing.'

I swallowed. There was no doubt she knew who my father was. But it was clear she was covering for me. I took a breath of relief and then nodded. Miss

Galán walked towards the door, so I stood up. 'And please know that what you tell me about your family is private.'

'Thanks.'

'One last thing, when you come back from your break, we should have lunch again.' She winked at me.

'I would like that. Can I bring Gabriela this time?'

'Of course. And speaking of her, I recommend you don't share anything about your father with her either.' She walked me to the door.

My shoes squeaked from my sudden stop. 'Why?'

'Her father is one of the ones who has been inquiring.'

Gabriela was getting her uniform ready for Monday when I walked in. 'What happened to you? Your hair, it's all wild.' She smiled.

'I'm going home.' I said, still nervous about what I had just learned about her father.

'What? When?'

I dropped my books on my bed. 'Friday.'

'So, what's the matter with you? Why the long face?'

To change the subject, I asked, 'Are you going to see your boyfriend?'

'He is not my boyfriend. I only have friends, and you are my best friend.' She touched my arm.

I realized then that she wasn't using me to get to my father. But her father still worried me. 'I was just teasing. You know, aside from you, I don't have any friends here. They are all rich and stuck-up.'

'Ay.' Gabriela shook her head. 'Try harder.'

'Try harder? What do you mean?'

She whispered, 'It's that your head is always inside a book.'

'Well, I have to study,' I grumbled.

'I know, but you don't come out and play with the rest of us, so people think you are the one who is stuck up.'

'What? Why didn't you tell me this before?' I sat on the floor in disbelief.

Gabriela sat next to me. 'Because you are always sad, and I didn't want to make things worse. Don't feel bad. I just thought that now that you are happy because you are going home, you should know.'

She was right. I was most unhappy at school, frustrated chasing after my father, missing my family, and mourning Mario. In the process, I had ignored almost everyone else. All that brought me joy were my books. My only rewards were my grades, spending time with Gabriela and my sister, and having a sporadic lunch with the principal.

Friday arrived with chatter, giggles, and activity as the girls packed to go home. Outside, parked cars waited for students to come out of the gates.

'I'm leaving soon,' Gabriela said, and embraced me.

'I'll walk you out.' I grabbed one of her bags.

'Are you sure your grandfather is picking you up? Because if he doesn't, you can come to my house.'

As appealing as it was to get to know her brother, Ricardo, I felt terrified to come across her parents. I couldn't trust her father and maybe not even her mother. Besides, I was yearning to see my family.

'He'll be here soon. I know.'

When we arrived at the entrance of the school, the crowd was thinning out. Only a few cars remained. I was about to leave Gabriela's bag and go back to the dorm to avoid running into her family when Ricardo jumped out of his polished car.

'Hey, Gabby!'

It was too late for me to run away. So, I placed my friend's bag on the floor and looked back towards the school as if I were expecting someone else. Ricardo approached us, kissed his little sister, and took her bag. She hugged me goodbye and waved at the gray-haired lady sitting in the back seat, then ran to the car.

'Hello. I'm Gabriela's brother, Ricardo, and you are?' He smiled and extended his hand.

Our eyes locked for a brief moment. Suddenly, my legs felt weak.

'Rocío.' I shook his hand.

Looking at me from head to toe, he said, 'So you're Rocío.'

'Yes.' I turned to leave, trying to hide my burning cheeks.

'Let's go,' Gabriela's mother called from inside the car.

'Bye, Rocío.' Ricardo said.

I waved and continued walking. Once I was back inside the building, I peered through a first-floor window. Ricardo was riding in the front of the car, on the passenger side, his gaze moving up and down the school, almost as if he were searching for me.

My feet felt heavy as I watched their car creep away. I couldn't get Ricardo's smile out of my head.

For two hours, I waited for my grandfather, standing by the window where I had watched Gabriela and her family drive away. Traffic came and went. But as the sun set, my heart raced. To distract myself, I went back to the empty dormitory. A chilly breeze came through the open window. The bedding was being washed, leaving the mattresses naked. Only my bag was left. On it lay my folded ruana. I grabbed the shawl and wrapped myself in it.

Outside, the park across the street was mostly empty. Only one girl and her mother were there. The girl's ponytail swayed in the wind as the woman pushed her swing. I thought of my grandparents' yard and their home in the city. Swinging was like flying without wings. From up above, everything seemed small and unimportant. I envied that girl.

It was not until the bells of the nearby church tolled six o'clock that I realized that the park was deserted.

Please don't let me down, Grandpa.

'Rocío,' Miss Galán called.

I turned around.

The principal approached me. 'Your grandfather called and apologized. It seems that his car broke down, but he will be here soon.'

I couldn't conceal my delight. 'How soon?'

She was now standing in front of me. 'I don't know. He was trying to catch a taxi.' She gave me a faint smile. 'Would you like to have dinner with me?'

'No thanks. I'd rather wait.'

'All right, let me know if you need anything,' she said before leaving the dorm.

Half an hour later, I heard someone honking outside the school gates. A taxi with three people. Liliana emerged from one side.

I opened the dormitory window and peered out at her. 'Liliana.'

'Sorry we're late,' she said, looking up at me.

I bolted downstairs where my sister and I embraced as if we hadn't seen one another for years.

'Sorry, Rocío,' Grandpa said, and gave me a hug. 'I liked my car at first because it's a classic. But as your grandmother said, it is only for show. I would've been here long ago if it hadn't been because the stupid car left me stranded.'

'It's all right. I'm just glad you are here now.'

'C'mon, girls. It's getting late.' Grandpa Miguel patted my back.

As we drove away from the city, the stars shone like scattered crystals in the dark sky. I couldn't wait to see my brothers and grandmother.

'Did you ever get to read the papers that Mario sent you?' Liliana whispered.

'No. And I don't want to talk about it now.'

'Why not?'

'Because we can get in trouble,' I said. Miss Galán's words of advice spun in my head.

Grandpa turned around to face the back seat. 'I suggest you throw away anything Mario gave you.'

Our mouths dropped open in surprise. Apparently, Grandpa's hearing wasn't as bad as Grandma had thought.

'Why do you say that?'

'Just get rid of it.' Grandpa's voice had turned harsh.

Liliana shook one hand. The signal for; *Is he upset with us?*

She gazed at Grandpa.

I twisted my mouth to one side, meaning; *I don't think so.*

Our grandfather turned around again and gave us a wary look. 'If I were you, I'd forget all about Mario. Nothing good happens to people who support the commies. I told him many times, and I've also told you this before.' He straightened up and continued giving directions to the driver.

When we arrived at our grandparents' home, all the lights were off. Liliana and I kissed Grandma, then immediately went to bed close to midnight.

The next morning, I woke up with Jaime and Orlando jumping on my bed.

'Are you awake?' Orlando pulled my eyelids up.

I stretched. 'I wasn't, but now I am. How are you?'

'We're fine.' Jaime pulled the pillow from under my head. 'Let's go to the pool.'

My brothers' daily pranks used to annoy me, but not today. I got up and hugged them both. They said they were fine when I asked them how they were doing.

'Not true, Jaime is getting really bad grades,' Orlando said.

'Are you?'

He put my pillow back on my bed. 'They aren't that bad.' He stared at his feet.

'Yes, they are,' said Orlando. He was about three inches taller than Jaime, who was a year older.

Grandma came into my room. 'My girl, how are you? I missed you so much.' She kissed me on the cheek.

'I'm fine.'

'You seem thinner, but your skin color is still rosy.' Grandma gazed into my eyes. Even though the wrinkles on her face were now more noticeable, she was as elegant as Audrey Hepburn. Every day, she would take a shower and dress before breakfast. Her father had taught her never to go to the dining room until she was ready to be in public. This day wasn't any different. Her dark, short hair, in contrast with her white cotton blouse and ruby lipstick, made her look stylish.

'Go get cleaned up and let's have breakfast,' she said.

Jaime held my hand. 'But what about the pool?'

'That's going to have to wait. First, we want to hear all about Rocío and Liliana's school.'

On my way to the dining room, I heard the macaw, Rebecca, calling my grandma.

'Emilia… Emilia.' I went out of the house to watch the colorful bird dangle on the tree when I noticed that where once stood Mario's house, only rubble had been left behind.

Breaking Ties with Papá

Devastated by the emptiness left by Mario's absence and the demolition of his house, I collapsed on the ground. I picked up a handful of gravel, slowly releasing it through my fingers.

Is this all that is left when we are gone? Do people forget about you so soon? It was as if someone had wanted to erase all traces of his existence and, in some odd way, that of my father. The scorching sun on my back, compounded with the feeling of betrayal, left me perspiring and shaky.

'Niña Rocío, what are you doing?' Avelina asked as she approached me.

'What happened to Mario's house? Who did this?' I brushed my hand over the fine sand.

Avelina raised her arms up in the air. 'You better talk to your grandmother. It's not my place... come, get up. You are getting dirty.' She attempted to help me stand up, but I pulled away.

'This is not right.'

I felt my chest stiffen with sadness. His library and all the hidden articles, gone. My only contact to Papá's world, wiped out.

'But, niña Rocío... he has passed...'

'So what? Does that mean we have to get rid of everything he had? Why didn't someone tell me?'

'I better go get your grandmother.'

'No. I'll go.'

Avelina walked briskly ahead of me until we arrived at the dining room, where the others were having breakfast. She rolled her eyes to show my grandmother that I was upset and then disappeared into the kitchen.

'What happened?' I demanded.

'I'm sorry,' said Grandma. 'We had to do it.'

'Why didn't you tell me?'

'Tell you what?' Liliana rested her chin in her hands and gazed at me.

'They bulldozed Mario's house. Didn't you notice?'

Orlando raised his shoulders. 'It was actually kind of fun to watch them flatten it.'

I covered my ears with both hands. 'Oh my God, it's like no one cares. I can't believe it. What about his paintings and his things?'

'Rocío, sweetie, calm down.' Grandma's voice softened. 'I'll explain if you give me the chance.'

When I took my hands off my face, I saw my siblings staring at me with worried eyes. Grandpa pretended to read the newspaper. He lowered it, peeked at me, then raised it back up.

'Fine.' I sat down.

'The house had many cracks, so we had an engineer check it. After a lengthy study, the man told us that the house was unsafe to live in, and that the repairs would cost more than building a new house. We had to demolish it. We didn't want you kids to get hurt, or anyone else.'

'But what about everything inside?' I couldn't tell my family that losing Mario was more than mourning a great uncle. It was as though someone had turned off the last glimmer of light left inside a dark, endless tunnel, leaving me behind, scared and with no hope of finding my father.

'We gave most of it away to the poor.'

'His books and his drawings?'

Grandpa brought the newspaper down to his chest. 'I already told her it was all revolutionary propaganda. Karl Marx, Friedrich Engels, Mao Tse-tung.'

Grandma gave my grandfather a piercing look before answering me. 'We were planning to tell you about what we found and all about the house today.'

Grandpa folded the newspaper, placed it on the table. 'Look, I am a councilman in town, and I can't take the risk of having communist books and editorials on my property. I would probably be kicked out of the association. Even worse, the police could arrest me for being a communist sympathizer.'

'But didn't you save anything for me?' Tears rolled from my eyes, and my throat closed.

'The books were donated to the library in town, and some of his art… we kept, including your portrait. The rest we gave away to friends and family.' Grandma held my hand.

I wiped my eyes with a napkin. 'Can I have my picture?'

She smiled. 'Of course.'

With my heart still aching, I let go of her hand.

She tried to console me. 'How about if we have breakfast, and then you and I take a walk?'

I was waiting by the water fountain when Grandma came out of the house. She was wearing an enormous hat, boots, and gardening gloves. In one hand, she carried her pruning shears. 'Aren't you going to wear a hat?' she asked me.

'No, I'm fine.'

'If you don't take care of your skin, you'll get wrinkles.'

'It's not too hot.' I didn't want to talk about my skin or how the sun could make me look old. Had they found any documents at Mario's house with my father's name? I didn't believe he had sent them all to me.

'Walk with me, Rocío. I need to prune some bromeliads.'

I followed her to the entrance of the property. From the young trees that don Rogelio had planted along the cobblestone estate entry, grew short-stem, spiny-leafed plants.

'I love their flowers and to think that in Spain, they didn't even have them until Columbus brought them back from one of his trips.' She cut a couple of dead leaves before continuing. 'When Mario realized he was not going to make it, he made me promise I would help you.'

A floating sensation of hope and gratitude rose in me.

Grandma will help me?

'I need to find him. I want to know what he is doing.'

'Look, Rocío, there is a cold war going on. And even though I said I would support you, I feel that the best thing for you to do is to forget about your papá… at least for now. Trust me.'

'I can't do that,' I replied, on the brink of tears.

Grandma turned to me. 'Calm down, please. Listen to me. I will help you by sharing information about him. However, you cannot look for your papá because he doesn't want to be found. Has that occurred to you?'

I shook my head.

'Besides, your grandfather wouldn't be happy if he knew I was aiding your search. He was livid when he realized Mario was a supporter of the whole leftist movement. So, whatever I tell you has to stay between you and me.'

'But Grandpa needs to understand he is my father.'

'He understands, but he is also opposed to the guerrillas. And, I must admit, I agree with him. There are other ways to fight against injustice.'

'I won't tell him. I won't tell anyone. I promise.'

Grandma lifted her hat, then sighed. 'To understand what drove your papá to become who he is, you need to learn more about life, history, politics, and so many other things.'

'Why can't you just tell me?'

'I wouldn't even know where to begin. You are going to have to be patient. To find out about your papá is not going to be easy.'

A light breeze swept the dry foliage around us. My body relaxed. Grandma perked her head up. 'You don't want to put us all in danger, do you?'

'No. But, at least, I should know what's so important to him.'

'It's hard to say because the media doesn't cover everything. And the underground publications are not only hard to find but also, I don't feel comfortable buying them.'

I held my hands tight, impatient about my grandmother's refusal to help me find my father and now her less-than-hopeful support.

She continued, 'There is one more thing. You are the oldest, and therefore, it is your job to protect your siblings. This includes keeping all information regarding your papá from them. They are too young to understand.'

'You mean lie?'

'It is not lying. It's protecting them. Boys look up to their fathers. You don't want your brothers to grow up and follow in your papá's footsteps, do you? Your mamá would die if that happened. You must not allow problems to deter you from your goals. Your mission is simply to keep them safe. I understand you want to know about your papá, but you should also focus on school, succeed, and make your mamá proud.'

'I am trying.'

'Don't get sidetracked searching for your papá. Go to college and travel. Take advantage of the opportunities life brings to you. Don't let challenges hold you back.'

'I'm confused. First, you tell me to protect my siblings, and now you want me to go to college and travel the world?'

'Those two things go together. Focus on the long-term goal. The most important thing is for you to ensure your future. Become an independent woman. This way, you don't have to rely on a man to support you. You cannot let any of this keep you from achieving your goals.'

A profound emptiness traveled through me thinking about Mamá working in another country to pay for our expenses.

'You must be a role model for your brothers and sister. Promise me,' Grandma said.

'All right, I promise. But please help me learn more about Papá.'

'I'll do my best.'

The sun was directly overhead when I arrived at the pool. Liliana, Jaime, and Orlando were betting on who could stay underwater the longest. I sat on the boulder next to the pool to reflect on what Grandma had asked me to do. Could I somehow have the strength to pave the way for my siblings? Orlando and Jaime already pretended Papá didn't exist. However, Liliana had followed in my footsteps. I knew that, like me, she still hoped that our papá would return one day.

'Come in, Rocío,' Jaime called out. 'You need to play too.'

'Yea.' Orlando waved from the other side of the pool.

'One moment. I need to warm up first.'

Liliana's head popped out of the water. 'How long was I under?'

'One minute and ten seconds.' Jaime checked his watch. 'It's your turn, Orlando.'

Orlando came out of the pool, walked to the deep end, then dove in.

'One minute sixty-two seconds,' Jaime called when Orlando burst out of the water with a loud gasp.

Orlando wiped the water from his eyes. 'I'm winning,' he said with a smirk on his face before getting out of the water.

I thought about the cornea transplant ordeal and silently thanked Monique, the cornea donor.

Because of you, my brother can see and play like a normal eleven-year-old boy.

In that instant, a pair of doves flew out of a tree. I smiled and gave Monique an imaginary hug. So much had happened since that winter day at the train station, when we waved goodbye to our father, Mamá's car accident, Jaime's fishing ordeal, the men trying to kidnap us, Mamá leaving, and me being separated from my siblings. I felt a knot in my throat just thinking about Hanukkah at Grandma Sarai's home.

I shook my head, trying to erase all the sad memories. Then I joined Liliana, who was standing by the pool next to Orlando.

'It's my turn.' Jaime gave the watch to Liliana.

He stayed underwater for some time.

'One minute and fifty-two seconds,' Liliana sputtered, looking at me with worried eyes.

I sat by the edge of the pool to see if Jaime was all right. He was floating face-down. My muscles tightened, fearing something had happened to him.

When I was about to jump in to pull him out, he turned over and caught his breath. 'How long?'

I covered my mouth in relief.

'Wow, two minutes and two seconds,' exclaimed Liliana.

'I win.'

'Not so fast. It's my turn. Check the time,' I told my sister, then dove in. With a flip in the air, my body tumbled down to the deep end of the pool. The cool water refreshed my aching heart, erasing the sadness away.

When I couldn't hold my breath anymore, I came up to the surface.

'One minute and thirty-six seconds,' said Liliana.

'Ha. I still win,' Jaime boasted, his chest puffed up as he paraded by the edge of the pool.

'You cheated.' Orlando pushed him.

'No, I didn't.' Jaime shoved back.

Liliana tried to separate our brothers, who were now wrestling. The boys turned on her, and a moment later, they were falling into the pool, punching and screaming. I swam to them and pulled them apart, yelling.

Gasping for air, we got out of the water and sat on the lawn. With water dripping down our bodies, we remained quiet for some time, trying to regain our strength.

I said, 'Look, guys, all we have is—'

'I know, each other,' Liliana interjected.

Jaime and Orlando's chests were still wheezing.

'That's right. So, you can't fight anymore.' My voice cracked.

My brothers stared at me.

'He started it,' they said in unison, pointing at one another.

'You pushed me first,' said Jaime. Blood was dripping from his lip.

Liliana grabbed a towel and pressed it against his mouth. 'Hold it there,' she said.

'Your head was up enough to breathe,' Orlando said.

Jaime moved the towel away from his lip. 'No, it wasn't.'

'Enough!' I screamed.

'I was trying to separate them, and you punched me in the eye,' Liliana squealed at me, pulling down her lower eyelid. 'See what you did.' Her eye and its surroundings were red and puffy.

'I'm sorry, I didn't mean to.' I tried to get close to my sister, but she moved away. 'I said I was sorry. Mamá would be very unhappy if she was here today.'

Orlando moped. 'When is she coming back?'

Trying to lift my siblings' moods, I guessed, 'She should be back by the end of the year.'

'Grandma just got another letter from her. I saw it on her night table.' Jaime twitched.

I propped my head up in delight. 'What do you mean, another letter? I've never received a letter from her.'

'We've read two already,' Jaime admitted.

Why Mamá hadn't sent me anything puzzled me, but stopping the bickering was more important at that moment. 'Look, let's make a deal not to fight. We promised Mamá, so we have to keep our promises, right?'

'Yea, just like Papá kept his promises?' Jaime snapped.

Suddenly, I felt as if my grandmother were speaking to them through me. 'Apparently, he is out there saving the world, whatever that means, and he isn't coming back. We all need to accept that.'

They kept their heads down as I told them we should move on and forget about our father. I also assured them that the only way we could succeed was if we stayed together.

'At least we have Grandma and Grandpa,' said Liliana.

'Let's have lunch,' I said, 'and then we can ask Grandma to let us read Mamá's letters. Is that a deal?'

No one responded. We walked back in silence and went to our rooms to get ready for lunch.

In her letters, Mamá mostly described everyday occurrences. She worked at a hospital assisting dietitians with meal planning. After work, she trod over heavy snow to get to her secretarial school, four days a week. In her spare time, she studied, leaving her little time for other activities.

The third, and last, brief letter Grandma read to us left my siblings and me restless: 'My dear children, I am happy to know you are healthy and doing well in school—'

'Ha.' Orlando interrupted. 'I guess Mamá doesn't know that you are failing all your classes.'

Grandma lowered the letter she was holding. 'That's enough, boys. Jaime is going to do better in school so that I don't have to tell your mamá, right, Jaime?'

I gave him a nudge.

'I guess I can do that.'

'Of course you can,' Grandma said.

Orlando was about to say something else, but I fixed my eyes on him, so he desisted and looked away.

'All right then, let me continue reading.' Grandma cleared her throat. '"I know that our life has not been easy with your papá gone. However, we are blessed to have a great family. All I want now is to finish school, go back to Colombia, and then find a job so that I can buy us a house. Also, I hope that one day, I can find a good man. Please write and have your grandfather send me your letters. It would make me very happy to hear from you. I love you and miss you dearly. Your mamá."'

'What does she mean by finding a good man?' Jaime stood up from the couch, where the four of us were sitting.

'Well, your mamá will have a job and eventually buy a nice home. And, hopefully, get married. Just like she wrote,' Grandma said.

Inside, I felt my chest wheezing with sadness.

Find a good man; the words pounded inside my head.

She had accepted that Papá was never coming back. I slumped onto the couch and glanced at Liliana. Her rounded shoulders showed me she, too, had understood that Mamá wanted to move on.

Jaime stared at me, digging for answers. 'What man?'

I raised my shoulders, hoping he would stop inquiring about our mother. But my brother wouldn't look away. So, I picked up an envelope that was on the nearby table and began fanning myself. There was nothing I could say that would make him feel better. Nor was I ready to admit aloud that our mother was interested in having another relationship.

Jaime stormed out of the room. Orlando leaned on me.

'Why hasn't Mamá written letters to me?' I asked.

'Your mamá doesn't want anyone to know where you live in the city. She wants to keep the family affairs private.'

'Why?' Liliana sat up.

Grandma took a deep breath. 'Those are her wishes, and we have to respect them.'

The weight of Mario's house being gone, Jaime's problems at school, our fight, and Mamá's letter left me feeling ill.

'Tomorrow I'm planning to take you all on a hike to the river,' Grandma said. 'Doesn't that sound like fun?'

I thought of the bromeliads. Like a dry leaf, my family wanted to cut my father off, pretend he had never been there.

Taking Responsibility

Drizzle and sunshine accompanied us most of the way to the river. Bella ran ahead of us, wagging her tail, distracted by all the fresh smells on the road. The boys followed, busy searching for walking sticks. Determined to find a four-leaf clover, Liliana strolled behind my grandmother and me. Suddenly, Orlando stopped to pick up a dry branch, which Jaime quickly took away from him.

'That's mine,' Orlando said, chasing after Jaime.

Grandma confided, 'Jaime's behavior makes Orlando mad, and that's why they get into fights. Jaime is trouble. He's always coming home with ripped shirts and bruises. When I ask what happened, he makes up all sorts of excuses. He says he tripped over things and tells other less believable stories. The principal called last week and said that after school, Jaime and other students meet behind the building where Jaime fistfights with different boys while the spectators cheer.'

'He wasn't like that before,' I said.

As a young boy, Jaime had been a talented singer without even trying. A powerful voice flowed out of his small body. He was the comedian who found humor in simple events and even in our bodily functions. He imitated all those who met him with great accuracy. Liliana, Orlando, and I were his loyal audience, which sometimes got us in trouble. Jaime was the caring one. Once, he saved a piece of candy a friend from school gave to him so that he could share it with the rest of us. He'd always give us his turn riding our one and only bike if we asked him. He'd let us serve our food at dinner before he did.

'Please talk to him,' Grandma said, 'because he doesn't listen to me. And I don't want to tell your mamá. She already has a lot to worry about.'

'What do you think is going on?' I asked.

'Well, you saw him act out when I read your mamá's letter. It's like he is angry inside. And it doesn't help that the other boys at his school challenge him to fight. He could get seriously hurt. Plus, during the fights, he leaves his bags lying around. I've had to buy him books and school supplies several times because others stole his things while he was fighting.'

I was relieved to hear that Grandma agreed with me. Still, I didn't know how to help my brother without hurting him even more.

'That's not good. But I don't know what to do.'

'You should spend more time with him and see if he will open up to you.'

'I'm trying. At least I was able to convince him to come with us to the river.' I took a deep breath. 'By the way, do you think Mamá has met someone?'

'I don't think so, but she is still young and pretty. Being alone is difficult, and she has the right to find a good husband.'

Like a recurring bad dream, the picture of my mother sobbing over the kitchen table in Montréal spun in my head.

Sometime later, we arrived at Avelina's sister's property, which had a shortcut to the river. Avelina's nephew, Tomas, with his German Shepherd at his side, opened the rusted metal gate. Bella padded over to sniff the other dog. Pretty soon, they were frolicking on the ground.

Grandma smiled. 'You can tell they are friends.'

A small tin-roof house was on one side of the property. On the opposite side, scattered orange trees overflowing with ripe fruit brightened the lush greenery around them.

'Look at the oranges.' Liliana caressed one that was hanging from a nearby branch.

'Take all you want. We have a lot,' said the barefooted boy.

'Really?' Liliana snapped the orange from the tree and began peeling it.

'Thank you for allowing us to use this shortcut,' said Grandma. 'Otherwise, we would have to walk a couple of miles to get to the river.'

'No problem. Come anytime,' Tomas said.

The rest of us picked oranges and dropped them in Grandma's basket. Then Tomas walked us to the ledge of the hill. At that point, we again thanked him. Below, the faint sound of water traveled across the canyon. We went downhill through a dense forest of banana and coffee trees, sometimes using them as handles so that we wouldn't slip on the muddy soil. But then, midway through our descent, Grandma slipped. The small wicker picnic basket rolled down the hill, spilling all its contents.

'I'll get it.' Jaime slid on his bottom, like a toboggan, until he reached the food. Orlando joined him, and together they picked up our water container and the snacks.

The sun shone when we arrived at the riverbank, like flickering glitter. The rapids washed over the enormous boulders. Bella jumped into a nearby shallow pond formed by rocks. Orlando and Jaime kicked off their shoes and joined the dog. Orlando broke his walking stick in half and threw it for Bella to fetch. The sound coming from the cascading water made conversation difficult, so Liliana, Grandma, and I quietly sat by the shore and dipped our feet into the cool water. Around us, heavy vegetation and grand trees.

Grandma raised her voice and said, 'What do you think about planting coffee plants in Mario's lot?'

'I think that would make him happy,' I said, as I thought of Mario's fondness for coffee.

In the water, my brothers wrestled over another branch to decide who would play fetch with Bella. At that instant, I remembered my grandmother's warning about not allowing my brothers to develop Papá's traits. But Jaime was fearless and determined, like Papà. He didn't rest until he had taken the branch away from Orlando. In my mind, I heard Mamá's voice say, 'Soldier.'

A vision of Jaime wearing fatigues and boots made me jump. I hurried to separate my brothers. They stopped for a moment. Then they laughed and continued wrestling.

'Rocío, don't worry, I think they're just playing,' I heard my grandmother say. I took a deep breath and walked back to where Liliana and Grandma were, now feeling the sharp rocks carving into the bottom of my feet. Grandma handed me a towel.

'What if we told them you are going to call Mamá?' asked Liliana.

'I can't lie,' Grandma said. 'And I don't want to call your mamá and make her upset. Right now, they are both acting out, but Jaime worries me. He is going to have to change. My hope is that he'll listen to you, Rocío.'

I hated the responsibility everyone was heaping on me, like I had to clean up the mess of our entire family.

After we ate our snack and the sun dropped, Grandma got up. 'Let's go back before the mosquitoes come out.'

For the rest of the six-week school break, I kept my eyes on Jaime. During the day, he enjoyed swimming and the hikes we took with Grandma. We often rode the neighbor's horses. One day, Jaime was trying to stand up on a moving horse to show the man's young daughters he was a skilled rider, but the horse trotted under a tree, throwing Jaime into the air. When we confirmed all he had were a few scratches, we roared with laughter. He didn't smile, though. Clearly, he didn't like to be laughed at.

In the afternoons, he slumped into a chair in front of the TV to watch *The Saint* with Roger Moore. Orlando built cities and parking lots with his miniature cars. Meanwhile, Grandma, Liliana, and I retreated to the study. There, Grandma read to us from history books and showed us maps in geography books.

Three days before we went back to school, I found Grandma looking at some childhood pictures. I swiped my hand over the bookcase that was behind the sofa.

'Grandma, it's obvious that you are fascinated with the tsars, Napoleon, and Latin American novels. But we never got to talk about Papá.'

She closed the photo book and said, 'You should know that history helps us understand the present. Take China, a communist country, where they imprison or kill anyone who disagrees with Mao. We don't want that for Colombia, right?'

'No. Are you saying the same thing could happen to this country?'

Grandma sighed and was about to respond when Liliana walked in and said, 'History is boring.'

'We read novels to remember.' Grandma held my sister's hand.

'I liked the story you told us about Désirée, Napoleon's girlfriend,' said Liliana. But before we responded, she blurted out, 'Rocío likes a boy!'

'Do you?' Grandma grinned.

'It's not like that—'

'Well, you blush when you talk about Gabriela's brother,' Liliana said.

Grandma tipped her head to one side. 'Oh, is that so?'

'No, I don't.' I flinched, just thinking about what Ricardo's father could do to Papá. 'Besides, I don't think I want a boyfriend. Romantic stories always end up bad.'

Grandma consoled, 'Not always.'

'Yes, just like Napoleon left Désirée for Joséphine.'

Like Papá left Mamá. The words got trapped inside my throat.

Liliana's smile disappeared, then we exchanged glances.

My sister and I were packing our clothes to go back to the city when Jaime entered the room.

'When are you going back to school?' he asked.

'Tomorrow,' I said.

He put his hands inside his pockets and walked away. After I finished packing, I went searching for Jaime. I found him standing by the pond. He picked up a flat rock, and like a disk, he made it fly into the air. The rock skipped across the water before sinking.

'That's a nice trick. Where did you learn to do that?' I asked.

'With friends.'

'Can I try it?'

'Here.' He handed me a stone. 'Bend your elbow but keep your forearm at shoulder height.' He modeled for me.

I took the flat stone and threw it as hard as I could, but it tilted in midair, sinking as soon as it touched the water.

'That was terrible. You just need practice.' He took another stone out of his pocket. It spun in the air, then skipped on the surface of the water before sinking.

'Speaking about practice, how are you doing in school?'

Jaime looked away. 'Not so good.'

'What's going on?'

My brother hunched over, pretending to search for more stones. 'Nothing.'

'I was told that you cut school, get into fights, break windows with a slingshot, and you are not studying. I know you don't like it when Mamá is gone, but it is not my fault. So, I don't want to hear that you are in trouble all the time. So, cut it out. Okay?'

Jaime twisted his mouth to one side. 'I hate school.'

'Why?'

'Adults are always telling you what to do, even Grandma and no matter what, I'm always blamed for everything that goes wrong.'

'Who blames you?'

'The teachers, Grandma and Grandpa… everyone.'

'But you are doing bad things. You can get hurt. You know that, right?'

'I won't.'

I tried to make him feel better. 'The end of the year will come soon, and Liliana and I will be back. And probably Mamá will be done with her school by then too.'

Jaime kicked a piece of branch. 'That's a long time.'

I bit my lips, feeling uneasy about giving hope to my brother that I, myself, didn't have. 'It'll go fast. You'll see.'

Jaime turned away. 'I'll be fine.'

'Please promise me you'll be good. Think about Mamá.' I embraced him.

His body stiffened. When I let go, he walked away.

Swirling clouds mixed with burned orange and yellow rays loomed over the mountains far in the distance. Honking geese woke up the ducks lying by the shore. One of them jumped into the lake, flapping its wings. Ducklings, that was the nickname Papá had given us.

Now, more than ever, I have to find Papá.

My chest tightened with sadness just thinking we could also lose Jaime. Bella must have sensed it because she licked my hand.

The following day, Grandma, Orlando, and Jaime walked behind my grandfather's new station wagon until we got to the gate. Sticking our heads out from the rear windows, Liliana and I waved goodbye. As we turned onto the highway, I looked down the hill toward the property. Small coffee plants covered Mario's lot. Standing by the entrance, Grandma and Orlando kept waving. Jaime had left.

Kindred Spirits

A loud quarrel near the school entrance made me flinch. From the empty dorm window, I could see two men who looked like detectives wearing raincoats and hats. Grandpa had brought me a day early, so I was the only student around. Miss Galán was inside the school gates, yelling and flailing her arms around. I ran downstairs and hid near an open window so that I could hear what they were saying.

'No, you are not coming in. I'm calling the police!' she said.

'We *are* the police!' said the lighter-skinned man in a heavy foreign accent.

The other one took one step forward, put his arm through the gate bars, and held up a photo. 'Do you know this man?'

The man's hand was so close to Miss Galán's face that she had to move her head back to examine it.

She shook her head. 'No.'

'We believe he is the father of two of your students, Liliana and Rocío Velásquez. All we want to do is speak with them.'

I swallowed with fear. Visions of the nightmare I'd had years earlier appeared, blood dripping, Papá on the floor unresponsive. My body quivered.

Miss Galán lowered her voice so I could no longer make sense of what she was saying. The trio argued for some time. In the end, the darker-skinned man handed a document to Miss Galán, then the two men got in their car and drove away. Immediately after, she stormed into the building and called my name. I pretended to be searching for a lost notebook.

Fanning the paper in the air, she asked, 'Rocío, did you see those men?'

I cleared my throat to force the words out of me. 'Yes, what did they want?'

'They wanted to speak with you.'

'To me? Why?'

'They are looking for your father.' She rolled the paper tightly.

The words squeaked out of me, 'What did you tell them?'

'I tried to convince them you weren't related to the doctor, but I don't think they believed me.'

My head suddenly felt heavy. As I looked down, tears fell on the hardwood floor.

Miss Galán held my arm. 'I'm sorry. It must be hard for you.'

I nodded. 'Do you think my sister and I are safe?'

'Don't worry. Nothing will happen to you here. They can't get into the school without some type of official document.'

I tightened my fist to get the strength I needed to ask, 'What's in that paper they gave you?'

'It just says that your father has been a powerful ally of Che Guevara. They link him with a guerrilla group that supported the Congolese liberation movement last year, the separatist group in Québec, and many other revolutionary movements. But I suppose you know most of it. Am I correct?'

Understanding my father's pursuits had somehow become less important than finding him. My shoulders sagged.

'I know some things.'

'I thought so.' She let go of my arm.

'Please, Miss Galán, help me find my father.'

She turned to me. 'What?'

'I have to let him know they are after him,' I blurted out.

Her posture turned rigid.

'I see. These men are going to come back. You know that, right? And I don't want other students, let alone parents, to notice that the school is in the middle of some political scandal.'

Miss Galán paced around the room, shaking her head.

'Can I at least read the document the detective gave you?' I begged.

'No.'

'What about the daily newspaper?'

'I don't want more trouble,' she said, but when I dropped my head in disappointment, she softened. 'There is a copy in the library. I cannot keep you from checking it out. When you are done, return it to the librarian.' She patted me on the back and left, waving the document in the air. 'Now, I need to call a lawyer.'

The library was closed on Sundays, so I went to the empty dorm and lay on my bed.

How did the detectives find out where I go to school? Is that why Mamá never wrote to me?

'Stay strong,' were Mamá's last words the night before she left for Chicago. I had tried to keep my promise, but the sense of helplessness was weighing me down. The more I thought about Papá, the more anguish I felt. I sat down on my bed, trying to catch my breath, and glanced out the open window. Families with children were coming out of the nearby church. The world outside seemed so peaceful, while inside of me, everything was chaotic.

Late that afternoon, a swarm of girls began coming in through the school gates, talking and laughing. I stood by the school entrance, waiting for Gabriela to arrive. For the first time, I felt a strong desire to share with my friend the truth about my family, more importantly about my father. I needed someone to talk to. I also needed all the helpers I could get; finding my father had become an obsession.

When the dinner bell clanged, my shoulders dropped. Gabriela wasn't coming. However, as soon as I began walking toward the dining room, I heard a car approaching. I went outside and waited for my friend. Gabriela rolled down the window, and her face lit up when she saw me. 'Rocío,' she shouted, leaping out of the car.

We hugged as if we had been apart for years.

'You are so tanned,' she said.

'You look great too.'

Gabriela had cut her waist-length hair to her shoulders.

'Did you have your hair done?' I touched a strand.

Highlights made her brown hair shine with the sunlight.

'No. It's just the sun.'

My throat tightened. 'I thought you weren't coming.'

'We were at la hacienda, and there was a lot of traffic coming back to the city.'

'I'm glad you are here.' Then I glanced towards the car, hopeful her brother would be inside, but he wasn't there. The driver was pulling a bag out of the trunk.

'Ricardo went back to college. But he sent his regards.' She smiled.

I tried to hide my disappointment.

'Let's go inside. I have a lot to tell you.'

She took her bag, thanked the driver, and walked with me into the building.

'You have five minutes to be in the dining room, or you'll have to go to bed without dinner,' said Miss Rodriguez with her hands clasped on her waist.

'Go leave your things, and I'll see you in the dining room,' I said.

Gabriela sneered and sped upstairs.

That night, when the dorm was quiet and the rest of the students were sleeping, Gabriela and I got up and went to our hiding place, the advisor's office, on the first floor. There, Gabriela told me how heartbroken she and all her relatives were when her father confessed that life in la hacienda wasn't safe anymore. As a result, the children and their mother couldn't come back, the war had intensified.

Sounds of gunfire coming from nearby towns woke them often. Day and night, her father and newly hired armed men patrolled la hacienda. Her father suspected that one day soon, they would have to evacuate their property for fear of getting caught in the middle of the crossfire between the guerrillas and the military.

All I could think of was how her family was being threatened by the war in which my father was actively involved, and how much Papá despised the very system that kept landowners wealthy, while many of their workers had to bury their young children for lack of good medical services and medicines. Yet, there we were. The two of us, coming from opposite worlds, caring for one another.

After she finished, there was a long pause. Gabriela brought her knees closer to her chest and embraced her legs. To hide the overwhelming conflict I felt inside, I rubbed my eyes.

Am I a traitor? What would Papá think if he knew I was friends with the daughter of a man who was fighting the guerrillas and could even hurt him? My thoughts swirled.

What was Gabriela going to do when she found out that I longed to be reunited with Papá, a lead activist and supporter of the revolution? The movement that was threatening the assets of her family and even the life of her father.

'What's going to happen to la hacienda?' I finally asked.

'We don't know. Even if we try to sell it, no one will buy it. At least not now. But enough about me. Tell me about you. What did you do at home?'

Outside, the sound of a siren made us both jerk in our seats.

'I'm sorry about what's going on with your family,' I said. 'I've been scared too. This morning two detectives or policemen, whoever they were, came to the school looking for me.'

Gabriel fixed her light blue eyes on mine. 'What? Who?'

'Well, actually they are after my papá.' I chewed my lower lip to stop myself from crying. As soon as I calmed down, I recounted my family's story and all that had happened with the detectives.

As if she had seen a ghost, Gabriela sat still until I finished my confession. When I was done, she closed her eyes for a moment.

'I'm sorry, amiga. But why didn't you tell me this before?'

'I was afraid,' I said.

'Of what? You don't think I am a spy, do you? Or that my father somehow—'

She raised her chest and squinted as if she were trying to read my mind.

'No. Of course not.' At that instant, I knew she had nothing to do with the detectives' visit. Neither did she have anything to do about selecting this school. I suspected then it was all by chance that the two of us met, both a product of the armed conflict that was devouring our country. However, I still suspected that her father was the one who was trying to find out about my true identity. What for? I had yet to find out. But I wasn't about to tell Gabriela about my suspicions. I didn't want to hurt my friend.

With a sinking feeling, we curled in our chairs, waking up hours later, before the morning bell.

Gabriela and I told Liliana what we had learned about our fathers the previous day. I also told her about the detectives. My sister confirmed that she, too, had seen a silver car.

'They followed us on our way back from Fusa. I hope they never find Papá.' Liliana stiffened.

Gabriela embraced my sister. 'Hopefully, they won't. The whole country is in trouble.' She let go of Liliana and explained how the civil war was spreading like an invasive vine, smothering everyone and everything in its path, leaving nothing but devastation, loss, and many casualties.

We sat on the lawn. The sun hid behind the clouds. A group of students were jumping rope, others stood around the playground, laughing and enjoying their first day back. In us, however, there was only stillness. Perhaps, in one way or another, we were all trying to make sense of our friendship after what we had learned about the conflict between our fathers' ideals.

We made an unspoken deal that day. Above all, we were preserving our friendship. Gabriela took the lead.

'We need to sign up for basketball.'

'But we don't know how to play,' Liliana sighed.

'I know, but who cares? We'll learn.' Gabriela shrugged.

Liliana raised her eyebrows. 'But they'll destroy us in the first game.'

'Not if we practice every day,' I said, and bumped my elbow against Gabriela's.

'We'll eat lunch fast, so we have time to practice at noon,' Gabriela said. 'After school, Rocío and I will practice some more.'

'What about me?' Liliana protested. She argued she wasn't at school for enough hours to practice.

'Find a hoop near where you live and practice shooting the ball through the hoop,' said Gabriela. 'Borrow a ball from the school.'

'You mean steal it?' Liliana's eyelashes fluttered faster. 'I can't do this. What if I'm caught? I'll be expelled. No, we will all be expelled.' She began to hyperventilate.

'Come on,' I said. 'You'll be fine. Remember what Mamá did in Canada? She forced Canadian immigration officers to give us a visa so that we could join Papá in Montréal.'

'What does that have to do with anything?'

'That the goal justified the risk,' I said, then winked at her.

That day, Gabriela and I concocted a plan to have Liliana take a ball home without being caught.

A week later, we had completed a fake art project, a treelike Papier Mâché. We hid a ball inside the base. When we finished, we walked Liliana to the bus.

Gabriela carried my sister's lunch box, and I took her schoolbag. This way, all she had to worry about was the artwork.

Miss Rodriguez was standing by the gates with a clipboard in her hands, checking to see which students were boarding the bus.

In a shrill voice, Liliana said to me, 'I'm afraid.'

'Keep walking and don't look at her.' I stepped in front of my sister to make her feel protected.

'Smile,' cheered Gabriela.

Once we arrived at the gates, Liliana hesitated. Gabriela and I glanced at one another, then at Miss Rodriguez. The gray-haired woman stood on her toes to look at my sister, who was behind me.

'What is that?' Miss Rodriguez asked, approaching us.

Liliana licked her lower lip.

'My sister is taking our art project home so she can show it to the family,' I quickly responded.

Liliana tightened her grip, making her knuckles turn white.

'I don't know what it is, but it's very creative.' The woman tilted her head, inspecting our work.

At that moment, the driver called, 'Let's go.' The bald man waved for Liliana to board the bus, but her feet seemed glued to the cement.

'He's calling you. Go.' I gave my sister a light push.

Liliana stumbled when she stepped onto the first step of the bus, but the driver quickly grabbed her by the arm. Gabriela and I held our breath until she was safe inside.

Liliana peeked out the window and, rolling her eyes at us, said, 'I'm fine now. Give me the bag and lunch box.' I handed it to the driver, keeping my eyes fixed on Liliana, hoping there would be no problems. Once they drove away, Liliana smirked.

For weeks, my routine was to finish my homework at the library and then scan *El Tiempo*, the daily newspaper, in search of news about my father. Reports of other newly formed guerrilla groups, as well as private counterrevolutionary units, paramilitaries, filled the front pages of the newspaper. But no mention of Papá.

Gabriela and I met at the court with other beginners and played until dinnertime. Among rubber shoes screeching against the wooden floor and balls bouncing, Liliana, Gabriela, and I began our basketball practice.

Three months later, the coach selected the players. Training by herself, my sister had spent the afternoons dribbling and shooting the stolen ball at the hoop, earning her the shooter's position. Because I was the oldest and tallest, I became the center, blocking the opposing players from shooting. She selected Gabriela to be the small forward. The Speedy Blond was her nickname because she moved around the court so fast no other player could block her.

On the day of our first interschool game, I went to the library to take a peek at the daily newspaper before heading to the court. The librarian was organizing files.

Without looking at me, she said, 'There's no newspaper today. And Miss Galán wants you to meet her in her office after the game.'

'Do you know why?'

The round-faced woman stopped filing and twisted her lips to one side.

'I don't know what for. And even if I knew, I wouldn't be able to say anything. That's between the principal and you.'

She's found Papá.

The words swirled in my mind until I heard the coach calling my name. Liliana must have noticed because she motioned toward the mounted scoreboard: 2-6, first quarter. We were losing. To focus, I pretended our father was one of the spectators. Suddenly, a gush of energy transformed me into an eager player, often stealing the ball from the other players. The other team stayed ahead in the next quarter, but we tied it up in the third quarter. At the end of the last quarter, I tossed the ball to my sister. She dribbled it, swerving past one of the other team's very aggressive players. When she was blocked, she made a pass to Gabriela, who made the victorious hoop.

The Dark Art of Deception

After the game, Liliana and I excused ourselves and ran to the principal's office. When we arrived, Miss Galán's office door was closed, and we knocked excitedly. After a moment, Miss Galán opened the door of her office.

'Come in, girls. Have a seat.' She showed us two empty chairs, then walked around her desk to sit across from us. On her desktop was a stack of folders, and next to it was a newspaper. Miss Galán was pale, and her lower lip was trembling. 'I am afraid I have bad news.'

Liliana and I held hands. My knee started bouncing out of control.

'I don't know how to. Oh my, I'll just read it.' Miss Galán unfolded the newspaper and read aloud, 'October 21, 1966. Bucaramanga. The authorities confirmed the identity of a group of outlaws who perished during the military operation that took place in this city. Among the ones killed in combat was Doctor Jaime Velásquez along with fourteen other insurgents—'

After this, her words lost all meaning. Liliana and I placed our heads on the principal's desk and wept. Miss Galán stopped reading, came around, and hugged us. She tried to console us. But her voice suddenly became muffled, as if it were coming from afar. Only the pain ripping through me was real.

A while later, I forced myself to stand up, hoping to calm Liliana's sobbing, but my legs felt weak. The room began to spin out of control, so I sat back down and closed my eyes. Grinding my teeth with anger combined with debilitating sadness, I finally asked, 'Do you know if our mother, brothers, and grandparents know?'

'I'm sure they do. It's on TV, the radio, it's everywhere. But I'll send them a letter anyway. I'm reluctant to call because the phone could be tapped.' Miss Galán's eyes narrowed behind her glasses.

I forced myself once more to get up. 'Let's go, Liliana.'

My sister nodded and glanced at me, tears rolling down her cheeks. As we were walking out, Miss Galán handed me the newspaper.

'Please let me know if there is something I can do for you. Also, remember that you can always come and see me.'

The bus was already outside, waiting for Liliana. Near the entrance of the building, Gabriela and some of our teammates were chatting. As we walked by, we felt the girls' prying eyes fall upon us, so we hurried until we arrived at the gate. Then, holding our tears back, we embraced. No words were necessary.

This time, my sister didn't wave goodbye or look out the window as she left. Hunched over, she simply sat in the back of the bus. I didn't watch the bus leave either. Instead, I ran to my bed and sobbed. All I'd hoped for was to bring my family together. But the contrary had happened. Papá was dead.

The following day, I awoke to the loud thump of my heart. I reached for the pillow and put it over my mouth so I wouldn't wake others up with my crying. Dark clouds and angry rain had choked the sunlight, leaving a hazy blanket across the sky. The chilly wind whistled as it filtered through the cracks of the historic building. Then I pulled the covers up to my chin to stay warm and stared at the wooden beams of the colonial ceiling. I envied the massive buttress because it kept the building together, something I hadn't been able to do with my family. I imagined the arch collapsing and heavy boards falling over me, leaving me caught underneath the rubble.

For three days, I wrapped myself in the ruana Grandma had given me, and stayed in bed, complaining that I was too ill to attend my classes. In the afternoons, Gabriela brought my homework to the dorm and sat next to me until she and I finished our assignments. In the morning, she took my work to the teachers. On the second day, I tried to tell her what had happened, but the words got caught in my throat. How could I expect compassion from her when her own father was fighting the guerrillas, my father's men?

Gabriela studied my eyes and then hugged me. 'I'm sorry you are sad. And you don't have to tell me anything if you don't want to. It's all right.' She stroked my back.

There were no phone calls from my grandparents or my mother, most likely because they, too, feared that the phones were tapped. All I had was the newspaper that Miss Galán had given me. On several occasions, I attempted to retrieve it from inside Mario's leather bag, where I kept all documents related to my father, but I quickly dropped it back inside as if I'd pricked my hands with sharp thorns. After many tries, I decided that I didn't want to know anything about Papá's final moments. I didn't even want to know if he had been right to fight for what he believed in. Accepting that Papá had been taken away from us, the man I looked up to, my mother's first love; the doctor whom everyone admired was all I could handle. I took the leather bag and shoved it into the trunk I had under my bed, leaving my hopes buried under clothes and books.

In the afternoon of my third day in bed, Miss Galán came to see me.

'How are you feeling?' she asked.

'Not good.'

'The nurse doesn't believe you are sick. And you and I know she is correct.' My eyes filled up. 'Listen, it is never easy to lose our parents. I lost both of mine last year. But life goes on for us and for our family.'

'I know.' I wiped my eyes.

'Please understand that I am taking an enormous risk. I do it because I like you both and because, as I said before, my mission is to protect my students. But, by you and Liliana missing school, it may become obvious that you are related to the doctor, and we don't want that. Somehow, we need to convince everyone that you are not family. The other parents could put pressure on the board to have you removed from the school to avoid a scandal. I could also lose my job, you know? Therefore, I need you to go back to class.'

My suspicions were correct. It wasn't just us she was trying to protect. She was afraid for herself.

'But I can't,' I said. 'Not right now. Can't I just go home? Please? I beg you.' I covered my face with my hands.

'No, I'm sorry. I have orders from your mother to keep you here until she contacts me.'

'But why not? Why doesn't she call me?'

'I don't know. It's her wish and I must respect it. She is only trying to keep you safe.'

An intense desire to run away left me agitated.

She continued, 'I don't know how much longer I can keep up this lie.' She shook her head. 'TV and newspaper reporters are after me. My secretary has explicit instructions to dismiss them, but these people are relentless.'

'So, all you want us to do is to pretend that he wasn't our father, correct?'

That was what my sister and I had been doing, but apparently, we hadn't been convincing enough.

'Yes, deny, deny.' She flapped her hands in the air. 'That way, we will avoid a scandal. Most importantly, you need to get back to school so that you can help Liliana through this difficult time.'

'How is my sister?' I stared into the principal's narrow eyes.

'I spoke to your mother's friend, Mrs. María Raquel, and she told me that Liliana is not eating well. She even got sick one day.'

'I'll go to class tomorrow,' I said.

'Great, I will let your sister know. Hopefully, she will attend too.'

With only a few hours of sleep, I kept dozing off until the morning bell rang. Between moans and groans, students got up and stood in line for the morning shower. I waited in bed until Gabriela came and pulled my blankets off me. 'Let's go, sleepyhead.'

'I'm not feeling—' I took the covers back from her and rolled to one side.

Animated, Gabriela made up the lyrics to a song.

She sang, 'Today we can do something fun, and maybe we can do it with Liliana.'

I dragged myself out of bed.

'I'm coming.' I grabbed my toiletries and followed my friend.

After breakfast, I sought cover from the downpour under the portico, my gaze glued to the gate, but it was difficult to see. All I could make out were clusters of girls carrying umbrellas, squealing as they ran for cover. Suddenly, someone wearing a yellow poncho ran towards me. Liliana lifted the hood and, staring at me with her dark, solemn eyes, said, 'I'm glad to see you.'

'I'm glad you came.' I embraced my sister and helped her take her poncho off. 'How are you?'

'Not so good, I guess. And you?' She faked a smile.

I took a deep breath and said, 'Like you.'

'What about Mamá and the boys? Do they know?'

'I think so. The principal said she would send everyone a letter. Plus, it's all over the news.'

We went inside the building, where I relayed the conversation I had with Miss Galán.

For days, the torrential rains continued to pound the city. As a result, the basketball tournament was postponed. Having no other place to hide from curious looks during recess, I sat with Gabriela on a couch in the students' lounge. We listened to songs by the Beatles, Bob Dylan, and the Beach Boys on Gabriela's new Philips cassette tape recorder her mother had bought in the United States. The louder we played rock and roll, the less I could hear the voice inside my head reminding me that Papá was dead and that my family was shattered. Captivated by the sounds of the African drums mixed with harmonica, guitar, and piano, I daydreamed of a foreign city where no one knew me, where I didn't have to pretend, where my heart didn't hurt. If Gabriela let me borrow the recorder, late at night I'd sneak into the counselor's office and listen to music until I fell asleep. Each time, Gabriela woke me up so I wouldn't get in trouble.

Soon after, girls wearing peace-symbol necklaces joined our rock and roll group. One day, Liliana rolled her eyes at us in disdain. 'Only hippies listen to that music and hang around with druggies.'

'What are you saying? We don't use drugs.' I got close to Liliana's face.

'I've heard that some of them do,' Liliana whispered, then started to walk away.

At first, I was upset about my sister's comment, then I thought it might be a way to get us home.

'That would be a good way to—'

'Get expelled,' she said, completing my sentence. 'Then we can go home.'

'Exactly. Although I wasn't planning on getting expelled. All we should do is to get in some sort of trouble, so they call our grandparents. And if Miss Galán calls enough times, they will at least come to check on us or maybe even have us go home.'

'Yea.' Liliana held my hands tight inside her hands.

Our plan to get into trouble was short-lived. One afternoon, when the air smelled musky-fresh and heavy clouds threatened the city with rain, the basketball team met at the gymnasium for training. The coach, a powerfully built young woman with legs that resembled those of soccer players, blew the whistle at every incorrect pass, dribble, or shot we made. An hour into our training session, the piercing, long, steady sound of the whistle made us all halt and turn to our coach, who was now screaming, 'We'll never win the championship if you don't pay attention to what you are doing. Go to the benches now.'

The twelve of us ran and did what the coach ordered.

'If you can't pass the ball and shoot, how do you plan to beat other teams?'

Liliana and Gabriela were sitting so close to me, one on each side, that I could hear their heavy breathing. Like me, they were in shock by the coach's angry outburst.

'But Coach Acosta, we are trying—'

The coach's eyes protruded. Then she walked towards us, keeping her eyes on Liliana's. When she got close to my sister, she enunciated each word, 'Trying. Is. Not. Good. Enough.'

The sound of the metal-framed door opening made us all flinch. The principal was now standing by the exit. She waved at the coach to join her. They spoke for a few minutes. The coach shook her head and then came back.

When I saw the coach's somber eyes, I felt an intense desire to hide. I knew that Miss Acosta wasn't someone who scared easily. Something horrible had happened. I couldn't handle any more bad news.

The coach's eyes softened when she looked at my friend. 'Gabriela, the principal would like to speak with you.'

Liliana and I glanced at one another.

'You'll be all right,' I whispered when I noticed Gabriela's tense facial muscles.

When Gabriela got up, she faced Liliana and me. We held hands in a small circle until the coach urged, 'The principal is waiting for you.'

Gabriela let go of us, and hunched over, walked to the exit door. Miss Galán said something to her, then embraced her. Our friend let go of Miss Galán, and squatting, she broke out crying.

At that instant, Liliana and I got up to see what was wrong with our friend, but the coach ordered, 'Sit down.'

'But we have to help Gabriela,' I pleaded.

'Sit.' The coach pointed at our bench.

I looked towards the exit again, and the principal was helping Gabriela stand up.

'Can't you see there is something wrong with Gabriela?' I tried to walk, but the coach's strong finger dug into my arm.

'You are not going anywhere. The principal's orders. Please sit down.'

With all my strength, I pulled my arm away from her and closed my eyes tight in frustration. I was replaying in my mind the scene we had just witnessed, Gabriela torn with pain, when I felt my sister's touch.

'Come on,' she said. Liliana was now sitting down. Brokenhearted for my friend, I sat down too. For the remainder of the training session, Liliana bit her nails, and I stared at the door, hoping Gabriela would be back.

She didn't come back. We heard her father had been wounded, caught in the crossfire between the guerrillas and the armed forces, and had been shot several times. He died later at the hospital from complications.

The Stranger

September 1967

One evening at home, I began skimming over some of my early diary entries. From the family room where I was, I could see Mamá cooking and humming a tune I didn't recognize. My siblings listened to the music coming out of the small R.C.A. transistor radio while they worked on their homework. I felt my chest tense up when I read several sections in which I described my struggles to adjust to my new school and the longing I felt for my family. I inhaled and exhaled slowly.

Each entry reminded me that things were different now. Our mother had arrived home a year after she started her secretarial course, as she had promised. Soon after that, she had rented a small apartment in the city for the five of us. Her well-paid job as an executive secretary for an international corporation allowed her to pay for nearby private schools. On Saturdays, she'd dress up while humming some of her favorite songs to meet her boyfriend.

'When I feel ready, you'll get to meet him. He seems like a good man,' she told us one evening.

My siblings and I refrained from saying anything to her. But when she left, we didn't go out with friends. We stayed in our apartment consumed by what each of us was doing until she returned.

Even though we all missed Papá dearly, we never spoke about him. All we did was deny we were related to him, as Miss Galán had suggested. Mamá agreed; she said that even though Papá was gone, it was a matter of safety. People believed me sometimes, but at other times, they didn't. I think it's because they could see the pain deep inside my eyes.

Jaime stopped fighting at school after he began taking martial arts. His grades improved. Still very competitive, he challenged Orlando all the time to different competitions, who could run faster, who could swim the length of the pool more times, and so on. Now that Orlando's eye was better, he was eager to sign up for Jaime's endless games as long as he could keep his new glasses safe.

My sister and I never played competitive basketball again. After Gabriela left, Liliana and I lost interest in the game. With only three games left to play, they had pulled our friend out of school. We finished fourth and received a small medal for our effort. I hid the little silver plate inside my trunk with the rest of my memoirs. Without Gabriela, an award was meaningless. In the afternoons, I had watched the neighborhood kids play, and I thought of her and the many days we played until dinnertime.

Just like Jocelyne, Gabriela and I had become sisters of the heart. We never spoke about our fathers or their political views. Could it be that Mamá was right? Angels exist, and when our paths cross with theirs, those angels become part of us forever.

I closed my diary when I heard Mamá calling.

'Rocío, dinner is ready.'

I went to the dining room, hoping that food would ease the discomfort I felt about Mamá being involved with someone other than my father. Mamá was pouring guava juice into our glasses. When she finished, she dried her hands with the apron she was wearing over her pencil skirt. 'How was your day?'

'Fine,' the word dragged out of my mouth. I noticed that Liliana and Orlando were staring at their food while Jaime was nervously spreading it around the plate.

'As I told you,' Mamá said, 'Saturday afternoon, we have a visitor. His name is Howard Dresser. He is a delightful man, and he wants to meet you.'

'I don't want to meet anyone.' Jaime's chair screeched as he abruptly stood up.

'Sit down,' Mamá ordered; then her voice softened. 'Please, Jaime.'

He obeyed. His head dropped to his chest, allowing his long bangs to block his eyes. Liliana, Orlando, and I stared at our food while our mother told us all about the man she had met at a party. Unhappy with his engineering work in Greece, he had visited his friend in Bogotá, who was married to a Colombian woman, one of my mother's coworkers. Mr. Dresser had decided to make Colombia his new home after receiving a job offer from Texaco and meeting our mother.

When Mamá finished, my brothers looked at her suspiciously. We all had doubts. Why now? Papá had passed almost a year ago. What if this man did not like us and wanted to take Mamá away from us? He was an American. Could he be a spy? What did he want from us?

'Rocío, are you listening?' Mamá interrupted my thoughts.

'Yes, Mamá. I'll meet him.'

I knew I had to find out everything I could about this man before I could feel comfortable with him. But for now, I wasn't going to share my suspicions with my mother. I didn't want to upset her. For the first time after Papá had left, her face was glowing again. Besides, she deserved to be happy.

I remained quiet until Orlando made us jump when he said, 'That man is not my papá.'

The tears made his long eyelashes stick to the side of his eyes.

'And no one will replace your papá,' Mamá said. 'I know that. But please give him a chance. That's all I'm asking. If you don't like him, I won't see him anymore.'

'I'll meet him. And you should all help Mamá too.' Liliana struck the table with such force that she scared us.

We kept to our chores for the rest of the week, never bringing up the impending meeting with our mother's boyfriend. When Saturday arrived, I awoke at dawn. Outside, the city lights struggled to glimmer behind the dense fog. On my tiptoes, I went to the kitchen. I was writing a letter to Jocelyne, telling her all that was happening when Mamá walked in.

'You can't sleep either?' She kissed my forehead.

I shook my head.

'It is natural that we want things to stay the same, but it doesn't always happen that way, I guess. Unfortunately, your papá isn't with us anymore.'

My mother's words ripped open the wound that I was trying so hard to heal. I dropped the pen I had in my hand and wept.

Her voice cracked with grief. 'I lost him, too, you know? But we need to move on. And I need your help.'

I moved away from her. How could I support my mother without feeling like a traitor? The thought of having another man at home who wasn't my father made me feel faint. However, when I heard Mamá sniffling, I forced myself to say, 'I'll try.'

She fixed her robe and said, 'Thank you. That means a lot to me. Now help me make breakfast.' It surprised me to see how fast she transitioned from grief to thinking about preparing food. Almost like some sort of chant, I heard her words in my head.

Move on. That's what we've always done, and that's what we should continue to do.

So, I helped her in the kitchen, making an effort to hide the painful ache inside me.

Later in the day, the sound of the doorbell ripped through our apartment.

'I'll get it.'

Our mother opened the door. Playful curls bounced from her now short hair. The pencil skirt and blouse she had made for herself made her look like a much younger woman.

A tall, heavyset man with glasses stood outside the door.

'Good day. Is this a good time?'

'Yes, please come in.' Our mother hugged the man and nervously showed him in. 'Come, say hello to Mr. Dresser.' Mamá gave me a light push. 'And speak English, because he doesn't speak Spanish.' Her mouth tightened when she noticed that my brothers were rolling their eyes. She was about to reprimand them when Liliana took one step forward.

'Hi. My name is Liliana.' She shook the man's hand. At almost fourteen years old, her body still resembled that of a boy, flat-chested and with thin legs. The silky short dress she was wearing appeared too big for her fragile body.

'And mine is Rocío,' I said, following my sister. 'I'm seventeen.'

We turned to my brothers. Orlando fiddled with his collar, pretending it was uncomfortable. And Jaime placed his hands in his pockets and rocked as he looked away.

Mr. Dresser walked up to them and said, 'You must be Jaime. Your mother told me you are twelve years old. Correct?'

Jaime nodded.

'It's a pleasure to meet you.' The man smiled, showing his dimples. 'And you must be Orlando.' Mr. Dresser approached my other brother. Orlando looked around the room as if he were searching for a way to escape, but he didn't move. Mr. Dresser continued, 'For an eleven-year-old boy, I hear you are very studious.' The man extended his hand, hoping to shake hands with my brother. But Orlando kept fiddling with his collar.

For an hour or so, Mr. Dresser did most of the talking. He told us all about his work in Greece, the dark and heavy coffee they drink in that country, and about his new job in Colombia. He had been asked to build the oil camps in the southern part of the country, and as a result, he was required to live at the camp Monday through Friday. Relief washed over me and I sighed when I learned Mr. Dresser was not going to be around during the week. Liliana and my mother tensed up from seeing my reaction. At the end, he surprised us all when he asked Mamá, 'So would it be all right if I took the kids to the movies?'

Going to the movies was expensive, so we rarely went to the theater.

Mamá grinned. 'Whatever they want is fine with me.'

I also smiled because I could tell our mother would have liked to go out on a date with him or even accompany us, but it was clear she wasn't invited.

'What movie?' Jaime finally mumbled.

'How about Aladdin's Magic Lamp?' Mr. Dresser said in a playful voice, trying to motivate us.

Orlando and Jaime glanced at one another.

'I'll go.' Orlando played with his hands.

'I'll go too.' Liliana lifted her chin to me, signaling; *Come on, you too.*

'Yes, we will all go. Thank you,' I said.

Even though Mamá seemed very confident about the man's intentions, my loyalty to my father, and the fact that this man was an American, still made me feel apprehensive. I wasn't about to let my siblings go out alone with a person I couldn't trust. As if someone had pushed me from behind, I scurried to the door.

'Shall we go, then?'

'Sure.' Mr. Dresser winked at our mother.

Before the movie, Mr. Dresser asked us to choose a restaurant. My siblings and I couldn't think of one, because we never ate out. To avoid being embarrassed, I croaked in a voice I didn't recognize, 'You decide.'

Liliana raised her eyebrows, thanking me.

'I know the perfect place. My friend took me there a few days ago, and the food was delicious.' Mr. Dresser gave me a pat on the back. 'It's a few blocks from here.'

At the Restaurante las Olas, waiters moved around the enormous room, buzzing with talkative people. One agile man, dressed in white, went by us, swinging a tray with barbequed steaks, roasted potatoes, corn on the cob, and my favorite: fried ripe plantains.

That day, my brothers ate like I'd never seen them eat before. Orlando ordered beef with vegetables and corn. Jaime had become a vegetarian after watching don Rogelio kill a chicken for dinner, so he ordered the same dish as Orlando, but instead of the meat, he had fried yuca, a starchy, creamy root similar to a potato. Mr. Dresser joined Orlando and ordered beef. Liliana and I shared a large dish with fish, corn, and plantains. We ordered Colombiana, a traditional soda. At first, I felt uneasy disobeying Papá's wishes that we never drink sodas, but soon the guilt dissipated as the sweet drink calmed my thirst.

Little by little, we told Mr. Dresser about our new schools. Orlando joked that Jaime had been called to the principal's office because he had been caught kissing a girl. Liliana joined in and shared that a boy at school carried my books. I thought of Ricardo, Gabriela's brother. After his father was killed, the police blamed the guerrilla, and the guerrilla blamed the police for his death. Regardless, Ricardo and I never looked at one another in the same way.

Liliana must have noticed that I was reminiscing about the past, because she gave me a little nudge. And so, I tried, though unsuccessfully, to convince everyone that I had nothing going on with the young man who, for one day, had carried my books. Pointing at me, Jaime choked on his drink from laughter. Orlando joined in and said he didn't like any of my friends. Mr. Dresser didn't take sides. He smirked at our silly jokes.

After we enjoyed the movie, we took a taxi home. Like a tight restraint, a suffocating silence swathed my siblings and me. I opened the window, letting fresh air inside. We all inhaled. I didn't have to ask my brothers and sister why their early bliss had turned into a serene sadness. We couldn't replace our father, no one could, not even this charming stranger. That would be a betrayal. I couldn't trust him or anyone else. More importantly, I wanted to know what he thought about Papá.

Mr. and Mrs. Dresser

For the next few months, every Sunday, Mr. Dresser, my siblings, and I went out to lunch, followed by a surprise outing. Sometimes we went sight-seeing in Mr. Dresser's car. On other occasions, we explored the museums. While in the Bogotá Gold Museum, we entered a dark room that resembled a vault. Once everyone was inside, the large, heavy door closed, leaving the room for a second or two in complete darkness. Then slowly, the lights brightened, allowing us to see the circular room we were in. Thousands of pre-Colombian gold pieces covered the walls. In the middle of the room, a large, round table contained additional gold figures. We laughed when Mr. Dresser, mesmerized by the sight of so much gold, rubbed his eyes, then cleaned his thick glasses as if it were all a dream. When he heard us giggle, he twisted his mouth to one side, trying to stop himself from laughing too.

Sometimes, the five of us came home carrying large bags of items he had bought for us during our adventures. Pretty soon, we had new backpacks, shoes, balls, and other toys. Papá would have considered them extravagances. Each time, Mamá questioned us, trying to find out if we had asked for these gifts. Each time, we gave her our word that we had never asked for anything. They were all Mr. Dresser's ideas. And then one day, a delivery man surprised us with a new refrigerator.

'A gift from Mr. Dresser.' was all the serviceman said. And Mamá understood. Saturday was Mamá and Mr. Dresser's date day. Our mother and her boyfriend joined other couples and went out for the night. Every time I watched them leave, my heart and my head entered a long and heated debate. Part of me wanted to stop this nonsense with Mr. Dresser courting our mother and invading our family. The other part of me heartened when I saw his expression soften at the sight of our mother, his eyes turning glossy with admiration and joy.

Still not convinced of the stranger's true intentions, I called his company to check if he worked there. He did. When his friends came over to our place, men and women fluttered around him like bees seeking pollen. It angered me to realize that deep inside, I, too, was slowly becoming fond of this man. And I wasn't the only one. My brothers and sister never planned activities with friends on Sundays anymore, always hoping to go out with Mr. Dresser. The day he asked us if he could marry our mother, we cheered.

I found Grandma and Lola arranging the centerpieces for the wedding in my grandparents' dining room. The bouquets of roses and lilies made me think of spring. When I came in, Lola blurted out, 'Oh my, you are such a young lady now.' Small wrinkles appeared around her eyes.

'I can't believe you came.' I gave her a hug. 'How is your mother?'

Lola's face turned serene. 'She is not with us anymore.'

'I'm so sorry.'

'She is in a better place now.' Lola inhaled and then slowly exhaled. 'This is Rodrigo. Do you remember him?' She pointed at the boy who was carrying some of the finished centerpieces.

'*Baby* Rodrigo? Wow! Of course, I remember him.' Rodrigo's chubby cheeks turned bright red. 'Hi, I'm Rocío. I met you when you were a little boy. Did your mother tell you that you were born at my grandparents' home in the city?' The boy nodded.

Grandma shook her head. 'What a crazy night that was! It was a very, very difficult birth.'

'Yes indeed. If it wasn't for—' Lola covered her mouth.

'For whom?' I asked, feeling limp, just thinking that Papá had something to do with the delivery.

My grandmother quickly intervened. 'Rodrigo was a surprise baby, that's all.'

'What do you mean? If Lola had the baby at home, who helped her?'

'My dear Rocío, leave it alone. Today is your mamá's wedding, and we still have a lot to do.'

When Lola avoided my eyes, I knew my suspicion was true. Because of my father, Lola and the baby were fine. A sudden warmth filled my heart when I glanced at Rodrigo. I didn't insist. Grandma was right. It was Mamá's day, and I wasn't about to do anything to make her sad.

The grounds of the estate were overflowing with guests when Liliana and I finished decorating the arch, where the ceremony was going to take place.

'I forgot to give you Jocelyne's letter. Do you want it now?' asked Liliana.

'What letter?'

'It arrived before we left the city, so I forgot to tell you.' My sister bit her lip. I felt my pulse increase with anger. 'I would've liked to read it now, but since you forgot, I'll have to do it later. There is no time now. The wedding is about to begin.'

'I'm sorry. I'll give it to you tonight.' Liliana shrugged her shoulders.

'That's fine. We need to get ready anyway.'

On our way back to the house, a light afternoon breeze made the tablecloths on the tables, which were scattered around the garden, flap. The petals, sprinkled along the path to the arch, danced. My sister and I waved at Papá's college classmate, Dr. Carlos Arango, and his wife and twin daughters, who were sitting at one of the front tables. At the next table was Gabriela conversing with other guests. I scanned the group, searching for her brother, but he wasn't there.

It's better this way. I sighed when I felt Gabriela's arms around me.

She embraced Liliana and me so tightly that we almost fell over.

'You don't want to get our pretty dresses dirty, do you?' I joked at Gabriela's outburst of love.

Grandma approached us, fixing her silk flower hat.

'Liliana and Rocío, your mamá is looking for you.'

'I'm glad you are here.' I kissed Gabriela.

She kissed me back. Liliana moved away from Gabriela.

'I'm happy you are here too. But now we must go. See you later, my friend.'

We rushed to Mamá's old room. Once there, we took one step back when we saw her standing in front of a full-length mirror. Her V-neck dress made of chiffon and beige lace seemed as if it had come out of a magazine.

'Please help me finish zipping my dress up.'

I hurried to help her. Liliana circled around our mother.

'You look like a princess. Did Mr. Dresser buy that dress for you?'

'Yes. He bought it in Medellín and had it shipped to Bogotá.' Mamá brushed her hand through the silky material. 'You both look very beautiful too.'

A seamstress in the city had made us identical rose-gold dresses with a beige ribbon.

'It's a little too puffy for me, and the crinoline itches.' Liliana rubbed her legs.

'Leave it alone, Liliana. You can take it off after the ceremony. Now help me with this, please.' Mamá handed my sister a ribbon that matched our dresses.

Liliana's skillful hands, like those of a professional, moved quickly around Mamá's waist.

'Done,' Liliana said.

I let out a, 'Wow!' when I saw the beautiful sash bow on Mamá's dress. 'It's lovely.'

Mamá looked at herself in the mirror. 'Thank you.' She kissed my sister, then placed Grandma's pearl necklace around her neck.

Liliana secured it and said, 'Done.'

'Not so fast.' I took the two-tiered veil that was lying on the bed and fastened it on Mamá's hair with bobby pins.

Our mother twirled around and said, 'What do you think?'

'Mr. Dresser is right. You are the prettiest woman ever.' I kissed Mamá.

'Maybe it is about time that you stop calling him Mr. Dresser. His name is Howard.' Mamá dropped the first veil over her face.

When the musicians began to play classical music, we knew it was our cue to go outside. Jaime and Orlando joined us at the main door.

As Ave María played, Mamá stepped into the garden, followed by the four of us. The guests stared at us with admiration while we walked down the path that led to the arch. Orlando, who disliked attention, fixed his tie several times. Once we arrived at the arbor, my siblings and I sat, and Grandpa joined our mother. Howard held his hands in anticipation.

When the musicians stopped playing, a Presbyterian minister, as per Howard's request, officiated the ceremony. Dancing and a three-course meal followed. Towards the end of the reception, under the moonlight, a pair of owls serenaded the couple. Everyone cheered at the sound of the nocturnal birds except me. I thought of the evening in Puerto López when I woke up to find Papá sleeping by my bed, still concerned about the minor surgery he had performed on my foot. In the distance, an owl hooted as a gentle breeze filtered through my open window. Suddenly, I remembered Jocelyne's letter. My head spun, and I sensed she had something unusual to tell me because she didn't write often anymore.

* * *

Near the mango tree, Mamá's cousins were playing their Spanish guitars while Liliana and others sang romantic ballads. I came from behind and pulled Liliana's arm. 'Give me the letter, please?' I whispered in her ear.

'Which letter?'

'Jocelyne's.'

'Can't you wait?'

'No.'

She rolled her eyes at me and impatiently charged ahead until we arrived at our old room.

'Here.' She found it on her desk and handed it to me. 'Can I read it too?'

'I guess.' I sat on my bed and read. My hands shook when I separated Jocelyne's letter from an official document. Apparently, our father had been at the Saint-Luc hospital that same year in June requesting a previous employment verification letter. The clerk knew Jocelyne's family and so she kept a copy for herself before handing the original to our Papá. The clerk later gave the letter to Jocelyne's father and warned him that two officers had been asking questions about Dr. Velásquez. I stopped reading Jocelyne's letter and checked the date on the typed document. 'June 7, 1967,' I mumbled.

'Go on,' Liliana insisted.

'I can't. I don't believe it. I'm scared.'

'I'll do it then.'

Liliana took the envelope and its contents from me and read it quietly. Then, breathing heavily, as if she had seen a ghost, she said, 'But I don't understand either. The dates are all wrong. How could Papá go to the hospital this year if he was killed October 21 last year?'

'That's what I thought. What if Papá is *alive*?' A cold sweat covered my body.

'We need to let Mamá know. This means she is not really married, because she never divorced Papá.'

I was about to run out, but my sister grabbed me by my skirt, pulling so hard that it ripped.

'No. We can't tell her. It's her wedding day.'

'I can't do this anymore. I'm tired of being sad, worried, and afraid. I'm tired of living a double life,' I blurted out.

'Let me read Jocelyne's letter again. Maybe we are wrong.' Liliana skimmed our friend's letter. 'It is true. Apparently, Papá was at that hospital that day. And there is more. He wasn't alone. A woman named Suzanne Bernard was with him.'

'Papá is alive? Another woman?' Overwhelmed by a whirlpool of emotions I collapsed on the floor.

Liliana sobbed as she, too, fell next to me.

When we calmed down, I asked, 'Who sent the hospital's official letter to Jocelyne's father?'

'The clerk at the hospital. He knows Jocelyne's family and wanted to warn them.'

Lola's calling startled us.

'Señorita Liliana and señorita Rocío, your mamá and Mr. Dresser are leaving.'

We jumped to our feet, and Liliana stuffed the letter and envelope into the night table.

Wiping our tears, we ran outside where we joined our brothers, who were together with remaining guests and family members, throwing rice at the couple. Mamá looked around until she saw the four of us and blew us a kiss.

When everyone was gone, my siblings and I sat on the same steps we had sat on the day of Mamá's accident. Although this time, instead of going to the hospital, Howard and she were driving to the airport to catch a plane for their honeymoon. Orlando broke the silence. 'Where are they going?'

'To San Andrés.' I placed my arm over my brother's shoulders. 'An island in the north of Colombia. They say it's very pretty.'

'I want to go.' Orlando frowned.

'You are so naïve.' Jaime burst out laughing.

Liliana intervened. 'They'll be back soon.' She glanced at me, sweeping her hand across her forehead.

Events had turned our world upside down again.

Wrestling with Anguish

A few days after Mamá and Howard left for their honeymoon, my sister and I were watching *The Flying Nun.* A well-groomed commentator appeared on the screen, interrupting our show. The man stared into the camera, showing a deep furrow that ran across his forehead. 'We apologize for the interruption, but we just received confirmation that Doctor Jaime Velásquez was not killed during the military operation that took place in Bucaramanga on October 21, 1966.'

Liliana and I both gasped.

'I knew it,' she whimpered. 'What are we going to do?'

I felt the muscles in my chest tighten with anguish. 'Nothing. We do nothing. And why is it such a surprise to you?'

'I thought maybe it wasn't true.' My sister sobbed.

'After a long investigation,' the reporter said, 'the authorities have concluded that the guerrillas used the body of another dead rebel and made everyone believe it was the doctor's remains. It has also been confirmed that the doctor left the country soon after the October confrontation. Stay tuned for additional details. And now, we return to our regular programming.'

When *The Flying Nun* reappeared, I raced to turn the TV off so that my brothers wouldn't hear any possible new updates, but it was too late. They were standing by their bedroom door, faces ashen.

When I approached Orlando, he pushed me away and growled, 'I don't want to talk about him.'

'Why?'

Orlando went back into his room and slammed the door. Following his lead, Jaime kicked the wall and also left. I understood to an extent. After the initial elation of the news had settled in for me, a slew of questions arose. It felt even more like Papá had abandoned us, that he had faked his own death in part so that he could start over. But still, at the bottom of my heart, I wanted to see him again.

Grandma came into the room.

'I just heard the news on the radio. I don't know what to say.' She took a handkerchief from inside her pocket and blew her nose. The phone rang then, and she hurried to answer. 'Hello,' she said, still sniffling.

I heard Mamá's frantic voice coming out of the receiver, but I could not make out the words.

Grandma muttered, 'Hi, dear. Yes, Rocío and Liliana are standing next to me. Yes, here she is. I love you.' She passed me the receiver.

Still shaking inside, I said, 'Hi, Mamá. Where are you?'

'My dear Rocío. We are still in San André, but we will be home soon. How are you?'

'I'm okay,' I said.

The truth was, after reading Jocelyne's letter, I had lost my appetite and had trouble sleeping. At night, I tossed and turned while questions flashed in my mind.

Should I look for Papá? And if I find him, what will I say or do? Should I tell Mamá about Jocelyne's letter? What about Howard? Will he stay?

'Are you sure?' Mamá insisted after a momentary silence.

'Yes.'

'And your siblings?'

'Liliana is here. She is okay too.' I glanced at my sister.

Liliana shook her head, signaling that she didn't want to speak with our mother.

'And your brothers?'

'Not too good.'

'Can I speak with them?'

'I'll get Orlando,' Liliana said, and walked out of the room.

When Liliana came back with Orlando, he took the receiver from me.

'Mamá? I want you to come home,' Orlando said while he played with the phone cord. He listened. 'Can't you take a flight out now?' Listening some more, he stared at the floor. 'I hope you can make it tomorrow.' My brother looked around the room. 'No. Jaime is not here.' Then he mumbled, 'I love you too.'

'I'll get him.' I left the room in search of my other brother. 'Jaime, Jaime,' I kept calling around the house.

No response. From the kitchen window, I saw him squatting by the lake and drawing on the dirt with a rock.

I sprinted down the back stairs and joined him outside. 'Hurry. Mamá is calling long-distance and wants to talk to you.'

Jaime continued etching the soil with the sharp rock.

I pleaded, 'Phone calls are expensive, and Mamá is waiting. Did you hear me?'

'I don't want to—'

'You don't want what?'

'I don't want anything to do with him.'

'You mean Papá?'

My brother nodded and then looked away.

'But it's Mamá calling.'

'I know.' He flung the rock into the water.

'So go talk to her.' I tried pulling him by his arm.

Jaime pulled back, screaming at me, 'Leave me alone!'

And so I did. When I went back to the family room, we had lost the phone connection. Through the open door, I could see Grandma in the garden speaking with Grandpa. He stopped sweeping leaves, his favorite and only chore, then he dropped the rake. Astounded by the news, he first tapped his head, then made a fist in the air out of anger.

They never really liked Papá, and now they'll like him even less.

It was all surreal. Tormented, I sat back on the couch where my sister was flipping between channels. Every station had the same breaking news. Our father had fooled the authorities and was alive.

Each time the reporters said our father's name, my sister and I cringed. Just envisioning what the headlines of the newspapers would say the next day gave me chills. Some small part of me was glad, though, to learn that it was all over the news. It wasn't my responsibility anymore to inform my family about

Papá's reappearance, something I couldn't understand and had no proof of other than the letter Jocelyne had sent.

'Now what?' Liliana smiled at me with tears in her eyes.

'I don't know.'

My sister's painful look ripped through me like a dagger. For years, I had babysat her and my two brothers, always trying to protect them from harm, but this time, I had no consoling words and no explanations to offer. Once more, something trapped us in the political scandal that had hovered over us for so many years.

Two days later, Howard entered our grandparents' home carrying suitcases and presents. Under his tanned, unshaven complexion was a tense face. Our grandparents hurried to help him, but Howard stumbled, dropping all the packages on the floor.

'Hi, everyone.' His eyes shone behind his thick glasses when he turned to my siblings and me and said, 'I'm so glad to see you. All you need to know is that I am here for you. You don't have to worry about anything.'

Jaime took a step back.

Orlando puffed up his chest and said, 'Thank you, but you are not my father.'

'And I don't pretend to be. I just—' Howard's voice faded.

I sensed that Liliana, like me, felt as if our feet were stuck to the floor and our mouths were sealed with tape. So, we remained still and silent until Mamá came in holding a handbag and her coat. I felt as though we had been adrift in a river and suddenly we were approaching a high waterfall drop. My siblings and I ran to our mother and embraced her like she was our last hope for survival. Mamá dropped to her knees, let go of her purse and coat, and embraced us back. 'I heard about your papá.'

'I don't want to talk about him.' Jaime walked away.

'I don't either.' Orlando followed Jaime out of the room.

From the corner of my eye, I saw Grandma pulling Grandpa's hand. He resisted for a minute, but after she whispered something in his ear, they left the entryway and went to the dining room.

Howard picked up the packages and, on his way out, said, 'Honey, I'll take these to the room. But please let me know if there is anything I can do to help.'

'Thank you, darling.' Our mother winked at him. After he was gone, she turned to Liliana and me. 'How are the two of you?' she said. 'Are you two feeling better?'

Suddenly, as if I had just been struck by lightning, I screamed, 'He doesn't care about us. He not only left us but is also willing to die for his stupid cause without regard for the impact that all of this would have on us.'

Mamá placed her hands in prayer. 'Please, don't say that.'

'I forgave him because I thought he was dead. But now that I know he is alive, I know for certain that he just doesn't care.'

Like poison, anger left me feeling so sick, I gagged. I hurried to the bathroom. Mamá and Liliana followed me there.

'My poor baby.' Mamá took rubbing alcohol from the bathroom cabinet, poured some on a small towel, and handed it to me. 'Take a deep breath.'

When I placed the towel over my nose, the powerful smell made my eyes water, but somehow eased the nausea.

'Talk to me.' Mamá caressed my head.

I stood up and faced her. 'Why can't you accept Papá doesn't care about us?'

'Don't say that,' she begged. 'He was always a good father.'

'He hasn't been a father for a long time,' I said.

Mamá turned her face to one side as tears rolled down her cheeks. 'Well, he is a good man.'

I threw my hands into the air.

'I can't believe that you are still defending him.'

'Stop it,' Liliana said.

My mother's shoulders sagged.

Sobbing, she said, 'I've done everything for you, for this family. I've always protected you, did everything I could, so that there was food on the table. Everything, everything I do, is for all of you.' She shook her head.

An intense guilt for upsetting her made my voice crack.

'I'm sorry. It's not your fault, I know.'

I just wanted her to be mad at Papá, like I was, but she wasn't. She *never* was. I couldn't understand why she never complained about him not sending money, or about him being a bad husband or father. Instead, when he left, she had taken on the role of both mother *and* father. She read to us and did homework with us. She even spoke to us like he used to, about the future and the world. 'No one is better than you are. You can achieve any goal as long as you work hard. If you fall, you get up and keep going.' After a moment, Mamá moved away from me and said, 'I don't even know what to do.'

Grandma startled us when she knocked on the open door and said, 'Let's have something to drink.'

I felt queasy but followed my grandmother to the living room. Liliana and Mamá trailed behind us. Avelina was holding a tray with several glasses of cold lemonade. As soon as we went in, the men placed their glasses on a small table and studied us with curious eyes. Outside the window, Rebecca, the macaw, rocked from side to side on a branch. She must have noticed that I was looking at her because she began to move her head up and down playfully. But when I sat down, she shouted, 'Quiero cacao.' That made us grin.

'Avelina, please finish here and feed Rebecca.' Grandma waved a hand in the air as if she were happy to have found an excuse to dismiss her dedicated maid.

'Yes, Ma'am.' She served the rest of the lemonade and went outside.

Mamá tried to keep the upbeat mood by telling us about some of the fun adventures from her honeymoon. She told us about riding a motorcycle and swimming, but soon the conversation turned back to the issue at hand.

'We need to decide what to do now that we know your papá is alive.'

'Would you like me to go get Orlando and Jaime?'

'I'll talk to them later. The boys need a little time.'

Howard said, 'I'm so sorry they are having a rough time. Is there anything I can do?'

'Not for now. They'll come around, darling. For now, we need to worry about all the legal documents and about their new schools.'

Howard replied, 'You are right, because the company will only pay for their insurance and schools if I am legally married to you.'

'I know. We can talk about this later.' Mamá sighed.

A few months later, my parents' divorce was final. Because of our father's issues with the law, the dissolution of their marriage was treated as a special case. They shared none of the details with my siblings and me. Nor did we ask. Immediately after, Mamá and Howard remarried in a civil and private ceremony. This time, they didn't go away; together we drove to our new home. Nestled in a sea of elaborate gardens, our new neighborhood, which was in the northern part of the city, stood out against nearby colonial buildings. Trucks carrying sand, paint, and other building materials were parked on the streets. Dusty workers with stained overalls were working around different homes, completing the final details. Some children were playing in their not-yet-landscaped front yards. Other homes were vacant. They posted large For Sale signs on the windows.

Our house was on the last street next to a park. When we went inside, the heavy smell of fresh paint made my siblings and me cough.

'It's brand new, so we should air it out.' Howard opened the windows.

My brothers, sister, and I were keen to help. Soon after, a light breeze brought in the scent of fresh-cut grass from the nearby park. I took a deep breath, filling my lungs with clean air. As I exhaled, peacefulness, something I hadn't felt for a long time, replaced the sadness and confusion that had troubled me for so long. It was over. Mamá was remarried.

This is my life now.

I toured our home, captivated by the openness of the high ceilings and the brightness of the sunrays filtering through the windows. There was something liberating about this place. Everything was new. No memories, no unresolved issues, only clarity.

'I hope you like it.' Howard grinned when I walked into the room. He was inspecting the second floor.

'I do.'

'Good. You kids and your mother deserve the best. Your mother and I looked for a comfortable place for a while. And we both liked this one because it is in a great location, plus it's spacious.'

'Yes, it's big.'

'I think it's perfect. Especially this room.'

'What is this room for?' I noticed it had more closets and drawers than the others.

He moved his hips from side to side and smiled. 'This is my airplane room.'

Confused, I asked, 'What airplanes?'

'Model planes, you know, like the ones you fly with a radio.'

'No, I don't know.'

'Well, I have an event this weekend, so we'll go.'

On Sundays, we went with Howard to the Floresta Flying Club. What he didn't tell us was that he was learning how to fly the balsa models, so he crashed a lot. And every time his plane collapsed, he asked us to run through brush, hike hills, and jump fences to pick up the pieces. 'Make sure to retrieve the motor. They're expensive.'

Sunday evenings, he rolled up his sleeves, tied an apron around his large waist, and cooked a special meal for us. Among flour dust, Howard baked bread and apple pie while listening to Tom Jones or Engelbert Humperdinck. The main dishes were usually beef chili, ribs, and other times, our mother's meal of choice: New England clam chowder. After spending several hours chasing Howard's airplanes, Orlando, Liliana, and I were hungry for his culinary specialties. At first, we looked forward to those Sunday dinners. But after a while, however, we all pretended to be busy, hoping we wouldn't have to spend the day running around, getting pricked by the sharp bushes and shrubs that covered the endless field adjacent to the flying club. It never worked. Our mother argued that Howard had only two requests, that on Sundays we went to the club and that we spoke English, and as a result, neither was optional.

On Mondays, Howard went to Orito, a town in the southern part of Colombia, where he worked as an engineer building oil camps. He did not return until Friday as he had previously told us. Although we enjoyed the four days Howard was away because we could speak Spanish and spend time with friends, we seemed delighted to have him back. Friday mornings, Mamá and Margarita, our new maid, decorated the house with bouquets of flowers, leaving a spicy fragrance in the air. They stocked the kitchen cabinets with strange foods like peanut butter, mayonnaise, ketchup, and pickles, which Howard couldn't live without. Like a teenager, Mamá stood, humming, in front of the full-length mirror and tried on different dresses until she felt pleased with her looks. Then she would drive to the airport to pick Howard up. Jaime followed Howard around, watching him build planes. Fascinated by automobiles and planes, Orlando also spent many hours studying my mother's new Chrysler. Howard often joined him in the garage, where they examined the motor and other parts. Other times, he showed my brother how to change tires and take care of the interior.

Liliana and I always volunteered to go shopping with Howard. Each time, I brought back a new rock and roll album. 'Let's hear it,' Howard would say, pouring himself a glass of rum. Proud of my purchase, I'd start dancing at the sound of the first notes of what I considered heavenly music. Each time, Howard waved at me to stop the music. Smiling, he'd say, 'That is noise. Where is the music?' Then he'd shake his head and throw his hands up in the air.

I realized we were becoming a *family*.

But our new peaceful life came to a halt one day at nightfall. We were upstairs, except for Howard who was at work, when the doorbell rang. Margarita opened the door. Mamá and the four of us were standing by the railing of the second floor, looking down at the foyer.

'Who is it?' Mamá leaned against the banister, trying to see who was there.

Margarita left the door partially open, then turned towards us and, touching her chin, said, 'It's the kids' Grandma Sarai with a message from their father.'

He Will Always be my Papá

'I don't want that woman in my house!' Mamá shouted.

Grandma Sarai pushed the door, trying to force her way inside. 'Please let me see my grandchildren.'

Margarita held the door tight with both hands.

Mamá began walking down the stairs with flared nostrils. 'I said don't let her in.'

'You heard Mrs. Dresser. Stay out, please,' said Margarita apologetically.

Rooted to the stairs, my brothers, sister, and I watched the exchange. But when I saw my grandmother's face peeking through the opened door, I thought of Papá, the angry shield I'd built in an attempt to protect myself from all the pain of losing him, suddenly crumbled.

'I'll talk to her.' I sprinted halfway down the stairs. Mamá grabbed me by my arm. 'Please, just let me see what she wants?' I begged.

As if she were searching for an answer, Mamá looked up at my siblings, who seemed to have turned into stone, then at me.

'It will be all right, Mamá. I promise. Please?' I pulled away from her and made my way down the rest of the stairs. She didn't try to stop me but stayed vigilant.

A much older Grandma Sarai was standing outside on our porch. Hunched over like a woman carrying a heavy load, she wasn't the same tall and elegant lady I remembered. Dark halos around her eyes and deep wrinkles revealed that she had lost weight.

'My dear Rocío, I'm so happy to see you,' she exclaimed. Her clear eyes narrowed. 'I've walked all over the neighborhood trying to find your house.'

Overwhelmed by a storm of emotions, I thought of telling her to go away and to leave us alone. But when she moved, and the streetlight illuminated her face,

I saw again the undeniable resemblance between her and Papá, the defined cheekbones and broad mouth. I wept freely.

My grandmother rubbed my shoulder. 'I'm so sorry you've had to go through all of this.' She held her hands, then said, 'It has been difficult for all of us.'

'Why are you here?' I finally gained the strength to ask.

'Your papá wrote these poems for you,' she said, and handed me a large envelope.

I pushed her hand away. 'I don't want them.'

She held the envelope back against her chest and then murmured, 'You know your papá loves you, right?'

'No. He doesn't care about us.' The words burst from my throat.

Grandma Sarai looked at me with hurt eyes and said, 'He does. He just—'

'Just what? Cares more about his cause than us?'

'No. He wants to make this a better country… for you and for all the children.'

'Are you still covering for him like you did when we went to visit you?'

'What do you mean?'

'He almost kidnapped us and took us to Russia, remember?'

'He just wanted to be with you; he has every right. He is your *father*.'

I thought of Howard and how he was teaching me how to drive.

'Not anymore. Howard—'

'Howard is not your father. Jaime is,' she said angrily. 'He will always be your papá, and you will always be a Velásquez. Whether you like it or not.'

Astounded by her outburst, I didn't respond.

'Read the poems he wrote for you. You'll see that he thinks about you all the time.'

I took one step back. 'I'm sorry. Tell him that we don't want them. We wanted *him*, not some ridiculous poems.'

'I told him this would happen.' The creases on her face deepened. 'I begged him to go back to you kids, but he didn't listen… never did… because he is stubborn.' Tears filled her eyes.

Silence.

Then she scoped the street. 'I have to go.'

A station wagon drove by us at that moment. My grandmother kept looking at it until the car drove into a garage, a few houses after ours.

'Where *is* Papá?'

'I don't know, and even if I did, I wouldn't tell you.'

'Why not?'

'Do you have any idea how dangerous it is?'

'Yea, but—'

Grandma Sarai frowned. 'No *but*s. They've tried to kill your papá and will do the same to whoever is involved with him. Do you understand?'

I felt a lump in my throat. All I wanted was to be with my father even if it were for just a short moment, but no one would let me, not even my own grandmother.

'Please tell your brothers and your sister that their papá cares about them and that I do too.' My grandmother then turned and watched a taxi pass us. She kept looking at it until the car turned around and passed us again, this time going in the opposite direction. The driver parked a few feet ahead of where we were. I squinted, trying to see who was inside. It appeared that, besides the driver, there was a passenger wearing a man's hat and sitting in the back seat.

'I've run out of time.' Mamá Sarai's hands had a slight tremor when she tried once more to hand me the envelope.

If I couldn't be with my father, I wanted nothing from him, so I pushed her hand away. 'No.'

Her lips trembled. 'It's your choice, but one day you are going to regret it. Goodbye, my dear Rocío. May God bless you always.' She kissed my cheek, walked away, and got into the cab. As they were driving away, the man in the back seat turned around to look at me.

Papá!

With my heart beating out of control, I ran after the taxi, but when I got to the corner, they were gone. My chest ached from sadness, the same feeling I'd had every time he disappeared. I walked back home, broken.

Mamá and my siblings were sitting on the stairs, waiting for me. Mamá jumped up when she saw me come in. 'What happened? What did that woman do to you? I know I should've never left you alone with her.'

Anguish trapped the words inside of me, so all I did was weep.

'I'm going to call the police, and I'm going to tell them to arrest her for hurting you.' Mamá went to the living room and picked up the receiver.

'No.' I darted after her and took the phone away.

'Why not? Give me one good reason why I shouldn't.'

'She didn't do anything wrong. She just wanted us to have Papá's poems.'

I couldn't tell my mother that my father was in the car, because that would devastate her once more.

Mamá's voice lowered. 'What poems?'

'Apparently, he wrote them for us.'

'And where are they?'

'I didn't want them.'

'What about your siblings? Why didn't you ask them?' She turned to them. 'Did you want the poems?'

Orlando and Jaime went back upstairs. Liliana shook her head.

'Well, I still feel you should've taken them,' she said. 'They are yours not hers. You can't trust those people.' Mamá paced.

'Which people? Papá's family?'

My mother looked away. 'They never liked me. I think they were hoping your papá would marry a woman from their city.'

Grandpa Miguel and Grandma Emilia had never been fond of Papá either, but I couldn't fight with my mother anymore. All my energy had been drained out of my body. And with Papá's image still engraved in my mind, I remained quiet.

Mamá continued, 'Did she say anything else?

'No.'

'So why are you so upset?'

'I can't do this, Mamá, not right now.' I went to my room.

Liliana followed me and closed the door behind her.

'Something else happened,' she said. 'I know. You just don't want to tell us.'

It felt as though I was mourning my father all over again. I cried, holding the pillow over my head so my mother wouldn't hear me.

Liliana sat by my side. 'You saw him! Oh my God!'

I put the pillow down and nodded.

'You can't tell anyone,' my sister said. 'Not even Mamá.'

Liliana didn't see monsters in the room like she used to, nor did she ask me to go to her bed to protect her. That night, however, she fell asleep at the end of my bed, curled up like a newborn.

Holiday candy and bright lights decorated the store windows when Mamá, Liliana, and I went shopping. Upon our return, we found Howard in the kitchen tasting his homemade tomato sauce. Margarita was washing a pile of utensils he had used.

'When I cook, you all have to clean,' he had told us the first time he cooked for us. In the beginning, we had stayed out of the kitchen until dinner was ready, thinking that it would be a good idea to give him space, but that quickly changed one evening when Mamá, Margarita, Liliana, and I spent several hours cleaning and putting the kitchen back together. Every spice Howard had used was all over the kitchen counter, dishes were piled in the sink. Flour, sugar, and other grainy powders were sprinkled like dust on the floor and on the stove. After this, Margarita's sole responsibility was to clean after him.

'How are my favorite ladies?' Howard asked as we walked in. He kissed Mamá, then hugged my sister and me.

Mamá kissed him back. 'We are great. We did all our errands.'

'Good, let's eat. Dinner is ready.' Howard announced.

Margarita finished bringing all the platters, then retreated to her small dining table in the kitchen. Once we were almost done eating, Mamá took a gulp of water, then said, 'We'd like to ask you all a question.'

Her grave tone of voice made us all halt. It had the same sound we'd heard whenever a life-changing event was about to happen, so we put our forks down.

Howard probably sensed our apprehension because he came to our rescue. 'Would it be all right if I tell them?' He held Mamá's hand.

Our mother tapped the table with her thumb, then nodded.

'All right, nothing like being straightforward. As you know, in order for you to be covered under my benefit plan, we had to be married. Which we did. But we didn't do it only because we wanted to fulfill some sort of requirement. I love your mother like no one I've ever loved before.'

Mamá smiled and pressed Howard's hand.

'I feel lucky because not only did I find a marvelous woman but also four great kids... now my children.' Howard's eyes flooded with tears.

Our mother looked at us with hopeful eyes, perhaps expecting a response from us, but my bothers, sister, and I said nothing. I wanted to tell Howard how much I appreciated all he did for us. But, somehow, I thought that by caring about my mother's husband, I was in some way betraying my father.

'Thank you, darling,' our mother said.

Howard took off his thick glasses and placed them on the table, then wiped his eyes with a napkin. Mamá and Howard exchanged looks and then grinned.

'So here it is, kids,' he said. 'I don't just want to be your stepfather. I'd like to adopt you and give you my last name. This way, people will stop bugging you and asking you intrusive questions. And best of all, we will be a real family.'

I felt as though my heart was going to stop beating.

Another father?

I liked Howard a lot, but I wasn't ready for this. I could deny knowing Papá, but this was different. We were being asked to renounce him altogether. I thought my brothers were going to be filled with anger and leave the table and scream. But they didn't. No one moved. Liliana, Orlando, and Jaime looked at Howard with blank faces, like they didn't understand what he was talking about, or perhaps they didn't want to know. I felt the same way.

Two weeks later, dressed in our best clothes, the six of us stood in front of a judge.

The man's elongated oval face was like those I had seen in comic strips, though there was nothing funny about what was going to happen. Liliana's empty eyes and my brothers' stillness made me think that, like me, they were present in body, but their hearts and minds were wandering elsewhere. Although we never talked about it, it was clear that we felt that we were betraying Papá. Then again, we justified the step we were about to take in support of our mother, and because we were exhausted by the drama that had stalked us for years. All because of our father's relentless pursuit of justice regardless of the cost. And so, on that drizzly day, we were adopted and changed our last name from Velásquez to Dresser.

While the judge was explaining to Mamá and Howard what the steps were to register all documents with the county, I watched the man, like a puppeteer, move his nervous hands shuffling legal formularies and pointing in the direction of nearby offices. Once again, my siblings and I, like puppets, danced in the hands of others.

Colors of Allegiance

In 1972, the principal took the microphone and called my sister's name, 'Liliana Dresser.' She stepped onto the stage to receive her high school diploma, blushing with excitement. From the audience, Howard, whom we now called Dad, my mother, Orlando, Jaime, and I cheered so loudly that those around us broke into laughter.

As a senior in college in California, I'd come back to find my siblings grown up. This was the first time I'd seen Liliana in heels. Orlando was now shaving and was a foot taller than Howard. On the shelves above his desk, awards he'd received from almost every subject covered the wall. Jaime, however, had none. His conquests were mostly of the romantic sort. With shiny, shoulder-length hair and athletic body, Jaime had lady visitors every day until Mamá forbade him to see anyone during the week. The only visitors he was allowed were his tutors. The extra help was working because, before Jaime greeted me, he cocked his head and told me he was passing all subjects. Mamá had also changed. She played cards twice a week with her now many friends. Her reddish, wavy hair and bangs gave her such a youthful appearance, people often thought she was my older sister.

At home, we never spoke about Papá, and we avoided listening to the news. But I continued my investigation at college, hoping that one day I would understand why my father had been willing to give everyone and everything up for his ideal world.

Jocelyne, who, by a small miracle, was attending the same college, bared her teeth at me every time she found me in the library behind a pile of dusty books on communism and socialism.

'Leave it alone,' she'd say. 'You know why my father and I had to move to this country, right? I can't have friends who might be considered communists. We don't want to lose our visas.'

The day I was going back home for Liliana's graduation, Jocelyne hugged me and said, 'I hate to say this, but you are just as stubborn as your father.' She rolled her eyes. 'Here.' She handed me a small booklet, which had been covered with butcher paper.

I opened it and read, *The Communist Manifesto*. I smiled.

'If someone asks, you found it. I didn't give it to you.' She took it from me, hid the pamphlet inside my folded pajamas, then frantically placed clothes over it.

'Calm down,' I said. 'It's not like I've committed a crime or something like that.'

At break of day, a few weeks after Liliana's graduation, I was awakened by someone's insistent knocking. I stumbled out of bed and went downstairs.

My parents were standing by the unopened front door.

'Who is there?' Howard asked.

A man screamed, 'Open the door! I have news from Dr. Velásquez.' The man kept banging on the door. I joined my parents in the entryway, shaking with fear.

Howard held his breath and opened the door.

'Who are you and what do you want with my family?'

It was not one, but two rugged men. I recognized them immediately; they were the same ones who had tried to kidnap Liliana and me years earlier.

'Close the door!' I screamed.

When Howard heard my yell, he puffed up his chest and pushed the man so hard that he fell backwards onto the street. Two other men, who had come out of nowhere, stood under the door frame to stop Howard from closing the door. The younger of the two said, 'We are not going to harm you. We just wanted you to know that they've killed Dr. Velásquez.' He blew his nose with a handkerchief. 'If you don't believe me, turn on the TV. Those animals killed him. If someone asks you, say you haven't met him. They are after all his acquaintances.'

My whole body began to shake uncontrollably. To avoid falling, I leaned against the wall. In some odd way, which I couldn't explain, I knew that this time it was true. Mamá embraced me.

'It might not even be true,' she said, trying to console me.

'It's true. I know,' I murmured.

'You don't know. Remember what happened the last time? He reappeared.' Mamá blinked hard, almost as if she had a nervous tic.

In Montréal, we learned that snowflakes are less likely to fall during the bitter winter. That's how I felt. Paralyzed by the news, I couldn't speak, nor could I cry. All I did was listen to my parents argue with the men. Something had died inside of me. Once more, the hope that one day Papá would be back vanished. I would never understand his reasons for leaving us. I had missed the opportunity to truly get to know him, the man so many admired.

'So, what do you want from us?' Howard said, straightening his robe.

The man who had fallen peeked in and pleaded, 'You need to go to Quito and claim the body, because who knows what they'll do with his remains?'

Mamá choked, then swallowed several times to regain her composure. 'I'll go.'

Howard raised his eyebrows. 'You?'

'Yes, me. After all, he is my children's father.'

'But you can't go alone. I'll go with you.'

'I'll go, Dad,' I forced myself to speak.

Howard kissed my forehead. 'I don't like it, but that way your mother will not be alone.'

A few hours later, Mamá and I were on a plane to Ecuador. On our final descent, the airplane banked on its side, allowing us to see the Cotopaxi, a snow-covered active volcano that some say is the guardian of the ancient Inca city of Quito. Around it, green pastures and lush plants seemed unaware that one day the cone-shaped mountain could erupt and leave the land barren.

I didn't share my feelings with my siblings before I left. There was no need. I knew we were all heartbroken by Papá's death. I'd heard that identical twins have a unique bond. Even though we were not born on the same date, we had a bond of the heart, the result of our family history and the scar Papá had left on all of us.

After Mamá and I landed, we picked up our luggage and went outside the airport building. We had been told that someone was going to pick us up, but we were not given the name of the person, only the license plates of the car.

Now with gray hair and deep wrinkles, a much older Colonel Moncayo waited for us by the exit. He put out his cigarette and then tapped his cap. 'Ma'am.' He looked at me and bowed. 'Señorita Rocío.'

As if I weren't truly there, and feeling as though this was all just a long nightmare, I stared at the colonel but didn't greet him back.

Mamá's nails carved into my arm. 'You?' Mamá said. 'The day I met you in Puerto López, I knew that you were not just some ordinary army colonel. You got Jaime involved in this mess and look what happened to him.' She let go of my arm and wiped the tears from her eyes.

'Please, señora, you should know that when I met him, he was already committed to the—' He looked around, then continued, 'Can we talk inside the car? This is not a good place.' Colonel Moncayo waved to a driver who was sitting inside a small Renault idling at the curb. 'I beg you, get in.'

Mamá gazed at me. I suddenly remembered watching Papá pat the man's back, thanking him for bringing my dogs. So I nodded.

Still unsure about the colonel's intentions, Mamá read the license plates aloud. 'P-1193, just like the men at the door told us.' She raised her shoulders and handed her bag to Colonel Moncayo. I did the same. He took our luggage and placed it in the trunk of the car. At the same time, the driver got out, pulled his cap down, covering his eyes, then opened the back door for us. Once we were all seated, we drove away.

Mamá leaned forward and asked, 'So, where are Jaime's remains?'

To hear better, I, too, leaned forward.

The colonel cracked his knuckles in anger. 'Please let me tell you what happened first. Then I'll tell you our plan to get him out of the country.'

'Why? Is there a problem? He was a Colombian citizen.'

'We have learned that there could be complications. Apparently, the authorities, along with foreign agents, followed the doctor's Canadian wife to the house where he was hiding. On December 19th, a squadron stormed into the house and arrested everyone and then—'

'Shot Papá in the head,' I said. Just like in my recurring nightmare, I once more saw in my mind the blood dripping from one side of his face. I couldn't say anything else because I broke out sobbing.

My mother hugged me as the colonel explained that the assassins had called the media and told everyone that Papá had committed suicide. But he knew it was all a lie. The informant they had inside the prison had spoken with Papá's wife, Suzanne, and the others who were arrested, and they confirmed that Papá hadn't committed suicide. It was all a cover-up to avoid an international scandal.

When I thought the colonel had finished telling us the worst part of the story, I looked up, and from the rear mirror, I saw the driver's face. It was a bearded Leonel González. When he noticed that I was staring at him, Leonel sighed. 'I'm sorry, niña Rocío, that we have to meet again under these circumstances.'

'Do you know this man?' Mamá asked me as her voice cracked.

'Yes, he was Grandma Sarai's driver.'

Mamá shook her head in disbelief, perhaps thinking about our escape from Grandma's house.

'Your papá was my idol and many people's hope. You should know that.' He bit his lip. 'And, ma'am, I hope you can forgive me. I was just following orders.' He looked away.

'I can't talk about that now. Please, Colonel, finish. Where is Jaime's body?' Leonel wiped his eyes, then blew his nose.

The colonel continued, 'Let me finish saying what happened first. What I'm about to tell you is very sad, but I think you deserve to know.' He cleared his throat. 'After they shot him, like an animal, they dragged his body around the house, leaving a trail of blood. Then they threw him in the back of a truck.' He choked up. The four of us wept.

After driving through winding roads and hills, Colonel Moncayo took out a pair of sunglasses from the glove compartment and put them on. 'We need to get a grip on ourselves and do what we came here to do. Right now, Dr. Velásquez's remains are in a government building surrounded by guards. I worry that the Ecuadorian government might stop us from taking him out of the country. Or even worse... remember what happened to Che?'

My mother and I let out a loud, 'God!'

When Mamá regained her composure, she said, 'But you haven't told us what the plan is.'

'Leonel, stop the car,' the colonel ordered. 'Ma'am, see that van parked on the other side of the street?'

'Yes.' The tears had washed off my mother's makeup.

'We are going to place your bags inside. You are going to drive, and señorita Rocío will sit in the front with you. We will follow you in our car. First, we go to the government building where they are keeping him. This is the address.' The colonel handed my mother a piece of paper and pointed at the first line. 'At the gates, tell the guard that you are there to pick up a box and to please call Capitan Tabares. He is our contact. If they give you trouble, but only if they do, you give them this letter from the Colombian consulate requesting the doctor's remains. Once you have him inside the van, go straight to the Colombian Embassy.' The colonel showed my mother the second address and a hand-drawn map.

Mamá grabbed his shoulder. 'I don't want to put my daughter in danger.'

The colonel turned and said, 'Don't worry, Captain Tabares will not let anyone hurt you.'

'I don't think I want Rocío involved in this,' she said, shaking her head.

'We must do it. You don't want Dr. Velásquez to be chopped up as they did with Che, right?'

'No!' I spluttered. 'Please, Mamá, I'll be all right. I beg you.'

Mamá looked away for a moment, then ordered, 'Let me see the letter.'

The colonel took an envelope out of his jacket and handed it to her.

After she finished reading the letter, she asked, 'So why the mystery?'

'No mystery. As I said before, they are trying to cover up the crime by saying that he committed suicide. And they don't want to release the body, because an expert would be able to figure out that he was shot.' Colonel Moncayo rubbed his eyes with closed fists. 'The truth is that they had no intention of arresting Dr. Velásquez. They knew that we would do everything in our power to take him out of prison or even to help him escape, so they assassinated him. It's all a cover-up. Can you tell? This is why they have been avoiding our calls.

However, with a letter and with you two here, they will have a hard time denying the release of the body.'

Mamá sat straight and said, 'All right, let's do this.' She had the same look I had seen at the border between the United States and Canada where we were detained. 'Give me the keys.'

Colonel Moncayo gave her the keys. 'Remember, this is where we are going first. It's only a few blocks from here. We'll be right behind you. Once we get out of that building, we go to the Colombian Embassy. Good luck!' He shook our hands.

Leonel transferred our bags to the van, then went back to his car. Mamá and I got out of the car and into the van. I looked back as we drove away to make sure the Renault was trailing behind us. But once we arrived at the gates of the governmental building, the Renault sped off. In panic, Mamá and I looked around, hoping to see our accomplices, but there was no trace of them.

The guard made us both jump when he knocked on the window. Mamá lowered it and stuttered, 'We are here to see Captain Tabares.'

'May I ask who is looking for him?'

Mamá inhaled and, looking at me, said, 'Colonel Moncayo sent us.'

The officer scratched the back of his head. 'I'll be right back.' He went to a telephone booth that was by the gate and spoke to someone. Mamá pressed my hand when we saw the guard nodding.

The electric gates opened, and we drove in. Inside, military personnel walked around us. No one acknowledged we were there. We waited for a short time and, when we were about to get out, a blemished-skinned man opened Mamá's door.

'Hi, I'm Captain Tabares.' Mamá smiled and was about to get out when he stopped her. 'There is no time for formalities. Get out of here and drive to the back of the building. When I open a metal door, drive in. We will load the coffin. When we finish, drive away and quickly go to the embassy.'

'But I have a letter.'

'I know. That's fake. That was Plan B. We were hoping that if the original plan failed, we could pressure them to release the remains to you, the family.'

Mamá gasped. 'They lied to us.'

Mamá tried to give the captain the letter.

'Forget the letter. I'll see you in the back of the building.' The captain left.

Mamá's hand trembled, trying to turn the key in the ignition, but when the car took off, we both sighed.

Like a skilled thief, Mamá drove us out through a desolated alley. The metal door went up, and we pulled into a large storage space. She was about to turn the van off when Capitan Tabares opened the back door. Four soldiers came with the coffin and slid it into the back.

'Go and don't stop until you arrive at the embassy.' The captain tapped the side of the car.

We drove in silence through busy streets for what seemed like an eternity. It wasn't until we saw the yellow, blue, and red Colombian flag flapping in the wind, almost as if it were saluting us, that Mamá and I cried with joy.

When we stopped, Mamá jumped out and went to speak with the guard. I couldn't hear what she was saying, because she had left the motor running. She handed the guards our passports and Papá's old driver's license. The guard talked on the radio, then handed it to my mother. She played with her hair nervously as she spoke to the person on the radio. When she was finished, she shook the guard's hand and ran back to the van. 'We are going in.'

The sky had lost its colors by the time a group of soldiers pulled the coffin out of the van. As I heard the rhythmic sound of their heels against the marble, I envisioned a procession. Only that in this one, there were no flowers and no mourners, except for my mother and myself. When we entered one of the chambers, the soldiers laid the coffin on a large, ornate table. Four large candles, one in each corner of the room, dispelled the nocturnal darkness. Mamá and I embraced each other. Then, with my heart pounding, I watched as Mamá walked away and opened the top of the coffin. She quickly closed it. Then, from her purse, she pulled out a Colombian flag, shook it, and laid it over my father's coffin. 'We are taking you home, where you belong. To your country, the one you adored.' Mamá caressed the wooden lid.

I bent down and hugged Papá's coffin.

The Real Hero

In 1974, the first glimmer of light filtering through the curtains woke me up. Outside, the storm had faded away, leaving only stillness. I went upstairs and showered. As the warm water ran over my body, I thought about the previous night and the woman who came to the door with the package. She had looked at me and a picture she had in her hand several times, insisting each time there was a strong resemblance between my father and me. Each time I denied being related to him.

When I got out of the shower, I tightened a towel around me in anger. Then I stood in front of the mirror and brushed back my hair. Even though throughout the years many people had commented on how much I reminded them of my father, I never thought we looked alike. Now I knew we did. Perhaps it was our straight nose and our arched eyebrows, but mostly it was our character, our uncontrollable desire to achieve our goals. I was writing my master's thesis then and submitting applications for doctoral programs. Surprised by my self-discovery, I blinked several times and went to my bedroom.

Once I was dressed, I lay on my bed, thinking about how to find the woman with the package. I had no idea where to look for her. And if by some miracle I found her, it would distress my family. The wound that Papá had left us, although sensitive, was healing. No one spoke of him, not even when he was mentioned in the news. We had changed our last name. My parents and siblings had relocated from Bogotá to Quito. I was living in California but was visiting the family at that time. Orlando was in high school. Jaime and Liliana were in junior college. We were all surrounded by people who didn't know our story. And we liked it that way. It was easier. No sorrow. No unfulfilled expectations or hopes. However, I couldn't stop thinking about the package Papá had sent us. It was the only thing that was left of him, and I had refused it.

I jumped out of the bed with my heart hammering inside my chest. Suddenly, I was staring at the picture Mario had painted of me when I was a young girl, which was hanging on the wall next to the door. I thought of the old man and how I had upset him with my constant questions.

I spoke to Mario in my mind, *I'm sorry I bugged you for so long. But I needed a friend. I miss you, old man.*

I looked closer at the painting and noticed it didn't have his signature, so I took it down and turned it over. A number was carved on the wooden frame—

452548. As if I had seen Mario's ghost, I dropped the painting on the floor. I quickly picked it up and read the number again.

It was a phone number. But whose?

I tiptoed downstairs, hoping not to wake my family. Once in the office, I picked up the receiver and called the operator. Because Mario had passed before my parents moved to Quito, I assumed it was a Colombian number.

'I need to make a call to Bogotá, Colombia.' I read the number to the female operator.

'The phone is ringing,' she announced.

'Hello,' said the man on the other end of the line.

'You have a call from Quito, Ecuador.'

'Who is it?' asked the man in a hoarse voice.

'Go ahead, miss, you are now connected.'

I whispered, 'Hello, I'm Rocío and I got your number—'

The man interrupted. 'Please speak up. I can't hear you.'

I cleared my throat. 'I am Rocío. Dr. Jaime Velásquez's daughter.'

The man dragged a chair, maybe to sit down. 'How do I know it is you?'

Nervous, I stuttered, 'A woman came with a package. And so, I thought that you might—'

'When?'

'Yesterday.'

Silence.

'Sir, are you there?' I finally asked.

'Yes. You don't recognize my voice, do you?'

'No.'

'I'm Colonel Moncayo. I know a woman who had a package for you, but that was two years ago.'

'Who?'

'She owns the house where—'

'Which house?'

'That's not important.'

'But who is she? And why now?'

'This was his wish.'

I wondered why Papá had wanted the package held for so long, but I decided not to question the colonel anymore. It was evident by his short answers that he didn't want to say more than was necessary.

'Would you please help me?' I asked. 'I need a name and phone number.'

The colonel coughed again, then said, 'I guess things didn't go well yesterday.'

'No.'

'Her name is Libia, and her number is three, four, nine, two, zero, eight. She lives in Quito.'

My mother walked in, still yawning. 'Who is calling this early? I didn't hear the phone ring.'

'No one,' I said to her, and then into the phone, 'Bye.' I hung up.

I knew I couldn't hide the truth from my mother for very long, but I had to stall the conversation while I decided what to do. 'I was trying to—'

'What is going on?'

Tense, I clasped my hands.

'Come on, I'm waiting.' Mamá stared at me.

I realized that I wouldn't be able to ignore the fact that Papá had sent something to us. I'd always regret not accepting his poems. Even if it hurt us all, I had to find out. An avalanche of sorrow fell over me as I told, my mother about the woman with the package and my conversation with the colonel. Howard joined us but said nothing until I was finished. Then he glanced at my mother and said, 'My dear, you must do whatever your heart tells you to do. Right, honey?' He glanced at my mother.

Mamá paced with the tip of her index finger between her teeth, as if she were searching for ideas. 'I don't like it. What if this is all part of a police raid trying to find some of your papá's supporters? I think calling this woman is a terrible idea.' Mamá stopped pacing.

'She is just an old lady. I don't think she could harm anyone. What if you met her?' I pleaded with my mother.

'As long as we go with Rocío to the woman's house, I don't see the problem.' Howard held Mamá's gaze.

She finally exhaled in defeat. 'Okay, call her, but tell her we will meet her at her house.'

After breakfast, I went to the office and called the woman. 'Hi, my name is Rocío Velásquez. Are you Libia? The lady who came to my house last night?'

'I don't know what you are talking about. What did you say your name was?'

'Rocío Velásquez.'

I heard background noises, but no one spoke.

'Are you there, ma'am?' I asked.

'Yes.'

'Can I speak with you in person?'

'No.'

'Why not?'

'How do I know that you are who you say you are?'

'I promise.'

'That's not enough.'

'Please, I need to know what Papá left for us. Can we meet at your house?'

'No. I'll come to yours. Give me your address.'

'But you were here last night.'

'Give it to me anyway. I can't trust anyone.'

I figured my mother would be upset with me, but I was determined to get the package. 'My address is Calle de Los Pinos, one, three, zero, two. Can you come tomorrow afternoon?'

'I'll try.'

Click.

As I expected, Mamá was furious about setting the meeting at our home. I tried to explain to her that the woman gave me no other option, but Mamá kept flapping her arms, telling me all the reasons why we should never invite strangers into our house. When Howard saw how flustered she was, he put his cup of coffee on the kitchen counter and embraced her. 'Calm down, honey. I won't let anything happen to you or the children.' He kept holding her until the redness of her face faded away. 'Let's have some breakfast.' Howard grinned.

'Crazy gringo.' Mamá kissed him and went to the refrigerator to take out the eggs.

Howard winked at me.

I moved my lips without sound. *Thank you.*

He smiled back.

The next day, Mamá and I were helping Howard prepare his famous meatloaf when we heard the doorbell ring. Howard, Mamá, and I dropped what we were doing.

Orlando was already by the entrance. 'I'll get it.'

When my brother opened the door, Libia dropped her purse on the floor and threw her arms around Orlando. 'You look just like him!'

My brother stood still until she let go of him. 'Hi. I'm Orlando.' He shook her hand.

Mamá hugged me and Howard in relief. 'She can see the resemblance between the two of them... that means that she knew Jaime.' She turned to Libia and said, 'Please, come in.'

The woman stared at Orlando as she walked around him. 'You could be your father's double. I'm so glad I found you.' She embraced my brother again.

That day, we learned that Libia owned the house where Papá had been assassinated.

'I loved Dr. Velásquez like my own son.' She blew her nose and then told us what happened after the military and foreign agents took Papá's body.

Her son, Ramiro, a twenty-three-year-old university student, and Suzanne, my father's wife, had been put in prison and brutally tortured. Dripping in menstrual blood, handcuffed, and with her eyelids taped opened, Suzanne was dragged to an office where she was repeatedly interrogated under a blinding light. After these long brutal sessions, she was thrown back into her flea-infested, dark dungeon. Her cry for food, water, and blankets was denied over and over as she sat on the cold cement floor. Like a clam in its shell, she wrapped her arms around her knees waiting for the next round of interrogations. This went on for months.

Suzanne begged the authorities to let her contact the Canadian Embassy, but her requests were denied. She found out later that Canada had closed the embassy in Ecuador. The British consul, as an emissary of the Canadian Government, finally intervened on her behalf. When Suzanne and Ramiro were finally released, they were so frail that they came out in wheelchairs. Many other prisoners were killed or had disappeared. When she arrived in Canada Suzanne published a book titled *Quand les vautours... Récit d'une québecoise emprisonnée en Équateur (When the Vultures... Story of a Québecoise Imprison in Ecuador)* accusing Velasco Ibarra's dictatorial government of killing my father and of torturing prisoners. A year later she mysteriously died in a car crash.

Libia choked with emotion.

At the end, she explained that she hadn't brought the package for fear that it would be a trap. As we spoke, a group of Papá's sympathizers were surveying our home to protect Libia. She inhaled. 'I'm sorry, but I had to be cautious.'

'We understand.' Howard adjusted his glasses.

The woman stood up, pulled her knitted sweater down, and said, 'A lot of people are looking forward to meeting you. So, if it's all right with your parents, I would like to have all of the children over for dinner on Saturday. This way I can introduce you to our friends and give you the package.'

'Liliana is in the United States, and Jaime is out for the week with friends.' Mamá stood up and then said, 'I don't know if I feel comfortable with this. What do you think, darling?'

'I'll drive them there and pick them up if that makes you feel better,' said Howard.

'Mamá, if you haven't noticed, I am a man now.' Orlando smirked.

Libia interjected, 'Look, ma'am. I think Mr. Dresser's idea is good. This way you know where I live. You can also come in or wait outside until we finish or come back later. Either way works for me.'

With her hands on her hips, Mamá insisted, 'Why is it so important that Orlando and Rocío go to dinner?'

'Very few people knew that he had children until after his death. Don't ask me why because I don't know. All I can think of is that he was trying to protect you all.' Libia picked up her purse. 'Listen, Dr. Velásquez was our hope for change, a leader, and our comrade, so we all want to meet his children. It would be an honor to have them at my house.'

My parents lived on the outskirts of the city in Los Chillos Valley, a residential area with spacious homes and well-kept gardens. To get to Libia's house, we had to drive through several communities. As we approached midtown, traffic slowed us down near one of the main plazas. Weathered-skinned women and men moved around small tents, selling fruits, vegetables, and other farmed goods. Wearing several layers of necklaces, bracelets, and wool hats, many women carried their babies swaddled and strapped to their backs. Some toddlers ran around, jumping in puddles while others played with homemade toys. The sweet smell of food being roasted on portable coal-heated stoves filtered into the car, reminding me how hungry I was.

A few blocks after the plaza, the steep street narrowed.

'We have arrived,' Howard announced as he parked the car.

I looked around, trying to find Libia's place, which she had described as a modest, burnt-yellow home. 'Which one is it? They all look alike.'

Mamá pointed at the one across from us. 'That's the number.'

I broke out in a cold sweat when I saw the house. It scared me to think that behind that framed, dark, heavy, wooden door were Papá's secrets, his life's work, his ideals, his friends, and even his last breath.

'Come on, Rocío.' Orlando got out of the car.

I kissed Howard and Mamá, then stood on the sidewalk with my brother.

'Are you going to wait for us?' asked Orlando.

Mamá replied, 'Of course. Every so often wave to us from the window. That way, we know you are all right.'

'We will. Let's go.' Orlando elbowed me. 'I thought you wanted to come.'

'I do. I do.' I tried to gain the fortitude I needed to face whatever truth was behind those doors.

'It wasn't my idea, you know?' Orlando said.

I pushed back my shoulders and said, 'Here we go.'

Libia greeted us. 'I can't believe you are here. Come in, please.' She closed the door behind us and showed us the way to the dining room.

As we walked through the poorly lit hallway, I thought about the terrible crime that had been committed inside these walls and felt faint. Orlando must have felt the same way, because when we arrived at the dining room, he grabbed onto my arm.

'Your father would've been so proud to see you two all grown up, such a fine young woman and man.' She brushed her hands down our arms as if our existence was some sort of miracle. 'I haven't met Jaime and Liliana, but I imagine they are just like you.' She kept staring at us. Her carefree smile made her look younger than the woman I had met that stormy evening 'Would you like a tour of the house?'

Orlando tightened his grip on my arm. 'No.'

'Not right now, maybe later.' I tried to ease my brother's and my own angst.

Libia's eyes filled with tears. 'He was happy here, but I understand.'

The buzz of the doorbell loosened the tension in the room. Orlando let go of my arm, and Libia's facial muscles softened.

'I'll be right back.' She turned and left.

She returned with so many guests that they overflowed into the living room and the kitchen. The strangers mingled as they waited for their turn to introduce themselves to my brother and me. When I glanced at Orlando, I noticed tiny drops of sweat peppered around his face. I knew how uncomfortable he felt in places with poor ventilation, so I excused myself and went to the nearest window, hoping to open it and wave at Mamá and Howard, confirming we were fine. My heart started thumping inside my chest when I noticed that my parents' car wasn't there anymore.

My thoughts were racing when I heard Libia say, 'Are you all right?'

'I'm just a little hot.' I kept looking outside, searching for my parents' car. Dusk had fallen, and it was drizzling.

'I'll let some air in. I just don't want the nosy neighbors to wonder what is going on in here.' She cracked open the window. Libia turned around and called the guests. 'Hello, everyone. Welcome. I'm so glad you could make it tonight.' When people quietened down, she continued, 'We prepared a simple dinner in memory of Dr. Velásquez and to welcome his children, Orlando and Rocío.'

The crowd clapped, and I took a big breath of relief. I convinced myself that perhaps my parents had only moved the car.

People sat wherever they could find an empty seat. Others stood by small tables where they placed their plates. A very animated man with large ears toasted and proceeded to tell us all about his brother's accident. Apparently, he was accidentally shot in the head by an acquaintance. My father had worked all night to remove the bullet. At the time, the family had few resources, so they paid Papá very little. The man squinted and told Orlando and me that he was indebted to our father. With all the sniffles, laughs, and chatter, the room turned noisy until we heard the clinking of a knife against a glass.

A short man wearing a loose tie and dark sweater stood up, looked at Orlando, then at me, and said, 'Perhaps you have already heard this, but for reasons that I don't understand, he never told anyone he had children.'

Everyone in the room nodded. The words felt like daggers in my heart, and I smiled sadly. I couldn't understand why he would pretend not to have children. Orlando began perspiring and became restless. Perhaps I would find out the reason my father never wanted to keep our picture in his office.

The man took a gulp of water and then continued, 'He was like a brother to me. And I know he must have had his reasons for keeping his family a secret. Jaime was the most loyal, dedicated, and honest person I've ever known.' The man proceeded to tell us he was the director of a hospital in Cuba where Papá had been a surgeon. He had been so impressed by my father's skills that he videotaped his hands during one of the procedures. The director had used that tape for years as one of the main training tools for medical students at the University of Havana. After serving as a minister of health, Papá went back to Colombia, arguing that his country needed him. When the director finished speaking, everyone cheered.

Farmers, peasants, priests, dentists, and other intellectuals followed, all recounting stories of our father's commitment to the indigenous people, the poor, children, and all of those he thought were neglected by their governments. They also described him as having an unusual intellectual ability as well as being a great orator.

Libia's son, Ramiro, who had been quiet, stood on a chair and said, 'One more toast for the doctor, a man without borders, a man who believed the land belonged to its people.'

When the crowd was dwindling, Orlando approached me. 'Are you ready to go?'

I remembered then that our parents' car was gone. 'Oh no. I need to see if they're back.' I peeked out the window. When I saw their car, I gasped in relief. 'They are here.'

'Why wouldn't they be?' Orlando asked.

'Never mind. But to answer your question, I can't go yet. She still hasn't given us the package, remember?'

'I've heard everything about Papá I can take for one day. I will wait for you in the car.'

Libia joined us. Orlando extended his hand. 'Thank you for dinner. I will wait for Rocío outside. I need some fresh air.'

Libia shook his hand, and my brother left.

'I'm sorry, but this is very difficult for all of us, especially my brother,' I explained to Libia.

'I understand. It was devastating for us too.' She closed her eyes for a moment, then said, 'I'll be right back.' She went to her room and returned with the package. Her eyes lost their shine when she told me how, after Suzanne and Ramiro were put in prison, she had hired a handyman to hide the few items Papá had left us inside the bathroom wall for fear that the authorities would confiscate them. After the colonel contacted her and told her that our family had moved to Quito, she had chiseled part of the wall away until she found the hidden metal box with the package inside. Like her most precious possession, Libia handed me the wrinkled, large envelope. We embraced; then I left.

I kept the folder next to my chest, as if I were holding my father's ashes, until we got home. Mamá told us that when Orlando waved at them, which I wasn't aware of, they had gone out to dinner. That explained why I hadn't seen them when I looked out the window. Tired and emotionally drained, Orlando and I closed our eyes and leaned our heads back. Mamá and Howard must've thought we were sleeping because they didn't ask us questions.

When we arrived home, I promised my parents that I would tell them all about it the next morning. Mamá frowned, so I told them it had gone well and once more excused myself. Howard pulled Mamá aside and whispered something in her ear.

'I can't wait to hear all about it,' Mamá said before closing her bedroom door. Orlando had already gone to his bedroom when I went to the study, and under a faint light, I opened the package.

I first pulled out Suzanne's book, which I recognized because it was written in French. Then I pulled out another book and read the cover aloud: *Contrainsurgencia y guerra revolucionaria, Jaime Velásquez Garcia.* Short of breath, I placed the books to one side. I took a deep breath, then pulled out a letter, a pen, and a pair of Papá's old scrubs and hat. No poems. With clumsy hands, I unfolded the letter and read.

My dear ducklings,

The news might sadden you, but do not let my death stand in the way of your goals. I did what I was meant to do. Some people watch the bureaucrats, supported by military puppets, steal the money and resources that should be used for social programs and to improve the living conditions of the poor, and do nothing about it. Children and adults die of curable diseases, and those in charge also ignore the problem. People who look the other way are worse than those committing the crimes. I refused to stand by while others were getting hurt. I am not making excuses for myself. I just strongly believe in taking action.

It is important that you also know that once my involvement with the revolution became known, I had two options: stay with my family, putting all of you at risk, or going away. The most difficult decision I have ever made was to leave my family. I learned then that the greatest sacrifice one can make is to let those we love go so that they can thrive. Even though I was not at home, I never abandoned you. I knew all about you. Every time I could, I would watch you come in and out of your schools. Indirectly, I was involved in Orlando's surgery and your mamá's recovery. I feel pleased to know that Mr. Dresser is now part of the family. He is a fine man, and I am certain that he will take care of you and your mamá.

Now the most important thing for you to remember is that you are lucky to have your mamá by your side. She is the best mother in the world. From the day you were born, she loved you and protected you unconditionally, never complaining about how hard it was to raise four children. I dedicated my life to our country, but she dedicated hers to you. All I ask is that you honor her and that you remain close to one another. Lastly, always fight for what is right. Your papá who will always love you,

Papá

'I love you too and I will always be Rocío Velásquez,' I whispered.

The moonlight shone through the window, and that's when I saw Mamá in her maternity nightgown, leaning against the door. I dropped what I had in my hands and embraced my mother. I wept.
Papá was right. *She* was our hero.

Author's Note

This book is based on our story. My only role was to transcribe the words and experiences of my family onto paper. I feel honored to have grown up with my siblings, Liliana, Jaime, and Orlando, and, later on, Kenneth Enrique. Although our professions differ and even some of our life views, there is one thing that unites us, a commitment to helping those in need.

Our mother, Cecilia Dresser, who fought to protect us from the claws of the political war of the time, continues to make us proud. She is the head of a large family, with nine grandkids and eighteen great-grandkids. Our adoptive father Kenneth H. Dresser passed, but his kindness remains very much alive within all of us.

After our dear grandparents, Emilia and Miguel A. Diaz's passing, my siblings and I kept their property *Emilia María* for over twenty-six years, reluctant to let go of the place that became our childhood refuge for so long. Some of the trees that were as tall as I was now stand more than forty feet tall. From many of them hang my grandmother's giant bromeliads keeping a watchful eye on the lush and colorful grounds.

I wish my father could see Colombia today. Cities and towns grew and are like a work of art, Gothic churches, colonial neighborhoods, and Spanish plazas mingle with modern buildings. The one constant has been our warm, charming, and welcoming people.

He would be proud to know that his efforts and unyielding search for justice and that of many others, determined to fight for what they believed in, the emancipation of the less fortunate, were not in vain. Social justice causes and the push for a more equitable society continue to be at the center of the political discourse.

As for me, I will probably never understand why Papá chose his cause over us. But, I have made peace with my past. I've been in touch with him through his writings and that of many others. I've seen him in the eyes of all of those he touched. I embrace him every time I hug someone he knew. Most importantly, learning that he stayed away to protect us showed me his immense love for us, this way easing the pain left by his absence.

And yes, I did recover the poems years after Papá's passing.